Doors of the Veil

BOOK 1: A NEW LIFE

By G.L. Ruby-Quartz

FriesenPress

Suite 300 - 990 Fort St
Victoria, BC, V8V 3K2
Canada

www.friesenpress.com

ISBN
978-1-5255-9845-6 (Hardcover)
978-1-5255-9844-9 (Paperback)
978-1-5255-9846-3 (eBook)

1. *Fiction, Literary*

Distributed to the trade by The Ingram Book Company

We all get knocked down...

Doors of the Veil is dedicated to anyone who has had the courage to get back up, shed the victim role and cast off society's judgment and expectations.

INTRODUCTION

HAVE YOU EVER wondered how the human race has survived for centuries, despite human nature and all its hypocritical flaws?

In this book I set out to show how modern-day society has been molded and shaped through one of the most powerful books ever written. Many organized religions are built with this book as the centerpiece. Our morals and values are based on it; even modern law derives its roots from this one very influential book: the Bible.

But what if...

What if the Bible was simply a collection of ancient people's journals or diaries?

What if Judgment Day, as it's written in the Bible, never existed in the first place? How would society be different if people knew that heaven and hell weren't real places where our eternal souls go?

If that is the case what happens to our spirits after we die?

It is through the main characters in this story that I try to open the reader's minds to the possibility that there is a finely crafted veil that has been pulled over all our eyes... a conspiracy that was crafted ages ago to control and manipulate the masses.

The story starts off in the mid-1990s in the Oklahoma Bible Belt. Small towns in the area were notorious for being technologically and socially behind the times. There was very little separation between church and state.

Society revolved very much around Christianity, with pastors, priests, and cardinals all looked upon as prophets of God, incapable of being anything less than perfect.

Children were to be seen and not heard, and should a child choose to exercise their freedom of speech, adults would often discount those words or become greatly offended. God forbid that a child ever brings an abuse accusation against a church leader, a teacher or a parent.

A patriarchal society was the social norm, especially in small towns. The distinction between right and wrong was a well-defined line that was not to be crossed, or else one would suffer the wrath and ridicule of the Christian horde. Non-Christians were thought of as sinners.

Lucinda, Mary and Damien don't know each other, but through their experiences they have one thing in common: they have all seen the doors of the veil. In doing so, they slowly find out the truth of creation, the veil that has been carefully crafted and pulled over all our eyes for centuries.

Through the experiences of the main characters, I intend to give you, the reader, insight into yourself. To question how you feel about the experiences the characters go through. To sit in judgment of society, its norms, its expectations and how society judges each and every one of us in turn. To bring into view the very values that society and religion binds us with.

You, the reader: you are the judge...

CHAPTER 1 –

Telling her Parents

IN RILEY, A small town in Oklahoma, Lucinda Hall had a secret that was eating away at her for over a month. She approached her mother with tears in her eyes and her hands trembling. "Mother, I have to tell you that Uncle Bill touched me."

"What do you mean, he touched you?" Before Lucinda could answer, she was interrupted. "Where? When? I can't believe my ears," her mother said. Lucinda ran to her room, a room shared with one of her four sisters.

Margaret chased after Lucinda. When Margaret reached the now closed and locked bedroom door, she began banging her fists on it, yelling, "Lucinda-May Hall. Open this door!" She could hear Lucinda inside, crying. "Are you going to come and open this door?"

When no answer came, Margaret went downstairs to fetch tools to unlock the door. Upon returning, she tried once more, this time in a calmer voice: "Lucinda honey, please open the door."

After waiting for a short time, Margaret used a scribe tool to unlock the door. Upon entering the room, she saw Lucinda in the corner behind the bed. She was sitting upright with head buried between her knees which were pulled to her chest, her long blonde hair covering her face as her entire body rocked back and forth, all the while sobbing and crying. Margaret sat on the bed near Lucinda.

1

"Tell me, daughter, what happened. All the details—don't leave anything out." At first Lucinda would not respond. "Lucinda, I don't know what to say." A lightbulb went off in Margaret's head. "Lucinda, it's better that you tell me before your father comes home." Lucinda jumped up and tried to run past Margaret, who caught her around the waist, pulling her back and onto the bed beside her.

"No, no, don't tell Father, he'll be angry." More tears and sobs came from her. "Please, Mother, please don't, please do not tell Father." She leaned into her mother; Margaret leaned away and put a hand between herself and her daughter.

"I must tell your father; he will want to know."

Lucinda burst into tears again. Margaret knew she should hug her distraught daughter; but she just couldn't bring herself to be comforting to Lucinda, or any of her five daughters. Margaret moved over, putting some space between them.

"Mother, are you that cold that you can't even try to comfort me? Why'd you move away?"

"Lucinda, you know I'm not comfortable with affection, and considering your accusation against your Uncle Bill, what do you expect from me?"

"Maybe just a little compassion and understanding, Mother, just one time."

Margaret turned her body so she was partially facing the girl. "Ok, is this better? Now tell me everything. I need to know all the details so I can save you from having to tell your father."

"If you tell Father, he will kill me." Lucinda's tears started flowing again.

"Lucinda, I need to know what happened. What do you mean Uncle Bill touched you?" she said in as soft a voice as she could muster. The child continued to sob but didn't say a word.

"Lucinda, I am starting to lose patience." Margaret raised her hands in a gesture that looked as though she was about to shake her daughter by the shoulders.

After what seemed like an eternity, Lucinda slowly spoke. "He—he touched—my—" More tears began to well up in the girl's eyes. "Touched—my—touched me down there." She pointed down towards her groin area. Looking up at her mother Lucinda knew she had passed the point of no return. Her mother's eyes met with hers and Lucinda had a sinking feeling in her stomach; she kind of knew what her mother would say next. In a pre-emptive maneuver, she blurted out, "I asked him not to touch me." Lucinda sobbed. "I cried when he touched me, but—but—but he wouldn't never stop," she said. Margaret quickly corrected her daughter.

"We don't use double negatives, saying 'wouldn't never' is not proper grammar, Lucinda, you know better."

"I shouldn't have told you; I knew you wouldn't believe me," Lucinda said in an offended tone of voice. Margaret sat silently listening. Lucinda again broke down crying, trying to mutter out words to explain. "I told—him—to—stop—Mother, he didn't stop—he just touched me and kept touching me."

"Lucinda, that is a serious accusation against your uncle. Are you absolutely certain he touched you? Could it have been an accident?"

"No! It wasn't an accident, I know what happened," the girl said through her tears.

"Lucinda, I think it's best if you don't tell your father. Leave that up to me."

"Thank you, Momma," she said appreciatively.

"I'll tell your father after dinner when all you girls are in bed sleeping." Lucinda smiled. "Now off you go Lucinda-May; chores wait for no one we have wasted enough time on this."

⁓

Later that evening as the family sat down to eat at the dinner table, John said grace. There was an echo in the room as the five girls and two parents all said, "Amen."

"Ok, girls, who knows what time it is?"

"Bible Verses!" the three youngest shouted out excitedly.

"'The Lord is my light and my salv—'"

Before John could finish the quote, two girls, Suzanne and Bethany, blurted out, "Psalm 27:1."

John smiled at his girls and had to choose which one earned the point, despite the fact that the girls both answered at the same time. "Point to Bethany."

The nine-year-old beamed with pride while sneering at Suzanne. The game continued for several more rounds, with Lucinda not even attempting to join in. Her thoughts were clearly elsewhere and John noticed.

Every night the game ended on the exact same quote. "Now girls, this is the last verse, remember to wait for the entire quote before giving an answer. Ready?" As the eager girls awaited, John smiled and said, "'Honor—'" He stopped as one of the girls started blurting out the answer.

"Ephes—" Suzanne yelled out. John interrupted to politely scold the overzealous eleven-year-old.

"I told you to wait until the whole quote is finished," said John.

"But Father, you always end the game with Ephesians 6:2, 'Honor your father and mother,'" Suzanne said.

Although only seven years old, little Barbara was smart as a whip; she stepped up to correct her sister Suzanne. "There are more verses that say 'honor your father and mother,' like Exodus 20:12 and what about Deuteronomy 5:16? It says: 'Honor your father and your mother, as the Lord your God commanded you, that your days may be long, and that it may go well with you in the land that the Lord your God is giving you.'"

Hearing his second-youngest speak so eloquently and seeing her put one of her older sisters in her place, John declared, "And tonight's winner is Barbara." Clapping his hands loudly, with most of the family cheering along with the daily announcement of the Bible Verses winner.

After being properly excused from the dinner table, the two youngest girls, Barbara and Charlotte, fetched their father's slippers and newspaper as John moved from the kitchen into the living room. He sat in his chair as Charlotte handed him the slippers and Barbara gave him the daily newspaper.

John could hear his wife clearing the table and the familiar sound of dishes being washed in the kitchen sink as the three eldest attended to their chores of washing, drying and putting the dishes away.

At precisely 8pm, the family once again gathered around the table for their nightly Bible reading.

John set his Bible on the table and opened it. "Alright family, who volunteers to read tonight?"

Suzanne gleefully put her hand up. "It's Sunday Father, that makes it my turn to read."

John clapped his hands together and pointed at Suzanne. "That's how you step up and take responsibility! Yesterday we left off at Psalm 50:20. Suzanne start us off at Psalm 50:19 and go from there."

"Yes Father." Suzanne cleared her throat as the family followed along in their own Bible's.

"'You use your mouth for evil and harness your tongue to deceit. You sit and testify against your brother and slander your own mother's son. When you did these things and I kept silent, you thought I was exactly like you. But I now arraign you and set my accusations before you.'"

"Now stop right there. Who wants to tell us all what that last passage means?" John looked at Lucinda who seemed lost in thought. "Lucinda, what is your interpretation of the passage your sister just read?" Lucinda looked down to quickly reread. "We're waiting Lucinda." John said impatiently.

"Father, deceit means to trick someone, testify means to tell on someone, slander is saying something false and arraign means taking someone to court. I think it means—" John interrupted.

"You think? Or do you know Lucinda?"

"I know Father." She paused long enough to check her father's facial expression. "It's about someone who stayed silent at first when their friend talked badly about their family. Then they felt guilty and told the truth about what happened."

"That's good Lucinda, and what is the moral of that passage?"

Bethany blurted out. "I know, I know. The moral is not to talk badly about your family to other people."

John smiled. "I will agree with that, family is the most important thing in your life, never speak ill of them to anyone."

Lucinda thought to herself, *Will Father be proud of me for telling the truth about Uncle Bill?* She watched her father's eyes closely as Bible study continued. *'When you did these things I kept quiet,'* A sinking feeling washed over Lucinda as she thought about those words over and over in her mind. *Father won't be proud, he'll be angry.* She shivered at the thought.

An hour later, the girls were all tucked into bed upstairs in their two rooms: one room shared by Lucinda and Suzanne the other shared between Bethany, Barbara and Charlotte. Margaret would dutifully tuck the girls in each night at 9pm and then return to the kitchen to make the nightly tea. Usually, Margaret relished the precision of the routine; however, tonight was different, she could barely control her anxiety, her hands were shaking as she poured the tea into cups and very carefully placed them on saucers on the serving tray. Margaret put her unsteady hands on the handles of the serving tray, looked to the ceiling and said a silent prayer in her mind. *God give me the strength to tell my husband the truth.* With a deep breath she picked up the tray and went to the living room.

Margaret's hands still shook slightly as she placed the tray on the small round table between the two chairs. John looked up and thanked his wife for the tea, but just as he was about to return to reading his newspaper, he saw a look of concern on Margaret's face. John folded the paper in half and placed it between his leg and the arm of the chair. Looking at Margaret, he said, "Out with it, wife, what is bothering you?"

Margaret froze as her fears gripped her. She tried in vain to think of a lie, a way not to tell him, if she could only come up with a believable story. She knew the look on her face gave her away.

"Well?" John said, staring straight into Margaret's eyes.

"John, I don't want you to be mad." She paused to gauge his reaction.

"Now!" John raised his voice.

A wave of terror washed over Margaret as she stammered to get the words out. "John, don't be angry. It's about your brother Bill." John continued to stare into his wife's eyes as she told him the news. "Lucinda told me today that Bill touched her."

Time seemed to stand still as Margaret looked at John's facial expressions. She waited for John to reply, expecting him to ask for more details, but John did not reply. His face flushed red as he waited for her to continue, but she did not.

John's nostrils flared. Bill was his little brother and John was very proud of him; Bill had worked hard to become a priest and the pastor of the local church in Riley. The words he was hearing from his wife painted his brother in the most negative light. Raising his voice further, he said, "Margaret, what do you mean? Bill touched her? How? What? Where? Answer me, woman!"

Margaret's worst fears were realized; she had known in her heart of hearts that John would be furious, that he would demand answers, answers that she didn't have. In a shaky voice, she continued, "John, he touched her nether regions, I don't know when or how or where, I only know that Lucinda was upset and crying. She came home early from Sunday school." Margaret spoke as fast as she could to get the story out before John could interrupt. "Lucinda was in tears and related to me that Bill had touched her. I asked where and she pointed to her groin."

John stood mere feet from his wife, well within striking distance. Suddenly an idea popped into Margaret's head. "John, you know it's probably nothing, just a little girl's imagination, she probably mistook a hug for sexual touching." She tried to laugh it off with a half-hearted chuckle as her left eye twitched.

At the top of the stairs, Lucinda sat listening to every word her parents said. She just heard her mother betray her, telling her father that it was just her imagination. Hearing those words hurt more than any physical pain of Uncle Bill breaking her hymen. Her thoughts were interrupted by the sound of flesh contacting flesh. Lucinda turned just in time to see her mother's head snap back and to the left.

John yelled at his wife, "What kind of girls are you raising?" With one hand holding her by the blouse he was stopping her from fleeing. Margaret just stood there, not even daring to try to escape, her eyes blinking constantly as if trying to protect themselves from the next backhand. She felt the sting on the cheek that John had already hit and she regretted telling him anything.

As John raised his hand for a second time, she begged him, "Please, John, I'm sorry, please don't." John held his hand and, somewhat coming to his senses, he refrained from a second strike; instead, he chose to push her back into the chair.

Standing over her he screamed. "That is my one and only brother, he has worked hard to get where he is and he's well respected." John's tone was angry as he continued to berate his wife.

Margaret cowered in fear and nodded occasionally. "I agree John, I agree."

The verbal barrage went on for some time and Lucinda heard every last word, including when her father said, "Lucinda has always been out of control; you were slack on raising her and now we are reaping what you have sown."

John continued, barking, "She's a liar! There is no way on God's green earth that my brother, the pastor of our church, molested our daughter, no way!" John stormed into the kitchen with Margaret following close behind. He continued his tirade, saying things like, "That lying harlot is going to ruin me, my brother, and our family!" John's rage seemed to grow with each word he spoke.

Even though her parents had now moved into the kitchen, Lucinda could still hear every word clear as day; she heard her father accusing her of lying, and doing so without even hearing her side. His condemnation of Lucinda continued for what seemed like forever to the young girl sitting atop the stairs with her knees pulled to her chest, arms around her knees, slightly rocking as tears streamed silently down her cheeks.

Lucinda struggled with her own feelings of guilt. She thought to herself, *Maybe I shouldn't have said anything.* She could hear her mother crying as her father continued yelling; she thought she heard another slap. The emotions she felt were almost unbearable when at that very moment a thought popped into her head; she didn't think it through rationally but just reacted and bounded down the stairs. Making her way into the kitchen, she yelled at her father.

"Stop!"

Both John and Margaret stopped and stood there as if frozen. Lucinda was also surprised at her own bravery. A braveness that would be short lived.

John broke the silence as he looked at Lucinda with complete disdain. In a loud voice—not quite yelling, but loud and commanding—John exclaimed, "Your mother tells me that you accuse my brother William of molesting you!" Taking a step closer to the girl, John added, "That is a serious accusation, little girl!" Raising his voice with each new statement, he scared Lucinda with every forward step. She felt as if she were prey being stalked by an alpha predator. Lucinda heard every question her father asked; but in her mind, she was consumed with how physically close he was getting. Subconsciously she continued to step back while her every instinct was telling her to run away.

Seeing her daughter slowly backing out of the kitchen, Margaret remembered that earlier in the day Lucinda had run upstairs, slammed and locked her bedroom door. She also knew that if she did the same thing now, John would surely give chase and matters would get worse.

Margaret moved slowly around the table to get to the other side of Lucinda, just in case she tried to make a run for it.

Lucinda's eyes were watching every move her father made, so much so that she didn't see her mother slide in behind her, essentially blocking the doorway out of the kitchen.

John's final step startled Lucinda as she stepped back directly into an obstacle. She turned to see her mother standing behind her. Turning her back to her father was a mistake; suddenly she felt his hand grab her by the hair, pull her back and closer to him. Lucinda shrieked out in pain as her hair was almost yanked from her skull; she could feel the tension on the roots of each hair, then she felt his hand gripping the back of her neck with hair still entwined in his fingers. He squeezed tightly, so tight she couldn't move.

"What happened, Lucinda? Tell me the truth now, girl!" Lucinda struggled to break free of the hand gripping her neck as her mother watched, not saying a single word.

In a pained voice, Lucinda answered, "Uncle Bill touched me and made me touch him." Desperation rang out in the girl's tone, her body fighting to break loose of the hold on her neck. She felt his fingers digging into her flesh as she struggled.

"No! He did not!" John bellowed.

"Let me go, please!"

"Will you tell the truth if I let you go?"

"Yes, Father, please let me go!" Hearing those words, John released the grip on her neck. Lucinda jerked her head forward and turned to face her father. Her head still hurt from having her hair pulled so hard, but she found the courage to stand toe to toe with the massive man. Her bottom lip quivering she cried out, "Uncle Bill touched me, he—he made me touch him and it hurt when he touched my privates with his saddle horn."

John couldn't believe what he was hearing; this is not what he was expecting. He wanted the truth, even if it wasn't the truth; he wanted his truth, the truth that wouldn't make him the laughingstock of the town and a pariah at church; and most of all, he wanted his perfect little organized world to stay the same at all costs.

John grabbed the girl's wrist, twisting it behind her back. She cried out in pain while her mother was imploring her to be quiet. "Hush girl, hush now, don't wake your sisters," Margaret pleaded.

"Tell the truth!" demanded John, twisting Lucinda's arm further behind her back. She begged for release.

"I'm telling the truth, Father. Uncle—AHHH!" John twisted her arm further. "It's the truth, Father, Uncle—" Before Lucinda could say 'Bill,' her father would twist even harder, pulling upwards with the girl's body twisting and trying to escape. John wrapped his free arm around her, closing that arm around her neck to hold her body in place. He continued to wrench on her arm; all the while Margaret stood by, watching and pleading with the child to be quiet despite the fact that Lucinda's arm was literally being ripped from its socket.

Lucinda was always taught not to tell a lie. She had never lied before and she wasn't going to now. "Uncle Bill raped me!" she yelled out, despite the fact that she knew this would bring more of her father's rage down upon her. She had had spankings and beatings before, but never had she felt so much pain. She knew she had to stand up for herself, if only this one time.

The second John heard Lucinda yell those words, he pulled so hard on the arm, Margaret heard two horrific sounds: the first was a loud snap as if a large rubber band had been pulled past the point of breaking, the other sound was a blood-curdling crack as if a rock was being broken apart by a sledge hammer. She jumped as she let out a startled gasp.

Lucinda screamed only for a second, feeling the pain shoot through her arm tingling through her body as she passed out from the intense pain. Feeling the girl's body go limp, John released the arm and let her fall face first to the floor. Looking down, he could see a trickle of blood leaking from under her face. He turned to Margaret and, for a third ne that night, he struck her with a backhand across the face. "This is all your fault. You're the worst mother and wife a man could have."

John left and headed to his room. As soon as she heard the door close, Margaret dropped to her knees, holding her now swelling and bruised face. John knew to hit exactly where it hurt the most, right on the high cheekbone. Her eye felt as though it was about to pop out of the socket and she had a throbbing headache.

She knelt there for quite some time before looking over at her daughter. Seeing the young girl motionless on the floor with a small pool of blood starting to form just beside her face. Margaret took one look at the blood and thought to herself. *I better clean that up in case John comes back.* She moved over to Lucinda, leaned over and put her ear to Lucinda's back; she felt relieved to hear that her daughter was breathing. She turned the girl over, cradled Lucinda in her arms and rocked her back and forth. "Why did you have to—" She shed some momentary tears before remembering about the blood on the floor.

Margaret moved Lucinda to a chair in the living room and cleaned the blood, snot and tears from her face using a cold damp cloth. This woke Lucinda up and she felt major pain in her chest, ribs and back, but mostly in her shoulder and arm; when she tried to lift the arm, she couldn't due to the pain. Looking at her arm, she saw swelling around the elbow and she thought, Maybe my arm is broken. She sobbed softly, replaying the incident over and over in her head, asking herself, *What did I do wrong? What's wrong with me? Why don't my parents love me?*

Margaret handed another cold cloth to Lucinda. "Hold this to your face." Lucinda took the cloth with her left hand, as she could hardly move her right hand without feeling a tremendous amount of pain.

Margaret left her in the chair and went to clean the kitchen. After cleaning the kitchen, Margaret walked back to the living room where Lucinda was still in the chair. Margaret saw her daughter's swollen arm starting to bruise and could hear the girl whimpering in pain under her breath. Without saying a word, Margaret removed the afghan blanket from the couch, covered Lucinda and went to bed.

CHAPTER 2 –

First Contact

THAT NIGHT LUCINDA stayed in the chair, too sore to move. She didn't get much sleep due to the pain coursing through her body, slipping in and out of consciousness all night long.

During her bouts of unconsciousness, it was as if her mind disconnected from her body and she couldn't feel the pain. She drifted in and out, sometimes waking to intense pain. She knew that she was blacking out and not really going to sleep; when she was unconscious, it was as if she were in a waking dream state.

She felt the pain in her shoulder, like an electrical current was pulsing through the joint; then she would pass out and the pain would go away. The house was silent yet Lucinda could swear she heard faint whispers. In her peripheral vision, she saw small bursts of green and yellow flashes like mini lightning bolts. She opened her eyes, which awoke her body and brought the pain back. Lucinda would try to stay conscious, but eventually the pain won out and she would black out again.

Lucinda blacked out and found herself in a dark hallway. Off in the distance, she could see a small bright white light at the end of the hallway. She focused on the light, felt her heart starting to race and blood pump faster as she walked closer to the light, which got bigger the closer she got. As the hallway ended, it opened up into a vast space.

Straight in front of her was the white light; to the right off in the distance a green light shone; she turned to her left and saw a glowing blue light.

"I must be dead. I've heard people say when you die, go towards the white light; that's what I'll do." She spoke to herself. Taking one step towards the white light, an overwhelming feeling of fear invaded her thoughts. *This is my Judgment Day. What if God doesn't forgive my sins?* In her fear she turned away from the light and walked back down the hallway.

At thirteen years of age, this was a terrifying experience for the young girl. She always thought that when you died and went towards the light, you would have a feeling of peace and tranquility. Instead, she felt the exact opposite: she felt frightened and alone, cold inside and out.

This went on throughout the night. Lucinda would wake up, momentarily feel the pain and then pass out again. In those times she would see the dark hallway, with the white light shining straight ahead, off in the distance.

"What is happening? Am I dying?" Lucinda called out, speaking to no one, but hoping someone would answer.

CHAPTER 3 –

Tell the Lie

EARLY IN THE morning Lucinda stirred and opened her eyes slightly to see a crack of light peeking in through the window and then she heard footsteps coming down the stairs. It was one of her sisters; Lucinda closed her eyes, pretending to still be asleep.

Charlotte's voice carried, "Good morning, Mother." Margaret was already in the kitchen preparing the day's breakfast. Soon Lucinda could hear the bustling of the whole family sitting down to breakfast. She heard her father call for grace and Barbara was the one who said the prayer blessing the food.

Charlotte asked, "Why is Lucinda in the living room on the chair?" Lucinda listened for her mother's answer.

"Lucinda felt sick last night and when she went to go to the kitchen for some water, she fell down the stairs and hurt herself."

"Is she alright?" Suzanne and Bethany asked in unison.

"Yes, children she's fine. After you all go to school and father goes to work, I'll take her to the doctor to be examined. She'll be just fine, don't you worry." Lucinda felt relieved to hear her mother's words saying she would take her to the doctor, and more relieved that her father didn't object.

With her newly relieved feeling, Lucinda decided to try and drift back to sleep while waiting for everyone to get on with their day. A short while later, she was awoken by her father's booming voice.

"Goodbye girls, have a good day at school and be good." John walked past Lucinda and she heard his footsteps. She closed her eyes just a little bit tighter so as not to have to see her father, or worse yet, to have him talk to her. He walked right by and out the door. Shortly afterwards she could hear the hustle and bustle of her sisters rushing to get ready for the school bus. Charlotte was always the early bird, and she often chided her sisters to "hurry up, we're going to miss the bus."

After the house had gone silent, Lucinda could hear the clanking of dishes being washed in the sink. She tried to sit up in the chair and as she did, the pain in her shoulder came back worse than before. She moaned out, "Argh!" She used her good arm to remove the blanket and sit up in the chair.

Moments later, her mother came out of the kitchen into the living room. "Go get changed, I'm taking you to the doctor."

Lucinda could see the bruise on her mother's face—she had a very black eye—and she knew her mother would be wearing her big sunglasses to go out. She was kind of amazed that her mother would actually go out in public so soon after receiving a black eye. She had seen her mother with these types of bruises on many occasions. This brought a frightful thought to Lucinda: *I must be hurt pretty bad if Mother is going to take me to the doctor.*

She then looked at her arm. With the sun shining in through the living room window, she could see that her flesh was black and blue, very bruised, very sore and definitely swollen. Her arm looked to be as big as her thigh, with the swelling going from just above her wrist all the way up past her elbow.

She made her way upstairs on wobbly legs. She got to the bathroom, looked in the mirror and saw her lip was fat and split. She then opened her mouth and could see one of her front two teeth had been chipped on the corner. Lucinda felt sadness overtake her as the memory of her father's attack on her came flooding back. Looking in the mirror again, she turned her head to the side but couldn't see the bruises on the back of her neck where her father had squeezed so tightly.

She went to her room and changed out of her flannel night gown. Lifting it over her head proved to be very difficult and painful as she had to move her swollen arm; but she knew she had to get dressed, that her mother most certainly wouldn't take her out in public dressed in her night gown. Lucinda went to her dresser, picked out a pair of sweat pants and a loose-fitting sleeveless tank top, as she knew it was going to be hard to put the shirt on without a whole lot of pain.

Sitting on the bed, she gingerly pulled the sweatpants on, one leg at a time, pulling up with her good arm. She lifted her bottom and pulled the pants into place. Then came the moment she dreaded. She took the tank top in her left hand, raised it over to her bruised right arm and very slowly pulled the shirt over the arm as she maneuvered the garment over her head and onto her body, finally poking her left arm through its hole. She then went to the bathroom and stood once again in front of the mirror.

"I wish this never happened," she said to her own reflection. She washed her face, brushed her teeth with her left hand and tried almost in vain to brush her long straight hair.

She heard her mother calling, "Are you ready Lucinda? Hurry up." Lucinda walked out of the bathroom and down the stairs, trying to be careful, yet still trying to hurry as much as she could.

She saw Margaret, who didn't say a word to Lucinda; she just got her purse and headed towards the door with Lucinda following behind. Once inside the car, the only thing her mother said to her was, "When we get to the doctor, you are to tell him that you got up in the middle of the night, it was dark and you fell down the stairs trying to go to the kitchen for a glass of water, do you understand?" Lucinda nodded and then hung her head down to hide her face.

It was a ten-minute drive to the doctor's office. When they arrived Lucinda could hear her mother whispering; although she couldn't make out the words, she assumed her mother was telling the reception nurse the false story Margaret had instructed her to tell the doctor.

Margaret then came and sat beside Lucinda. "The doctor is not busy this morning, he will see us soon. Remember what I told you." They waited in silence for what seemed like forever. Lucinda could feel shooting pain in her shoulder and her lip was still sore. Every now and then, Lucinda would run her tongue over her lips to feel the large split and how dry they were.

CHAPTER 4 –

Mortified Doctor

THE NURSE CALLED out Lucinda's name. She stood and followed the nurse with Margaret following behind. They were led to a small patient waiting room with a typical patient examination bed covered with fresh brown paper, a small circular chair and a chair in the opposite corner near the door.

Once inside the room, Margaret again reminded Lucinda, "Remember what you have to tell the doctor."

Lucinda replied sarcastically, "Yes, Mother, I heard you the first three times." Again, there was silence as Margaret glared at her daughter's obvious disrespect.

In a short time, Dr. Watkins entered the room, greeting the pair as he closed the door behind him. "Good day ladies, what seems to be the issue today?" Dr. Watkins immediately noticed the large sunglasses Margaret was wearing.

She looked at Dr. Watkins and explained, "Our daughter Lucinda was thirsty in the middle of the night; in the darkness she fell down the stairs."

"Uh huh," Dr. Watkins said, turning to look at the young girl. He saw her bloodshot eyes looking at him as he moved closer. He saw her twitch slightly as he moved his hand to take the hand of her injured arm. Being in a small religious town, Dr. Watkins knew the family well, having been the family doctor who delivered all five of John and Margaret's girls. He felt sadness as he looked over the girl, realizing that he had never seen Lucinda so timid. She pulled her hand away and he saw her wince.

He gave the girl a comforting smile. "May I please take your hand?" Lucinda reluctantly moved her hand back within the doctor's reach. He took her hand very slowly and gently. Slowly he turned the hand inwards to gently twist the arm; the very second he did, Lucinda let out a painful sigh. "Oh, there, there, it's alright. I know it hurts." He stepped closer to get a better look at the arm. Using his free hand, he gently touched the wrist, "Tell me if this hurts." Tap-tap on the wrist, Lucinda didn't say a word; moving up to the forearm, tap-tap. "Does this hurt?"

"No" replied Lucinda.

Moving to the side, he stated the obvious. "That's a nasty swollen bruise on your elbow. Are you sure this doesn't hurt?" he said as he tapped her upper arm again.

This time Lucinda changed her answer, "It hurts a little." She winced as Dr. Watkins tapped her arm.

"I see your lip is also swollen and split open. What hurts more, your lip or your arm?" the doctor's attempt at humor drew a slight smirk from Lucinda. Then Dr. Watkins tapped her shoulder ever so lightly and Lucinda let out a shriek.

"Owww-ccchhh!" she cried out, her breathing labored. Dr. Watkins put on a very calm, collected face while deep inside he was enraged.

He smiled at Lucinda. "Just relax and hang tight; we are going to need x-rays." In the background he thought he heard a sigh from Margaret. Lucinda looked up into the doctor's eyes with gratitude.

Dr. Watkins picked up the phone in the room. "Nurse Leslie, please inform the hospital that we will need x-rays as soon as possible, I will be right over with my patient."

Dr. Watkins turned his stare towards Margaret. "An ambulance will come to transport Lucinda to the hospital." He turned back to

Lucinda. "Wait here, little lady, we'll come get you when it's time to go." He smiled at the young broken girl. "Margaret, I need you come into my office to sign some in-patient forms." Margaret hesitated, "We need the forms signed to admit Lucinda for the x-rays." Dr. Watkins' tone reinforced the importance of his request.

Margaret followed Dr. Watkins out the door and closed it behind her. He led her down the hall to his office; once inside he closed the door. "Have a seat, Margaret."

"No, thank you, Dr. Watkins, I'll stand."

Dr. Watkins stepped closer to her. "Margaret, would you kindly remove your glasses please?"

"Why, Dr. Watkins?"

"You know why, Margaret. Examining your daughter, I can tell you those injuries did not come from a fall down the stairs." Margaret hung her head as Dr. Watkins continued, "I suspect that you have another nasty shiner hiding behind those dark glasses, and once again you're lying to cover for him." He paused.

"Uh, no, I just have a migraine, the sunlight bothers my eyes."

Dr. Watkins pursed his lips and shook his head. "I have seen this so many times before. What was it this time? You walked into a door? Slipped in the shower? A coffee cup fell out of the cupboard onto your eye?"

Margaret still wouldn't remove the glasses, "Bradley." She called the doctor by his first name as if she were speaking to an old friend. "You can't say anything, the scandal would be an embarrassment to—"

Dr. Watkins cut her off. "These are serious injuries to your daughter. I suspect her arm has been pulled from the socket and is broken in at least two places. I have to make a report of my findings."

Margaret pleaded "Bradley, you can't. It would ruin our family. John—"

Dr. Watkins put his hand up as he tilted his head to the side. "Stop, Margaret, just stop. John has major anger issues; he's incapable of controlling his emotions."

"But you know him, Bradley, he would do anything for his family, his friends, his—"

Dr. Watkins interrupted loudly. "Margaret! Facts are facts. Your daughter is in the other room with her arm mangled, ripped from the socket with what I suspect is multiple fractures."

"Bradley, she fell down the stairs."

"No, Margaret, stop with the lies!" There was silence as Dr. Watkins waited for Margaret to admit the truth. Breaking the silence, Dr. Watkins pushed Margaret to near hysteria when he said, "I have to report this to Sheriff Brown."

Margaret burst out into tears, wailing, "No, no, no, Bradley, it will ruin John."

"I have a duty as a medical practitioner, it's my responsib—"

Margaret interrupted. "What about doctor-patient privilege, Bradley?"

"Margaret, I'm offended that you even bring up doctor-patient privilege." Shaking his head, breathing in deeply, he said, "It's futile for me to even try to convince you to tell the truth. You would rather place yourself and all five of your daughters in harm's way than to admit your husband is a family annihilator. The Hall family name means more to you than your own children." Margaret looked pitiful, tears streaming down her face. Dr. Watkins thought for a moment, then said, "Doctor-patient privilege is only part of my oath. I also have a duty to report findings of abuse and—"

Margaret tried to interrupt. "But—"

"Shut up, Margaret, and listen!" Dr. Watkins barked. Margaret sobbed and did as instructed. "As I was saying, I have a duty to report injuries and suspicions of abuse!" Dr. Watkins paused a moment, expecting to be interrupted. "Your daughter's injuries are very suspicious."

Just then, there was a knock on the door.

"Dr. Watkins, the ambulance is ready."

"Thank you, Nurse Robinson."

He opened the door, walked down the hall and entered the room where Lucinda was. Behind Dr. Watkins, the paramedics from the ambulance appeared in the doorway with a gurney. Dr. Watkins helped Lucinda to her feet and over to the transport gurney, helping her to lay down. "Lucinda, it will all be over soon and we'll have you all fixed up," he said with a warm smile.

Margaret stood in the background, trying to compose herself. As they wheeled the gurney past her, she placed her hand on it, stopping it momentarily while she leaned over and whispered in her daughter's ear. "Stick to the story, Lucinda." After whispering, she spoke loud enough for everyone to hear. "We all love you Lucinda, it will all be alright." Dr. Watkins saw right through Margaret's façade.

"Ok, let's go," chided Dr. Watkins.

The hospital wasn't very busy and Dr. Watkins walked beside the gurney as the paramedics wheeled Lucinda into the emergency room. They transferred the girl to another gurney-type bed used in hospitals. She winced a little as she was moved from gurney to gurney and Dr. Watkins could clearly see she was toughing it out. He turned to Margaret and sharply said, "You can stay in the waiting room. I'll come get you once I see the x-rays."

Margaret sat nervously in the waiting area, hoping that her perfect organized Christian world would stay intact.

After about thirty minutes, Dr. Watkins came to the waiting area. "Follow me Margaret." She stood up and followed him down the hallway to a room where Lucinda was sitting up in a bed. On the wall was a light board used to view x-rays. Dr. Watkins went to the counter, picked up a folder, opened it and placed four x-rays up on the board. With a pointer stick he began to explain the damage. "You see here at the shoulder; the arm is completely dislodged from the socket." Margaret sat emotionless as she listened to Dr. Watkins describe the x-rays. "Further down at the elbow, we see a dislocation — this is what's causing the swelling and bruising in the elbow — and right in the middle of the forearm, you can clearly see two fractures, one on the radius and one on the ulna. These are three very serious injuries."

Lucinda started crying. Margaret sat there stoically as she took in the news. Dr. Watkins went on, "We will need to put a cast on the arm from the wrist to the elbow." He further explained, "We'll sedate Lucinda and adjust the shoulder socket to pop the arm back into place, and then put the cast on." Lucinda was still sobbing as she heard the news. Dr. Watkins then lightened the mood. "The good news, Lucinda, is we don't have to put a cast on your swollen lip, as there are no broken bones in there." Lucinda's sobbing was momentarily interrupted by a slight giggle at the joke.

Margaret asked, "When will I be able to take her home?"

Dr. Watkins knew that he could send the girl home that very same day. "Margaret, we will need to keep her overnight for observation, to ensure the cast sets properly and the bones will have the best possible chance to heal."

"She can heal just fine at home, Dr. Watkins."

"Doctor's orders, Margaret. Lucinda will stay overnight in the hospital. You can come to see her in the morning. You should go now so we can get her prepped for surgery."

Feeling insecure, Margaret felt she had no other choice. The tone in Dr. Watkins voice was resolute, and she felt there was no point to argue. She looked at Lucinda. "Lucinda, sweetie, God bless you, that you may have a successful operation and come back to your loving family soon." Lucinda cracked a smile as fake as her mother's words. Margaret left the room, leaving Dr. Watkins with Lucinda.

Margaret's fears weighed on her mind. As she was walking out of the hospital, she crossed paths with Pastor Bill.

"Margaret!" Bill said with a smile as they approached each other. "What are you doing here at the hospital?" Bill completely ignored the dark sunglasses.

Margaret was upset and tried to compose herself as she explained. "Lucinda was thirsty in the middle of the night and in her sleepy state she fell down the stairs and broke her arm."

"Oh no, how horrible. I hope she's going to be alright."

"She'll be just fine, William. Oh, look at me, holding you up from your business." She stepped to the side as if to go around him and exit, he stepped in stride with her, not wanting to let this opportunity pass by.

"I'm just here to visit the widow Agnes. It shouldn't take too long; if you need a shoulder to lean on, I could be there for you."

Margaret thought with only a moment to decide. "That would be wonderful William, why don't you stop by the house after you're done here? I'll make some tea."

Bill grinned. "You're on Margaret, see you shortly." With that they went their separate ways.

CHAPTER 5 –

Afternoon Delight

MARGARET WAS EXCITED to see Bill at the hospital, even more excited to have him come over for tea. She could really use a shoulder to lean on right now. She rushed home then hurried around the house making sure everything was clean and tidy for her afternoon guest.

About half an hour later, Bill walked right in the front door without knocking. He called out, "Hello, anyone home?"

Margaret felt a jolt of excitement as she heard Bill's voice; she called out from the kitchen, "The tea is almost ready, be right out."

Bill had been to the house many times. He was familiar with the layout and took no time at all to make himself comfortable on the sofa while waiting for Margaret.

She came out of the kitchen carrying a silver tray with teapot, two tea cups, a bowl with sugar and a smaller pot for the cream. As she saw Bill, she beamed a smile as she placed the tray down on the coffee table. She sat in the chair adjacent to the sofa where Bill sat. "Thank you for coming over William, it's been a rough morning."

"Oh?" Bill asked. "Is there something more than just Lucinda's terrible fall down the stairs? He knew why she was wearing the sunglasses; she had in the past confided to him that John hit her sometimes. He saw an opportunity.

"No William, I'm just grateful you're here to comfort me." She smiled rather slyly.

"I feel that I must ask, what are Lucinda's injuries?"

"Nothing much William. Dr. Watkins said she broke her arm, which is to be expected in a nasty fall like that, she'll probably end up with bruises all over her body, knowing her like I do." Margaret laughed.

"Well Margaret you're a good mother and God will be there for Lucinda; she'll heal quickly. I am more worried about you and the emotional trauma you must be going through."

"You're concerned for me?" Margaret feigned surprise.

Taking the cue perfectly, Bill saw an opening. "Of course Maggie." He knew that calling her Maggie would be a test. "You have always been very important to me Maggie, my concern for you is genuine."

"You called me Maggie." She beamed. "You haven't called me that since..."

Bill grinned as he saw her face light up. "I haven't called you that since our affair ended and yes Maggie, I've never forgotten our time together."

"You mean torrid love affair, Bill." Margaret winked.

As Margaret leaned in to take the teapot, William placed his hand on hers. "The tea can wait; I want you now!" he exclaimed.

Margaret felt giddy inside as she saw Bill lean in, place a hand on the back of her head, drawing their faces closer together as he kissed her. It started slow and a bit awkward then quickly turned into an erotic passionate kiss with Margaret moving over to straddle Bill while he sat on the sofa. Within minutes the pair had removed their clothes.

"I've missed you, Bill," Margaret gasped in between kisses.

"I never stopped lusting for you, Maggie, you're the most beautiful woman in the world."

"Take me Bill." Margaret moaned.

"Oh, Bill," Margaret panted as she attempted to catch her breath. "That was amazing. It's been so long since John touched me."

"I know the feeling, Maggie. Stephanie is the same—quite the prude, if you know what I mean."

Margaret and Bill finished putting their clothes back on.

"Maggie, do you feel better now?"

"Actually Bill, I do; but I still don't know what to do."

"Do about what Maggie?" Margaret feigned embarrassment.

"Dr. Watkins is insisting on reporting Lucinda's accident to Sheriff Brown." She purposely quivered her bottom lip. "He seems to think something nefarious happened even though there is no incident to report." Bill nodded. "It's silly to think that anything but a simple accident happened; but if Bradley reports to Sheriff Brown, there will surely be an investigation."

Bill realized where this was going. "And you're worried that there'll be a scandal." He smirked. "Riley townspeople do love their scandals." Bill sensed another opportunity. "I could certainly see how Dr. Watkins would be concerned, considering that not only Lucinda had an accident; but it seems that you also had an 'accident.'" He motioned with his fingers making the quotation signs as he held his hands in the air.

She realized that Bill could see through her story. A tear started to form and roll down her cheek.

Bill saw this and went into support mode. "Margaret, tell me the truth, what really happened? I'm here to support you; I love you, after all, and I worry about you and your daughters."

"John flew into a rage last night. He hurt Lucinda, but it was in the heat of the moment." A seductive devious smile crossed her lips. "Will you help, Bill? Talk to Dr. Watkins, get him not to make a report to Sheriff Brown, please."

"Of course, Maggie, I can do that for you," he said, making it seem as though he was doing a great favor for her.

Upon hearing Bill agree to help, Margaret stood up, offered her hand to him. "Come to bed with me, Bill." He didn't need to be asked twice. The pair went upstairs to the master bedroom, to the very bed that Margaret shared with John. They took their time removing each other's clothes before embracing and falling together on the bed. After a few intense kisses, lips locked, tongues entwining, Bill casually asked, "So, what exactly set John off?"

Feeling aroused, Margaret had completely let her guard down and answered without thinking. "John got angry because Lucinda accused you of molesting her." As the words came out of her mouth, she realized her error. She looked deep into his eyes, waiting for him to be upset. He was not at all shocked to hear Margaret's words; in fact, hearing her say it out loud excited him even more. Margaret expected Bill to deny the accusation immediately; but not hearing anything, she thought for a moment as Bill was licking and nibbling on her neck. "It's not true is it?" she asked and Bill quickly responded.

"You're right Maggie, it's completely absurd." His hands roaming all over her body, he cunningly followed up his comment, "Why would I want a little girl? When I have the sexiest woman on the face of the planet, naked and in bed with me?"

The compliment not only made Margaret blush, it also disarmed her fleeting concern that there may be some small truth to Lucinda's accusation. Bill's vehement denial of the accusation set her mind at ease and she allowed herself to enjoy the physical connection the two would share that afternoon.

CHAPTER 6 –

Religious Influence

BILL LEFT MARGARET'S house just before the children arrived home. He had no fear, secure that his word would be believed over that of a child. Yet he still wanted to put a lid on the Lucinda situation before it became the scandal Margaret feared. He went straight over to the hospital, walked in and talked with the reception nurse.

"Hello, Bonnie, how are you on this fine afternoon?" Bonnie was a young mother who was a devout Christian, so she thought nothing of giving Pastor Bill any information he asked for.

"I'm fine, thank you for asking, Pastor Bill. It certainly is a lovely afternoon."

"Bonnie, I was wondering if you could tell me about Lucinda Hall."

"What about Lucinda, Pastor Bill?"

"What is she in the hospital for? I would like to go and visit my niece; offer moral support, you know," Bill said with a sly wink.

Bonnie the ever-dutiful Christian looked at the computer screen and gave Bill the information he needed. "Well, right now she is in surgery having a cast put on her arm. She'll be out at around 5pm, then in recovery for an hour. And then back to her room around 6pm."

"What's her room number?" Bill said with a narcissistic smile.

"It's room 109." Bonnie smiled up at him. Bill returned the smile.

"Thank you so much, Bonnie. That being the case, I will come back after dinner to visit my niece. See you then."

~

Lucinda was now prepped for the operation. She was wheeled into the operating room. Dr. Watkins' smiling face greeted her, using words to comfort and ease any fears she may have. "Hello, little lady, are you excited to get all fixed up?"

"Yes, Dr. Watkins, thank you."

Dr. Watkins spoke to everyone in the operating room. "My friend Lucinda here is a little bit scared, but we're here to make her feel all better."

One of the nurses assured Lucinda, "You're in good hands with Dr. Watkins."

The girl smiled as Dr. Don the anesthesiologist spoke. "Lucinda, can you count out loud for me from ten down to one?"

She started counting, "Ten... nine..." and that was all it took. Lucinda's eyes rolled shut and she was out.

Soon after, she was dreaming as she had the previous night. She saw the green flashes, heard the whispers and felt an overwhelming feeling of calm surge through her. In her dream, she again tried to communicate with the whispers. In a soft non-threatening voice, she called out, "Hello, it's me again, Lucinda, can you hear me?" The whispers continued but sounded like complete gibberish. She closed her eyes tight and saw the green flashes; it was as if her body was floating and she felt no pain, only pure comfort. She reveled in the feeling as she lay there listening to the whispers, the tone, the tune, it was a song unlike anything she had ever heard, it was as if heavenly angels were singing to her.

~

At quarter past six, Bill returned to the hospital. As the town's pastor, it was very easy for him to get in to see his niece. He walked into room 109 and saw his niece sleeping. He approached the bed, Lucinda's eyes opened slightly. She blinked a few times, trying to adjust to the light in the room. Bill saw this and went to the dimming light switch, turning the brightness down enough so that Lucinda could open her eyes. He returned to her bedside, waiting for her to focus and see him. Eventually as she became more aware and alert, she opened her eyes to see Bill standing over her. Her body twitched as if in fear, "Wha-what are you doing here, Uncle Bill?"

Bill smiled at the thirteen-year-old. "Well Lucinda, I had afternoon tea with your mother and she told me how you fell down the stairs, and how Dr. Watkins wants to make a report to Sheriff Brown."

Lucinda's body started to tremble in fear and she lied. "I kept our secret, Uncle Bill, just like you told me."

Bill frowned. "That's not what I heard from your mother."

Lucinda tried to stammer out an excuse. "My mother made me tell her." Lucinda realized she had just lied; she felt horrible about it, she had never told a lie before and now she lied to save herself. Bill, recognized that she was scared; he saw that she was already feeling guilty about telling her mom.

"Lucinda, what's done is done, but it can be undone."

"How, Uncle Bill?"

"Well, Lucinda, you just need to tell the doctor that you fell down the stairs, that's all that happened. Have you already talked to the doctor? What did you tell him?"

"I promise, Uncle Bill, I'll tell him I fell down the stairs, I won't say anything about you and me."

Bill pushed further. "Lucinda, what we have together is extremely private." He emphasized the word private. "We share a bond between pastor and parishioner; when you're with me, the things we say and do together are private and confidential." The girl looked at his face as he spoke. "You wouldn't want the people in town or at church to find out that you're a harlot who seduced her pastor, would you?" He continued on. "Wearing those tight clothes, showing off your body, giggling and asking to play horsey with Pastor Bill."

Lucinda had a shameful feeling. She thought, *did I really seduce Uncle Bill? I thought it was just a game.*

Pastor Bill pulled the covers back, revealing her arm in the white cast. He looked at her. "This is what happens when you betray a confidence, Lucinda." She looked at her arm in the cast and felt as though it were her own fault. Pastor Bill continued. "When you betray confidences, God will visit upon you retribution." He chided, "You told your mother that I molested you, which is not true! The truth is that you smiled and wanted to play with me, you knew what you were doing and you knew exactly what you wanted; it made you feel wonderful."

Lucinda started crying. Pastor Bill moved closer, leaned over, wrapped his arms around her and hugged her. "There, there, Lucinda, it's going to be alright, just be sure to tell the doctor that you fell down the stairs, and never again tell anyone about our special relationship."

Lucinda stopped crying long enough to speak. "I promise, Uncle Bill, it's a secret." Bill looked at her.

"And what will you tell the doctor?"

Lucinda stumbled slightly over her words. "I will tell him I fell down the stairs, Uncle Bill."

Bill smiled wide as he released the hug and looked into her eyes. "That's a good girl. God will be with you and love you."

Just then, Dr. Watkins walked into the room. "Ah Lucinda, I see you have a visitor. Hello, Pastor Bill."

"Hello, Dr. Watkins." Bill paused a moment. "I will let you take care of your patient. When you're done, would it be possible to meet in your office privately?"

Dr. Watkins agreed. "I should only be a few minutes. Her operation went well and she is well on her way to healing. One night in hospital and she'll be good as new."

"That's great news. I'll wait outside for you, Doctor."

Pastor Bill left the room, pretending to close the door behind him; he closed it so that it was still open about four inches. He then stood leaning against the wall just outside the door so that he could listen in on the doctor's conversation with Lucinda.

Dr. Watkins examined Lucinda's cast. "How are you feeling Lucinda?"

"Hungry," she replied with a smile.

"Anesthesia has a way of doing that to a person. I'll have the nurses bring you some food right away, but first I would like to talk to you about how this all happened."

Lucinda answered very quickly and in as confident a voice as she could muster. "I fell down the stairs Dr. Watkins, honest." Another lie, but this time Lucinda didn't feel guilty; she was lying to cover a wrong she committed.

Bill heard this exchange and moved away from the door, stepping across and down the hall so that he would not get caught eavesdropping.

When Dr. Watkins came out, he walked towards Pastor Bill. "I'm all yours now, Pastor, step into my office." He walked down the hall to the nurses' station. "Nurse Laura, would you please take some food to Lucinda in 109."

"Yes, Doctor, right away."

Dr. Watkins continued to his office, ushering Bill inside. "I'm glad you're here, Pastor Bill, your niece sustained some bad injuries that are not consistent with her description of what happened."

Bill feigned not to know what he meant. "What exactly do you mean, Doctor?"

"She said she fell down the stairs, yet her wrist is severely bruised as if a hand was tightly wrapped around it."

Bill sat listening to the doctor, feeling a bit like a poker player watching his adversary play all his cards at once.

"And the back of her neck has bruising consistent with a large hand squeezing around it." Dr. Watkins looked at Pastor Bill's expression for signs of outrage; he only saw a look of focused intent to hear the doctor out. The doctor continued. "As for her arm, it was ripped from the shoulder socket—one simply doesn't get a separated shoulder from falling—her elbow is dislocated—and there are two breaks in her arm, one on the ulna, and the other on the radius. These breaks combined with the shoulder dislocation all point to her arm being violently twisted behind her back and pulled very hard in an upwards motion."

There was a silence in the room as Pastor Bill pretended to be pondering what was said. "Did you talk to Lucinda, Dr. Watkins?"

"Yes, I talked to her, but she's too scared to tell the truth."

Bill knew he had the doctor exactly right where he wanted him. "What did Lucinda say happened?" he asked.

Dr. Watkins rolled his eyes. "She said she fell down the stairs."

Pastor Bill perked up in his chair. "So, let me get this straight, Dr. Watkins. The girl says she fell down the stairs, her mother says she fell down the stairs, and you want to make a report to the sheriff stating what exactly?"

"I didn't say anything about making a report to the sheriff." Bill watched closely as he saw the doctor's facial expression come to a sudden realization.

"Well, Doctor, no, you didn't say you were going to tell the sheriff, I guess I assumed that was the direction you were heading."

There was tension in the room as both men were contemplating their next move, it was like a game of chess with the truth on one side and a lie on the other.

Dr. Watkins began to speak. "I have a duty to inform—" He was quickly interrupted by Bill.

"You have a duty to your patients. At this point your suspicions are pure speculation." As Dr. Watkins tried to speak, Bill again interrupted. "Without absolute proof, even a reported suspicion would cast a shadow over the family, Lucinda would become the gossip of the town and my brother's wife would forever be thought of as a child abuser—"

Dr. Watkins interrupted. "Margaret was also a victim, Pastor. Her eye is black, and she was also abused."

"Dr. Watkins, have you thought that perhaps when John found out Margaret had abused their daughter, whom he loves dearly, that maybe he was overcome with situational rage, and in that rage, he struck Margaret out of pure animal instinct to protect one's offspring?" Bill could see the gears turning in Dr. Watkins' mind. "Think of it this way, Bradley. If you make a report to Sheriff Brown, the sheriff opens an investigation. Who exactly would prosecute if Margaret was found to be an abuser?" He paused to allow his words to sink in. "Joseph Bain is the Crown Prosecutor, he's on the Deacon Board with John and myself, Judge Ivy plays golf with me every week, and I don't believe Margaret abused her child, and certainly knowing my brother, I know beyond a shadow of a doubt he doesn't have a violent bone in his body." Dr. Watkins sat there brooding; having picked up on the veiled threat. "Finally, Dr. Watkins how would you recover from the scandal? Riley is a small town; people would see you as a whistleblower and they would lose faith that you would uphold doctor-patient privilege." He paused again, waiting for a response from the doctor. "No one wins, Dr. Watkins; I urge you to consider all the consequences."

"Alright, Pastor Bill, you're absolutely correct. Lucinda says she fell down the stairs, that's what my report will reflect. After all you can't fight City Hall, or in this case, the Church." Dr. Watkins glared at Bill.

Pastor Bill gave a graceful victory smile and a nod.

"I want you to know, Pastor Bill. I don't believe for one second that any of those girls in that house are safe. That man, your brother John, is a family annihilator. He will eventually destroy that family and when that happens, the church and you will again circle the wagons and protect your violent brother at all costs."

Pastor Bill stood up, headed towards the door, then turned his head and replied to the doctor's statement. "God will protect those girls and that family, and God will ease my conscience, Doctor." He smugly walked out.

⁓

The next morning Margaret picked Lucinda up from the hospital.

"I'm sorry I lied about Uncle Bill, Mother."

Margaret was pleased with the obvious change in the girl's demeanor. "You will need to apologize to your father, Lucinda, he'll be happy to hear it."

"I will, Mother, as soon as father gets home from work."

CHAPTER 7 –

Meeting Mary

PASTOR BILL WAS the youngest parish priest in Oklahoma history, so it came as no surprise to him when on Tuesday morning he received a phone call from a junior pastor in the next county.

"Hello, Pastor Bill speaking."

"Hello, Pastor Bill, it's Conrad here. I need your help with something."

"Sounds serious, Conrad, what's happened?"

Conrad was a young pastor of a small town not unlike Riley, where Pastor Bill lived.

"I think we might have a legitimate demon possession here in Champion," Conrad stated seriously. Pastor Bill let out a half chuckle of disbelief.

"That would be very rare; give me all the details."

Conrad sounded relieved to hear that Pastor Bill would hear him out. "Well, Pastor Bill, I have a sixteen-year-old girl, Mary Jones, she claims to have died and gone to heaven." He paused, waiting for a response.

"Go on Conrad, I'm listening."

"Nine days ago Mary was struck by a motor vehicle while she crossed the road. She was taken to hospital and was in coma for a week.

"When she awoke, she was delirious. Doctors said she might be suffering from a lack of oxygen to the brain. This might explain her mania, but it doesn't explain what I would categorize as stigmata." Again, Conrad paused, knowing that there are very few cases of actual reported and proven stigmata.

Hearing the word 'stigmata,' Pastor Bill wasn't sure if his apprentice priest was being dramatic or if this might be an actual case.

"Describe the bodily wounds you're seeing, Conrad."

"At first the bruises were on the girl's thighs, the inner thighs. The doctor thought that maybe she was raped, so he examined her and found no evidence that she was raped, in fact the doctor believes she is still a virgin as her hymen seems intact."

Pastor Bill felt his own excitement as Conrad talked of the young girl's sexual examination. "Tell me more, Conrad."

"Well, after a few days Mary showed bruises on her neck. It was as if someone had grabbed her by the back of the neck, causing finger-shaped bruises to appear. Here's the weird part, Pastor Bill, Mary has been held in the hospital psychiatric ward and has not left the hospital. These bruises appeared out of nowhere."

"Could these bruises be a result of the automobile hitting her?"

"Not very likely, Pastor Bill, the shape of the bruise is that of a large handprint, and the only injury she suffered from the accident was a small bump on the back of her head where she fell back and her head bounced off the pavement." Conrad realized that he needed to expand more on the vehicle accident. "Mary was walking across the street when old Mrs. White's car bumped into the girl. The car hit Mary's right thigh and tossed her body a few feet away. She landed on her backside with her head snapping back and hitting the pavement."

Conrad continued. "I have personally interviewed all the witnesses, and they all report the same thing: the car was hardly moving. She did have a slight bruise on her right thigh from where the car's bumper contacted her, but other than that, the only other injury is to her head."

"Interesting," Pastor Bill said.

"The doctors couldn't understand why Mary was in a coma. The bump on her head wasn't that bad, but it took a week for her to recover. When she finally woke, she was hysterical, screaming and yelling. She couldn't tell what day or month it was; she barely knew her own name. I sat with her for three days after she woke. While I was talking with her, she would forget things that we spoke of minutes before, she would ask the same questions she had asked a few seconds ago. At times her tone of voice would become very deep and sounded evil. She would say horrible things to me, telling me she wanted me to..." Conrad paused, stammering to get the next words out. Pastor Bill realized that he was beating around the bush.

"Just say it, Conrad."

"Pastor Bill, she wanted me to procreate with her, not in those words, she used profane sickening language; but she has several times asked myself, the doctor, orderlies and even the nurses to defile her body." Conrad let out a breath as he felt relieved to get over the hump and make his point.

Pastor Bill was even more intrigued. "So, you think that her personality change is pointing towards demonic possession?"

"Yes, Pastor Bill, Mary has always been a devout Christian girl, she has never been in trouble at school or home and is always involved in church activities and youth groups." There was genuine concern in Conrad's voice as he explained the changes in the girl and all he could think was that Mary was possessed.

"Well, Conrad, what you have said sure sounds serious, most definitely serious enough for me to make a special trip out to Champion."

Junior Pastor Conrad sounded excited and relieved to hear that Pastor Bill felt it was important. "When can you come, Pastor Bill?"

"I'll be there tomorrow morning. I will meet you at the church, and then you can take me to the hospital to introduce me to your Mary."

"Thank you, thank you very much, I'll see you tomorrow, Pastor Bill..

That evening after dinner, Lucinda approached John. "Father, may I please speak with you alone?" she said in as reverent tone as she could.

John agreed. "We can talk in my study after your chores are complete."

"Yes Father, I will tend to my chores first."

"Come see me when you're done." John sat down in his chair and read the newspaper.

A while later Lucinda again approached John. "Father, I have finished my chores. May we please talk now?"

"Alright Lucinda, let's go to my study." John led the way with Lucinda following.

"Father, I'm sorry for lying about Uncle Bill. I don't know what my mind was thinking, it was all just a misunderstanding."

"What I don't understand Lucinda is, what made you think that way?"

"Father, I was mistaken. We were all wrestling around with Uncle Bill and I thought he touched me; it was my mistake, I overreacted." Lucinda was doing her best to smooth over the incident. "Please don't hate me."

"Again, those were very serious accusations, Lucinda, accusations that could ruin a man of William's stature, not to mention the shame and embarrassment it could bring to our entire family."

"Father, I am truly sorry, I feel so guilty."

"I can see your apology seems sincere. Have you learned your lesson? God's will is for his children to be honest, and when you are dishonest there are consequences," John said, pointing at Lucinda's arm.

"Yes, Father, I deserved everything I got and more. I only pray that God will forgive me of my trespasses, and that you and Mother will also forgive me."

"And Uncle Bill, don't forget you need Uncle Bill's forgiveness most of all."

"Yes, Father, Uncle Bill as well."

"I'm relieved to have this resolved. Now run along and get ready for bed, Lucinda."

"Thank you, Father."

Lucinda left the room as directed.

⁓

The next morning Pastor Bill left at 6am for the one-hour drive to Champion. In his mind, he replayed the entire conversation he had with Conrad. He was excited to meet this Mary, to see and hear her story. He wondered if the girl would exhibit the same symptoms with him, if she would demand to procreate with him. He thought about the possibility of reporting to the church a legitimate possession, and how it would put him in the spotlight, how his religious career would profit from it.

Just then, he heard sirens. He looked in the rear-view mirror and saw red and blue flashing lights; he looked down to see he was doing 75 miles per hour, and realized he was speeding and about to be pulled over.

He guided his car to the shoulder, stopped and waited for the state trooper to approach his window. Upon arriving at his window, the trooper saw Bill's collar. Immediately the trooper asked, "Father, do you know how fast you were going?"

"Yes sir, I didn't realize it until I heard your sirens."

"Well, Father, I really should write you a ticket, but seeing that you're a man of the cloth, I think this time I'll let it slide. Just watch the speed, carry on and have a nice day."

"Thank you, officer," Pastor Bill went on his way. He chuckled to himself. "It's good to be a priest."

Once he arrived at the church in Champion, Bill went to the back through the corridor towards the office of the junior pastor. "Pastor Conrad," Bill greeted him. Conrad was delighted to see Pastor Bill;

he leapt out of his seat and offered his hand, the men shook hands as Conrad invited Pastor Bill to sit down.

After reviewing the case, Pastor Bill spoke. "Take me to the hospital, its high time I meet this Mary Jones." The two men left the church and went to the hospital's psychiatric ward where Mary was being monitored closely by medical staff.

The men walked into the room. Conrad entered first with Pastor Bill following. Bill noticed the girl was lying in the bed with her wrists in restraints. He looked at the restraints and then at Conrad, who picked up on the quizzical look on Bill's face. "Ever since she came out of her coma, the hospital staff keep her restrained most of the time."

Just then, Mary turned her head to see Conrad and the strange man. She recognized Conrad and asked in a sharp combative tone, "Have you come to put your seed in me, Conrad?"

Conrad gave a look to Bill that said *I told you so*.

"And who's that?" Mary hissed as her restrained hand attempted to point at Bill.

"Mary, this is Pastor Bill from Riley. He is here to help you." Mary perked up, looking Pastor Bill up and down.

"Help me?" she quizzed.

Pastor Bill stepped forward, introducing himself. "Conrad is right, I am here to help. My name is Pastor William Hall; you can call me Bill."

Mary's demeanor seemed to change once she heard the man's voice. "Well, Bill, can you help with this?" She used her legs to push the blanket covering her body, until it was down past her knees. Pastor Bill's eyes immediately focused between her thighs, where she had her legs spread wide, showing her naked vagina. Conrad immediately moved in front of Pastor Bill, replacing the covers just far enough to cover her groin area. Pastor Bill motioned his hands in a downward and back-off motion, signaling to Conrad that it was ok and for him to step back.

Bill engaged the girl asking, "Help with what, Mary?" He spoke softly.

Mary's tone became enraged. "Are you bloody blind?" Bill looked puzzled. "Look at my arm, dumbass!" Conrad gasped as he looked at her arm. Bill turned his focus to her right arm and saw that it was swollen and bruised.

"Ouch, that looks very sore, how did it happen?"

Mary snapped, "I don't know! I went to sleep last night, this morning I woke up and my arm hurt like holy hell! And I'm thirsty and no one will bring me anything to drink!"

Conrad offered. "I can go and fetch you a glass of water Mary. I'll be right back."

"No rush Conrad, take your time." Mary sneered.

With Conrad out of the room, Bill took advantage of the situation. "Mary, I have been told that you have other mysterious bruises as well, may I ask where those are? I see the bruise on your wrist." He moved his body around to better see her head. "I also see the bruise on your neck. Are there any other bruises?"

Mary bluntly said, "Down there," as her finger pointed to her thighs.

"Would you mind if I examined the area?" Pastor Bill was getting excited.

"Not at all, Bill, take a look." Mary's tone was more suggestive and almost alluring. Bill smiled at Mary and slowly moved the blanket down her legs, exposing her groin area. Trying as much as possible to appear professional, he moved even slower once the blanket had exposed her vulva.

The girl sensed the pastor's excitement; her next words startled Bill as her tone became very deep, just as Conrad had reported.

"Do you like what you see Bill?" When she said his name, she would drawl it out, "B-iii-LLL," saying the "i" shortly and emphasizing the "Ls" as if to mock or challenge him with a disrespectful tone. She paused with her eyes locked onto his, seeing that he was clearly gazing at her vagina. "Would you like to dip your man tool in there, Bill?"

Hearing footsteps coming down the hall, Pastor Bill lowered the blanket further down to expose the bruises on the girl's inner thighs.

He took another blanket and quickly folded and placed it over her vaginal area, covering it just before Conrad came back into the room with a nurse.

"Nurse Terry, meet Pastor Bill." Bill turned and smiled at the nurse.

"Pleased to meet you, Nurse Terry." Bill offered his hand politely.

"I think he wants to fuck you, nurse," Mary rudely blurted out.

"Mary!" Conrad exclaimed, disgusted with her comment. "Please control yourself, Pastor Bill is here to—"

Bill interrupted, saving Mary from admonishment. "Conrad, not to worry. Mary is right, Nurse Terry is very pretty; but what I'm wondering about is, why exactly is Mary in restraints?"

Nurse Terry explained. "The restraints are for everyone's protection. Last night she woke up screaming and was roughly rubbing her arm against the bedrail. The night shift gave her a morphine drip for the pain as well as a sleeping sedative so she could get some rest."

Mary chimed in. "Yeah, Bill," she said sharply, "they gave me drugs, good drugs." Bill saw Mary's wide-eyed grin; he smiled and nodded at her.

"What is your professional opinion on this case, Nurse Terry?"

Mary yelled out. "That stupid bitch doesn't know shit!—"

Conrad interrupted Mary, trying to calm her down. "Mary, you know everyone is here to help you, including Nurse Terry." The nurse didn't say a word, although Bill noted that her facial expression seemed to suggest that she was accustomed to this type of verbal abuse from Mary.

"Perhaps we should talk out in the hall, Nurse Terry."

"Of course, Pastor Bill, I wouldn't mind getting out of this room right about now." She walked out into the hall with Bill following behind.

"I realize that may have been uncomfortable for you Nurse Terry, I appreciate you taking the time to talk with me. What can you tell me about Mary?"

"Mary's case is an odd one, Pastor. Mysterious bruises have appeared on her the past three nights. Sometimes she is sweet as apple pie and the next moment she's off-the-rails nasty, foul-mouthed and rude."

"Go on, tell me everything," encouraged Pastor Bill.

"She can be violent, which is why we have her in restraints and check on her every hour. Pastor Conrad was called in because the girl seemed to need an exorcist. She even bit one of our intern nurses so hard that she drew blood."

"Interesting case indeed, Nurse Terry. What does the doctor say?"

"Dr. Moffatt is baffled; he can't understand how the bruises are happening, since she has pretty much been in restraints since she awoke. At first, he thought it was my staff physically abusing Mary, and that is just not the case."

"I can see how that thought would cross a person's mind."

Nurse Terry's tone became a bit defensive. "I can assure you, Pastor, my staff are professional at all times. None of them caused those bruises!"

"I didn't mean to accuse or offend anyone."

"But you did, Pastor. There is no reason anyone would think my staff to be abusive, we are professionals at all times. This is a small town, everybody knows everyone's business; if my staff were abusing a patient, it would-be-all-over town before you could say Johnny Appleseed."

Pastor Bill backpedaled, trying to ease the tension. "Honestly, I didn't mean anything by it, Nurse Terry."

She accepted the half apology with a nod. "It's a very stressful case; no one knows what's going on. She is a very healthy young lady except for the mysterious bruises. I hope you can help. We certainly need it."

Bill sensed the frustration in Nurse Terry's voice; he saw this as an opportunity to boast his experience. "I have been a pastor for years and I assure you I am here to help. We will get to the bottom of this soon enough." Nurse Terry smiled appreciatively.

Just then, the nurse was paged over the loudspeaker. "I have to go, Pastor Bill, let me know if you need anything."

"Will do," Bill said as he smiled at the nurse and watched her hips swing as she walked away.

Going back into the room, Bill had already started to formulate a plan. "Conrad, this is certainly an interesting case you have here."

"Yes, Pastor Bill, now you see why I called you."

"For sure, Conrad, you did the right thing, and now I think you should go back to the church, I'm sure you have work to do." Conrad looked at Pastor Bill, wondering why he was being dismissed. Reading Conrad's facial expressions, Pastor Bill knew he had hurt Conrad's feelings. "Let's go out in the hall, Conrad." Nodding in agreement, Conrad exited the room with Bill.

"Conrad, I suspect that a fresh set of eyes is what is needed here. You did the right thing to call me in." Conrad nodded. "I feel as though Mary could be faking it, and I feel with you there while I interview and talk with her, it could influence her to continue with the facade." Conrad seemed to understand and was still nodding slightly.

Pastor Bill went on to explain. "I do believe this could be a possession. If it is a possession, we will need to move the girl out of the hospital and into the church."

Conrad stopped his affirmative nodding. "Why would it be necessary to move her to the church?"

"Conrad, for Mary to remain in hospital, her mind believes she is sick, and the longer she remains in hospital, the more it will reinforce to Mary that she is sick. I'm not a medical expert, but I have had experience with demonic possession. If this is a demonic possession, surely the best place to deal with it is in a holy environment such as the church."

Conrad could now see exactly where Pastor Bill was going.

"Very good points, Pastor Bill. I will head back to the church."

Bill smiled, knowing his deception had worked.

"I'll contact you later, Conrad, and fill you in."

"Sounds good. The church has guest bedrooms in the back. I'll have two of them made up, one for you and one for Mary."

"That would be excellent, Conrad. I'll talk with Dr. Moffatt and tell him what we suspect."

Conrad left the hospital at just after 9am. Pastor Bill went back to Mary's room. When she saw he was alone, her eyes grew wide.

"I'm glad you came back." Mary licked her lips slightly.

"I'm happy to be back, Mary." Bill smiled. "Would you mind if I move this chair beside your bed?"

"Fill your boots Bill." Her eyes looked him up and down as he bent over, picked up the chair and moved it. "So, you think you're the hero that's going to save me?"

"I don't know about that Mary, what I do know is that I was asked to come and help you. I am pleasantly surprised to find a beautiful, obviously intelligent young woman who at this time may or may not be possessed by a demon."

"You came to help me Bill, how about you start by removing these fucking things?" Mary pulled on the restraints holding her wrists to the bed rails.

"Unfortunately Mary, I'm not authorized to do that; but if you're really good." Bill winked. "I'll see about asking Nurse Terry to remove them after we talk. Deal?"

Mary pursed her lips and wiggled her nose. "Ok fine, we have a deal; but first you have to do something for me." She licked her lips and rubbed her thighs together as she stared directly into Bill's eyes. Bill instinctively put his hand to his collar and gently tugged it as he ran his finger inside to allow for some air flow. "Oh, does that make you uncomfortable when I do this?" Mary licked her lips again.

Bill smiled confidently. "You do have very nice lips Mary and no it doesn't make me uncomfortable. It tells me you need a drink of water. Would you like me to hold the glass for you?"

"Well, it's about God damned time, I'm so thirsty and it's a little difficult to lift the glass to my mouth with my wrists bound to the bed."

Bill laughed. "Alright, let me." He stood up and reached over grabbing the glass of water Conrad had brought. He moved to stand directly beside the bed, leaning over he slowly moved the glass to Mary's lips. "Ok slowly now." Just as he bent over the bed railing, he felt Mary's hand fondle his crotch through his pants. "Oh, careful." Mary's bottom lip contacted the glass as Bill raised the bottom so the water would come out slowly. "How's that?"

Mary took her sweet time drinking the water. "Just a little more Bill, please." Mary took advantage of Bill's vicarious position and continued fondling him as he gave her water.

"Ok Mary, I think that's good for now." Bill removed the glass and stepped back. As he returned the glass to the bed table, he saw the devilish expression on Mary's face.

"Thank you Bill, that was amazing."

"The water was amazing?" Bill asked.

"Yes, I meant the water." Mary sarcastically quipped. "It was like drinking Holy Water blessed by the almighty himself. Hallelujah, praise the Lord." She mockingly laughed.

"You have a sharp tongue Mary, do you enjoy—" Mary interrupted.

"I'll tell you what I enjoy if you bring your ear over here so I can whisper it to you." Another seductive lick of her lips which again excited Bill. "Stand up, come let me whisper in your ear."

"I don't know about that Mary." Bill feigned fear, to cover up his attraction to the young woman.

"Just do it Bill, I promise you won't regret it."

"But Mary, I understand you have already bitten a nurse. What's to say you don't bite my ear off?"

"Oh come on Bill, I'm possessed by a nymphomaniac not a cannibal. Let me whisper in your ear, please." Her alluring eyes begged the Priest. "Take a leap of faith Bill, I promise I won't bite."

"I tell you what Mary, I'll take that leap of faith as long as you promise to return the favor should I ever ask for the same from you."

"Deal!" Mary excitedly shrieked.

"Ok, here goes." Bill stood up, looked suspiciously into Mary's eyes as he moved closer, he placed a hand on the bed's guard rail and leaned over slowly moving his right ear ever closer to her waiting lips. "Remember you promised not to bite."

Mary spoke softly. "A little closer Bill." He responded and bent over just a little farther. "What I enjoy Bill is touching. The feeling of hot flesh contacting hot flesh." Just as she finished her sentence, she seductively licked Bill's ear lobe. "Hmm, you taste good Bill. Did you like that?"

"Ah—" Bill didn't have time to answer before Mary again licked his lobe, only this time as she did it, she placed the palm of her hand on top of Bills hand which was holding onto the bed rail. "Oh my God!" Bill moaned out loud as his mind flooded with erotic feelings and his manhood became instantly erect. He moved his head up and looked at Mary to see her eyes had turned the brightest shade of emerald green he had ever seen in his life.

Mary gasped. "That's it, that's the feeling. Flessshhh on flessshhh." Mary caressed the back of Bill's hand the best she could while in the restraints.

Nurse Terry shouted out as she came in the door. "Is everything alright in here? I heard someone—"

Bill interrupted. "Everything's fine." He thought fast and grabbed the glass of water and put it in front of Mary's face before turning around to show the nurse. "I was just helping Mary have a drink of water and some spilled."

Mary helped with the deception. "Yeah, Nurse Terry, it's all good. Bill just got me a little wet is all, sorry to disturb you."

"Alright then, I'm just down the hall if you need anything, either of you." The nurse left and Mary giggled quietly. "You liked making me wet Bill, I could tell." She grinned as Bill sat back down in the chair breathing heavy. "Did you feel it Bill? The electricity between us?"

Bill took a swig from Mary's water and returned the glass back to the table. "Oh yes Mary, I don't know what happened; but that was—"

Mary interrupted. "Euphoric." She smiled.

"That about sums it up Mary, wow!"

"So, will you ask the nurse to remove my restraints now?" Mary flashed her best puppy dog eyes at him.

"Yes Mary I will; but I'm curious about something." He paused a moment. "Have you done that to anyone else, like the doctor or—?"

"Done what Bill?" Mary played coy.

"Touched them and made them feel—" Mary interrupted saving him from having to finish his awkward question.

"Yes I have Bill, and to answer your next question. No! I did not have that same physical, spiritual explosion of erotic energy when I touched Doctor Moffatt, or when I touched Brian the orderly. You're special Bill, we have a connection. Now please tell the nurse to let me out of these damn restraints."

Bill chuckled. "I see." He nodded. "Ok Mary a deals a deal, you've been amazing so I don't see how you pose any danger to yourself or others around you." He pressed the call button and within minutes Nurse Terry came into the room.

"Thank you for coming, Nurse Terry." Bill smiled at her. "I think we can safely remove the restraints now; Mary seems to be in good calm spirits." He turned to Mary. "Isn't that right Mary?"

"Yes, Pastor Bill, I'll be good, I promise."

Nurse Terry began to object. "Pastor—"

Bill interrupted, "Nurse Terry, trust me, I have experience with violent patients. Mary poses no danger; please remove the restraints." The nurse shook her head but decided to do what was asked; she didn't want to be the nurse who defied a request from a man of the clergy. As Nurse Terry removed the restraints, Bill's eye caught Mary looking at him seductively.

Nurse Terry was about to leave the room when Pastor Bill made another request. "Could we get some food for poor Mary? She looks quite hungry." Mary was in agreement, interrupting the nurse's response.

"That would be wonderful, I'm famished."

"I'll get you some food, Mary, be back shortly." Nurse Terry left.

"Bill, thank you for having those infernal straps removed." Bill grinned at her. "They were starting to chafe my wrists." She demonstrated, holding her wrists out to show the pastor.

"You're most welcome, Mary. You're not going to make me regret my decision, are you?"

"Who, me?" Mary jested. "Never would I ever," she said with a sly grin.

"Good, I would hate to look the fool."

Nurse Terry returned with a plate of toast, scrambled eggs, bacon and orange juice, placing it on the tray beside the bed.

"Thank you, Nurse Terry." Mary was being pleasant and calm. The nurse smiled and moved the bedside tray over Mary's lap.

"Now, eat slowly Mary, we wouldn't want you to get sick now."

"Got it, Nurse Terry, slow and steady."

Bill watched as the nurse left the room; he turned back to see Mary slowly eating her meal. He wondered to himself how he would convince Dr. Moffatt to relinquish custody of the girl to the church, to him. He then thought about how he would get the girl's parents to allow him to keep the girl overnight at the church.

CHAPTER 8 –

Teamwork Manipulation

EVERY MORNING FOR two-weeks since the accident, Sally and James would go to the church around 9:30am, they would say their prayers and then go to the hospital to check on their daughter. This morning was no exception. The two parents walked into the church, made their way to the front and knelt before the altar. There was a large wooden cross hung on the wall with a ceramic Jesus figure mounted to it. As Sally and James held hands, they began to pray. "Oh Lord, our father in heaven, we come to you in our time of need."

Pastor Conrad heard noises coming from the cathedral. He went to investigate, and as he walked through the doorway, he saw Mary's parents and exclaimed, "I have wonderful news, James and Sally!" As he moved closer, they stood and moved towards Conrad. James shook his hand, but Sally passed on the handshake; instead, she moved to hug Conrad. It was clear these parents loved their daughter and were in much distress. "Come sit here." Conrad pointed to the front cushioned pew. The three sat down with Sally in the middle. James leaned forward and listened as Conrad explained.

"Yesterday I contacted our parish priest Pastor Bill. I told him of Mary's plight and he agreed to come and investigate." James let out a sigh of relief.

Sally quickly tapped James on the knee. "Don't interrupt, dear, let the pastor finish. Go on, Pastor Conrad, we want to hear everything."

Conrad's facial expression was upbeat and excited as he continued. "Pastor Bill arrived this morning just before 8am."

Sally shrieked. "He's already here?"

James returned the favor to Sally tapping her on the knee. "Let the man talk, dear." Conrad chuckled, as did Sally.

"I share in your excitement, James and Sally. I felt as though we needed help and the good Lord provided." He placed his hands together, bowed down slightly before looking upwards. "Thank you, Lord." Mary's parents followed suit, placing their hands together, bowing and looking upwards.

"Pastor Bill is at the hospital now; he has had time to meet and talk with Mary and is waiting to meet with Dr. Moffatt."

"What does he say?" James asked. "Does he think Mary is possessed?" Sally's eyes focused intently on Conrad's.

"First I must tell you that this morning there were new bruises on Mary's body." Sally gasped as James winced as if in pain. Conrad saw the reaction of the parents and immediately comforted them. "No, no, it's a good sign. The new bruises gave us insight and we, myself and Pastor Bill, feel that we are one step closer to solving the mystery." The parents again perked up, hearing hope in the pastor's voice.

"Pastor Bill feels that Mary being in the hospital is reinforcing the idea that she is sick, when in fact she's in perfect health. We discussed it and feel that it would be best to move her to the church for a few nights." The parents looked puzzled. "If it's a demonic possession, what better place than our church to cure Mary?" Conrad said.

Sally agreed immediately. James had a question. "For how long would Mary stay at the church? What happens if she doesn't get better?"

"The hospital doesn't know what to do with Mary. Ever since she bit Nurse Ramirez, they have pretty much kept her in restraints. We need help that goes beyond modern medicine. It is often best in matters such as these for the parents to step back and put their faith in God, the church and its priests."

James and Sally listened, nodding affirmatives as Conrad explained. "Pastor Bill is one of the best, most respected priests in the whole church. He is well known for helping families come together in times of trauma. What Mary is experiencing is well beyond anything Dr. Moffatt and his staff have ever experienced; and the longer she stays in hospital, the more people are going to hear, and gossip."

Conrad's words resonated with the parents. "Can we meet this Pastor Bill?" Sally asked.

"Of course, let's go over there now."

"Thank you, Pastor Conrad," James said, followed by Sally, who stood and hugged Conrad.

~

Mary finished eating and laid back with a smile on her face. "That hit the spot," she said, with a satisfied grin.

"I'm glad you liked it. How long has it been since you ate?" Mary paused and thought for a moment, her eyes looking up and to the left as she tried to remember.

A knock at the door came and in walked Dr. Moffatt. Pastor Bill stood up, turning to face the doctor, who was followed into the room by Nurse Terry.

"Dr. Moffatt, this is Pastor Bill." Said Nurse Terry. Bill extended his hand out to the elderly doctor.

"I'm glad you're here, Pastor Bill. This is a curious case indeed, and it would be nice to have some direction from the church."

Nurse Terry informed the doctor, "There were new bruises on her arm this morning." Dr. Moffatt rolled his eyes in disbelief and didn't say a word. He walked over and examined Mary's new bruises.

"When did this happen, Mary?"

"Dr. Moffatt, it happened last night while I was sleeping."

The doctor looked baffled. There was a long pause. He shook his head. "I have no clue what's going on here, this makes absolutely no sense. In my fifty-two years practicing medicine, I have never seen anything like this."

Pastor Bill smiled inside as he recognized an opportunity. "Dr. Moffatt, may I speak to you in private?" He looked at Mary and asked her, "Would that be alright with you Mary?"

The girl picked up on Bill's angle. In her best, sweetest voice, she responded, "Of course, Pastor Bill, I'll be just fine. I will be a good girl, won't be a problem at all. I really don't want to go back into those restraints."

Dr. Moffatt saw the empty food tray beside the bed. "Did you finally eat, Mary?"

"Yes, Dr. Moffatt, I was famished. It was so good."

He laughed loudly. "You're the first person who ever said hospital food was good."

He turned to Pastor Bill, remembering that the pastor had requested to see him. "Yes, yes, of course, Pastor Bill, let's go to my office."

While the doctor met with Bill in the office, Mary's parents and Pastor Conrad arrived at the hospital.

⁓

Sally walked into the room first and saw her daughter sitting up in the bed, a bright shiny smile on her face. She looked so much better today than in past days. Sally rushed to hug Mary. "You look so good. How are you feeling Mary?" A tear of joy ran down James' face seeing his daughter in this state.

Mary hugged her mom, telling her, "I feel much better, I think I can go home now."

Sally sat on the side of the bed beside her daughter as her father stood and watched in awe at the complete reversal in his daughter's demeanor. "Pastor Bill came to help and I feel so much better, Mom."

Sally said a silent prayer thanking God for sending an angel to save her daughter.

～

"Thank you, for taking the time to speak with me, Dr. Moffatt."

"Think nothing of it, Pastor Bill. I'm grateful for your assistance."

"Seems that Mary's physical injuries are healed."

"Yes, her injuries were minor, other than a slight bruise where the car struck her, a bruise that has since gone away. She suffered a slight bump on the head but the neuroimaging shows no brain damage at all, we have run every test on her. Her CT scan is negative, everything is as it should be, yet we see curious bruises forming on her body and an oddity that I have never seen in my many years in medicine."

"What was the oddity, Doctor?"

"I was in Mary's room checking on her and for a moment she flat-lined. She was for all intents and purposes dead." Bill saw from the man's facial expression that he was truly mystified.

"I was told that she was just in a coma."

"She was, but for an instant she flat-lined. Then suddenly out of nowhere she sat straight up and yelled; she then slumped back on the bed. I checked her immediately and found she was still alive, yet still in a coma."

"Very interesting. What did she yell when she awoke?"

"No!"

"No? You won't tell me?"

"No, that's what she said. 'No.' that's all she said, Pastor Bill. It was the strangest thing. I just can't put my finger on it. When Conrad suggested demonic possession, I didn't believe it possible, but it's the only explanation left."

"Conrad was wise to call me. I have spent a lot of time reviewing Conrad's written reports and I have talked with Mary, as well." Bill stated facts like he was reciting his resume.

Dr. Moffatt listened with hope in his eyes.

"Honestly, Dr. Moffatt, I'm with you. I have only ever seen one demonic possession. It was very early in my career." He watched as Dr. Moffatt's eyes lit up. "The young lady that was possessed showed many of the same signs Mary shows." Bill carefully watched the doctor's body language as he related his experience. "She had bruises appear on her hands, feet and across her chest. She was violent, combative and used profane language, much like your Mary."

"I believe that you have gone above and beyond, Dr. Moffatt. You have done every possible test, checked and rechecked your findings." Dr. Moffatt nodded in agreement.

"Yes, I have done everything I possibly can to get to the bottom of it all."

Bill smiled like he was holding a royal flush in his hand. "Dr. Moffatt." He placed a comforting hand on the doctor's shoulder. "You've done all you can do; it's in the hands of God now." There was a long pause before Dr. Moffatt answered.

"I agree, Pastor Bill. We have done all we can; it's now in the hands of God. Will you help?"

BINGO! Pastor Bill thought to himself. "Of course I'll help. The first thing we need to do is discharge Mary from the hospital." Bill watched the doctor, closely measuring his reaction. "As long as she is in hospital, she will believe she is sick. I know that Pastor Conrad has guest rooms in the church; he suggested we move her to the church for a few days."

~

Mary was pleasantly conversing with her parents and Pastor Conrad. Sally and James were elated to be having a casual conversation with their daughter, one in which she wasn't shouting obscenities.

Walking into the room, Dr. Moffatt approached the bed. He spoke to the girl. "Mary, you seem much better today." Mary saw a pathway out of the hospital and she took advantage.

"Dr. Moffatt, I feel much better. Pastor Bill explained to me that I need God's help to get better. You have done everything you can, but I need to put my faith in God now."

"I'm glad you feel that way, Mary," Dr. Moffatt said. "We'll be discharging you to the care of your parents." Upon hearing that, Pastor Bill went into a panic; he thought that he had convinced the doctor to release Mary to him. "I've had a conversation with Pastor Bill and he feels he can be helpful to you. He's offered for you to spend some time at the church so that you may return to a relationship with God." Pastor Bill's panic was diminished as he saw where the old doctor was going.

Dr. Moffatt turned to James and Sally. "I've done everything I can; Mary is clearly in good health. I strongly recommend you spend some time talking with Pastor Bill. He has a solid plan of action, which I believe will benefit Mary greatly."

Mary's smile did little to conceal how excited she was.

Dr. Moffatt turned to leave. "I'll inform Nurse Terry to process Mary for discharge. If there are any other issues, don't hesitate to come see me." He walked out the door.

James looked over at Pastor Bill, then turned and offered his hand. "I'm James and this is my wife, Sally. We're Mary's parents."

"Very nice to meet you." Bill thought to himself. *Where do I know Sally from?* He looked closer. "Sally, I can't shake the feeling that we've met before." Bill's mind was trying to recall a memory from long ago.

"I don't remember ever meeting you Pastor Bill." Sally turned her eyes away from him.

"Ah yes! Have you ever been to Riley? I think it was the Mother's Day spring carnival back in nineteen seventy-sev—." Bill was interrupted.

"Honestly Pastor Bill, I have never been to Riley." Sally's cheeks flushed slightly.

James added. "You couldn't have met Sally then; every Mother's Day she spends a week at her mother's house in Tulsa."

Bill looked puzzled. "I could have sworn..." When he looked at Sally, he realized her eyes were pleading with him to keep her secret. "You're probably right James, I see so many people in my life, sometimes it becomes a blur." Conrad sensed the awkwardness. "My apologies, I guess I should have made proper introductions."

Pastor Bill saved face for Conrad. "There's no fault here, Conrad, we were all anxious to listen to Dr. Moffatt's recommendation. Besides, we've met now, so it's all good. I suggest we go to lunch together, all of us." Bill looked at Mary. "Would you like to go for lunch?" Mary practically leaped out of the bed.

"Oh, yes, Pastor Bill, I could do with some more food, the hospital food is not as good as I said before." She opened her mouth, making a gesture with her finger pointing into her mouth as her tongue stuck out. To her parents and Conrad, the action was received as Mary saying the food was not all that great; to Pastor Bill, he sensed that Mary might be sending him a personal private message.

Pastor Bill suggested, "I think the men should leave the room so Sally can help Mary get dressed." Everyone agreed and the men sauntered out of the room and waited in the hallway.

Nurse Terry came down the hall with a wheelchair. "This is standard procedure for discharging patients."

"I can walk just fine," Mary blurted as she saw the wheelchair.

"Standard procedure if you want to be discharged, Mary." Nurse Terry smiled.

Conrad suggested. "Pastor Bill, we could go on ahead to the local diner and meet James and his family there."

"I'm good with that." Said Bill.

James stated. "We'll see you shortly."

"Yes, see you there Pastor Bill," Mary called out as the nurse wheeled her out of the hospital room.

Sitting in the diner with Conrad, Pastor Bill basked in the conversation.

"Pastor Bill, I can't believe the change in Mary. Just yesterday she was a complete mess, and now after spending a short time with you, it's as if she's all healed."

Bill realized that things were going well, too well. He needed to dial back the narrative, to present a reason for him to stay the night in Champion. He knew that Mary wasn't possessed; he thought he understood exactly why there was a change in her, but he didn't want to let this opportunity slip away. He was excited at the prospect of spending some alone time with Mary. He had to bring the narrative back around to Mary's issue, and he had to convince Conrad and Mary's parents that he needed more time with Mary.

"I don't think she is healed, Conrad, far from it. I believe that she is responding well to accepting God back into her heart." Conrad hung on every word Pastor Bill said. "She seems better because the one thing I have given her is hope."

"Hope?" Conrad quizzed.

"Yes, hope that God will forgive her and that she'll have a place in the kingdom of heaven."

This all made sense to Conrad. "There they are," he said as he saw James, Sally and Mary enter the diner. He stood and waved them over to the table.

As Sally approached the table on Conrad's left side, Mary was to the left of her mother, nearest to Pastor Bill. The priests stood up, Conrad pulled a chair out for Sally, Bill did the same for Mary. James moved behind Conrad as the ladies were being seated. He took a seat to Conrad's right.

During lunch there was much discussion about Mary. She was certainly the star of the show.

Conrad opened the conversation. "I'm happy to see you feeling better, Mary." The girl beamed looking over at Bill as if to give all the credit to him. Bill saw her looking but he played the humble card, shooting her a sympathetic smile in return.

Sally was elated. "Pastor Bill, we can't thank you enough for coming to our aid."

James chimed in. "Yes. Thank you, Pastor Bill."

Bill looked at Conrad. "I can't take all the credit. Conrad is the one who suspected there might be an issue beyond modern medicine. He called me and I came, that's all." Bill desperately needed to put a stop to all this 'Mary is cured' type of talk.

The parents went on and on about what Dr. Moffatt said and how God was the answer to their prayers. Conrad seemed to feed the narrative even more and Bill realized it was slipping further and further away.

"In cases such as Mary's, it's often prudent to not let your guard down. We must be vigilant," Bill injected into the conversation.

Mary enjoyed watching the verbal chess match of manipulation that she could clearly see Bill was spinning. She picked up on the fact that if her parents thought she was cured; they would take her home and she might not see Bill again.

"I think Mary's change is not as much of a miracle as you would think."

Sally interrupted. "Of course, it's a miracle, Pastor Bill, she was down and depressed, angry and lashing out at everyone. She even bit a nurse." Sally looked at her daughter, patted her knee. "It wasn't you dear, you weren't yourself." Mary gave a sheepish smile, pretending to feel sorry for biting the nurse. "James will tell you how close we were to giving up, how we thought the devil himself had taken over Mary's body, and now she's all well."

Pastor Bill was almost beside himself now; he seemed to be fighting a losing battle. He thought to himself, *one downside of extremely devout Christians is they look for religious meaning in everything. When things go wrong, they pray to God, and when things get better, they give credit to God and think it will never happen again. How can I turn this around? They need to believe their daughter is still in danger.'*

"Conrad, what do you think? Should we have a parade for Pastor Bill?" James said in a jovial manner. Mary watched Bill's reactions closely; she could see he was struggling to make his case.

Mary changed the tide with a simple speech. "When I was hit by the car, I thought I was going to die. It felt like I was dying; there was a white light that I was drawn to." Everyone at the table listened intently to every word Mary said. She'd never had so much attention in her life and she relished it.

"It was the scariest thing that I've ever felt. I thought that if I could only make it to the white light, I would be ok, that God and Jesus were waiting for me." Mary paused for effect, looking at the faces around the table all fixated on her. She played it up even more. "Before I could reach the light, I had a feeling of abandonment and an extreme feeling of being alone and in that moment, I was angry with God, angry because I didn't understand what was happening."

Tears flowed down Sally's face as she had heard about the white light before; she'd heard it from Mary when she first came out of the coma. Sally feared that Mary was going to again tell the story she told of how God didn't exist, how dying is cold and painful, and how the church lied to her all her life.

Mary saw her mom's tears and knew she had everyone eating from the palm of her hand, including Pastor Bill.

"When I awoke, the first thing that people did was crowd around me, asking lots of questions. I didn't know how to handle that so I lashed out."

Bill realized what Mary was doing. She was casting shadows of doubt; she was opening the door for him to step through and they played well off each other.

"I see what Mary is saying," injected Pastor Bill. "Conrad and I spoke earlier." He looked over at Conrad as if handing off the football.

Conrad took the ball and ran. "Yes, what we think is that Mary had lost hope. Pastor Bill's arrival and the time he spoke with Mary gave her back the hope she'd lost."

"Exactly right!" Mary exclaimed loudly.

Bill saw a pathway now. "Champion is a small town. When Mary awoke, she was inundated with people she knew all asking her questions at the same time. She answered those questions the best she could. After a period of time without having food, and having just awoken from what could only be described as a near-death experience, it's understandable how Mary would feel let down by God," Pastor Bill explained. "I'm not quite sure there was a demonic possession, but if there was, surely the demon has retreated even if only temporarily."

Mary got in step with Bill. "I agree, I wasn't myself. It was as if someone or something had taken over and was speaking for me. I would never use profanity, but yet I said awful things to people—to you, Mom, and to you, Dad." Mary looked at her parents with remorse, "I'm sorry, I just didn't know what came over me." Bill took the handoff from Mary right on cue.

"Mary, it wasn't within your control. You had an out-of-this-world experience that would be more than enough to shake anyone." Sally watched as Pastor Bill comforted her daughter; she felt as though this man was sent by God himself to help Mary. James sat listening to the conversation and he too felt great appreciation for Pastor Bill.

Bill looked at Sally and then turned to Mary. "Mary, if you feel that you're all better, then my work here is done." Bill was starting to enjoy the cat-and-mouse game he was playing with Mary, leading her down a path to give her the power to make a choice. In doing so, he knew it would be removing the decision from her parents, which they would go along with whatever Mary wanted to do. Mary picked up on the twist, realizing what Bill had done.

"I don't think your work here is quite done," Pastor Conrad chimed in. "You've really only had a few short hours with Mary, and you haven't yet proved or disproved a demonic possession."

Bill was happy that Conrad had clued in. He sensed that Conrad was afraid that if Bill left, Mary could relapse and Conrad would be left holding the bag.

James then stepped into the conversation. "I thought the plan was for Mary to spend some time at the church with Pastor Bill, to help her reconnect with God, and make a determination whether or not there is a demonic presence within her."

Pastor Bill had to respond. "Yes, that was the plan, but you're her parents and it's up to you." He paused for effect. "Ultimately, the choice is Mary's."

Another pause, only longer this time. Bill noticed that everyone was looking at Mary. "Mary, you haven't had the chance to tell me much about your experience while you were in the coma. Would you like to talk about that?"

Mary feigned hesitation; she knew everyone was eating it up like pumpkin pie at Thanksgiving. "Pastor Bill, I would like to talk about it. I still don't understand it all."

James addressed Sally. "I think we need to ask Pastor Bill to continue with the original plan. Mary needs to make sense of her experience, and Pastor Bill seems to be able to relate well to her."

Sally agreed. "Pastor Bill, will you stay awhile? To help our daughter to understand, help us to understand what she went through, please."

Conrad also joined in. "Bill, I think it's in Mary's best interest for you to stay."

Mary did everything she could to stop herself from bursting out in laughter. She saw Bill's facial expression; it was like he was a fisherman reeling in his catch.

"Of course, I'll stay. I'm a tool of God," said Pastor Bill. Mary chuckled inside at his use of the word "tool."

"Then it's decided. After lunch, Mary will return home, just long enough to gather her overnight clothes and toiletries, then you will drop her off at the church and leave her in our capable hands." Conrad's words were directed at James and Sally.

"Yes, that's a wonderful idea," Sally said gleefully, looking over at her daughter and the wide smile on her face.

CHAPTER 9 –

Mary's Experience

AT 4PM SALLY and James dropped Mary off at the church. They walked her inside and went to Pastor Conrad's office. Seeing them appear in his doorway, he stood up from behind his desk and ushered Mary to the room she would be staying in at the end of the hall.

"Mary, you can put your overnight bag in this room and once you're settled, you can come to my office."

"Where's Pastor Bill?" Mary asked.

"Oh, he's in his room writing reports and sending emails. He could be a while as our Prodigy server is kind of slow, it takes forever to send email." Conrad chuckled.

Mary went into the room and looked around. There was a single bed, a night stand, a desk with a chair, a lamp on the desk and a small dresser in the corner under the window. She put her bag on the floor and then flopped herself on the bed. "Well, this isn't too bad." She did a snow angel on the sheets.

In Pastor Conrad's office, James and Sally spoke with Conrad. "We can't even begin to express our appreciation for everything, Pastor Conrad, we really were at the end of our rope."

"We should go and get out of their way, let them do their work, Sally."

"Yes, James, you're right, we should go."

Conrad assured, "Your daughter is in good hands."

The parents left the church.

～

Pastor Bill was emailing his wife:

Dear Stephanie,

I've arrived in Champion and have met the girl Mary. Pastor Conrad may be right, this could be a legitimate demonic possession. I will need to stay one, maybe two nights. It may become necessary to admit the girl to Hopewell Asylum. I will contact you again tomorrow.

Love William.

It took at least ten minutes for the email to send. Bill sat and waited while the bar on the screen read, "Sending..." He could hear the dial-up tone and thought how marvelous this technology was that would allow him to send a message in mere minutes, rather than days through the US Postal Service snail mail.

Bill came out of his room to find Mary leaning against the wall across from his doorway.

"Darn, you surprised me, Mary—a pleasant surprise mind you. Have you just arrived?"

She shook her head. "No, Bill I've been here about a half hour."

"Wow! I had no idea, sorry to keep you waiting. Follow me, Mary." Bill walked down the hall to Conrad's office. He poked his head in. "Would you care to join us in the sitting room, Conrad?"

Conrad looked up from his desk. "Of course, Pastor Bill, I'll be right there."

Bill then walked further down the hall, past the archway off to the left that led into the cathedral of the church, past the church kitchen and into the last room at the end of the hall. With Mary following close behind, she almost bumped into Bill when he stopped to open the door. As Bill stepped back, he inadvertently bumped into her. "Oh, pardon me, I didn't realize you were that close, Mary."

She grinned and looked at Bill. "I wouldn't mind getting even closer, Bill."

Inside the sitting room was a wall of shelves full of books, and two leather couches with four end tables, one on each end. The two couches faced each other with a long rectangular coffee table spaced evenly between them. About ten feet away was a set of two high-back leather chairs, a table between them facing a fireplace. The room was set up for reading; a single King James Bible was on the table between the chairs.

Pastor Bill moved over to the couch farthest from the door; he sat in the middle of three cushions, leaving enough room for Pastor Conrad to choose one side or the other. "Have a seat Mary." He pointed to the couch opposite of the one he was on. He watched as Mary eyed up the couch, carefully choosing her spot. She chose the middle seat. "Ah, I thought you'd choose the middle seat." Bill smiled victoriously.

Mary kicked off her shoes, turned her body and lay across the couch, scooching up to the right of the couch so her head was using the arm as a pillow. "So, Bill, is this how you want me?" She bent her legs at the knee, then playfully spread them apart as she stared directly into Bill's eyes, this time clearly licking her lips seductively.

Bill was stunned; he thought that maybe Mary had some interest in him, but now he knew for certain. She acted like she knew exactly what she wanted and she was going to get it, come hell or high water. Just then, Conrad came into the room. He took one look at Mary and chuckled.

"That's funny, Mary, this is not a psychiatric session. You don't have to lie down, unless of course you want to."

Mary was calculated in her actions; she had purposely chosen to lie down so as to occupy the entire sofa. She didn't really want Pastor Conrad sitting beside her. "Pastor Conrad, I feel comfortable just like this." With that, Conrad moved to the other couch, sitting to the left of Pastor Bill, directly facing Mary.

Conrad took the initiative and started the session. "Mary, we would like to hear about your experience after the accident when you were in a coma. Would you like to tell us about it?"

Mary played coy with Pastor Conrad. "Well Pastor Conrad, I tried to tell you when I first woke up, but you didn't believe me..." She paused. "Remember?"

Conrad looked at her, puzzled. "Whatever do you mean, Mary?" Bill found this intriguing; the girl was going straight at Conrad, basically calling him out.

"Remember when I said God doesn't exist? You didn't believe me!" Conrad tried to speak. Mary continued talking in a raised voice, completely ignoring the fact that Conrad had started to speak. "You said that I didn't really mean that, I was just in shock. You didn't believe me."

Conrad paused for a moment of thought. "Mary, it was a shock to me, I guess I didn't react very well." Mary sat up and began to feign emotional distress.

"Do you know how much that hurt? How it felt for me to have my own pastor dismiss me, to basically call me a liar, in a room full of people no less?"

Conrad tried not to get defensive; he didn't want to escalate the tension in the room. "I know, Mary, in that moment I failed as your pastor. I apologize from the bottom of my heart."

In a firm tone, she demanded, "Pastor Conrad, since you didn't listen to me then, what makes you think you'll listen to me now?" She paused just long enough to allow Conrad to start speaking.

"I don't—" he said before Mary rudely interrupted him.

"Pastor Conrad, you're right, you don't, and you simply don't believe me. This was very personal and scary for me." Bill saw a few tears had started to well in Mary's eyes. "Pardon me, Pastor Conrad, I think you are a wonderful man and a great pastor, but I believe it would be best if you left the room. I don't feel that I can be honest with you here, I don't trust that you would take me seriously. I wouldn't want to become the laughingstock of Champion." Mary's words were precise and sharp. Bill looked over at Conrad and could almost see his ego shrinking as it deflated.

The three of them sat in silence for quite a few awkward moments. Conrad finally stood up and gathered his composure. "Mary, you're absolutely correct, I should've been more sensitive to your privacy. We should've talked privately in the hospital and for that I sincerely apologize."

Mary stared at the pastor for what seemed an eternity. She knew that if she accepted his apology too quickly, it could be an invitation for him to stay, which is the very last thing she wanted.

Conrad felt unwanted. "Maybe I should go now and leave you in Pastor Bill's capable hands."

Mary nodded. "I agree, Pastor Conrad, I feel Pastor Bill will listen and be of great benefit to me."

Conrad looked over to Bill. "With your permission, Pastor Bill, I will take my leave and head home now. I'll see you in the morning."

Bill nodded and added, "How about we meet at the diner at our appointed time? I plan to sleep in a while, this day has been exhausting for me." Conrad nodded and left the room.

Mary sat up facing Bill. She whispered, "I thought he'd never leave." She followed up with a giggle.

The school in Riley was the only one they had. It housed students from Grade 1 all the way to Grade 12. When Margaret's girls got off the bus, they would come into the house put their bags, jackets and shoes away and then meet their mother in the kitchen.

Suzanne was excited to tell her mother of the scandalous news. She rushed in the front door, quickly put her belongings away, and rushed to the kitchen. "Hello, Mother, how are you?"

Lucinda was next followed by the three youngest to file into the kitchen, each taking a seat at the kitchen table.

"Hello, girls, how was school today?"

Suzanne could no longer hold it in. She blurted out. "You know Norma-Ann Rodgers?"

Margaret knew everyone in town and their children; she thought it was an odd question coming from her eleven-year-old. "Of course, I know Norma-Ann," Margaret replied indignantly.

Suzanne saw that her younger sisters were all hanging around; she realized that maybe she shouldn't break the news with them present.

"What about Norma-Ann? Did something happen?" Margaret was curious.

"It can wait, Mother," Suzanne said, looking at her younger sisters.

Lucinda commented, "Probably for the best with young eyes and ears watching and listening."

John came home from work soon after. The three youngest girls Barbara, Charlotte and Bethany all greeted him at the door, hugging his legs and waist as he hung up his jacket.

"Hello, Father, how was your day?" Charlotte asked cheerfully.

"I had a fine day, little one, now why don't you and your sisters run upstairs and play before dinner?"

"Yay!" the three girls gleefully cheered as they hustled up the stairs to their room for some play.

John entered the kitchen as Lucinda and Suzanne were getting the dishes and cutlery to set the dinner table. "Hello, Father," the two girls greeted him.

"Hello, girls." John moved to his wife and whispered. "Did you hear about the Rodgers girl?" Suzanne heard enough words to understand what her father had just whispered.

"She's pregnant!" Suzanne excitedly blurted out. John swung his body around to face her. Lucinda stepped back out of sheer instinct. She watched her father closely.

"Where'd you hear that, Suzanne?" He stepped towards Suzanne as Lucinda backed away to stay out of John's reach.

Suzanne saw the look on her father's face and her body began to tremble. "I-I-I—"

Lucinda interrupted, helping her sister out while standing just behind her. "Father, it's all over the school, everyone's heard; that's why Norma-Ann hasn't been to school in over a week."

Margaret shook her head in disgust. "How old is Norma-Ann? I don't even think she's seventeen years old yet, and so young to be with child." Margaret bought into the gossip immediately.

John's eyes narrowed as he stared down his two eldest daughters. "It's not just all over the school, girls, it's all the talk in town. Everyone's talking about it. You know it's a sin to have relations before one is properly married, and to have a child out of wedlock is not in God's plan. The girl has brought shame to her family and herself."

Seeing Lucinda and Suzanne intently listening, John continued on with the lecture. "I feel very blessed that I have such good daughters; they would never shame their father in such a way."

Lucinda was moved by her father's words and she began to weep as she brought her hands up to cover her face.

It was rare for John to become involved in a heartfelt moment so it was a shock for Lucinda when he moved closer and hugged her. "There's no need to cry, Lucinda, the Rodgers girl made her bed and now she'll have to lay in it."

Lucinda composed herself, thankful that her father had drawn his own conclusion, for the truth behind her tears would be far more devastating.

～

"Did I do good, Bill?" Mary asked as she giggled again.

"Yes, of course you did good, I love your style," he said with a wink and a smile. "Mary, I would really like to hear about your experience. I need some details for my report."

Mary teased, "You're making a report, are you?" She stood and sauntered around the coffee table to sit on the sofa beside Bill. All the while she would not take her eyes off the man; she moved like a stalking predator.

"Ok Bill, I'll tell you. But, what do you want to hear? The truth or the placating lie that all pastors want to hear?"

"How about we start with the truth, Mary? Remind me again how old you are?"

"Sweet sixteen, Bill, I turn seventeen next month," she said with a wink.

"You're very intelligent and composed for a sixteen-year-old; it's very impressive."

"Well, thank you, Bill. I try." The girl tossed her long straight brown hair over her shoulder, slightly pulling her elbows back to push her chest outward. Bill noticed the girl's obvious flirt.

Mary crossed her arms across her chest with her hands on her shoulders; she pretended to shiver as she patted her shoulders. "Bill, I'm feeling a bit chilled. Would you mind making a fire in the fireplace?"

Bill looked over between the two large chairs at the fireplace. He stood, looked to the left and saw a cabinet in the corner. He walked over to the cabinet, opened the doors to find stacks of chopped firewood. "I think I could arrange a nice warm fire for you, my lady," Bill said as he looked back over his shoulder at Mary who had a big, wide-eyed grin on her face.

Bill set to work making a fire, his back turned to Mary. "It's been a while since I made a fire; but have no fear, I'll get the job done for you Mary." Bill focused intently on the task. "Here goes nothing, wish me luck." He lit a match and put it under the crumpled-up newspaper and moments later a small flame started to grow into a larger flame while Bill watched with hope in his eyes. Eventually the chopped logs caught fire and Bill felt victorious and exclaimed, "May I present to you, you're fire my lady." He turned around and saw no sign of Mary. Seconds later she appeared in the doorway. She had changed into a big warm terry cloth robe with fluffy slippers on her feet. She walked towards Bill. He stood there as if mesmerized, watching her every move towards him. She stopped right in front of the fire and stood facing him. Mary reached her arms up around his neck and hugged him. "Thank you, Bill." She released the hug soon after and sat in the chair to the left of the fireplace; Bill took his place in the other chair.

"Well, Bill, it's your show, what do you want to know? The truth, you said?" Mary kicked off her slippers as she leaned back, then pulled her legs up to bend at the knees as she curled up in the chair facing Bill. She moved herself into a comfortable position, wiggling around like a cat clawing and adjusting a blanket into a cozy little nest.

"Tell me about your experience, Mary. The truth, please."

"Please?" Mary chortled. "So formal, Bill. Just relax, I'll tell you the truth, but you have to promise to try and have an open mind. Promise me, Bill!"

Bill held up three fingers. "Scout's honor, I'll keep an open mind."

Mary was pleased to hear his words and she went on to tell the story of her experience. "Bill, I remember seeing the car hit me. I flew through the air and next thing I know, it feels as if I'm floating. It's dark and I can hear faint whispers. I opened my eyes and I could see that I was in a hallway. I looked ahead and saw a small white light. I looked behind me and saw nothing but darkness. I tried to listen to the noises around me; I heard whispers off in the distance; but I couldn't make out what they were saying." Mary paused for a moment to see that Bill's eyes were focused on hers, he was listening intently.

"I saw the light and I was drawn to it, a thousand thoughts were going through my mind, but one thought rang out more than all others: What was the light? I felt compelled and I walked towards the light and when I came to the end of the hallway, the space opened up and I saw the white light; it looked like the outline of a door."

Bill sat up in amazement. "That's very detailed, Mary, and you speak so eloquently and with such confidence; please continue."

Mary went on. "I turned to the right I could make out a rectangular shape that looked like another door; this one was green. When I looked to the left, I saw another shining light; this one was blue and again it looked like a door from a distance." Mary stopped to check Bill's reaction. "So, Bill, what do you think? Am I crazy?"

"Not at all, Mary, I'm fascinated with your experience. I want to hear more."

Mary smiled wide and continued. "I found myself walking towards the white light door, ignoring the blue and green ones. In that instant, I thought I must have died and was on my way to heaven to be with God. I felt relieved to be going to heaven. But..." She paused and a concerned look of fear came over her. Bill saw this and quickly encouraged her to continue.

"Mary, there's nothing to worry about. I'm here for you, and you're safe."

"That's comforting, thank you, Bill. The closer I got to the white light, the colder it felt. It felt like my bones were freezing. I thought that if I could just open that door, I would feel the warmth of the Lord envelop me and everything would be fine. I continued walking towards the door, faster now than before. My only focus was getting to the light. It was right in front of me. I felt myself reaching out, I touched the door and the second I did, I heard a voice clearly say, 'Do you give yourself over?'" Mary emphasized the question, stopping her story to check Bill's reaction.

Bill was so immersed in Mary's words that he didn't realize she had stopped; he was in a trance, vividly picturing every detail she described. "Bill!" Mary scolded. He shook his head as if to break the trance. Mary giggled. "I don't think anyone has ever been that engrossed in something I have to say."

Bill regained his senses. "Of course, Mary, your experience is amazing, I'm hanging on your every word. Please continue; what happened next?"

Mary felt very comfortable in Bill's presence as she related the rest of her experience.

"'Do you give yourself over?' the voice asked me again. It was like that old record player skipping to the same line over and over. I didn't know how to answer." Mary's expression became somber and almost sad. "My hand felt stuck to the door, I felt regret, sadness and pain. Time stood still; it felt like days, weeks, months, even years. I could feel a force holding me in place; I tried to step forward and I couldn't; I tried to step back and again I found myself frozen in place. I felt my neck being grasped; I couldn't break away. The light spoke again. 'Do you give yourself over?' 'Come with me now.' 'Just step through the doorway.' I became angry, very angry to hear that question again, those words over and over. I couldn't speak but somehow, I managed to yell out, 'No!' The next thing I know, I'm above myself, looking down. I can see the light has grasped me by the back of my neck—" Bill interrupted.

"Mary, do you know what astral projection is?"

Mary looked at Bill and coyly replied, "I didn't, but I know now." Bill was puzzled at Mary's words. "Bill, astral projection is separating one's spirit or soul from one's body. I didn't know then, but I most certainly do now. Shall I continue?" Mary said with an arrogant tone; Bill nodded.

"As I was saying, I separated my spirit from my body. I could see the light holding me by the neck, and my spirit tried to fight. I tried to break its hold on me, but every time I tried, I couldn't break free. For days I tried to figure out how to escape from the light, and finally I realized that my body might be stuck; but my spirit wasn't. I decided to leave my body and go find help. I explored everywhere for weeks on end, looking for anyone that could help me. There was no one. I traveled back to my body. I could see the light and my body were still frozen in time. I realized to break the hold, I had to face the light. It wanted me to give myself over and I had denied it. In that moment, I had an epiphany, the light needed me to willingly give myself over and when I refused to give myself over, somehow my body and the light became fused together.

"It was then that I knew the way out. I spoke to the light. 'I do not give myself over, I will never give myself over!' I screamed at the light. The white light cracked and in the center of the crack was an orange hue, and shortly after I saw a spirit not unlike my own rise from the light. I could speak to the spirit and it could speak to me."

"This is all very fascinating. I must hear more, Mary."

She sounded relieved. "You're not going to say this was all a dream, Bill?"

"No, Mary, I don't believe this sounds like a dream. I'm truly enthralled by your experience. Please continue."

"The light spirit said to me, 'You must give yourself over.' It repeated the phrase over and over until it realized that I would never give myself over. Finally it asked. 'What do you want, Mary?' I told the spirit I wanted to be free, to let me go."

"'Impossible!' The spirit's voice boomed. 'Well, I will never give myself over, ever. God is on my side and I will never give myself over to you, Satan.' The spirit became amused at my words.

"'You think I'm Satan? There's no such thing as Satan. There's no heaven, no hell, and even God himself no longer exists.' 'You're lying, spirit, God does exist.' We argued for days on this topic. I finally asked the spirit to prove to me that God did not exist.

"'Fine then, if I prove it to you, will you give yourself over?'

"'Never!' I screamed at the spirit. 'Prove it! Prove that God doesn't exist, I dare you.' The spirit went on to explain it this way. In the beginning, God created the universe, the planets, the stars, the earth, everything. God created the world and all the beings in the world were fashioned in God's image, with God's will and instincts. God's will is to create, or as we would know it, to procreate."

Mary paused and asked Bill, "Do you believe it's Gods will to procreate?"

Bill thought for a moment. "That makes perfect sense; it's natural instinct for humans to procreate."

"Exactly!" Mary said as she smiled seductively at Bill.

"Is there more?" Bill quizzed.

"Yes, Bill, there's more. The spirit said that God created the beginning of all things, but then was consumed by that very creation. I asked the spirit how that was possible. I couldn't believe that God was destroyed by his own creation. The light spirit went on to explain that all beings have a body and soul. The body is a vessel for the soul to grow inside and once the soul ripens, the body dies and releases the soul. The released soul turns to energy, once that energy passes through the doors of the veil that energy can then be absorbed. I was starting to understand what the light spirit was saying, but I also sensed that something was wrong with it; it seemed to be growing weaker, the longer it was out of its body. I urged the light to feed me more information. I asked what the veil was. The light spirit told me to think of the veil as a curtain between what you would call the spirit world and the incubator world. 'So, what are you saying, light? Are you saying that the earth is an incubator for our souls?'

"'Yes.' the spirit explained. 'Once your soul passes through the veil, it becomes pure energy, which is then consumed by powerful beings on the other side.' I became very angry hearing that from the spirit. I questioned it, saying, 'So you're saying that heaven isn't just over there, on the other side of that door? That there's no heaven? That once our bodies die, our spirits don't go to heaven or hell?' The light spirit told me my description was not even close to the reality that is the universe. 'Remember God created everything in God's image and God's instinct, and God's instinct is the same as all animals: we're all driven to procreate, to add to our power to consume what is necessary to fulfill our goal of procreation.' It was then that I saw the light fade and I realized what was happening was the very thing that the spirt told me of: it needed to consume me, but it couldn't do so without my consent. I figured it out—the longer the light spirit was out of its light body, the weaker it grew."

"Fascinating, Mary," Bill interrupted.

"Do you want to hear the story or not, Bill? Don't interrupt me when I'm on a roll. I called out the light spirit. 'You said God created everything in God's image, including a desire to procreate, and clearly God also gave all beings free will, and that is why you're unable to convert my spirit into energy for you to absorb; you need my consent.'"

Mary looked at Bill; he was ghost white.

"Are you ok, Bill?" Mary asked. He didn't answer; it was as if he were stuck in an intense memory. "Bill!" Mary raised her voice and he shook his head slightly, snapping back to attention.

"What's wrong, Bill? Did I touch a nerve?" Mary's eyes narrowed as she was laser-focused on his body language.

"No, nothing, nothing is wrong, Mary. Please continue; tell me what happened, how'd you get out?"

"I said to the light spirit, 'I will not give myself over to you, not now, not ever! What I will do is break your will; you're coming to an end.' I then willed my spirit back into my body. Once my body and soul were reunited, I was able to pull away from the weakened light spirit. I turned to face the light once again. I knew the light spirit was out of its body and I knew that my will was much stronger now than before. I used all my willpower to envision the implosion of the light spirit, and right before my eyes it came to fruition as I watched it shrink into itself and then fizzle out into nothingness. It was then, with my body and soul reunited, that I was able to slam that damn door shut. I made my way back to the darkened hallway. The next thing I knew, I saw a bright light. I couldn't open my eyes because it hurt, the light burned. Then I heard voices, familiar voices calling my name over and over: 'Mary, Mary, are you awake? Mary.'"

Bill interjected: "And that's when you woke from the coma." Mary nodded. "What I don't understand is your recollection of time, Mary. You said it was days, weeks, months—"

Mary interrupted. "It felt like years!"

"And yet you were in coma for what, six or seven days?"

"Exactly, Bill. When we die, time becomes meaningless. For all I know, I was stuck there for an eternity."

"And that door is a gateway between our world and heaven?"

"No, Bill, that door is a veil between our world and the spirit world, where spirits become energy. Strong spirits absorb weaker ones and become more powerful. If you go through that door, you're giving yourself over and your spirit will be absorbed by the light spirits on the other side."

"I just..." Bill paused. After a moment his facial expression changed and Mary saw a sadness wash over him.

"Bill, something happened to you, didn't it? You've seen the door, haven't you?"

He stared directly into her eyes, paused for thought and then spoke. "Yes, Mary, I had a very similar experience when I was a young boy."

"Tell me about it, Bill, I'm curious."

Bill swallowed hard. "Ok, Mary, but you're the only person I've ever told; I haven't even told my wife about my experience." He paused and looked over at the young woman. "I was nine years old and my brother John fell into the river. I tried to save him and in doing so, I drowned. Very similar to your experience, I saw the white light, only I didn't go towards it. Instead, I found myself drawn to the green door. Once I opened it, I was enveloped in a swarm of green fireflies who communicated to me."

This piqued Mary's interest. "Tell me more."

"I was told that it wasn't my time and that I had an important role to play. And the next thing I know, I woke up with a huge jolt from the defibrillator that the paramedics were using on me. I went on with life, thinking that it was all a dream, until now." Bill's face had gone white again.

"Sounds to me like you had a near-death experience, Bill, and tell me, how did you feel when you came back?"

"Honestly, Mary, that's when I decided to dedicate my life to becoming a priest and serving God."

"Really, Bill? So what happened?" Mary said in a combative tone.

"What do you mean, Mary?"

"Bill, you're now a Catholic priest. Your life has been dedicated to serving God and teaching the Bible to others, right?"

He was on his heels as he answered. "Yes, of course, Mary."

"You teach the word of God, right?"

"Yes, Mary."

"And you pray to God, for comfort, for understanding, and you place your faith in God, and you believe that you are made in God's image, with his traits, his desire, his will, his very nature?"

Bill tried to answer but he was lost and no words came out.

"Bill, you believe that there is a heaven where people's spirits go to when they die, you believe that God has a destiny for you, but yet you have free will?"

Hearing those words, Bill answered quickly, "Yes, we all have free will."

"Bill, you have free will, yes. But do you have a destiny laid out by God?"

Bill was stumped and couldn't answer.

"Bill, it's a paradox. You cannot be destined to do something on one hand and on the other hand have free agency to make decisions. Which is it? Is your path a choice or is it preordained? A paradox, like I said."

Bill sat in stunned silence.

"Bill, is it reasonable to believe that there is one God controlling all living things? To what end?" She paused; Bill was still dumbfounded.

"Listen, Bill: yes, there was a God as we know him. There was a creator; he created all living things, so why is it that humans believe we are above all other beings? What makes a human more important than, say, a dog or a fish?"

Bill's head was spinning as he found the girl's logic overpowering.

"I can prove it to you, Bill, if you open your mind."

"How, Mary? How will you prove it to me?"

Mary smiled with confidence. "Do you agree that it's human nature, nature itself that we are driven to procreate?"

"Yes, I agree with that, Mary."

"Are you married, Bill?"

"Yes, I am," Bill responded.

"Were you married in a church, did you say vows to your wife and her to you?"

"Yes, Mary, we did."

"And did you promise to love her, forsaking all others?"

"Yes, Mary, of course."

Even though Bill was a master at mental chess, he felt like he was already in checkmate. He'd forgotten all about his sinful lust for the beautiful girl; he was captivated with the discussion and felt as though he was being schooled. Schooled by a sixteen-year-old girl.

"Then, Bill, tell me why you have fornicated with so many others?"

Bill's eyes shot wide open. "What'd you mean? I haven't—"

Mary interrupted him sharply. "You have! I saw into your soul the very first time we touched. You're the quintessential example of a man created in God's image. Your drive to procreate is exceptionally high."

Bill looked to be in absolute shock.

Mary stood up in front of Bill. She removed her terry cloth robe, revealing her completely naked body.

"You see, Bill, when I awoke from the coma, at first I couldn't make any sense of how I felt. I'm a virgin, yet I awoke with a burning desire to have sex, lots of sex, with anyone, with everyone. I was out of my mind trying to make sense of it all. I felt no attraction to anyone, until you showed up. That's when it all came together, the fine jagged points filling in the puzzle; I had an epiphany. I didn't just need to procreate, I needed a like-minded soul, and you were it, Bill. I was attracted to you the very second I saw you."

Bill felt a stirring between his legs as the girl stood naked before him, speaking of her desires.

"But I'm more than twice your age. How can you say you're attracted to me?"

"Bill, we've both seen the veil; you know that age doesn't mean a damn thing. I'm attracted to your soul."

"Age might not mean anything to you, but the State of Oklahoma might see it differently, they might charge me with statutory—"

Mary interrupted and smiled at him as she moved her body ever so slightly, seductively as if she was doing the dance of the seven veils. She swayed slightly from side to side, showing off her body, enticing the man before her.

"Bill, you're a Catholic priest in the Oklahoma Bible Belt, there's no judge that would ever allow you or any priest to be prosecuted, so prove me wrong! Can you deny this? You're a man of God, Bill. But can you deny your true desire to procreate? Can you resist my body?" Mary spread her legs slightly, placed her hands on her hips and moved them down to her thighs and then back up the inside of her thighs, framing her groin area with her hands as she spoke.

"Stand up, Bill," she commanded. As if in a trance, Bill did exactly as he was told. Mary smiled, moved in, pressing her body to his, and stepped on her tiptoes to whisper in his ear. "Take me, Bill, make me a woman."

She breathed softly in his ear, moving down to kiss his jaw and then his neck as her hands found their way to his collar, pulling the white cuff from his neck. She ripped his shirt at the buttons and then moved her hands down his ribcage to the top of his pants, where she slowly undid the button.

She whispered in between softly kissing his neck. "I want you, Bill, I want you inside me. I want our souls to mingle as we share our most erotic burning desires."

As Bill's pants dropped to the floor, he felt their groins touch, and Mary pushed him onto the chair. Standing before him, looking lustfully into his eyes, she said, "Bill, you must freely give yourself over; you must tell me that you want it, that you want me. Say it!"

Bill couldn't resist; he growled, "I want you, Mary!" In the blink of an eye, Mary straddled the pastor and proved to him that the desire to procreate is both the beginning and purpose of life.

"Do you have a condom Bill?" Mary was kissing his neck as she straddled him.

"Don't worry Mary, I'm pretty sure I'm sterile. Stephanie and I have been trying to have children for years."

CHAPTER 10 –

Lucinda's Nightmare

AFTER DINNER AND nightly Bible studies, Lucinda hit the sack. She had learned to sleep with her cast and found that sleeping on her left side was the most comfortable, considering she normally slept on her right side but couldn't due to the cast.

She thought about what her father had said about Norma-Ann, how she had shamed her family by getting pregnant. Her eyes closed and her thoughts became less vivid as she drifted off to sleep.

She dreamt of her wedding day; she pictured herself in a flowing white wedding gown. She imagined seeing her father walking her down the aisle, her mother in tears as she and her father walked past towards her groom standing just in front of the pastor's pew.

It was a joyous feeling. As she arrived at the pastor's pew, her father turned to face her, raising his arms and lifting the veil over her face. Lucinda saw this dream as if she were watching from overhead, floating just a few feet above everyone's head.

As the veil was lifted, Lucinda could see the smile on her father's face change to mortified disgust. She then looked at her own face and saw it was black and bruised with creepy crawly bugs crawling from her mouth up into her nose, with some bugs crawling into her ears.

She looked her body up and down and where she saw her legs meet her body; a small stain of red blood formed on the pure white dress.

The stain kept growing bigger as it rippled out from her groin until the entire dress was saturated in blood.

She heard gasps from the gathered crowd, and one person yelled out, "She's not chaste!" Another yelled out, "She's a sinner!" Lucinda watched but didn't move, she just stood there; she could hear more comments from the mob.

"A child born of the devil."

"Shameless."

"Look, God shows her virtue is impure and brands her with the scarlet letter."

Those were just a few of the comments Lucinda could make out.

She looked at her mother and saw her face was beet red with embarrassment and shock as tears flowed from her eyes, causing her black eyeliner to run down her cheeks. Lucinda looked back to her father who was now standing behind her. She looked at her sisters and all four of them were vomiting.

As she stood there unable to move, she suddenly felt extreme pain; she looked down between her breasts to see the tip of her father's 14" hunting knife, one side of the knife smooth and sharp, the other serrated and rough. She saw on the very tip of the knife her own beating heart. Her father had driven the knife in her back, clear through to the front, taking her heart with it.

The crowd, seeing the still-beating heart dislodged from the sinner's body, cheered.

"Yay!"

"Justice is served!"

"Kill the sinner!"

Lucinda woke up sharply, sitting straight up, sweating like a pig on the hottest day of the year. She was panting and trying to catch her breath. The noises she made woke Suzanne, who opened her eyes and looked at her sister.

"Lucinda, are you alright?"

Lucinda was practically hyperventilating; she just couldn't catch her breath.

Suzanne sprang from her bed and ran towards the door. "Hold on, Lucinda, I'm getting Mother."

Just as Suzanne was about to move past her, Lucinda reached out and tightly grabbed her sister's nightgown. Still gasping for air Lucinda was barely able to stammer out, "No, don't."

Suzanne then moved to sit beside Lucinda and rub her back as she tried to comfort and calm her sister. "Just relax, breathe deep."

It took a good fifteen minutes before Lucinda could regain her breath. "Thank you, Suzanne," she panted.

"What happened?" Suzanne said as she felt her own heartbeat returning to normal.

"It was just a bad dream. Sorry to wake you, sister." The girls sat in silence as Suzanne soothingly stroked her fingers through Lucinda's long blonde hair.

"Lucinda, I could sleep with you tonight if you'd like."

"I think I would like that very much, thank you, Suzanne." Lucinda then laid down on her left side with her cast above the covers; Suzanne gently slid in behind and, placed her arm carefully around her sister's waist, the two girls fell back to sleep.

⁓

6am came too soon for Lucinda; she heard her mother open the door and call to the girls, "It's time to wake up." As Margaret peered inside the room, she could see that the two sisters were in the same bed, and that Suzanne was spooning behind Lucinda with her arm around her sister's waist.

At breakfast Margaret spoke to Lucinda and Suzanne. "Why were you two girls in the same bed?"

John lowered the newspaper long enough to peer over and look at Lucinda with raised eyebrow.

"Mother, it was nothing, I had a nightmare," Lucinda answered. Suzanne sat in silence. "Suzanne offered to sleep with me for comfort."

"Don't you think you girls are a little old to sleep in the same bed?" Neither of the girls answered. "Do not do it again." John said sharply. Both girls' faces flushed with shame.

Margaret echoed her husband's sentiments. "Both of you in the same small bed, you could've broken the bed."

"Yes, Mother," the girls replied in stereo.

After breakfast, the girls got ready for school and went to the bus stop. Once they got on the bus, Suzanne made a point of sitting beside Lucinda. "Sister, are you alright?"

Lucinda faked it. "I'm fine; it was just a silly nightmare."

"I've never seen you that scared, Lucinda. It must've been a really bad nightmare."

"I don't really want to talk about it," Lucinda frowned.

Just then, there was a loud screeching noise followed by a resounding bang. Without any notice, the bus driver slammed on the brakes causing every passenger to lurch forward. The noise was the buses tires screaming to a stop as a large gravel truck collided with the front left side of the bus. The truck had failed to stop as the bus was rolling through the intersection.

Children could be heard moaning and crying. Suzanne shook her head. Placing a hand on her forehead, she felt pain and could feel a welt forming. She looked to her right and saw Lucinda's shoulders, at first she couldn't see Lucinda's head; but upon closer examination she realized Lucinda's head was outside the bus as it had gone through the window.

"Lucinda!" Suzanne called out. She placed her hands on her sister's shoulders, pulling her head back inside the bus. She shook her, but Lucinda wouldn't open her eyes. "Help!" Suzanne screamed as she wrapped her arms around her sister, praying, "God, please help my sister."

Suzanne called out to her other sisters, "Bethany, Barbara, Charlotte." She repeated, "Bethany, Barbara, Charlotte!" as she called out through tears. She heard Charlotte crying as she answered.

"Suzanne, where are you?"

"Over here, Lucinda's hurt!" Suzanne called out again, "Barbara. Bethany!"

Barbara and Bethany yelled back at the same time, "We're here, we're ok!"

Suzanne looked around as she held Lucinda in her arms. Blood from Lucinda's forehead dripped onto Suzanne's arm and she realized that she needed to do something. She put her hand on the bleeding gash on Lucinda's head and pressed as hard as she could. One time when she had cut her finger, her mother wrapped it in paper towel and told her to press hard until the blood stopped. Through all the chaos, eleven-year-old Suzanne kept her composure. Through sweat and tears, she held her hand to Lucinda's forehead and kept talking to her sister. "Lucinda, wake up, wake up." She cried and pleaded again. "Wake up, sister, wake up."

It wasn't long before lots of people from Riley were at the scene, they pried the bus doors open. Suzanne could hear voices shouting commands, adult voices helping the children off the bus.

She heard the sirens of the fire engine, and in all the calamity she continued to hold her hand to her sister's head, slowing the loss of blood. "Lucinda, wake up, please wake up," she begged with tears streaming down her face.

She heard her three younger sisters all yelling from outside the bus. "Our sisters are still in there, help them!"

Just then, Suzanne saw the children in the seats in front of them being evacuated. She stayed there, holding her hand to her sister's head, still pressing hard even though her arm and hand was hurting badly from pressing so hard.

Bob the junior paramedic called out to his partner as he arrived at the seat where Suzanne and Lucinda were. Suzanne turned her head to see Bob; she heard him calling out, "Sherry, Sherry! We have a major head wound here, bring the kit!" Suzanne heard the urgency in Bob's voice and it scared her. She turned to look at her sister and saw her own hand was covered in blood. She could've panicked but she didn't; she continued pressing her hand to Lucinda's forehead until the other paramedic arrived.

Sherry put her hand on Suzanne's shoulder. "You're doing good. Keep your hand there just a little longer, and when I tell you, I want you to move your hand and step back and go with Paramedic Bob." She looked into Suzanne's eyes. "Can you do that, honey?" Suzanne nodded yes. "Ok, when I say three, I want you to move your hand and step back and away. Ready?"

Suzanne nodded. "Yes, I'm ready."

"One— two— and three." Suzanne stepped back. Sherry replaced Suzanne's hand with her own hand, which held white gauze, she reapplied pressure. Suzanne turned her head to watch her sister as long as she could before Bob ushered her off the bus.

When Suzanne walked past the bus driver's seat, she was mortified to see their driver Melanie covered in blood and not moving. She turned to Bob and yelled, "Help her!" as she pointed to the bus driver.

"I can't help her, she's gone," Bob replied, Suzanne's eleven-year-old eyes widened in horror.

As Suzanne stepped onto the pavement, she tried to focus her eyes in the bright sunlight. She saw children and adults everywhere, children crying as their parents hugged them. She looked for her younger sisters and found them huddling together with their mother.

Suzanne rushed over to them, crying out, "Mother, Lucinda's hurt real bad, she's still on the bus her head is bleeding." Margaret opened her arms to the girl as Suzanne rushed to her. She looked up and saw her mother with tears streaming down her face. "It'll be ok, Mother. Paramedic Sherry is with her now, she'll be alright." Suzanne said as she reached out for her three younger sisters.

Margaret and her daughters stood there watching the door of the bus, waiting for Lucinda to be brought out. Other children were being ushered out by Paramedic Bob and two firemen. Then Paramedic Bob went to the ambulance, opened the back doors and wheeled out the stretcher. Seeing that, Margaret panicked and rushed over to him. "Is that for my daughter, Lucinda? Is she hurt?" Bob knew Margaret from church and he tried his best to calm her.

"Yes, but don't worry, Margaret, Sherry is with Lucinda, we'll bring her out soon. I have to go now." Bob pushed the stretcher past Margaret to the opening of the bus door.

Sheriff Brown and his men were there creating a perimeter around the bus. "Stand back people, let them do their work!" Sheriff Brown barked in an authoritative voice.

Margaret wept as she stood waiting to see her eldest daughter. She prayed. "Oh God, please help my daughter." Others heard Margaret's plea and came to hold and comfort her.

Sherry appeared in the doorway with a blood covered Lucinda in her arms. The girl's head was wrapped in a white bandage that was already starting to bleed through. Sherry slowly stepped off the bus, being careful not to jolt Lucinda. As Sherry laid Lucinda on the stretcher, Margaret saw that her daughter was not moving and she burst into tears. Bob pulled the stretcher as Sherry pushed it; they hurried to the ambulance and loaded the stretcher inside. Margaret saw the paramedics secure the stretcher and watched as Sherry got inside the back as she closed one door while Bob closed the other door. Bob then hustled around and the next thing Margaret saw was the ambulance rushing away, heading in the direction of the town's only hospital.

Margaret then gathered up her other four girls, loaded them into the family station wagon and drove first to the factory where John worked. "Stay in the car while I go in and get your father."

She went to the front door, walked in and straight onto the factory floor to find John. Once she found John, he began to chastise her.

"Margaret! You can't be here," he bellowed before he saw that her face was blackened by running mascara; it was obvious she was crying.

"It's— it's— Lu-cin-da" Margaret managed to stammer out through heavy breathing and a flood of tears.

"What? What has happened to Lucinda?"

Margaret struggled to gain her composure as she gasped to catch her breath. "Hospital, we have to go to the hospital." John sensed the urgency and left immediately with Margaret.

The normally quiet hospital was in complete chaos with nurses and orderlies running everywhere when John, Margaret and their four youngest girls arrived at the hospital. The family rushed into the emergency room and up to the reception desk. John asked with a tone of panic in his voice. "Lucinda, my daughter, where is she?"

The nurse recognized the family and remembered Lucinda coming in just last week with Dr. Watkins.

"Dr. Watkins is in with Lucinda. They're assessing her injuries. We should get some information soon, if you'd like to just take a seat in the waiting area."

The nurse pointed behind the family to chairs in the waiting area. It looked very busy with many children around with bumps, bruises and minor abrasions, with one or more of their parents sitting patiently beside them.

CHAPTER 11 –

Hard–Luck Lucinda

DR. WATKINS HAD rushed to the hospital, and as he entered, he heard a commotion rarely heard at the hospital in this peaceful small town. He feared the worst as he scurried down the hall to the hospital men's locker room. As Dr. Watkins was just about finished changing into scrubs, the attending resident came in to give him a report.

"Oh good, you're here, Dr. Watkins. Are you ready for a status update?"

"Yes, Allen, what happened?"

Allen was a fourth-year resident attending physician, one of three on staff at the hospital. He was the physician on duty when the tragedy happened.

"A ten-ton dump truck collided with the school bus on Main Street. The bus driver, Melanie Maples-Radisson, was killed on impact and is en route to the hospital. I assigned Nurse Aikenside to receive the DOA body."

"Ok good," Dr. Watkins said as he pulled shoe covers over his hospital sneakers.

"Aside from the DOA, there is only one critical injury. A young girl named Lucinda Hall."

Dr. Watkins heart sunk. "That poor girl, she was a recent patient of mine. She's got to have the worst luck in the world."

"Her arm is in a cast that has been cracked, but the critical injury is, as reported by the paramedics, a deep laceration on her forehead caused when the bus came to a sudden stop. It's unclear if the girl's forehead hit the seat in front or the window to her right."

Dr. Watkins was now finished dressing. He headed out of the locker room and down the hall towards the pre-operating room where nurses, doctors and surgeons scrubbed clean before entering the adjacent operating room. Allen followed closely on Dr. Watkins' heels, continuing to deliver his report.

"The patient—"

Dr. Watkins stopped in his tracks and looked at the attending resident. "Allen, would you please call her Lucinda? I know she is our patient but call her by name so that we all remember that our purpose is to save a real person with a real name. Her name is Lucinda!"

"Check, Dr. Watkins," Allen replied.

As Dr. Watkins entered pre-op, he looked to the left through the big picture window that separated the operating room from pre-op. He saw the white bandages around Lucinda's head, and could see they were soaked in blood. He saw Helen, the lead trauma nurse, and the anesthesiologist Collin in the room. Helen was adjusting a saline bag, and he saw that she had already prepared an intravenous cannula placed into the veins on Lucinda's left arm.

There were three trauma nurses in pre-op already scrubbed, masked and ready to enter the operating room. Allen and Dr. Watkins were rapidly scrubbing down arms, hands, fingers and nails. Once they finished scrubbing down, Dr. Watkins walked into the operating room, with Allen and the nurses following behind.

Dr. Watkins approached the table beside Lucinda. He addressed Helen. "Do you have Lucinda prepped?"

Helen replied, "Yes, Doctor."

"Collin, what is the status of anesthesia?"

"She's sleeping like a baby, Dr. Watkins."

"You know that she had anesthesia just a few days ago, right?"

"Yes, Dr. Watkins, Helen gave me the chart and I adjusted accordingly. Pulse and heart rate are stable."

Before Dr. Watkins began his examination, he stopped to give a short motivational speech.

"Before we begin, I would like to encourage everyone to remain upbeat and positive, and remember our patient has a name. Her name is Lucinda, she is thirteen years old, she has four younger sisters and she is a brave girl who recently had a nasty fall down the stairs in which she dislocated her right shoulder and elbow as well broke her arm in two places. She loves horses, kittens and shiny red ribbons on presents." Dr. Watkins improvised the horses, kittens and bows, but the message was clear.

"And now a moment of silence as I say a prayer. Dear Lord, we ask that you steady our hands, calm our minds and guide us to help this young lady to a full recovery. Amen."

Everyone said, "Amen."

"Helen, hit the music, please!" Dr. Watkins exclaimed. Helen walked across the room to the ghetto blaster and she hit play, as Dr. Watkins pre-recorded mixed tape was in the tape player. As the music started Dr. Watkins commented, "Take me away, 'Most Relaxing Songs.'"

One of the nurses asked, "Dr. Watkins what do you mean? 'Most Relaxing Songs'?"

Helen answered the young nurse. "Dr. Watkins has a mixed tape for just such occasions as this. He hand-picked the songs because they are relaxing and peaceful."

Dr. Watkins waited until the broken cast was removed before he started unwrapping the blood-soaked bandage from Lucinda's head. Once it was removed, he could see the wound was still trickling blood.

"Hang a bag of blood please, type AB positive," Dr. Watkins calmly requested as he leaned over Lucinda. Looking at the gash on her forehead, he called for measuring tools to record the length, width and depth of the wound.

"Wound is approximately nine inches long, a quarter inch wide and looks to be one and a half inches deep. Poor girl is going to have a battle wound for certain."

CHAPTER 12 –

Enraged Father

OUT IN THE reception area. John looked at Margaret. "Take the girls over there and have a seat." He looked over at the door as he saw Sheriff Brown walk in heading directly towards John.

"Ah, John there you are." He approached John and offered his hand.

"Dave, what happened?" John asked the sheriff.

Sheriff Brown shook his head in dismay. "The school bus was going down Main Street and was about to enter the intersection when a gravel truck blew through the stop sign." John shook his head in disbelief.

"I've come here to check on your daughter and to inform the hospital we have a DOA coming in the back door." John was shocked.

"A DOA, oh my God, I've lived all my life in Riley and never heard anyone who died of unnatural causes. Who's the DOA? Who?"

Sheriff Brown grimaced. "Melanie Maples-Radisson, the school bus driver. We think she died on impact. All things considered, other than Melanie and your daughter, there were no other major injuries. Lots of cuts, bruises and scrapes though."

"Who was driving the truck that hit them?" John asked.

Sheriff Brown shook his head in anguish. "It was Charley Rodgers." John felt a chill run down his spine. Charley had been the town drunk ever since his wife passed away from cancer a decade ago. He was left to raise their seven-year-old daughter and he hit the bottle really hard.

The town did its best to help support Charley and despite his alcohol problem, he managed to raise his daughter Norma-Ann all by himself.

John then asked the obvious question. "Was he drunk?"

Sheriff Brown hesitated. "John, how about we move over here out of the way so we can talk somewhat privately." Sheriff Brown placed a hand on John's elbow and guided him to a corner opposite of main reception.

"Dave, tell me the truth, I have no idea how badly hurt my daughter is. Was he drunk?" John raised his voice.

Sheriff Brown moved closer to John and put his hand on his shoulder. "John, I need you to lower your voice; we don't know yet. My men have him at the station and are checking that as we speak. John, I have to go and inform the desk of the DOA so they can open the side door. We don't want to wheel Melanie in through main emergency. I'll give you an update once our investigation is complete."

"Alright thanks Dave, any information would be appreciated." John nodded.

Just as Sheriff Brown reached the reception desk, John looked back at the emergency entrance and saw one of the deputies walking in with Charley Rodgers. When he saw Charley, he pictured his eldest daughter laying on a hospital operating table, her arm already in a cast and God only knows what injuries she had from the collision. Something inside John snapped; a switch flipped and like a raging bull, he charged at Charley, easily outweighing the drunk by thirty pounds yelling, "Charley, you son of a bitch!"

John used a straight arm to the deputy, knocking him back as he tackled Charley to the ground. Within seconds John had mounted Charley and was raining down fists of fury on Charley's face.

Margaret yelled out. "John, stop!" She saw blood splattering from his fists with each blow; blood was casting off and landing on the nearby wall.

John was yelling at Charley. "You hurt my girl, you bastard!"

It all happened very fast. Within seconds the deputy, Sheriff Brown and two other men were on top of John, trying to restrain the angry man. John broke his right arm free and landed one final blow directly to Charley's orbital socket, crushing it with an audible bone-cracking sound. It took four men, including the sheriff, to wrestle John to the ground and cuff his hands behind his back.

John was still yelling at Charley. "You son of bitch, you better hope and pray my daughter is alright, or as God is my witness—"

Sheriff Brown interrupted. "John, calm down, you don't want to say anything you'll regret."

Margaret made her way over to the area. She could see Charley flat on his back lying motionless, his entire face covered in blood from the rapid and brutal beating John had just laid on him.

As Sheriff Brown and the deputy helped John to his feet, nurses and orderlies were rushing to Charley's aid. A flat board was slid underneath Charley; another orderly rushed out with a gurney and they used the flat board to lift Charley to the gurney.

Margaret spoke to the sheriff. "What are you going to do with John?"

John struggled with the deputy while responding to Margaret. "Don't worry about me, Margaret, pray for Charley. Pray that our girl is alright!"

Sheriff Brown ignored John and answered Margaret. "We have to take John to the station. We'll hold him there until he calms down and we find out if Charley Rodgers is going to press charges."

"Press charges?" John yelled. "I'm not the one who killed someone today. He deserves everything he got and more!"

Sheriff Brown addressed his deputy. "Take John to holding. I'll hang around here and see how Charley is." John was still enraged but he went with the deputy willingly. As he was being escorted out, John turned his head and spoke over his shoulder.

"Margaret, come tell me how Lucinda is the second you find out."

"John, I'll be there as soon as I can."

Just before the incident happened, Suzanne watched her father charge at Charley and she had the foresight to take her little sisters and turn them away. Margaret rushed back to her daughters and saw Suzanne sheltering the younger ones with their backs turned.

"Did you turn your sisters away, Suzanne?"

"Yes, Mother, I did. I've never seen father fight and I didn't want my little sisters to see."

"That was very wise of you, daughter." Margaret cracked a slight smile.

CHAPTER 13 –

Making a Tough Call

DR. WATKINS STARTED working on Lucinda, and within a few minutes there was a knock on the big picture window into the operating room. Malcolm, another resident physician, was holding a mask over his face looking through the big picture window. Once he had a nurse's attention, he called through the glass, "I need to speak with Dr. Watkins." The nurse went over to the door, opened it and leaned her head out to take a message from Malcolm.

She went over to stand close enough for Dr. Watkins to hear her. "Dr. Watkins, Malcolm says there is another critically injured person from the accident."

Dr. Watkins stopped, looked up at Allen. "I thought you said there was only one critical injury." Allen was shocked to hear there was a second critical.

The nurse then added. "It's Charley Rodgers, the driver of the truck. Malcolm wants you to come as soon as you can." Dr. Watkins knew that Lucinda was still critical, yet he had her far enough along that he could do a quick assessment of Charley.

Anesthesiologist Collin spoke up as Dr. Watkins stepped back. "If you're going to be longer than fifteen minutes, you need to let me know, Dr. Watkins."

Dr. Watkins replied, "I won't even be more than a couple of minutes. Besides, Charley is probably already anesthetized with alcohol." As the words slipped out of his mouth Dr. Watkins realized his mistake. "Apologies that was unprofessional of me to say." He left the operating room to go back through pre-op and out into the hall to an adjacent examination room.

He opened the door to the room and saw Charley on the gurney motionless. "Is he sedated?" Dr. Watkins asked Malcolm.

"No, Dr. Watkins he's knocked out." Dr. Watkins made a quick assessment of the man. "It looks like his orbital socket is crushed and he has some facial bruising, probably from his head slamming into the steering wheel or the dash of the truck."

Malcolm hesitated to reply.

"Clean his wounds and check for any deep cuts or lacerations. Put him on a low dose of morphine. When he wakes up that is going to hurt like hell."

Malcolm answered, "Yes, Dr. Watkins. I'll take care of it. You should know that the wounds on Charley are not from the collision."

Dr. Watkins looked at Malcolm then back at Charley. "Could've fooled me. What are they from?"

"They're from the father of the girl you have in the operating room." Dr. Watkins looked again at Charley and as he looked closer, he realized the bruises were definitely fist marks.

"Dr. Watkins, I believe that Charley is in more serious condition than your patient in the operating room. I believe Charley is hemorrhaging internally."

Dr. Watkins paused a moment. "Malcolm, the hospital only has one operating room. This is a very difficult decision of which one to treat first."

"Dr. Watkins!" Malcolm raised his voice. "This patient is almost most certainly going to hemorrhage to death within a short period of time, you need to get him in now!"

"Malcolm. It's my call!" he snapped at the attending physician. "The time it would take to relocate Lucinda and to reset the operating room, and the time it would take to reset again after Charley would put both patients at severe risk. We'll proceed as it is now. For the time being, I want you to sedate Mr. Rodgers, hang fluids and monitor him, is that clear?" Dr. Watkins was resolute in his tone.

"Yes, Dr. Watkins."

Once back in the operating room, Dr. Watkins went back to working on Lucinda. He worked on her at a much faster pace, but still careful to be exact and not make any mistakes. After a half-hour he addressed Collin. "Collin, she is stable enough to be moved out of the O.R."

Collin started to object. "It's risky to move her right now."

"Yes, I know, but we need the O.R. for Charley Rodgers now before he bleeds out internally. She's stable enough for now. You go with her to the other room."

Dr. Watkins addressed Helen. "Once the room is clear, we have ten minutes to sanitize and prepare the O.R. for Charley. Please make it happen."

"Yes, Dr. Watkins."

"Allen, you'll go with Collin to take Lucinda to exam room 3; you'll stay with her until I come see you. Collin, once you stabilize Lucinda in the exam room, I'm going to need you back here to anesthetize Charley and stay during his operation." Dr. Watkins spoke with absolute confidence and authority. Everyone executed their roles flawlessly.

Within an hour, Dr. Watkins and team had determined that Charley did not have internal bleeding. They stabilized his condition and sent him to recovery.

Lucinda was brought back in and was still stable. Dr. Watkins finished operating on Lucinda successfully, and then she was also moved into recovery.

"Good work, team," Dr. Watkins proudly announced in the pre-op room as everyone was cleaning up. Everyone applauded Dr. Watkins.

"You did an amazing job, Brad," Collin said as he patted him on the back.

CHAPTER 14 –

Margaret's Deepest Desire

IT WAS SHORTLY after 8am when Bill opened his eyes. Laying on his back he looked down to see the beautiful young woman beside him, her arm draped over his chest as she slept. As he looked at her, he used his free hand to gently stroke her hair. His thoughts were a bit jumbled, as he thought back on his night with Mary and how well they connected. Just then, Mary stirred and opened her eyes. As she gazed dreamily up into Bill's eyes, she said, "Good morning, lover, hope you enjoyed last night."

With absolute sincerity Bill smiled and assured the girl, "You're an amazing lover, I really enjoyed our time together." They lay in each other's arms for a while before they heard a clanging bang at the front church door. Before Bill realized that the clanging was keys hitting the door as another key was inserted in the lock, Mary had jumped up, gathered her robe and slippers, and had bolted down the hall into her own room where she closed the door, slipped into bed and pretended to be asleep.

Bill could hear loud echoing footsteps coming from the empty cathedral. The footsteps got louder as they grew closer. He got out of bed, put on a robe and walked out into the hallway just as Pastor Conrad was about to open the door to his office. "Good morning."

Conrad jumped a bit, clearly startled by the greeting. "Well, good morning, Pastor Bill, I see you're just waking up. Would you like me to make you some coffee?"

"That would be wonderful, kind sir." Bill smiled. "I'm going to grab a quick shower and see you shortly." Bill then walked down the hall to the bathroom that was between the two guest rooms. He closed the door, disrobed and stepped into the shower.

~

At the police station in Riley, John sat in a holding cell, still seething at Charley.

Sheriff Brown arrived at the station. He walked into the holding cell area where his deputy sat at his desk five feet away from the two holding cells. "Was he any trouble, Dale?"

"Not all, boss, he came along peacefully." Sheriff Brown walked over to the cell where John was pacing back and forth. The sheriff stood there in silence, watching the large man going from one side to the other inside the cell.

John saw the sheriff, stopped and yelled, "What?"

"John, you're a good man who loves his family, but you had no right to attack Charley."

"Dave, you know he had it coming, it was only a matter of time before that drunk killed someone. Someone had to stand up and set him right."

"That's not your responsibility, John."

John interrupted Sheriff Brown before he could continue. "It sure as hell is, Dave! Lucinda is my eldest daughter and I'm responsible for her. An eye for an eye," John exclaimed.

"But John, now you're here, and what good are you to your daughter here in jail?"

"Dave, that's my family! I will defend them to my very last breath, everyone knows that. Charley got what he deserved, end of story." John went back to pacing.

Sheriff Brown shook his head and walked away. As he passed the deputy's desk, he leaned over. "You! In my office now!" Sheriff Brown said, just loud enough that the deputy could hear but John wouldn't be able to.

Once inside the office, Sheriff Brown sat in his high-back chair at his desk while the deputy sat in the opposite chair across from the sheriff.

"Dale. Exactly what were you thinking to bring Charley out in public? Wasn't I clear when I gave you the order to take him to the station, book him and put him in the holding cell?"

Deputy Dale became worried. "Sheriff Brown, Charley got real sick in the back of my cruiser, he was choking and vomiting everywhere. I thought maybe he had a concussion so I took him to the hospital."

Sheriff Brown put his elbows on his desk at the same time, putting his hands on his forehead as he shook his head. Deputy Dale watched in silence, waiting for Sheriff Brown's next words.

"Dale, Dale, Dale... that's a pickle for sure. I can certainly see why you made the choice, but do you think you could've done it differently?"

Dale thought about it. "Yes, I suppose I could have."

"And what could you have done?" The sheriff removed his head from his hands and looked directly at Dale, looking down at the two-way radio on Dale's police-issued belt. Then he looked back up at Dale; he looked up and down a few times until Dale realized.

"Oh, I could have radioed to you for guidance."

Sheriff Brown smiled. "Exactly, Dale, you're a keen one."

Dale's body language became relaxed at hearing the compliment from his boss.

Sheriff Brown noticed. "You're not off the hook yet, Dale. While I can understand why you made that choice, you certainly didn't think it all the way through. And now because of you, we have a good man, John Hall, penned up in jail and another man, Charley Rodgers, in hospital with God only knows the severity of his injuries. This job requires us to always put the safety and well-being of the public first and foremost. You must always think, especially when you do the opposite of the order I have given you."

Dale's shoulders slumped. "Sheriff Brown, I'm truly sorry. It won't happen again."

"Good then. Consider it a lesson learned. Oh, and by the way, go clean inside that cruiser of yours before it starts to smell."

In the waiting room, Margaret waited with her daughters for news on Lucinda. Suzanne sat somberly beside her mother as her sisters played about with the children's toys on the table.

CHAPTER 15 –

Planting Seeds

CONRAD, BILL AND Mary made their way over to the diner to meet with Sally and James. On the short drive over, Conrad asked questions.

"So, Mary, how did your session with Pastor Bill go? Were you able to find comfort?" Mary was still giddy inside, basking in the afterglow of becoming a woman and the wonderful feelings she had because of it.

"Pastor Conrad, to be honest we only talked for a little while before I felt too tired and needed to go to bed."

"Oh?" Conrad said in an inquisitive tone. "So, did you get to tell Pastor Bill about your experience while in coma?"

Bill listened to the exchange as he sat silently.

"Yes, Pastor Conrad, there wasn't much to tell, though. I saw a white light and felt the warmth of God and then I was back in the hospital."

"Ok, Mary, I understand. So, do you believe in God again?"

Mary chuckled at the young pastor. "Of course, Pastor Conrad. God the Creator. I just wasn't myself when I first woke up in hospital."

As they arrived at the diner, Mary saw that her dad's car was already parked and she assumed her parents were inside. The three of them walked into the diner with Conrad leading the way, followed by Mary.

Sally and James sat at the table. At the table next to them sat a mother with her two teenaged daughters. Upon seeing Mary, one of the girls said to her mother, "Mom, that's the girl I was telling you about. The one that went crazy." The girl snickered.

Her mom saw that Sally and James were sitting at the very next table and she tried to silence her daughter from saying more. "Greta, shush, it's not polite to gossip."

Her other daughter Grace spoke up. "But Mom, it's all over school. 'Mary, Mary had a brain, hit by a car and now she's insane'".

Sally and James heard the cruel melody sung by the girls. They also heard Jeannie, their mother, say, "This isn't the time or place, girls!"

Sally wanted to turn around and admonish the girls for their cruel rhyme. Taking James hand, she said, "We should move to another table, James."

Conrad could see Sally and James stand up and move to a different table. Just as he approached Sally, he asked, "Was there something wrong with that table?" He pointed at the table that James and Sally had vacated.

"No, Pastor Conrad, I thought a little more privacy would be in order."

At that moment Sally looked over to see Mary walking by the two girls. Mary smiled and waved. Sally's heart shattered to pieces when she saw the two girls giggle and not wave back to her daughter. She took a step past Conrad and hugged her daughter, in part because Sally loved her and in part because she wanted to show Jeannie Klunkin that Mary was still very much loved. James also hugged Mary and then shook Pastor Bill's hand. "Hello again, Pastor Bill."

Bill greeted the parents and they all sat down to lunch. Again, Conrad was the initiator of conversation.

"I think we have some good news, Sally and James. Mary believes in God again, she told me so on the way over."

The parents beamed with happiness and looked at Pastor Bill for confirmation. Bill picked up on the quizzical facial expressions from Mary's parents. "Conrad is correct, Mary has made some excellent strides."

James wanted to know more. "Did you find out if she is possessed?"

Pastor Bill looked straight into James eyes as he confidently said, "I can assure you Mary is possessed."

Sally gasped. "Ahhh?"

Pastor Bill smiled and went on to say, "Mary had an experience in which she matured. With her experience, she has grown and become a woman." Conrad, James, Sally and Mary all hung on Bill's every word, especially Mary who enjoyed how Bill was stating his words such that only she knew his secret meaning. '*Become a woman*,' she chuckled silently to herself.

"What we all need to realize is that Mary had a traumatic experience and in order for her mind to make sense of the experience she had to blossom, much like the cherry tree blossoms in the spring and bears fruit in late May."

Bill's words were almost hypnotic to everyone at the table. "Honestly, I admire Mary for how well she has come to accept and make sense of it all. She's a remarkable young lady."

Sally was starting to forget the cruel rhyme said about her daughter as she listened intently to Pastor Bill. Mary wanted Bill to stay longer and she knew it was a good time for her to speak up.

"Pastor Bill speaks too highly of me. We really didn't have that much time to talk a whole lot."

James wondered, "Why not Mary?"

She smiled at her father and placed her hand on his. "Daddy, honestly I was completely exhausted yesterday and I went to bed at 7pm."

"I understand, Mary." James beamed a smile at his daughter.

Conrad then addressed Pastor Bill. "Pastor Bill, do you think you could stay one more night, spend a little more time with Mary before you go back home?"

Bill had larger plans in mind for Mary. He wanted her much closer to him than the hour-long drive from Riley to Champion, and Conrad had opened the conversation for Bill to lay his master plan down for everyone.

"While I have great faith in Mary, and believe that she'll make a full recovery, I feel that when she first woke up, she had lost all hope. The reason I think she lost hope was due to being inundated with questions her mind wasn't ready to answer."

Mary was a little lost. She did however enjoy the mental game of trying to guess where Bill was going with all this.

"It's clear to me," Bill spoke, "very clear, in fact, that Mary's greatest concern, whether or not she knows it, was that she was worried about what people would say about her and what she had said when she first awoke. The whole 'lost faith in God' comments. If Champion is anything like Riley, and I know it is," Bill paused for effect, "gossip runs rampant, and Mary, if she is not already, will eventually become a victim of petty small-town people who are so bored that at any little bit of excitement, they spread gossip like butter on toast."

Sally heard Bill's words and she broke down and started crying. She knew it was true; she had just heard a cruel rhyme about her daughter. *Mary, Mary had a brain, hit by a car and now she's insane.* The rhyme rang over and over through her mind. James put his arm around her, "Sally that was just silly little girls nattering rubbish."

Mary realized something had happened and she spoke right up in a demanding tone. "What happened? Tell me please!"

James kept his arm around his wife while he turned to face his daughter. "Mary, it was nothing really."

Mary wasn't happy with that response. "Father! I'm not a little girl. Tell me, I can handle it. After all, I came back from the dead. I think I can handle a little bit of gossip."

Bill placed his comforting hand on Mary's shoulder as Conrad spoke after coming to his own realization. "I see. That's why you moved tables. Did Jeannie Klunkin say something?"

James knew that it was best to say something as saying nothing would only cast shadows of doubt. "No, it wasn't Jeannie, her daughters were repeating a cruel children's rhyme that they heard in school."

"Was the rhyme about me?" Mary looked at her dad. Bill gently squeezed Mary's shoulder to comfort and calm her down. Mary saw an opening; she thought she knew the direction Bill was going and she was down with it.

"Ok, Dad, if you don't tell me, I swear I'll go over there." She pointed to the table where Jeannie sat with her daughters. "And I'll ask them myself."

James hesitated. "Mary, it's not worth it."

Mary took Bill's hand off her shoulder and sat straight up in her chair, pushing it back as she stood up. She walked past Bill as he tried to block her movement by gently grabbing her by the forearm.

Mary pulled her arm away as she marched over to the other table. She stood and placed both her hands on the table, her eyes looking at the two teenaged girls. "What did you say about me?"

Conrad went to stand up. Bill interrupted. "No, Conrad, leave it alone. This is good for Mary, trust me."

As Mary stood at the table, the girls sat dumbfounded and somewhat scared. When they didn't answer, Mary darted her eyes to their mother. "Clearly, Jeannie, your daughters are so cowardly that they can't even repeat their silly little gossip to my face. They can only snicker behind people's backs."

Mary stood straight up. With pride and dignity, she walked back to her table.

Bill made eye contact with Mary as he slowly and silently clapped his hands as if to applaud Mary for the scene she had caused. Conrad, Sally and James saw Bill's gesture. Just as Mary sat back down, Bill explained his applause.

"Mary, you were very well composed. How did you feel?"

Mary broke down; she put her hands in her face and started to cry. Through her fingers, she was saying, "They wouldn't even tell me what they said, it's sooo hurtful."

Sally was beside herself seeing the pain her daughter was going through. James stood up and was about to head over to the table and give Jeannie a lecture, but he sat right back down seeing the table was now empty.

Bill was impressed with the show Mary was putting on. Now that he knew more of Mary, he could tell that her tears were faked. He placed his hand back on Mary's shoulder and looked at Conrad.

"Conrad, I think you're right. It would be a good idea for me to stay one more day, to help Mary get her confidence back and the like." Sally and James both perked up and were pleased with Bill's decision to stay.

"That's great. Thank you very much, Pastor Bill," James said.

Bill was ready to plant the seeds for his master plan. "I believe that it would be good for me to assess Mary further. I have concern that she is still far too raw to be exposed to that kind of cruel gossip, after already witnessing people's cruelty rearing its ugly head. I will evaluate Mary further. I think that it may become necessary to have Mary voluntarily enter Hopewell Asylum."

Sally was shocked. "Hopewell? Why Pastor Bill? Do you think Mary is insane?"

Bill expected that very question, and before he spoke, Mary indignantly spoke. "Yeah, Bill, do you think I'm insane?" Bill shot Mary a look that only she could understand, a look that said, '*Trust me!*'

"Mary. No, I don't think you're insane at all. I think that small towns can be cruel, and although I feel you can handle the gossip and talk that is sure to follow you around; I think it might be an option for you to voluntarily enter Hopewell, so that you may fully recover in a positive, stress-free environment."

Mary realized exactly where Bill was going and she sealed the deal in agreeing with Bill. "I understand, Pastor Bill, so we'll discuss Hopewell and the pros and cons for me."

"Exactly right, Mary!" Bill responded.

After lunch, James and Sally returned home while Bill, Conrad and Mary went to the church.

CHAPTER 16 –

Breaking the News

IT WAS 2PM when Dr. Watkins came out to the waiting room. When Margaret saw him, she ordered Suzanne, "Watch your sisters while I go and speak with Dr. Watkins."

Margaret went over to Dr. Watkins. "Is Lucinda alright?"

"Yes, Margaret, she'll be fine. Can you come to my office please?" He led her down the hall to his office.

"Have a seat, Margaret." He breathed in deeply as if catching his breath as he watched her sit down. He sat at the small desk in the room, turning his chair to the side so he could be face to face with Margaret.

"Margaret, first of all I want you to know Lucinda is doing well. She's in recovery right now and when she wakes up you can see her."

Margaret let out a breath. "Oh, thank God."

Dr. Watkins went on to explain the injuries and how the operation went. "Upon initial examination, I recorded that Lucinda had a gash on her forehead nine inches long, a quarter inch wide and roughly one and a half inches deep." Margaret listened carefully so she could report as accurately as possible to John.

"The cast on her right arm was also damaged and had to be removed and redone after we completed the operation on her forehead. Later today we'll do some more x-rays to ensure her arm is still setting properly.

116

"As for the head wound, we operated to stop internal bleeding. She has dissolvable stiches on the internal laceration. As well, we have stitched her wound and she should recover nicely. We'll need to keep her in hospital for at least forty-eight hours for observation and to monitor for concussion."

"So, Dr. Watkins, will she make a full recovery?"

"I have every confidence that she'll make a complete and full recovery. Over the next few days, we'll take x-rays of her head and watch for brain swelling, but at this time we don't see any sign of swelling, she is again in perfect health." He smiled at Margaret.

"I'm sure John will be relieved to hear the news. Thank you, Dr. Watkins."

He looked at Margaret and his facial expression changed to a look of concern.

"Margaret, I should tell you that Charley Rodgers is also fine and expected to make a full recovery. I'm told that Charley's injuries were caused by your husband John, not by the collision."

Margaret just stared at Dr. Watkins with a callous expression. "So what? Charley killed the bus driver and injured our daughter; I couldn't care less if he makes a full recovery or not."

Dr. Watkins sighed. "Charley is a full-grown man, and the damage done to him is extensive. I understand why you wouldn't be concerned for Charley, but what I'm referring to is the fact that John lost his temper and was capable of doing that kind of damage to a grown man. I strongly recommend you get him some anger management help before it's too late and he loses it on you or one of your daughters."

Margaret became offended. "Dr. Watkins, I'll have you know that John is a very loving, caring and gentle man. If you were in his shoes and your daughter were seriously injured, don't you think you'd lose your temper as well?"

"Of course, Margaret, I understand. However, a rational person would be able to control their rage and not beat a man to within an inch of his life. Your husband has serious anger issues."

Margaret composed herself. "Dr. Watkins, I thank you for your concern. We'll be just fine, thank you," she said with a stern look on her face that suggested she didn't want to hear any more of this talk. She stood up. "Thank you again, Dr. Watkins. I'm going to be with my daughters and wait until we can see Lucinda."

"I'll have a nurse come and get you when Lucinda wakes up and is ready for visitors."

Margaret nodded, got up and left the office, returning to the waiting area to wait with her daughters.

CHAPTER 17 –

Mary's Choice

THAT AFTERNOON AT the church, Mary, Pastor Conrad and Bill sat in the sitting room talking about Hopewell Asylum.

Mary sat across from the two pastors. She knew that Bill had set it up so that they could spend another night together, she wanted to keep up appearances and pretended to entertain the thought of going to Hopewell.

"Pastor Bill. Why do you think Hopewell would be a good thing for me? Conrad, what do you think?"

The two men almost tried to answer at the same time. Mary laughed as she saw them both try to talk; it reminded her of two people bending over at the same time to pick something up. "Ah-ha-ha," Mary chuckled. "Sorry, pastors, I should have asked only one pastor at a time."

Bill nodded and rolled his hand palm up, "You go first, Conrad."

"Are you sure, Pastor Bill?" Bill nodded and for a second time made a hand gesture encouraging Conrad to speak.

Conrad sat up a little straighter and looked directly at Mary. "Mary, I haven't got as much experience as Pastor Bill. But what I do know is this town. Champion can be unforgivingly relentless when it comes to rumors and gossip. Like, for example, Jeannie Klunkin and her girls at the diner." Mary nodded her head in agreement.

"On one hand, Mary, going to Hopewell takes you out of the spotlight; on the other, it could actually add fuel to the rumor mill."

Bill's head was nodding in agreement. To him it didn't matter if Mary agreed to go to Hopewell or not. It would be nice if she did, but he didn't need to overplay and expose his hand.

"I thought I handled it well today, and then when I got back to the table, it felt like everything came crashing down on me."

"I one hundred percent agree, Mary, you handled that situation very well. The sad truth is that it won't be the last time you find people being rude. It can grind you down over time; that's what my only concern is, Mary."

Bill waited patiently to jump into the conversation. Mary knew that Conrad was absolutely right and thought that perhaps a change of address for a short time may be just what she needed.

"Pastor Conrad. At first, I was really mad at Pastor Bill for even suggesting Hopewell. But you make some good points. I'm not afraid of anyone, really; it's going to happen for sure. Champion can be so petty." She placed her right hand behind her head and scratched at her hair as to signal she was considering the proposal. Silence filled the room as the pastors watched Mary pondering her options. Bill decided it was the right time to jump in.

"Mary, you asked why I think Hopewell is a good idea. I visit there once a week," Bill said, dropping a hint to Mary that he would see her more often if she was in Hopewell. "It's not really an asylum so much as it's a sanctuary. It would give you time to relax and recharge your batteries. While I don't know Champion as well as Conrad, what he describes is very similar to how Riley is, where everyone is in everyone else's business."

Conrad and Mary both laughed at the comment. "Ha-ha, you're so right, Pastor Bill. Small towns don't leave a lot of room for privacy, or to even just blend in after a tragedy," Conrad added.

"I hate to admit it, but here in the Oklahoma Bible Belt it just makes small-town living all that much more difficult in situations such as this." Bill was on a roll; he had the attention of his two conversation partners.

Bill continued. "Maybe if you both provided me with more detail of what exactly happened when Mary came out of her coma."

Conrad made eye contact with Bill and then spoke. "I think that's a good discussion to have. I can tell you what was said to me, and Mary can maybe fill in some details."

"I don't mind filling in the details, Conrad." Mary smiled this time, both men noticed that Mary didn't use the word pastor before his name, leading them to believe that she was becoming more relaxed with Pastor Conrad to simply refer to him by first name only.

Conrad started telling his recollection of events. "I was in my office when I got a call from one of the nurses at the hospital. She told me that Dr. Moffatt had requested my presence at the hospital. When I arrived, I met with Dr. Moffatt in his office. He explained to me that Mary was his patient. That she was comatose for seven days and when she awoke her parents were there. Sally said something like, 'Thank God she's awake.' And that's when Mary became violent and irrational." Conrad stopped to let Mary interject.

She picked up on the pause and added to the recollection. "Yes, Conrad, that is what my mom said. I yelled at her: 'Don't thank God! God is dead!'"

"Yes, and that's when Dr. Moffatt decided to call me in. He recognized that a statement like that, even said while in shock, would be something that would interest the town pastor. Dr. Moffatt went on to tell me that once they calmed Mary down, she told them about her near-death experience. It was a spooky story. I told the doctor that I would talk to Mary. As I recall, Sally, James and a nurse were present in the room when I went in to speak with Mary."

"You're right, Conrad. You, me, Mom, Dad and that young nurse that stayed to monitor me."

"After a bit of small talk and getting Mary's blessing to speak with her, I asked her to tell me why she said God was dead. She was absolutely adamant that God was dead. She went on to tell me that she killed a light spirit and escaped back to earth."

Mary listened and so far agreed with everything Conrad was saying.

"The mere fact that Mary claimed to have killed God is why I called you in, Pastor Bill."

"Whoa, back up the bus, Conrad!" Mary said somewhat indignantly. "I never said I killed God. I said I killed the light spirit."

Conrad was taken aback at the comment. "That makes no sense. God is the spirit of light. On Mount Sinai, Moses came into contact with God. God was in the form of a light so bright that Moses was unable to look upon God. That's when God gave Moses the Ten Commandments. Mary, when you said light spirit, I assumed you meant God himself."

"Not at all, Conrad. The light spirit in my experience was definitely not God. Sorry you thought that's what I meant."

"Mary, you shouldn't be sorry, I'm the one who should be sorry. I could've asked better and more questions instead of jumping to a conclusion."

"It was a chaotic time, Conrad." He noticed that Mary had again used his name without his pastor title; this made him feel like he was starting to rebuild a connection with her.

"We all thought you said you killed God. I even talked with your parents in the hall about it. They thought that's what you meant too."

"And when you and Mom and Dad were in the hall is when I yelled at you."

"Yes, Mary, you did. Your voice was a completely different tone. It was deep and scratchy. You yelled out and kept repeating, 'God is dead,' over and over again. Your mother started crying and from there everything took a left turn."

Bill listened intently and interjected a few tidbits here and there so as to let both of them know he was still engaged in the conversation. "What took a left turn, Conrad?"

"In hindsight, Pastor Bill, I feel ashamed to admit this. When Sally started crying, I tried to comfort her by saying that Mary was not herself. I thought the change in Mary's voice was due to a demonic possession. When I said that to Sally and James, they seemed relieved that the things Mary was saying were not coming from her. They wanted to believe it was a possession as much as I did; because then that would explain the profanity Mary used. It would explain why she would say she killed God. It just seemed like a good fit."

In that moment, Mary understood why all the concern about the town gossip. She knew she was going to be front page headlines for all the town gossips and the grapevine would be relentless. She tuned out for a short time with her focus on the visions of the torment her parents would endure over this.

Conrad shook his head as he apologized profusely. "I'm so very sorry," he repeated several times. "Mary can you forgive me?" There was silence again. Conrad thought that Mary was pondering whether or not to forgive him. He looked at her and saw she was in deep thought. Bill saw it too.

The two pastors gave Mary some time. Bill broke the silence. "Mary— are you alright?" He said gently. Mary heard Bill's words but it sounded like an echo as she was so lost in her thoughts. She shook her head slightly as if to snap herself back to reality.

"Oh yes, yes, I'm fine, Pastor Bill." She then looked at Conrad.

"Pastor Conrad, of course I can forgive you. I was just thinking how mean the town will be with my parents, I was lost in that image." Her expression was one of genuine concern.

CHAPTER 18 –

IT WAS NOW 5pm. Margaret walked to the front desk and asked the nurse if Lucinda had awoken yet.

"Mrs. Hall, I'll go check with Dr. Watkins. Be right back." The nurse went to the back and to Dr. Watkins' office; he was not there. She went to the room where Lucinda was and found the doctor there. He was beside her, checking the monitors and speaking to himself. "This makes no sense." He scratched his head. "She should be awake by now."

"Dr. Watkins." The nurse startled him as she saw him jump and turn to face her.

"Oh my God, you scared me." Dr. Watkins placed a hand over his heart, patting it as he turned his head slightly to the right.

"Sorry, Doctor, I came to find you because Margaret is asking if Lucinda has woken up yet."

"I bet she is. Please tell her I'll be right out to come talk to her. Thank you."

The nurse nodded and left, leaving Dr. Watkins in the room with the unconscious girl.

She approached the front desk and informed Margaret. "Dr. Watkins said he'll be right out to talk with you."

Ten minutes later, Dr. Watkins came into the waiting room. He made eye contact with Margaret and pointed towards his office. Margaret patted Suzanne on the shoulder. "Suzanne, I'm going to talk with the doctor, watch the girls please."

"Yes, Mother," Suzanne said dutifully.

"Margaret, I can tell you that Lucinda is doing fine. All her vitals are good; the only thing is she hasn't woken up."

Margaret looked concerned. "Is that normal, doctor?"

"To be honest, I expected her to be awake by now, but with head injuries sometimes the body just takes more time to heal."

Margaret sat in stunned silence for a few moments before asking, "What should I tell John?"

"You should tell John exactly what I told you, Margaret. Lucinda had an operation that was successful. All her vital signs are good and we expect her to make a full recovery. She's just a little sleepy and we should know more by morning."

Dr. Watkins tried to be as factual as possible while at the same time he wanted to provide comfort that Margaret could take good news to John.

"Thank you, Dr. Watkins. I'll do that." She got up and left the doctor's office.

~

Mary rubbed her tummy as she exclaimed that she was a little hungry. "Oh my, seems I didn't have enough to eat at lunch."

Pastor Conrad offered his services. "I'm not a professional chef, but I make a mean grilled cheese sandwich if either of you are interested?" he said to Mary and Bill.

"I could go for a grilled cheese," Bill said.

Mary agreed. "Me too, if you don't mind, Conrad."

Conrad stood up. "I guess I'm off to the church kitchen. Be back in a jiffy."

Margaret stopped at the police station before taking her girls home. "Ok, girls, I have to go in and see your father. You be good while I'm gone."

Charlotte protested. "I want to go in and see Father."

Margaret answered quickly and sternly. "Absolutely not, Charlotte! The police station is no place for children. Stay in the car with Suzanne." She then looked at Suzanne and started to speak. "Suzanne—"

"Yes, Mother, I'll stay here and keep watch over my sisters."

With that Margaret got out of the car and went into the police station.

Walking up to the front desk, she met with Deputy Dale. "I would like to see my husband John Hall, please," Margaret said in a firm tone. She saw the deputy hesitate and turn his head to the right to look over his shoulder.

Margaret saw Sheriff Brown standing in the doorway of his office just a few feet away. She saw the sheriff nod to his deputy. Margaret looked past the deputy and addressed Sheriff Brown directly. "Thank you, sir."

The deputy opened the half door and let Margaret in. He led her down the hall and into the cell area. As soon as Margaret saw the cells, she gasped slightly. "Ahhh." Just to see her husband behind bars was a new experience. She pushed past the deputy and went directly to stand in front of John's cell.

"Hello, John," she said, as John was lying down on the single cot in the cell. Seeing his wife, he knew she was bringing him news of Lucinda. He sprang up and moved to the front of the cell just inches away from Margaret, with only the cell bars separating them.

"How's Lucinda?"

Margaret put on a brave face and buried any concern she might have deep down so that it wouldn't give John a scare. "Lucinda is fine, John." He didn't see through his wife's forced smile.

"Ah good." John felt relieved and let out an exhale as if he had been holding his breath the entire day.

"Dr. Watkins said that Lucinda's operation was a complete success and all her vitals are good."

"What happened to her, Margaret? Why did she need an operation?" John quizzed. Margaret realized that John didn't know that Lucinda had a head wound, all he knew was she was in hospital because Charley hit their bus.

"John, when the accident happened Lucinda bumped her head when the bus stopped suddenly. Dr. Watkins also said he had to remove her cast and put a new one on because the old one got cracked in the accident."

"Lucinda had a head wound and her cast got broken. Is that right, wife?"

"Exactly, John. Right now, Lucinda is sleeping and I'll go to see her in the morning. Dr. Watkins said they would need to keep her in hospital for thirty-six to forty-eight hours for observation. That is standard procedure in cases with head injuries. Concussion concerns, you know." Margaret was pleased with herself for communicating so confidently to John.

"And is she going to be alright?" John asked one more time.

Margaret smiled wide. "Yes, she'll be just fine, John. The doctor is pleased with her recovery so far."

"Thank you, Margaret. Where are the other girls?"

"They're out in the car waiting for me. I should get them home and make some dinner."

"Yes, that's a good idea," John agreed.

"Would you like me to see if the Sheriff will allow me to bring you a plate of food?"

"Not to worry, Margaret I'm sure these barbarians will feed me soon enough. Thank you for coming by; I was so worried about Lucinda."

"You're welcome John; I should be going. I'll see you tomorrow to come and get you after I talk to the judge." She sneered as she looked back towards the sheriff's office.

John smiled at his wife's dissatisfaction with the sheriff.

CHAPTER 19 –

Spiritual Connection Made

CONRAD RETURNED TO the sitting area with two plates, each with a perfectly cooked, golden grilled cheese sandwich on it, along with a dollop of catsup.

"Here we go. Grilled cheese by Chef Conrad." He bent over to put the plates on the coffee table, one in front of Bill, one in front of Mary. "Bon appétit."

Bill looked up at Conrad. "You didn't make one for yourself?"

"No, Pastor Bill, I think I'm going to head home and have dinner there, if you and Mary don't mind."

Mary spoke first. "Not at all, Conrad, we'll be fine here." Bill echoed the sentiment.

"Alright then, I shall take my leave. Goodnight to you both."

Conrad left the room and went to his office. A few minutes later, the couple heard the front door close and the lock being latched.

After eating their sandwiches, Mary got up. "Bill, could we have a fire again tonight?"

"Of course, Mary, I'll make one right now."

"I'll be back in a flash, I'm going to change into something more comfortable." She winked at Bill as she left the room.

A short while later. Mary returned to the sitting room and saw the fire but no sign of Bill. "Bill where'd you go? Are you changing into more comfy clothes as well?" She sat in the large chair by the fire.

After a while Bill returned, wearing a big terry cloth robe, one not unlike the one Mary was wearing. He ran his fingers through her hair as he walked by her chair. Mary cooed as his fingers touched her.

He sat down in the open chair and looked at Mary; she smiled the kind of smile that was alluring, with desire in her eyes.

"Mary—"

Mary put a finger to her lips. "Shush, now is not the time for talking." She then stood up and removed her robe, revealing nothing but her birthday suit.

She moved over, slowly stepping one leg then the other over Bill's lap. She leaned in and the couple embraced in a passionate kiss, which led to heavy petting, erotic caressing and eventually exciting chair sex in which they tried different positions and angles. Not a word was spoken, and they both felt the erotic energy of their souls entwined together in sexual ecstasy.

~

It was 8pm in Riley. Dr. Watkins checked in on Lucinda. He shook his head as he checked the machines. All her vitals were still good, yet she had not awoken from her surgery yet.

He left the room, went to the front desk and reported to the night nurse. "I just don't know why she won't wake up. But I'm exhausted, I need to go home now and get some sleep." The nurse looked at him sympathetically.

"Dr. Watkins, of course you're tired, it's been a long day. Go home, get some sleep. I'm sure she'll be awake by morning."

Dr. Watkins smiled and went to his locker, changed and left the hospital.

After an intense session of love-making, Bill sat in the chair with Mary curled up in his lap. The two exchanged passionate little kisses.

Mary looked up into Bill's eyes. "Bill, do you feel guilty at all?"

"Guilty for what, Mary?"

"Well, you're married and having an affair with me. Do you feel guilty at all?"

Bill paused for a moment as if to think of just the right words to say. "I suppose I should feel guilty, but honestly I don't at all. It just feels right; you feel right, Mary."

Mary was partially relieved to hear his words. "So, Bill, what is your intention as it relates to me?"

"A puzzling question, Mary. Let me think about it a moment." Bill stroked his fingers through Mary's long straight hair. "I have no intentions, Mary, other than to enjoy as much of you as I can for as long as I can." There was a silence as Mary slowly traced her fingers in a figure eight on Bill's chest. "Come on Mary, tell me where that question comes from? Are you wanting me to leave my wife?"

Mary burst out laughing as she playfully slapped Bill on the chest. "No! Are you on drugs, Bill? I would never want you to leave your wife, I'm just using you for sex, let's never forget that. No, what I'm wondering is why you want me to go to Hopewell?"

"Well, Mary, it would be absolutely wonderful to have you closer to me, yes. I go to Hopewell on a regular basis. I could see you often without having to make an excuse as to where I was going and why."

Bill could tell the gears in Mary's mind were turning. "Is there something else, Mary?"

"Yes, I suppose there is. Pastor Conrad said you had previous experience dealing with a girl in my situation." Bill looked even more puzzled. He was expecting the conversation to be about Hopewell. Not hearing a response from Bill, Mary restated with more detail. "Conrad said you were experienced with a girl who was possessed by a demon."

131

Bill now realized what she was asking. "Ah yes, I had an experience when I was a junior pastor, not unlike Conrad. I was called in to witness and work with two parish priests and a cardinal sent all the way from Rome."

Mary was excited and it came through in her voice. "Please, Bill, tell me all about it." Bill thought back in time for a moment, trying to recall the experience, a flood of memories filling his head.

"Well, Mary, it was about ten years ago. I was called upon to assist and keep a record of a suspected demonic possession. It was in Canada, out west in the prairies. I received a package from the Catholic Church, a large yellow envelope postmarked from the Vatican in Rome. I was so nervous to open the letter. I opened it and inside was a letter and a plane ticket."

"Wow, a plane ticket," Mary said. "I've never been on a plane."

Bill laughed. "I'd never been on a plane before either. I was excited and nervous at the same time. I went to Canada and met with the two parish priests. One I already knew as he was Pastor Flavio, who was my mentor pastor. It was at his suggestion that I be brought in to be the priest of record keeping."

Mary kept eye contact with Bill as he spoke; Bill continued to run his fingers through her long brown hair, stroking her ever so lightly.

"We met with Cardinal Carlos. He was from the Vatican and I was awestruck." Mary could see in Bill's eyes that he was traveling back in time as he told of his experience.

"Go on, Bill, tell me more. Did you get to talk to Cardinal Carlos very much?"

Bill laughed. "Actually no, he didn't speak English. The other parish priest's role was to be an interpreter for the cardinal. And also, he was the priest who requested the church send a cardinal. A few days into it, the cardinal became enraged with his interpreter. I think he actually fired him."

Mary's eyes flew wide open. "Why would he fire him?"

Bill chuckled as he continued. "As I understand it, the cardinal was exasperated because the case was not an actual demonic possession. The girl wasn't even Catholic, we came to find out."

"She wasn't Catholic?" Mary asked as Bill's mind continued traveling back.

"She was Christian, but not Catholic. She was of the Mormon faith. She was convinced that she was possessed by a demon. Her reasoning was that her flesh started to burn when she went out into the sun. As it turns out, she actually has a rare allergic reaction to the sun. It's actually called a sun allergy, something about light interruption, also known as sun poisoning."

"That's gotta suck, being allergic to the sun. Bill, why did the girl come to the Catholic Church if she is Mormon?"

"Well, Mary, she thought that she was possessed and the Mormon faith doesn't do exorcisms."

Mary sighed in understanding. "Ah, I get it now."

"The cardinal found out that she was not Catholic and he completely lost it on his interpreter. The next day he and the interpreter left. Pastor Flavio told me I had to stay for the entire week as my return ticket didn't leave until the end of the week. He told me to think of it as a paid vacation."

"What was her name? What happened to her?"

"Her name was Connie. Her skin was the palest white I've ever seen in my life, probably from never getting any exposure to the sun."

Mary realized that Bill had dodged the other half of her question. She thought that there must be a reason why. She prodded him further.

"Bill. Did you see Connie again after the other pastors and the cardinal left?" She saw Bill's facial expression change, as if he was deciding how much to tell her.

"Bill, you can be completely open and honest with me; I have certainly been open to and with you." She shot him an erotic smile.

"You're so right, Connie. You've been honest and open with me."

"Bill, you do know my name is not Connie, right?"

Bill paused, as if to rewind his mind a few seconds. He realized his faux pas, "Sorry about that, Mary." Bill emphasized her name. "My mind was so engrossed in the memory—"

Mary jokingly said, "Maybe you got our names mixed up because you slept with Connie as well." She chuckled.

Bill paused again; in his pause, Mary realized her joke wasn't too far from the truth. "Oh Bill, you dog, you slept with the Mormon girl." She laughed as she called him out.

Bill sensed it wouldn't bother Mary to know the truth so he confessed. "Yes, Mary, I slept with her every night until I returned home. It was the first time I had stepped outside my marriage; and honestly, I didn't feel guilty back then, either. Even though I was married, it just felt natural and I didn't even think twice about it. In the moment, it just felt right as if some force was drawing us together, not unlike you and I."

"So, Bill, what you're actually saying is that marriage is not the institution that society makes it out to be." Bill thought for a few moments. Mary explained further. "What I mean is that in my near-death experience, I learned that we are made in God's image and have God's desires and instincts. Procreation is natural. The desire to procreate is not attached to any marriage vows. Marriage is something that religion and society concocted to control the people."

Bill was taken aback by Mary's statement. "I've never thought of marriage as a byproduct of religion."

Mary further challenged Bill. "In fact, it seems to me that marriage, which goes hand in hand with monogamy, flies in the face of human nature, our desire and instinct to procreate."

"Perhaps you're right, Mary. It makes sense and would explain why I don't feel guilty about cheating on my wife."

"Now you're getting it, Bill. And don't expect me to fall in love with you. One thing I learned from my experience is that I don't want to live my life as others expect me to. I want to be a free spirit and squeeze every last drop of excitement out of life."

"So what you're saying is that you don't feel guilty about sleeping with a married man?" Bill smiled coyly.

"Yes, Bill, that's exactly what I'm saying. Tell me more about Connie."

"What do you want to know, Mary?"

"I wonder if Connie also had an afterlife experience like I had."

"That's an odd thing to think, Mary. Where's this coming from?"

She hesitated to answer and the look on her face alarmed Bill. "Mary what is it? Something is bothering you." She still paused and Bill could see her mind was processing. Bill remembered Mary's words from just a few minutes ago and he used them against her to loosen her tongue. With a cocky smile, he said, "Mary you can be completely open and honest with me; I've certainly been open to and with you." He grinned like a Cheshire cat.

"Checkmate! Ok, Bill, you win." She smiled, took a deep breath and explained. "Bill, I just think that there must be others out there in the world that have had the same or a similar experience as me, as us. We can't be the only ones."

"Mary, you're not alone." He emphasized some of his words. "I listened to you tell your story, and I didn't judge you. I accept that your experience was vivid and amazing and that it has changed your perspective on life. You're an amazing young woman and I will always be there for you whenever you need." Mary didn't answer; she only gave Bill a pleasant smile of appreciation.

"Thank you, Bill." She shivered.

"Oh, look at that." Bill pointed at the dwindling fire. "Looks like our fire has gone down. Maybe we should move this to the bedroom, crawl under the covers, snuggle up and share our body heat." He looked seductively at Mary, who again didn't say a word; she simply smiled and nodded.

Bill then stood Mary up, stood up himself and then reached down, picked her up, and cradled her in his arms as he carried her off to the bedroom.

CHAPTER 20 −

Enter Damien

AS BILL LAID on his back with Mary's arm draped over his chest, he found that he couldn't sleep as his thoughts drifted back to the past and his experience with Connie.

~

Connie married three months after her interlude with Bill. Alex was a good Mormon man, he knew that Connie was three months pregnant when they married. He loved her despite the fact that Connie had cheated on him throughout their two-year engagement.

Almost ten months after meeting Bill, Connie gave birth to a son. Alex raised Damien as his own child and never once was he bitter about raising another man's son.

Unfortunately for Alex, Connie was insatiable. She couldn't control her sexual urges and she continued to cheat on Alex throughout their marriage until, when Damien was five, Connie left for good, turning her back on her Mormon faith. Turning her back on her marriage, and her son.

Alex remarried two years later to another Mormon woman who had two girls of her own from a previous marriage. At seven years old, Damien had a new stepmother who was a staunch Mormon.

Rebecca insisted on living the good Mormon life. She ended her first marriage due to her husband being an alcoholic and causing many embarrassing incidents that caused her to become all the gossip in the Mormon Church.

Damien was nine-years-old now. He came home from school to find Rebecca waiting for him.

"Damien, we have to talk, son." Damien was a bit concerned with her tone as he came and sat in a chair at the kitchen table. Rebecca was sitting in an adjacent chair. From behind her back, she pulled out a Pepsi can, looked at the nine-year-old and began to lecture her stepson.

"Damien, I found this in your room." She pointed at the empty can of Pepsi.

Waiting for the boy to say something, Rebecca's face turned red with anger.

"Damien, the Word of Wisdom clearly teaches us that we shouldn't put things in our body that are unhealthy. Drugs, alcohol, coffee. Where'd you get this?" Damien stared at his stepmother, not quite understanding.

"A friend gave it to me, what's the big deal? It's just a Pepsi."

Rebecca nearly lost it when he said that. "Damien!" she yelled. "Pepsi has caffeine in it." She turned the can and pointed to the ingredients. "See that word there?"

Damien looked at where her finger pointed.

"It says caffeine and caffeine is not good for your body. Hence it's not acceptable for a good Mormon boy to drink coffee, Pepsi, Coke or Dr. Pepper, or anything with caffeine in it. Think of the example you are setting for Cindy and Carla."

"Mom, I'm sorry. I didn't know what caffeine was. Thank you for teaching me. I won't drink it again, I don't want to set a bad example for my sisters."

Rebecca looked into Damien's eyes. His shoulders were sunken, lips pouting outwards and he had tears starting to well up in his blue-gray eyes. In that moment, she felt almost bad for the lecture she had given.

"Damien, it's alright. You didn't know; how could you know? After all, you're only nine. It's okay, I forgive you, just don't do it again."

Hearing his stepmom's forgiveness, the boy perked up, smiled and asked, "I won't, Mom. May I be excused to go to my room? I have some homework to do before Scouts."

"Of course, Damien, you're excused, we'll leave at 5:30 for Scouts." Damien jumped up from the chair, moved over to Rebecca and wrapped his arms around her and gave her a hug.

CHAPTER 21 –

Mormon Boy Scouts

EARLIER THAT DAY, almost two thousand miles away in Alberta, Canada, Damien prepared for Boy Scouts at the Mormon Church every Friday night. He loved Scouts and conversing with his Mormon friends, but things were slowly changing for Damien. Tonight, was basketball night at Scouts. Two boys, Todd and Daniel, were selected to be team captains. A schoolyard pick ensued with Damien being picked last by Todd.

He felt badly about it as Todd was always his friend and whenever either of them was team captain, Todd would pick him first and he would pick Todd first. The game started and Damien ran hard to get to open spaces.

"Here I'm, open!" he called out to the teammate with the ball. He was ignored. The teammate then took a longer shot and missed.

"Oh come on, I was wide open!" Damien yelled at his teammate. At the half time, each of the teams huddled with their respective group.

Todd said. "Ok, guys, we're ahead, keep sticking and moving." The captain praised each player individually and when he came to Damien, he said, "Damien, you gotta stop yelling for the ball every time. No one wants to pass to a guy who the other team expects it to go to. Just be quiet and when you're open, we'll find you."

The whistle blew and the game was back on. For the rest of the game, Damien did as Todd said and didn't say a word, even when he was wide open with no one around for miles. No one on the team even looked his way, let alone passed him the ball.

After Scouts was done, Damien was leaving the gym and he heard Todd and Jacob talking about him.

"Yeah, Todd, he's just not getting it, no one wants to be his friend anymore. Why doesn't he get it? He must be dumb."

"I know, Jake. He used to be cool, but ever since I found out his mom isn't his real mom, he's been a loser."

"I didn't know Mrs. Solez wasn't his real mom." Jake said.

"Yeah, I found out last week my parents were fighting about it. My dad said, 'it's ok for Mormon's to get a divorce.' And my mom told him, 'It's not ok, no self-respecting Mormon would ever want to get a divorce.'"

"Wow Todd, so do you think your parents are getting a divorce?"

"I don't know; but they were talking about it because of Damien's mom."

"That sucks for you Todd."

"It's whatever Jake; hey you're still coming to my birthday party tomorrow, right? We're gonna ride motocross on the ranch. Don't tell Damien; I didn't invite him and I don't want him asking to come, if he finds out."

Damien overheard the conversation and he ducked into the washroom and looked into the mirror to see his bottom lip quivering as he fought back tears, composing himself before he went outside.

Rebecca was parked a few stalls away from the door. Damien went straight to the car. As Rebecca was talking with Heidi, Todd's mom, Todd stuck his head out the car window.

"See you later, Damien, good job out there."

Damien knew that Todd didn't mean to be nice; he was only putting on a show in front of his Mormon mother. Damien was already in the car by the time Rebecca got in and buckled up her seatbelt.

"Hey Damien, I saw you didn't say goodbye to Todd. I thought he was your best friend?"

Damien didn't answer.

"You know, Damien that was very rude of you to not say goodbye. Did something happen at Scouts?"

"No, I'm fine, Mom." Damien frowned. When they got home, Damien went straight to his room, walking right past his dad. He ignored what Alex had asked him.

"How was Scouts, son? Did you have—" He stopped talking when he saw Damien walk past him. He looked at Rebecca.

"Did something happen?"

"Alex, I don't know. Damien was incredibly rude to his friend Todd and when I asked him about it in the car, he wouldn't talk to me. If you ask me, I think the boy could learn some respect."

"That doesn't sound like Damien. He's usually so happy to go to Scouts and loves hanging with the boys."

Up in his room, Damien was having a hard time dealing with his feelings. He spotted the Cub Car he had made last year. Todd and he worked on their cars together for the annual Cub Car Races.

Every year the Scouts gave each boy a Cub Car package. The package consisted of a block of wood, four plastic wheels with holes in them and four shiny nails, long enough to act like single axles for each wheel.

The goal was for the boys to shape and build their own working Cub Car that would be raced down an elevated track. Each Scout Troop would determine the two boys they would send to the Scout City Championship.

Although the boys were supposed to do this all on their own, judging from the paint jobs and perfect curves on some of the Cub Cars, it was evident that there was help from an adult.

Last year, Damien and Todd built their cars together and painted them to be mirror opposites of each other. Damien's car was black in the back and came to a triangle point on the front hood area of his car, where the white would take over. Todd's was the exact opposite with white on the back and black on the front; both boys had silver lighting painted on the side. Damien's car was numbered sixty-six and Todd's ninety-nine.

He was so upset with Todd now. He couldn't believe that Todd didn't invite him to his birthday party and grew enraged at the thought. Looking over at the Cub Car proudly displayed on the center of his dresser, Damien went over, grabbed the car, placed it on the ground and started stomping on it, breaking the wheels off and scuffing the meticulous paint job.

Just then, Alex walked into Damien's room without knocking. He saw what his son was doing and yelled at him. "Damien, stop!"

Damien stopped and flopped on his bed, crying. His dad saw this and came and sat beside him.

"What's wrong, Damien? Why are you crying?" Damien didn't answer; he didn't want to talk about it.

"Your mother told me you were rude to Todd. Did something happen at Scouts?"

Damien still cried and didn't answer. His dad kept pushing.

"Stop crying like a baby and man up, Damien." Alex said, as he struggled to find the right words to comfort his nine-year-old. "What happened, Damien? Did you have a fight with your friend Todd? Tell me."

Damien could tell his dad wasn't going to leave it alone, so he turned over, sat up and yelled, "Todd is not my friend anymore, he's an asshole!"

Alex reacted on instinct and slapped Damien across the mouth. "Watch your language, young man. Even when you're angry, there's no reason to use profanity."

The two just stared at each other for what seemed like an eternity. Finally, Alex broke the silence.

"Damien, you can just stay in your room tonight. No supper for you, and you should think about how you're going to adjust your poor attitude."

Alex left his son with no food or water until the next day.

Damien thought a lot that night and he came to the conclusion that Mormons are all hypocrites. How can you pretend to be a good Mormon and treat someone as badly as Todd and others treated him? *'That's not what Jesus would do,'* he thought to himself. He was mad at Todd, his stepmom and his dad, but more than that he was disheartened with the Mormon Church for the first time in his life.

CHAPTER 22 –

The Great Debate

IN THE MORNING, Bill awoke again looking at the beautiful young woman lying beside him. He gingerly moved out from under her arm, allowing her to sleep in while he put his robe on, went to the kitchen and started making breakfast.

As he cooked bacon, eggs and toast, he thought about their conversation last night. How Mary brought up the theory of the impact of the church on the institution of marriage. His thoughts were interrupted when Mary walked in, rubbing her eyes with both hands.

"Good morning, Bill; you snuck out on me."

"I didn't sneak out, I thought you would like some—"

"It's ok, Bill, I just thought we could get in a quick morning session," she said alluringly.

"I— I—" Bill stammered as his mind swirled with thoughts of morning sex with her. He looked at the clock on the wall.

"It's only ten to seven, Conrad doesn't come in until nine, and we have time." Bill smiled wickedly. Mary stretched her arms over her head, pushing her perky breasts outwards. "Too late, Bill. Now that I can smell the bacon, sex will have to wait until you've fed me."

Bill pouted and frowned. "Well, then I guess I'll have to settle for a good morning kiss." He moved over to her and took her in his arms for a passionate morning kiss. Mary broke the kiss after a few seconds.

"Hmm, morning breath. Sorry, Bill, I haven't even brushed my teeth yet." She playfully pushed him away and skipped off to the bathroom.

Bill finished cooking breakfast just as Mary returned to the kitchen. As they sat and ate the meal, the conversation returned to the deep subject from the previous night.

"Mary. Last night you said something that I've been thinking about."

Mary politely waited until the food in her mouth was gone before responding. "What was that, Bill?"

"You said you think that marriage comes from the church."

Mary realized she had touched a nerve with the pastor. She thought for a long while before responding.

"I realize that my views on marriage and life in general might not sit well with the pastor in you, maybe this is a conversation better left alone."

Bill wouldn't let it go. "And why is that, Mary?"

"Why is what, Bill?"

"Why don't you want to have this conversation now?" Bill quizzed as he watched her facial expressions closely. Mary continued eating as he waited for her to get engaged in the conversation. Seeing Mary continue to eat with no apparent signs that she was going to talk anytime soon, Bill decided to push the envelope.

"Do you think that I won't listen to your views on the church and marriage, Mary?" She still didn't answer, just kept eating. "I think you'll find that I'm very interested in discussing your philosophy and debating the merits of it."

Mary finished eating; his last words resonated in her mind.

"Bill, you said 'debating.' That is exactly why I don't think it's a good conversation to have."

"Mary, debate is a good thing. We need to always be open to others' opinions and ideologies if we want to grow and develop."

Mary didn't answer.

"Mary, a while back I was at a religious conference. Not a Catholic one—it was an all-denominations conference. I met people from many different religions, different countries from all over the world. I had great conversations with everyone, including a long conversation with people from India and other parts of Asia who believe in reincarnation: that when we die, our souls, our essence is returned to the earth in another form; that we come back in another life as something else, a cat or a bird maybe."

"Ok, Bill, you win. You want to have a deep conversation, let's do this. Don't expect me to hold back; the gloves are off." She gave him a fun, combative smile.

"You said that marriage is an institution created by the church. Why do you think that?"

"Ok, Bill, when I had my experience, it felt as though I was trapped for years, giving me a lot of time to consider many of the things I have been taught so far in my life. I contemplated life on so many levels. Tell me this, Bill: what is the Bible?" Bill thought it was a rather obvious question.

"It's a book."

"No, Bill, you're wrong. It is not a book." Bill looked puzzled. "It's actually a collection of people's journals or diaries."

"I can agree to that; but all the journals together combine to form the Bible, which is a book in of itself."

"The Bible has been used over time by many religions. Even the laws we have stem from the Bible and are taken from the Ten Commandments."

"So far I cannot argue with your logic, Mary."

"Bill, picture this. Let's say I write a diary or a journal. I write about my life and my experiences, and let's say you write a journal. Could you imagine a post-apocalyptic world a hundred, five hundred, a thousand years from now? Now imagine that someone digs up a bunch of diaries and journals. They somehow figure out a way to decipher the language and then they put them together all in one book."

Bill looked intrigued.

"Now Bill. Imagine a religion being born from those journals and diaries. The Book of Mary." She chuckled. "Could you imagine? An entire society building laws, morals and ideas from reading my diaries?"

Bill sensed that Mary was going way off topic; he tried to bring her back to the crux of the conversation. "Mary, I think that is fascinating, especially your perspective and well-thought-out questions. But how does that relate to the church creating marriage to nefariously control people?"

"I'm glad you asked, Bill. Think about the Bible. It's only a collection of some ancient, uneducated people's journals. And yet the entire Christian religion—not just Catholicism, but all Christian-based religions—use a form of the Bible that they preach from. Tell me, Bill: when you prepare your next sermon for Sunday church services, where do you draw your information from?"

"Touché, Mary. The Bible." He smiled.

"Bill, let's play a game. No thinking allowed; I ask a question and you answer 'yes' or 'no.' Are you up for it?"

Bill was enjoying the conversation and wanted to hear it through to its conclusion. He nodded his head.

"Yes, Mary, I'll play."

"Alright then, let's do this. Question 1: God created the earth and all living things. Yes or no?"

"Yes, of course," Bill said and was quickly admonished by Mary.

"Bill, the game is yes or no only! Keep your comments to yourself." She coyly smiled at him.

"Ok, yes," Bill replied in a fun, snarky tone.

"Question 2: God created mankind in his image?"

"Yes."

"Question 3: God gave mankind free will?"

"Yes, correct." Mary gave Bill a stern look for not answering with a simple yes or no. Bill apologized with his eyes and she asked the next question.

"Question 4: God made Adam in his image?"

"Yes."

"Question 5: God then made Eve from Adam's rib?"

"Yes."

"Question 6: God presided over the marriage ceremony for Adam and Eve?"

"Uhm..." Bill hesitated. "There was no—"

Mary interrupted. "Exactly, Bill. Marriage was not mentioned in the beginning. It was an institution that was created later on by man, it was a way for wealthy families to increase their wealth by prearranging marriages for their offspring. Ok, Bill, a few more questions. The Bible is the word of God?"

Bill recovered and got back into the game.

"Yes."

"God himself wrote the Bible?"

"No."

"The Bible is the word of God?" Mary restated the question.

"You just asked that, Mary."

Mary stared directly into his eyes and sternly repeated, "The Bible is the word of God?" She emphasized the question.

Bill sat still with a stunned facial expression.

"Bill, the Bible is not the word of God! It's a series of ancient journals written by mere mortals, not by God himself but by men with limited knowledge of modern-day science. Hell, they thought the world was flat at that time."

Bill continued to remain silent.

Mary continued. "Some of the books were written over nineteen-hundred years ago. Organized Christian religion didn't exist before Jesus lived. Yet a mere forty years later, the writing of the first gospel of the New Testament was born, written by early Christians, who then organized religion based on the life of Jesus Christ. The concept of Judgment Day was skillfully designed to be the centerpiece of religion then and now: the idea that when we die, we are judged by God. The entire concept is written by early Christians who wanted to grow a concept, to have Christianity flourish and spread across the world."

Bill was speechless.

"The Bible, Bill, is not the word of God. You're living proof of that."

Mary recognized the expression on the man's face and knew she had offended him. "Before you get your underwear in a knot, Bill, think about it. You're married and yet you're here with me, and with others. You, Bill, are living proof that man is created in God's image with his desires and instincts. God is a creator with a will to create. In our case, we have a strong desire to procreate."

"Mary, I told you that I enjoyed discussion and debate, even on deep subjects like this one. It's clear to me that you had an experience in which you have grown and matured. I can't say I agree or disagree with what you said, but I can tell you I'm as always, amazed by you." He emphasized the compliment and smiled widely at her.

Mary returned the smile.

"I think you should go shower and change while I clean up things in here," Bill said.

"Good idea, Bill." Mary sprang from her chair, hugged and kissed him, then went on her way to the shower with a feeling that she might just have won the great debate.

CHAPTER 23 –

Leaving Champion

BY 9AM, BOTH Bill and Mary had showered and were in the sitting room enjoying morning coffee when Conrad came in.

"Good morning Pastor Bill, Mary," Conrad greeted the pair as he sat on the sofa beside Bill. "I just wanted to let you know that I think we should have James and Sally come to the church this morning."

Bill looked at Conrad. "I thought the plan was to meet for lunch, Conrad." Mary watched as the two men conversed.

"The plan needs to change, Pastor Bill. You're needed back in Riley as soon as possible."

Bill saw the look of concern on Conrad's face. "What's happened?"

Conrad shook his head in a manner that suggested something terrible. "Pastor Bill, there was an accident in Riley with the school bus. All I know is that a young woman has died and others were seriously injured."

"Well, that does certainly change my plans." Bill grimaced.

"Pastor Bill. Perhaps if I called Sally and James, they could meet us at the church right away. That would give you time to pack your things." Conrad had thought it through; he wanted Pastor Bill to give a final report on Mary to her parents before he left.

Bill paused, lost in thought.

Mary interjected. "Bill, I think that Conrad has a good idea; you'll need some time to pack up. I'll call my parents and ask them to come pick me up right away." Bill was still grappling with the situation.

"Alright—" He stopped. "Yes, that's a good plan." Mary could see Bill was stuck somewhere.

"Pastor Bill. I think it would be good for you to know that I have decided not to take you up on the offer to go to Hopewell. You need to go as fast as you can and don't have time to wait for me."

Bill realized that Mary was right. He was struggling between the need to leave as soon as possible and his desire to talk Mary's parents and her into letting him take her with him to Hopewell.

"Yes, yes, of course." Bill stood up and went to his room to pack his things. By the time Bill had his BMW all packed, Sally and James had driven up and parked.

They all went inside the church to the sitting room.

Conrad opened the dialogue. "James and Sally. There's been an accident in Riley and Pastor Bill is needed back home."

"Oh dear," Sally said. "I hope it's nothing serious."

Conrad responded to Sally's statement. "Well yes, it is serious, Sally. There was an accident and someone has died. Pastor Bill wanted to wait long enough to give you both a summary on Mary before he leaves."

"Thank you once again, Pastor Bill," James said.

"Yes, we can't even begin to tell you how much of a godsend you've been to our family." Sally smiled appreciatively.

Conrad sped the conversation up greatly, cutting through all the small talk and grateful thanks. "We talked with Mary and I believe she has decided to stay in Champion and decline the offer to go to Hopewell."

James and Sally listened closely.

Mary spoke up. "Yeah, I think that I can handle issues here in Champion. I don't need to run and hide."

Sally and James looked at Pastor Bill, who was clearly distraught. James said, "Pastor Bill. I know you have to go. But can you tell us, will the Hopewell offer still be available at a later time if Mary changes her mind?"

Bill snapped to attention and joined the conversation. "Absolutely, James. Honestly, I think that the hardest adjustment will be for you and Sally. Mary has more than convinced me that she has a good grasp on her experience and she's in full control."

The parents looked over at Mary, who was beaming with pride at hearing Bill's words.

"I think it's time for Pastor Bill to go now." Conrad stood up, causing everyone else to follow suit.

"Thank you so much, Pastor Bill," Conrad said as he shook his hand. James and Sally lined up behind Conrad. Once he moved out of the way, Sally and James in turn gave Pastor Bill heartfelt hugs as they thanked him.

Bill turned to see Mary. She quickly closed the distance, reached her arms up and gave Bill a long hug. She stood on her tiptoes so she could whisper in his ear, "We'll meet again, Bill." She then blew a kiss into his ear. As she stepped back, only Bill could see the sly, sexy grin on Mary's face.

The four of them all watched as Bill got in his car and drove away while they all waved goodbye.

CHAPTER 24 –

Back in Riley

BILL MADE SHORT work of the one-hour drive. Arriving back in Riley, he got home rushed in the house.

"Stephanie!" he yelled out. He stopped calling out as Stephanie came rushing down the stairs of the two-story house.

"Bill, thank God you're home!" She called out with relief in her voice. Bill rushed to meet her at the bottom of the stairs; they embraced in a hug and Stephanie began to cry.

Bill wrapped his arms around her as he walked in step with her, leading her to the sofa in the front room. Sitting with her close to him, he said, "Steph, I heard there was an accident."

"It was horrible, Bill, the school bus was crashed into by Charley Rodgers' gravel truck." Bill wiped a tear from his wife's face as she continued filling him in. "Melanie Maples-Radisson, the school bus driver, died instantly." Stephanie broke down crying and couldn't continue. Bill rubbed her shoulders as he let her weep.

"Riley has suffered a major tragedy to lose Melanie. I presided over her marriage ceremony not too long ago." Bill sighed.

"Melanie wasn't the only one, your niece Lucinda—"

"No! Not Lucinda, she died too?"

"No, no, Bill, Lucinda didn't die. She's just in the hospital. I hear she has a head injury."

Bill inhaled deeply. "Thank God for small miracles. I'll go over to the hospital to see Lucinda."

"Bill, there's more." Stephanie placed her hand on Bill's knee. "Your brother John is in jail." Tears again started to form in her eyes.

"What? John's in jail? What the heck for?" Bill asked in a slightly angry tone.

"He beat up Charley Rodgers."

"Why would he do that?" Bill asked and then answered his own question. "Of course—Charley was driving the gravel truck." He shook his head in anguish. "I can see John doing that, he loves his family so much. Is there anything else I should know, Stephanie?"

Ever the dutiful pastor's wife, Stephanie gave Bill clear instruction. "No, Bill. You need to go to the hospital and take as much time as you need to tend to your flock. The people of Riley look to you for strength and guidance. Go now, husband."

Bill stood up, kissed her on the forehead and left.

CHAPTER 25 –

The Day After

IT WAS 10:30AM by the time Bill arrived at the hospital. He went in through emergency and approached the counter where the charge nurse was sitting.

"Hello, Bonnie. I hear it's been a busy few days here at the hospital." The nurse was visibly happy to see Pastor Bill.

"Let me tell you, Pastor Bill, it's been a roller coaster. Good news is that Charley Rodgers woke up early this morning."

Bill pressed the nurse for as much information as he could get. "And how is my niece Lucinda?"

The nurse's tone became even more compassionate than ever. "That little girl has had a few rough weeks. Broken arm and now she still hasn't woken up from her operation yesterday." She lowered her voice and placed her hand by her mouth as if to direct the words only to Bill.

"Between you and me, Pastor Bill, I think Lucinda's in a coma." Bonnie read Bill's facial expression. "Oh sorry, Pastor Bill. I didn't mean it to sound like gossip. My mouth sometimes moves faster than my brain. Please forgive me."

Bill smiled, letting the nurse off the hook. "Don't worry about it, Bonnie, I know your heart is pure. May I see Lucinda?" Bill asked and could see Bonnie become nervous as she answered.

"You know, Pastor Bill, if it were up to me, I would; but Dr. Watkins has given orders that there are to be no visitors whatsoever for Lucinda or Charley without his authorization."

"Alright, Bonnie. I understand. Thank you for everything; keep up the great work." He gave Bonnie a thumbs up as he left the desk and exited the hospital.

～

Dr. Watkins was checking in on Charley Rodgers, who was now awake.

"Charley, how are you feeling this morning?"

"I gotta tell ya, it hurts all over, Doc."

"Oh, I bet it does. You have multiple lacerations to your face and forehead and your orbital socket is badly bruised, but the good news is, it's not broken. You're one tough, lucky guy." The doctor tried to be upbeat and positive.

"Hey Doc. Do you know what happened to me?" Charley asked.

"You don't remember, Charley?"

The man lay in the bed, trying to recall what happened that landed him in hospital.

"Maybe later today, when you're feeling better, Charley, we can talk about how you got here. For now, I need you to rest."

"Ok, Doc."

"Oh, and don't pick at that eye patch, leave it alone. Don't even touch it, Charley."

"Ok, Doc, I won't."

～

Sheriff Brown arrived at the hospital.

"Good morning, Bonnie, I'm here to see—"

Bonnie politely interrupted. "Yes, Sheriff Brown. Dr. Watkins is expecting you. Let me show you to his office."

The nurse led the sheriff inside and down the hall to Dr. Watkins' office. She opened the door and ushered the sheriff inside.

"I'll let Dr. Watkins know you're here, sheriff."

"Thank you, Bonnie." She left, closing the door behind her.

~

Dr. Watkins stopped in to check on Lucinda before heading to the front desk to see Bonnie. He walked into Lucinda's room and spoke with Nurse Laura, who was the one and only night shift nurse.

"Good morning, Nurse Laura. How's our girl doing? Has she woken up yet?"

Laura frowned as she answered. "Good morning, Dr. Watkins. There's been no change. She didn't wake up."

"That's a shame. Let's hope she wakes up today."

"I'll be praying for her, Dr. Watkins."

The doctor left the room and went to front reception.

"Bonnie. Have the lab results on Charley Rodgers come in?"

Bonnie was happy to report. "Yes, about fifteen minutes ago, Dr. Watkins." She handed him the results. "Oh, and Sheriff Brown is in your office."

Dr. Watkins smiled warmly at her. "Excellent work, Bonnie," he commended the nurse as he walked away, heading towards his office.

He opened the door to his office and stepped inside.

"Good morning, Sheriff Brown. I have the results you wanted to discuss right here," he said as he shook the envelope in the air.

Sheriff Brown stood up and shook the doctor's hand. "Good to hear. Let's get right down to it."

Dr. Watkins took a seat at the desk, opened the envelope and looked at Sheriff Brown. "As expected, Charley's blood alcohol was 230 mg per 100 ml. Or in other words, 0.23, which is well over the legal limit, as you know."

The sheriff was shaking his head at the news. "That's the results I was expecting; not what I wanted to hear, but it's what I expected." The sheriff went on to say, "Dr. Watkins, I need you to keep this information confidential. If it gets out to the public, I fear the town would form a lynch mob."

"I agree, Dave. Although that creates a problem in that in order for me to treat Charley, I have to be able to answer his questions. This morning he asked me what happened to him, and as per your request I couldn't give Charley any answers or ask any questions."

"Dr. Watkins. I didn't want him to talk about the collision because until we got the results of the blood alcohol content, we didn't know if we would be charging him. Now that we know, we're charging him, I can read him his Miranda rights. Is he awake and alert right now?"

"Yes, Sheriff Brown. I can take you to him if you like. But I also think we may want to consider asking him if he would like to transfer to another hospital in the big city. For his own protection, you know."

"I think that would be a wise choice if we could make it happen. But what about his daughter, Norma-Ann?" Sheriff Brown threw a monkey wrench into the mix.

"For now, Dave, I have to be able to talk to Charley about his treatment options, and he needs to understand the extent of his injuries. We can worry about Norma-Ann later."

"Once I have Mirandized him, it's up to Charley if he tells you anything. He can talk about his treatment, knowing that even though doctor-patient privilege applies, he should be careful what he says."

"Ok, Sheriff, I understand. Let's go see Charley."

Bill didn't see Margaret at the hospital, so he thought he would go on over to her house and see if she was there.

He walked in the door; he could hear the radio playing in the kitchen but he didn't hear any voices. He went to the kitchen to find Margaret. When she saw him, she practically jumped into his arms.

"Oh, Bill, you're back. So much has happened; I'm so glad to see you." She was holding him tight as she fought back the urge to cry.

"I heard all about the accident. Maggie, how are you doing?" He placed his hands on her arms, moving her back far enough that he could see her face.

"Oh, Bill, it's terrible. John's sitting in jail. Lucinda hasn't woken up and they won't let me see her—it's all a big giant mess. The only comfort I can find is having you here with me, Bill." Margaret then started kissing his neck, letting her hands roam over his body, fumbling to open his pants as she pressed her body to his.

Bill was pleasantly surprised that Margaret was acting so forward with him, especially while she was facing a pretty major family crisis, but he allowed it to happen. In reality, Bill couldn't say no to Maggie's affections—not now, not ever.

After a quick tryst with Margaret, Bill offered to help. "Maggie, I've been to the hospital. They wouldn't let me see Lucinda either. Doctor's orders or something like that." Margaret looked at Bill appreciatively as the two of them were getting dressed. "I can go over to the station and talk with Sheriff Brown and see about getting John out of jail, if you like."

Margaret felt a lot less tense now that Bill was there. "Yes, please, Bill, I'd like that very much."

"Ok, Maggie. I'm on my way." Bill kissed her cheek and left.

～

Dr. Watkins entered first into Charley's room while the sheriff waited outside to be called in by the doctor.

"Charley, are you feeling any better now?"

"Yes, Doc, I feel better. Can you tell me what happened now?"

The doctor was dotting his 'I's and crossing his 'T's as he chose his words wisely so that Charley wouldn't become scared or overexcited.

"Charley, I can certainly tell you how you came to be in hospital, but first I need you to talk with Sheriff Brown. Do you feel up to talking to the sheriff?"

"Yes, for sure, I would like to have a chat with the sheriff."

Dr. Watkins walked to the door and motioned the sheriff inside the room. With the sheriff standing at Charley's bedside, Dr. Watkins positioned himself near the foot of the bed.

"Sheriff Brown." Charley smiled. "Did you find my daughter Norma-Ann?"

Both Dr. Watkins and Sheriff Brown were taken aback by the question.

"Charley, I didn't even know she was missing. Did you file a report at the police station?" Sheriff Brown became concerned.

"No Sheriff Brown I haven't gotten around to making a report." Charlie said with guilt written all over his face.

The sheriff still had a job to do; Charley's missing daughter was important but he needed to read Charley his rights.

"Charley. As soon as I'm done here I'll go to the station and file a report on Norma-Ann; we'll then start a search for her. Charley, unfortunately I'm here on official business. I need to read you your rights."

"What?" Charley was surprised. "Why?"

The sheriff interrupted him. "Charley Rodgers, I'm charging you with vehicular manslaughter in the death of Melanie Maples-Radisson.

"You have the right to remain silent.

"Anything you say can and will be used against you in a court of law.

"You have the right to talk with a lawyer and have a lawyer present with you while you are being questioned.

"If you cannot afford to hire a lawyer, one will be appointed to represent you if you wish.

"You can decide at any time to exercise these rights and not answer any questions or make any statements.

"Do you understand each of these rights I have explained to you? Having these rights in mind, do you wish to talk to us now?"

Charley was in shock. He clearly understood that he was being charged with manslaughter, but he couldn't remember what had happened and he wanted to find out.

"Yes, I understand. Now tell me what happened. Please!" Charley begged.

Dr. Watkins looked at the sheriff as if to ask for permission to answer Charley's question. Sheriff Brown nodded.

"Charley, yesterday morning you were driving your gravel truck when you ran the stop sign and collided with the school bus. The driver was killed on impact." Charley started weeping as Dr. Watkins continued to fill in the blanks for him. "There were other minor injuries and one other critical injury. Lucinda Hall is hospitalized and is in a coma."

Charley completely broke down crying and blubbering. "So, you're saying I killed that bus driver and Lucinda Hall is in a coma." Charley knew John fairly well. "John has always been kind to me, he gave me a ride home from the pub one or two times when I was unable to drive myself. I honestly don't remember anything."

"Charley, remember you still have the right to remain silent."

"Sheriff Brown, I don't remember anything. It's not that I'm saying that as an excuse, I really don't remember."

"Do you remember how you came about your injuries, Charley?" the Sheriff had to ask.

"I think it was from the accident. Right?" Charley was guessing now, trying to fill in the gaps.

"No, Charley. My deputy walked you into the hospital and wasn't aware that John Hall was in the waiting area. John attacked you and beat you unconscious."

"I just can't believe that I killed someone." Charley sobbed.

"Charley, I need to know if you want to press charges against John Hall."

Charley didn't even think for a second. "No way, Sheriff. I can understand why John did what he did."

Dr. Watkins cringed. "Charley you have a long road to recovery; you're going to be in a lot of pain for a long time. Are you certain you don't want to press charges?"

Sheriff Brown followed up once more. "Charley, are you absolutely certain you do not wish to file charges against John Hall for his assault and battery on you?"

"Yes, I'm absolutely, one hundred percent positive, Sheriff, I do not wish to file charges or press charges or anything. This is all my fault."

"And will you sign a form releasing me from filing charges against John Hall?"

"Yes, I will, of course. Just give me the papers, Sheriff."

"Well, Charley, despite your issues with alcohol, you're a good man." Sheriff Brown smiled. "Now before I head back to the station can you give me some details for the missing person's report I'm going to file on Norma-Ann?"

"Sure, Sheriff Brown, anything you need." Charlie sounded relieved.

"When did she go missing?"

"I think it was seven days ago; but I can't be sure of that." Charlie frowned.

"Ok well Charlie, I understand you've been through a lot. I'll file the report and come back later if I have any questions. Ok?"

"Alright Sheriff Brown, thanks again. You're a good man."

The sheriff and doctor left the room.

Having been to the police station and found out the sheriff was at the hospital, Bill arrived at the hospital just as Dr. Watkins was walking Sheriff Brown out the door into the waiting area.

Dr. Watkins saw Bill approach the sheriff. As he saw Bill and Sheriff Brown talking, he stayed within earshot so he could eavesdrop on the conversation.

"Sheriff Brown, I'm glad I found you, we need to talk." The sheriff was still concerned about Charley's missing daughter and he wanted to get back to the station so he tried to brush the pastor off.

"Pastor Bill. I really have to get back to the station and file a missing person's report."

It was only natural for Bill to ask, "Who's missing?"

The sheriff didn't really have time to talk and his patience was growing thin, but he respected the priest and answered his question. "Charley Rodgers' daughter, Norma-Ann, is missing."

Bill let out a sigh of relief. "Oh, thank God."

Dr. Watkins overheard Pastor Bill's words. "What's your problem, Bill? The sheriff just told you that Norma-Ann is missing; it seems a little insensitive for you to be thankful that a young girl is missing."

"She's not missing, Dr. Watkins." Bill turned to Sheriff Brown. "Can we talk somewhere privately?"

"Yes, come in and use my office for privacy." Dr. Watkins led the two men to his office. Once inside, the sheriff got right to business.

"Ok, Pastor Bill. Do you know where Norma-Ann is?"

"Yes, of course I do. But before I tell you, I need some assurances of confidentiality. Do you agree to keep what I say in this room between the three of us only? It must be confidential even from her own father. She wants to remain safe and away from him."

"So, you don't want Charlie to know where his daughter is?" Dr. Watkins challenged.

"Not me Dr. Watkins. Norma-Ann is petrified of the man, she is the one who doesn't want her father to know where she is."

"Pastor Bill, I can't even—" Dr. Watkins was so frustrated that he couldn't even finish his sentence.

The sheriff stepped in. "Ok gentlemen, let's take a step back. Pastor Bill you've piqued my curiosity, why don't you start at the beginning?"

"Alright then," Bill said. "Ten days ago, Norma-Ann came to see me. She told me she was in fear for her safety living at home with her alcoholic dad."

Dr. Watkins rudely interrupted. "Bill, while I don't like to see anyone become an alcoholic, the man lost his wife to cancer. I can certainly see why he would crawl into the bottom of a bottle, there's no need to—"

Bill returned the favor and interrupted the doctor right back. "Hey, don't shoot the messenger. I'm only stating what Norma-Ann said. She told me she's afraid of her alcoholic dad, those are her words, not mine."

"Despite his drinking problems, Charley raised that girl all by himself for the past ten years. I doubt she would suddenly become afraid of him now."

"Well, Dr. Watkins, that's what she told me. She woke up one morning to find her dad passed out on the kitchen floor, which wasn't a big issue until she smelled gas in the kitchen. He had turned the stove on but passed out before lighting it, and that scared her."

"So, who planted the seed in Norma-Ann?" Dr. Watkins asked.

The question startled Bill. "I have no idea who got her pregnant." Bill's left eye twitched.

"Oh, now I see what's happening here. A seventeen-year-old girl gets pregnant and the righteous Pastor Bill steps in to help, and the next thing we know Norma-Ann is on her way to Hopewell with the shame of her born out of wedlock pregnancy well hidden from public view."

Sheriff Brown saw the confrontation escalating. "Gentlemen, let's dial it back a notch."

"Nothing to dial back, Sheriff. It's clear that Pastor Bill has stepped in and conned Norma-Ann—"

Bill rudely interrupted Dr. Watkins. "Yes! I counseled Norma-Ann, but I did not coerce or manipulate her. She truly feels like she is living in fear and she has even started proceedings to become emancipated from her father. I took her to Joseph Bain and he discussed her options with her. The next day she made an appearance in front of Judge Ivy in which he granted me temporary guardianship over the girl, in order for her to have an adult responsible for her and to sign off to allow her to enter Hopewell Asylum. I then drove her to Hopewell and checked her in under the name Jane Smith so as to protect her privacy and keep her father from finding her. She's been there ever since and that is where she'll remain."

"Well, that's a relief." Sheriff Brown was happy. "At least I don't have a missing girl on my hands."

"Ok, so Pastor Bill, you're telling us that you're Norma-Ann's legal guardian? How convenient for you." Dr. Watkins glared.

"That's exactly what I'm telling you. I have a signed court order stating that I'm Norma-Ann's temporary legal guardian and that Norma-Ann voluntarily admitted herself into Hopewell. And furthermore, I have a signed order from Judge Ivy, along with the permission and blessing of the Crown Prosecutor Joseph Bain, that Norma-Ann be admitted under an assumed name in order to protect her identity and keep her father from finding her."

Dr. Watkins thought of a different angle. "So even with all these signed documents you say you have, how's it fair to Charley Rodgers to be left in the dark to wonder if his only daughter has run away or is even alive or dead?"

"Dr. Watkins, we covered that base as well. Norma-Ann wrote a letter to her father stating that she has run away and started proceedings to become emancipated. Charley knows this from the letter Norma-Ann left him."

"Well, you certainly covered all your bases." Dr. Watkins sneered.

"Bradley, in my line of work, people come to me with their deepest secrets and problems; I try to help when I can. That's all. And now that the mystery of Norma-Ann is solved, I trust you gentlemen will keep your promise of confidentiality." Bill then turned to the sheriff. "I would like to talk with you about my brother John. You have him locked up in jail."

Sheriff Brown answered in a matter-of-fact tone. "Pastor Bill. Charley Rodgers has declined to file or press charges. As such, I was on my way back to the station to do the paperwork for Charley to sign in order for me to release John."

Bill clapped his hands together in triumph. "That's great! When can I come and pick up my brother?"

"It's just past noon now; how about you come at two o'clock?" said the sheriff before standing up. "I must be going back to the station; it seems I have some paperwork to complete that requires immediate attention." The sheriff left the room, leaving the doctor and Pastor Bill alone.

"Dr. Watkins." Bill started a new conversation. "I'd like to see my niece and have been told that no one is allowed to see her without your permission."

Dr. Watkins could see where this was going and wanted to avoid further argument, "Yes, for now I have her under observation. Lucinda is in a coma and I have a few more tests to run before I'll have more answers for the family. How about we say 4pm? You can bring the family to see Lucinda, I should be able to have all the tests done by then."

Bill smiled at the doctor. "It's a date. We'll see you at 4pm, Dr. Watkins." He left the office and went to tell Margaret the news.

CHAPTER 26 –

Free John Hall

BILL DROVE OVER to Margaret's house. He walked in and told her the good news.

"Margaret, I have great news!" he hollered as he entered the house. Margaret came running out of the kitchen, right into Bill's arms.

"Tell me, Bill, I'm so excited." Bill knew he had a few hours before he could go pick up John, and he used his time for his own personal gratification.

"But first before I tell you the news Maggie. How about you..." Bill winked at her as he undid the fly to his pants. Margaret knew exactly what he wanted and she complied.

~

Sheriff Brown arrived back at the station and went to talk with John.

"Hey John, I have good news." John hopped up from the cot and stood to attention. "I was at the hospital and Charley Rodgers has declined to press charges."

"Do you have news of my daughter? Is she alright?"

"Did you hear me say that Charley Rodgers has decided not to press charges against you, John?"

"Yes, I heard that. What I want to hear is how my daughter is doing." John stared at Sheriff Brown, waiting for a reply.

"As I understand it, John, Lucinda's operation was a success and she's in recovery. I just have some paperwork to do up and then I'm going back to the hospital to have Charley sign the document declining to file charges against you. Your brother Bill will be by in a few hours to pick you up."

"Thank you, Sheriff Brown." John smiled.

~

Margaret got up from her knees and sat on the sofa beside Bill.

"Ok, Bill, what's your news?" she said while wiping saliva from her lips.

"I got the sheriff to drop the charges against John. He just has to fill out some paperwork and we can go pick John up. John is going to be free and clear to come home."

Margaret shrieked with joy as she hugged Bill.

"There's more Maggie." Bill smiled. "I also talked to Dr. Watkins and we can go and see Lucinda at 4:00pm."

"That's great Bill. John will be elated."

~

Sheriff Brown stood at Charley's bedside as he asked one last time.

"Charley, are you sure you want to decline to file charges against John Hall?"

"Just give me the papers, Sheriff." The sheriff handed Charley the papers and a pen. He watched as Charley signed.

"Charley, I have asked Dr. Watkins to join us. We have something important to speak with you about."

"Have you found Norma-Ann? Is she alright?"

"Charley, you remember that you still have the right to remain silent, and to have a lawyer present while I talk with you?"

"Dave, I have known you all my life. You're not going to try and railroad me. Ask whatever you want. I don't remember much, but I'll try."

"Oh no, I don't want to talk about the details of the collision. I want to talk about your health and well-being—about your safety, Charley."

"What about my safety?" Just then, Dr. Watkins joined the men in Charley's room.

The sheriff went on to explain the big picture to Charley. "Charley, you know Riley is a small town of God-fearing people. There is strong sentiment that an eye for and eye applies."

Charley looked at the sheriff and doctor as he listened closely.

"You've been charged with vehicular manslaughter; there'll be a trial and quite frankly, Charley, I don't feel you'll get a fair trial in Riley."

Charley was absorbing everything. "Sheriff Brown, it doesn't matter. I killed that girl. I should go to jail." Dave knew his message wasn't coming through strong enough.

"Charley, the Crown would probably seek the death penalty in your case. The town's people would almost most certainly demand it, remember? An eye for an eye."

Dr. Watkins supported the sheriff's position. "The sheriff is right, Charley. Once news gets out, the town will form a good old-fashioned Christian lynch mob. You need to listen to the sheriff."

"Charley, I've already spoken with law enforcement in Oklahoma City. We can transfer you there tonight."

"I would be going to jail in Oklahoma City?" Charley sounded scared. Dr. Watkins again helped to support the idea.

"Charley, you wouldn't go to jail right away. But yes, you would eventually be in prison in Oklahoma City for the duration of your trial. You would be spending six to eight weeks in hospital recovering. Your injuries will take time to heal."

"I've talked with law enforcement in Oklahoma and they agree that you would be incarcerated in Oklahoma General Hospital during your recovery." Sheriff Brown wanted Charley to agree, knowing full well that the decision had already been made.

"But Sheriff Dave, I would be away from Norma-Ann." Charley's eyes started to well up.

"Charley, on that subject, Norma-Ann is safe. She's a ward of the state now and will remain so while you are on trial."

"What? Why is she a ward of the state, sheriff? Please, no!"

Sheriff Brown was trying not to agitate Charley.

"Charley, please stay calm," Dr. Watkins implored him. "I don't want your blood pressure to become unstable. Just take a deep breath and relax."

Sheriff Brown calmly explained, "Charley, when a single parent such as you is charged in a loss of life case like this, its standard procedure for the state to assign someone other than the parent as a guardian. Norma-Ann has been found and now has a legal guardian assigned to her. She's fine and doing well and she'll be financially cared for by the state for now. You really have nothing to worry about, Charley. Norma-Ann is in good hands."

Charley nodded. "When can I see her?"

"Charley, I'm going to tell you something that I shouldn't. This could get me in a lot of trouble. Please keep this a secret for me. Can you do that?"

"Of course, Sheriff Brown. Mum's the word." Charley held his hand to his lips as if to express zipping his lips shut.

"Ok, Charley here it is. Norma-Ann has been moved out of Riley into a safe place for her own safety. We have fears that the town might lash out at her over the death of Melanie; the town will want their pound of flesh."

"I understand, Sheriff. Why are you being so good to me? I don't deserve it." His eyes watered as he spoke.

"Charley, you're a citizen of Riley. It's my duty to protect the people of Riley, and honestly, you're a good man who has had a tough life. I want to help you. So, will you agree to go to Oklahoma City? You can get a fair trial there and a good lawyer to defend you."

"Yes, Sheriff Brown, I agree."

"Alright then, I'll leave you to rest, Charley. See you later."

The two men left the room. Out in the hall, Dr. Watkins called out Sheriff Brown on his stretching of the truth.

"Dave, you told him that Norma-Ann was a ward of the state. That's not true."

"Oh, but Dr. Watkins, it is true. A judge signed a piece of paper giving guardianship to Pastor Bill. The judge represents the people and the state." He winked slyly.

"I understand why you did that, Dave. You're a good man, like Charlie said."

"Thank you, Brad. I try to keep people as settled as possible. It makes my job a lot harder when people become agitated."

As they walked down the hall, Sheriff Brown realized that he should give the doctor a heads up.

"Just so you know, Brad, earlier at the station John Hall asked me how his daughter was."

"And what did you tell him?"

Dave winked at the doctor. "I told him that his daughter's operation was a success. Oh, and I also told him Lucinda was in recovery. You might want to prepare yourself because John will be coming to see his daughter and may be shocked to find she's in a coma."

"Gee, thanks, Dave," Dr. Watkins growled sarcastically.

"You're welcome, Dr. Watkins. His brother Pastor Bill is coming soon to pick him up. I'll talk to Bill before I release John; I'll remind Bill to keep John's temper in check."

~

At the station, Bill and Margaret walked in. They sat waiting for Sheriff Brown to return to the station.

Ten minutes later, Sheriff Brown walked in, saw Bill and Margaret and took the opportunity to talk with them before releasing John.

"Hello, Margaret and Bill. I'll go back and get John shortly, I just want to say this before I do. It was John's temper that landed him in this bad situation. You both need to help him to control that temper."

They both looked at the sheriff, nodding in agreement.

"Also, when you go to the hospital, you might want to prepare John before you get there. I just came from the hospital and Lucinda is still in a coma, again I remind you. Keep John's anger in check."

"Thank you, Dave," Margaret said.

"If you want to thank me, please make sure I don't have to put John back in this cell again." Sheriff Brown stared seriously at them both.

~

Once John was outside the station, he stretched his arms high and immediately wanted to go to the hospital.

"Thank you for coming and collecting me, Bill. Let's head over to the hospital, I want to see my daughter." Margaret took a hold of John's arm as she stood beside him in the parking lot.

"John, we won't be allowed in to see Lucinda for about an hour," said Bill. "Dr. Watkins has restricted visitors. I convinced him to let us come and see Lucinda and he has agreed to allow the three of us in to see her at 4pm."

"Bill, is there something you're not telling me? What's the issue? Why can't I see Lucinda now?"

Bill looked at his brother and placed a hand on each of his shoulders as he stood directly in front of John.

"John, Lucinda is still in recovery, which means she is still very delicate, and as far as I know she's still unconscious, so the doctor doesn't want too much commotion around her." Bill was smooth yet direct with John; he squeezed his shoulders as he broke the news to him.

Margaret whispered in John's ear. "John, there's nothing to worry about. God loves our daughter; she'll be fine." Margaret also worked to prepare John and keep him calm.

"Ok I get it, both of you. Lucinda is still unconscious. Can we go and see her now? Even if we have to wait, I need to see my little angel."

They all got in the car and went to the hospital. Upon arrival, Bonnie greeted the pastor. Margaret and John stood behind Bill as he talked with Bonnie.

"Hello, Bonnie, can you do me a big favor and go get Dr. Watkins?" Bonnie agreed and stood up with a smile. She went through the door to the back and found Dr. Watkins.

Dr. Watkins wasn't looking forward to this meeting, but he knew that he couldn't keep the Halls away from Lucinda forever and now was as good a time as any to get it over with.

He walked out to the reception area. "Pastor Bill, John, Margaret. You're early; but fortunately for you I've finished all the tests on Lucinda. Come follow me, please."

As soon as they arrived at Lucinda's room, John went to Lucinda's side while Margaret stood back a few feet with Bill behind her. Nurse Laura, who was in the room with Lucinda, stood up.

"Nurse Laura. How's Lucinda doing?" Dr. Watkins put the young nurse on the spot.

John looked at his daughter's face; her eyes were closed and she looked so peaceful. He could see her chest gently moving up and down in a peaceful rhythm as he tuned into the conversation going on behind him.

"Dr. Watkins, her vitals are all good. I can see her resting comfortably with lots of REM." The nurse smiled at Margaret to give the mother hope. "I think that she's just having an amazing dream, so amazing that she doesn't want to wake up just yet."

"Thank you, Nurse Laura, you can go now." The young nurse left the room.

Dr. Watkins addressed Margaret directly. "That Nurse Laura has really taken an interest in your daughter. She sits with her all the time, holding her hand and reading the Bible to her."

Bill spoke up. "That's very good to hear, Dr. Watkins, you have good staff here at the hospital."

As John listened to the conversation, looking down at his daughter, tears were rolling down his cheeks. He dared not turn around for fear of showing that he was crying.

"Yes, indeed, Pastor Bill. Laura isn't even on shift right now and she was sitting with Lucinda on her own free time."

"Wow, that's amazing." Bill emphasized the positive.

"Lucinda's operation was a complete success. We were able to repair the deep laceration on her forehead and quelled any internal bleeding. Her blood pressure and vitals are all good. I'm certain that she'll awaken soon and be back to her old self in no time. It's a very good sign that Lucinda is having REM, which means rapid eye movement. As Laura said, she's probably having a wonderful, peaceful dream while her body recuperates."

Margaret was overwhelmed and started weeping as she was overcome with appreciation.

"Thank you ever so much, Dr. Watkins." Bill softly placed a hand on Margaret's shoulder to comfort her—a gesture that did not go unseen by the doctor. He took it as a sign to leave the room and let the family spend some time with Lucinda.

"You're very welcome Margaret, you have a very resilient daughter, she's what I would call tough as nails. Be patient; she'll come around soon."

Bill patted the doctor on his back as he left the room. "Thank you, Dr. Watkins." He knew that the doctor wouldn't appreciate the gesture. "Thank you for letting us see her."

"I think that it's best you don't overwhelm Lucinda or yourselves. Just spend some time, maybe a half hour or so, and then I think she should get back to resting."

"Ok doctor, will do," Bill said as he smiled arrogantly.

John just sat there holding Lucinda's hand, not turning around, still with tears streaming down his cheeks.

After about forty-five minutes of almost total silence, Bill walked over to John, placed an arm around his shoulder and squeezed.

"Ok, brother, it's about time we go now. Lucinda's in good hands and there's nothing else we can do here."

"It's not fair, Bill. God is punishing me for my failures and he's using Lucinda to do it." John turned to face Margaret.

"I'm shocked, John, I've never seen you cry before."

He stood and moved towards her with his arms wide open. Margaret looked at Bill; she stepped away from John, avoiding his hug altogether.

"I need you, wife. Can't you see this is a traumatic time for me?" John whined through his tears.

Margaret's lips pursed together; Bill looked at her and could tell she was disgusted. "No, John, I can't hug you right now."

John broke down further, crying.

"Oh, stop it, John, you're an ugly crier. Stop it now before someone sees you."

After enough time had passed for John to compose himself, they left the hospital. In the parking lot, Margaret opened the passenger side door of the car for John, who got in and sat slumped over with his hands in his face. Margaret saw this and slammed the door.

"Maggie, don't be too hard on him. He's clearly distraught."

Margaret wheeled around to face Bill. "Yes, I understand he's sad, but he's blubbering like a little child. It's embarrassing and quite honestly, Bill, it makes him so undesirable. I wish it were you that I was going home with right now."

Bill hugged Margaret hiding the fact that he groped her ass as he hugged her, whispering in her ear, "I agree, I wish I were going home with you too; but hang in there, it'll get better."

That night, Sheriff Brown met Dr. Watkins at the hospital just before midnight. They greeted an ambulance that came from Oklahoma City.

Standing outside the ambulance area, Sheriff Brown saw an Oklahoma City police car drive up.

"That's the Oklahoma City police escort for Charley." He pointed to the car as he spoke to Dr. Watkins.

"Ah good. A police escort, that's a good thing. Oh, and there's the ambulance, that's my cue; I'll go check that Charley is ready to leave." Dr. Watkins scurried into the hospital.

The paramedics were the first to enter Charley's room, followed by Dave Brown and the two Oklahoma officers. Sheriff Brown addressed Charley.

"Ok, Charley are you ready to go now?"

"Yes, Sheriff Brown, I'm ready. I can't thank you enough."

"Well, good luck with everything, Charley."

"Take care of Norma-Ann for me. Watch over her." Charley's eyes watered.

"Of course, Charley, I'll be watching over her."

In the cover of midnight, the sheriff and Dr. Watkins watched as Charley was loaded into the ambulance and then escorted away with the police car leading and the ambulance following.

CHAPTER 27 –

Saturday Evening

JOHN AND MARGARET would visit Lucinda in the hospital, leaving Suzanne at home to babysit her younger sisters. John was beside himself with guilt. For Margaret, it was as if a switch had flipped. Seeing John acting so sensitive, she seemed to lose all respect for him.

"God is punishing me, Margaret," he said as he looked at his eldest daughter lying in bed, unable to wake up. "Why, oh why did I do that?" He pointed at the cast on her arm, visibly upset.

"You know, John, it wasn't your fault; you only did what a father should do when his daughter lies. All this crying over what, John? God is not punishing you at all, John; if anything, God is sending Lucinda a message."

"Margaret, our daughter is in a coma and you say these things. Have I done you so wrong that your heart has hardened and turned black?"

Margaret scorned him. "Oh poor, poor, pitiful me, John. I'm only saying that Lucinda's lie almost tore our family apart. If anything, God is punishing her for being a lying harlot."

John didn't answer; he just kept staring at Lucinda while he held her hand in one hand and stroked her blonde hair with the other. It was getting close to the end of visiting hours and Nurse Laura came into the room to give the sad father a fifteen-minute warning.

"Mr. and Mrs. Hall, visiting hours end in fifteen minutes. Don't worry I'll be sitting with her all night." The young nurse then left the room.

"For God's sake, John, pull yourself together. Our daughter is in a coma; she's not dead. She'll wake up and life will get back to normal before you know it."

"Margaret, I don't understand why you're so cold, but I'll pray for our daughter and for you."

John broke down in tears as they left the hospital. He didn't even try to hide his face from others. Margaret had never seen him so emotional and it embarrassed her.

Damien had gotten over the sting of his ex-friend dumping him.

It was Saturday night and as Rebecca entered his room, he rushed to give her a big hug.

"I love you, Mom," he said as he wrapped his arms around his stepmother. Rebecca was taken aback by the sudden turnaround Damien had taken.

"I love you too, Damien. What's got you so happy?"

"Tomorrow is Sunday school. I can hardly wait," he said with great excitement.

Mary's Saturday night was quite different; she was a bit nervous about going to church tomorrow. It would be the first time she had been back to church since her accident. She sat staring off into nothing in particular when Sally interrupted her train of thought.

"Mary, dear, I'll give you a penny for your thoughts." She smiled. Mary snapped back to reality as her mother's question registered in her mind.

"Nothing really, Mom."

"It can't be nothing, Mary, you looked as though you were lost in space. I'm here for you. You know that, right?" Mary appreciated her mother's sentiment.

"Mom. I'm worried about going to church tomorrow. People think I lost my mind."

Sally moved closer and hugged her daughter. "You have nothing to worry about, sweetie."

"Really, Mom? 'Mary, Mary had a brain, hit by a car and now she's insane.' It's all over town, Mom. I heard it in the soda shop and people keep singing it every time they see me."

Sally's heart was breaking, hearing her daughter's fears and knowing that there may be some truth to them. Champion could be a cruel gossip machine of lies and sensationalized stories. She pulled Mary tight into her as she tried comforting her.

"Mary, even if everyone in town is a cruel monster, you'll always have your parents, and we love you very much. We'll be at your side every step of the way."

CHAPTER 28 –

Sunday School Lessons

DAMIEN WAS UP and dressed for church an hour before the family even left. In the car on the way, he was a blabbermouth.

"I love Sunday school so much. Our teacher, Dewey, is so funny."

Alex and Rebecca listened as Damien talked in the back seat to his sister Carla. "What's your teacher like?"

Carla didn't really answer, other than saying, 'Fine.' She was more concerned with combing her Barbie's hair.

Damien continued babbling. "The church part is boring, but it's only one hour and then we get to go to Sunday school. I can hardly wait to hear what Dewey teaches today. Last week he told us about the Holy Spook."

Hearing that, Rebecca questioned the boy. "Your Sunday school teacher did not call the Holy Ghost a spook, did he?"

Damien giggled. "Yeah, it was funny, oops, but he said he shouldn't have called the Holy Ghost a spook. I think he just said it to be funny, Mom."

"Oh ok, well, as long as you know we always refer to the Holy Ghost with reverence and respect."

"Yes, Mom, I know."

Damien walked into Sunday school and high-fived Teacher Dewey. As Damien took a seat, he smiled widely, getting ready for another cool lesson.

"Good morning, children. Today we're going to talk about what happens when we die." Dewey made his lips into an 'O' shape, eyes wide with a funny grin on his face. The children laughed. "If you've lived a good life and followed the word of God, your spirit will be welcomed into the Celestial Kingdom."

Dewey went to the chalkboard and put a single dot on the board.

"In the Celestial Kingdom, you'll be given your body back, and you'll then be given a spot in the infinite universe." He pointed to the dot on the chalk board. "In your space you'll have the ability to create your own world, just as God created this one we live in."

The kids were all in awe of the lesson. One child blurted out, "We get to create our own world, that's cool."

Damien asked Teacher Dewey a tough question. "What happens if your body is cremated?"

Dewey thought about it for a moment. "Well, Damien you don't want to have your body cremated or God can't give you your body back when you go to the Celestial Kingdom. On your Judgment Day, if you have lived a good life and follow the commandments and the Word of Wisdom, and if you accept Jesus into your heart, you'll get into the Celestial Kingdom; you'll be exalted to the kingdom of God, and you'll be rewarded and given your space in the universe to create your own world, to be a God yourself."

Damien put his hand up. "What happens if we aren't good, Dewey?"

"That's a good question, Damien. On Judgment Day, you'll stand before God and he'll determine if you go to the Celestial Kingdom, the Terrestrial, the Telestial Kingdom or to Perdition. The Mormon faith teaches four levels of glory the spirit can go to when you die. Not just heaven and H-E-double-hockey-sticks." Dewey chose his words carefully because saying 'hell' is profanity to Mormons. The kids in the class all laughed at Dewey's comment about H-E-double-hockey-sticks.

"When you have your Judgment Day, you'll be given the opportunity to repent. Now on your Judgement Day when you stand before God, you'll be all knowing, you'll remember everything in your life and how your choices and actions affected you and others around you."

One of the students asked. "Dewey, how will we be all knowing?"

"Good question Zach, think of it like watching a movie. You'll see a movie of your entire life, you'll see all the bad things you did to other people, all the bad things others did to you and everything will be known to you."

"Will I see my dog?"

Dewey laughed. "Yes, you'll see your dog if you go to the Celestial Kingdom, all dogs go to heaven. Remember that movie?"

The kids all laughed. Damien asked the next question. "Dewey, what happens after you watch the movie of your life?"

"Very good question Damien. At this point you can repent and be forgiven of your sins, all except for two sins that God won't forgive. Does anyone know what those two sins are?"

Damien was quick to put his hand up. "I know one."

"Ok, Damien what's one?"

"Murder," Damien blurted out.

"Very good, and you're right, Damien. God doesn't forgive murder, which includes suicide. If you commit murder or suicide it's to H-E-double-hockey-sticks for you." The Sunday school teacher smiled and pointed his finger around the room, again bringing snickers from the students. "What's the other sin that can't be forgiven? Does anyone know?"

No one knew. "Ok, I'll tell you. God doesn't forgive those who deny Jesus. This means that if you deny that Jesus died on the cross so that we could have the right to repent, if you deny that Jesus was the one true son of God, or if you deny the Holy Ghost, then you will become a Son of Perdition and God will not forgive you and you'll be sent to where?"

The class responded. "H-E-double-hockey-sticks!" the students yelled out, followed by laughter.

After class, as the children were filing out, Damien saw Bishop Graham. "Hello, Bishop Graham."

"Hello, Damien." He patted the child on the head and watched him walk down the hall and outside.

"Dewey, we need to talk," the bishop spoke sternly to the Sunday school teacher. "Dewey, effective immediately, you are relieved of your duties as Sunday school teacher."

"Why, Bishop Graham? I absolutely love this calling," Dewey said.

The bishop grimaced. "Dewey, I've been told you referred to the Holy Ghost as a spook. Is this true?"

Dewey felt his heart sink. "Well, yes, Bishop. But I was only trying to capture the children's imagination."

"Nevertheless, Dewey, the calling of Sunday school teacher is one of great responsibility. Referring to the Holy Ghost as a spook is irresponsible and not something we want taught to our children. No matter what your reasons are, it's just plain disrespectful. You're relieved of your duties as Sunday school teacher, end of story."

CHAPTER 29 –

Laura's Ugly Discovery

NURSE LAURA WAS very attentive to Lucinda; she sat many hours by her side whether she was on shift or on her own time. On this night, Laura was the overnight nurse on duty, and with only one patient in the small hospital, Lucinda was the center of Laura's attention.

Laura had her own motivation for her interest in Lucinda. In Riley, almost everyone was Christian, it seemed to be a prerequisite to live in the small town. Laura went to church every Sunday, but that was nothing more than a facade she put on for the townsfolk of Riley.

In secret, Laura believed in Mother Nature. Although she was only twenty-one, Laura was proficient and educated in the art form of Wiccan energy healing.

There was a full moon this night and to Laura, this was her opportunity to use her healing energy. Full moons make it easier for a wiccan to channel the healing energy of Mother Nature.

After the day shift had left. She went to Lucinda's room, walked over and opened the curtains. She thought to herself, *it won't be long now*. She peered up at the beautiful full moon and said a phrase out loud as she raised her hands above her head. "If it harms none, do what you will."

Laura's hand hovered over Lucinda's body; she was sensing the girl's energy and looking for where the body would manifest pain. She started with her hands still above her head saying out loud, "Goddess Diana, channel your powers through my body. Help this girl to reveal her pain."

Laura had waited for the janitor to take his half-hour break before she started her ritual, little did she know that Nurse Helen would return to the hospital that evening to retrieve the cell phone she'd left at the nurses desk. Helen heard voices coming from Lucinda's room. She snuck down the hall until she was outside the girl's hospital room, she saw that the door was not fully closed. Helen peered through the crack in the door and silently watched the scene unfold.

Laura held her hands above her head. Her thumbs touched as her forefingers came together to form a triangle shape.

Helen watched as Laura moved her hands down to a horizontal position, keeping the triangle shape formed between the two hands. Laura started at Lucinda's head, hovering her hands about six inches above the girl's head for a long time.

She stared intensely at the girl and began a chant.

"Wrap thee in cotton,

"Bind thee with love,

"Protection from pain,

"Surrounds like a glove,

"Brightest of blessings,

"Surround thee this night,

"For thou art cared for,

"Healing thoughts sent in flight."

Laura then moved her hands to her own chest. Helen watched in fascination, not sure whether to burst into the room and break it up or to let it happen. She thought to herself, *I'll just watch unless something happens that I need to put a stop to.*

Laura moved her hands slowly, hovering over sections of Lucinda's body. Her neck and chest area, her shoulders, arms and legs. As Laura hovered her hand over specific parts of the girl's body, she was repeating over and over, "Harvest Moon, reveal to me this girl's pain." Sometimes she would say, "Goddess Diana, reveal to me this girl's pain."

Her hands always hovered about six inches above every body part, except for when Laura's hands moved over Lucinda's belly.

Her hands began to shake almost uncontrollably. Helen watched and became slightly worried. She could see Laura's hands and arms vibrating; she then watched as those hands slowly lowered until they were touching the girl's belly.

Just then, Laura cried out, almost in agony, "There you are!" Helen reacted by rushing into the room, scaring Laura out of her wits.

"Get your hands off her!" Helen yelled, not knowing what else to say. Nurse Laura jumped back, startled by the head nurse. Not saying a word, she just stared at Helen.

"What are you doing?" Helen demanded.

"Nurse Helen. I was trying to find where Lucinda's pain was hiding."

"Exactly how were you doing that, Laura?" Helen was speaking with great authority but was also curious.

"If you'll let me explain, Helen."

"Oh, by all means. Please explain this all to me."

"Nurse Helen, I was using energy healing to find where Lucinda's pain is hiding. I'm Wiccan."

"You're a witch?" Helen asked.

Laura immediately replied, "Helen, I wouldn't say witch like you're thinking. I'm not casting spells or making potions. I used my energy to connect with Lucinda's, so that her energy could communicate to my energy where the pain is."

"Devil worship!" Helen didn't know how else other than to be blunt.

"No, not devil worship. Wicca is about Mother Nature, natural energies and healing."

"Ok, so Laura, let's say for a second that I'm curious about this energy healing you speak of. What did you find on Lucinda?"

Laura was elated that Helen asked the question. "Helen, I found that Lucinda's pain is not in her head, not her neck, shoulder or arm where there has been clear physical damage. Her pain is in her stomach. She's conflicted inside and it shows in her belly."

Helen thought a moment and an idea popped into her mind to debunk the myth of energy healing and to bring Laura back down to earth. "In her stomach. Well, Laura, how about we put your theory to a test?"

Laura didn't know what to make of the question but she was positive that Lucinda's pain was in her stomach. "Ok, Helen, what do you have in mind?"

"Just stay here and I'll be right back. Oh, and don't touch her anymore."

A few minutes later, Nurse Helen rolled a cart into the room. On the cart was an ultrasound machine.

Laura looked at Helen as she saw the cart. "Excellent idea, Helen. Can I help you?"

The two nurses prepared Lucinda for an ultrasound of her stomach. Helen was looking to debunk Laura's mythological claim that the pain was in the girl's stomach. Laura was excited to see what the ultrasound would reveal.

Helen was moving the transducer all around Lucinda's belly. Laura watched closely. At one point, Helen stopped moving the tool. Laura moved closer to the screen, looking even closer at the image on the screen.

"Helen. Is that— is that—" Laura was clearly in shock as she tried to stammer out her question. "Is that what I think it is, Helen?"

Helen sighed and grimaced.

"Yes, Laura, it's a fetus. How old is this girl?"

"She's only thirteen." Laura had all of Lucinda's personal and medical information committed to memory.

The nurses sat in stunned silence for a long time before Helen removed the tool.

"Laura, wipe her belly clean, please." As Laura wiped it clean, she had one eye on the ultrasound screen and one eye on her task of cleaning up Lucinda's belly. She had an awful thought come into her mind.

"Helen, we can't tell anyone about this," Laura said in a panic.

"What are you saying, Laura? What'd you mean, we can't tell anybody? What about Dr. Watkins?"

"Helen, Lucinda is only thirteen years old. She was admitted last week with major physical injuries, and although the family and Lucinda all say it was from a fall down the stairs, I know Dr. Watkins doesn't believe those injuries were caused by a fall. I overheard him telling Lucinda's mother that she needed to get help for John's anger."

Helen was becoming horrified with every word that Laura spoke.

"If we tell anyone, it would surely be reported to her parents. I fear for her safety if her father finds out she's pregnant."

Laura's words resonated with Nurse Helen. She turned to the ultrasound machine, cleared the image from the screen and erased the history stored in the machine's memory.

"Ok, there, I just erased the memory. But surely we need to report to Dr. Watkins."

"Oh, and Helen, what are we going to say to Dr. Watkins? How will we explain why we did an unauthorized ultrasound?"

Helen found logic in the younger nurse's reasoning.

Laura had an idea. "Helen, I think we should say nothing to no one and when Lucinda wakes up, we'll tell her. After all, it's her body and she should be the first to know, and then she can decide what she wants to do and who she wants to tell."

"I really like that idea, Laura." Despite her deep religious beliefs, Helen, if anything, was all about a woman's right to choose what to do with her own body. "Laura, we tell no one, absolutely no one."

"I agree one hundred percent, Helen. We tell only Lucinda when she wakes up. I wonder if she knows who the father is." Laura's mind was churning and she blurted out a nasty thought that crossed her mind. "I wonder if she was raped, maybe by her father?"

"Bite your tongue, Laura, don't even think that. That's a horrible thought."

"It just popped into my head, sorry, Helen." Laura felt bad for saying her thoughts out loud.

The women left the room, having erased all evidence of the unauthorized ultrasound.

CHAPTER 30 –

Lucinda's Awakening

FOR THE NEXT few days, there was no change in Lucinda's status. She lay in the hospital in a deep comatose state.

On Thursday afternoon, as Laura was at Lucinda's bedside, she saw the girl's legs twitch. Laura's heart started racing; she moved closer to Lucinda, placing a thumb on her right eye and gently pulling the eyelid upwards. Lucinda's eyes began to open as her eyelids fluttered open and closed. Laura recognized that the light in the room might be too bright; she quickly went to the room's light switch, dimmed the lights and returned to Lucinda's bedside.

After about five minutes, Lucinda's eyes were open and Laura could see that she was trying to focus.

"Welcome back, Lucinda. Take it easy; don't strain yourself."

Lucinda shook her head slightly, looking around the room, assessing her surroundings. Laura keyed in on what she was doing.

"Lucinda, don't worry, you're safe. You're in Riley General Hospital. You're fine, just take things slow," Laura said in the most comforting voice she could.

"Whaaa—" Lucinda started to speak. "What happened?"

"Lucinda, there was an accident, but you're safe now."

Lucinda looked at her arm in the cast. "What happened to my cast? It's purple?"

Laura chuckled. "Lucinda." Laura patted her hand softly. "The doctor gave you a new upgraded colorful cast because you're special. Do you like the purple?" Laura was trying to be lighthearted and didn't want to make a big fuss that would stress the girl out.

"No, purple isn't my favorite color." Lucinda frowned.

Laura continued to comfort Lucinda for a few more minutes before she asked, "Lucinda, would it be ok with you if I go and get the doctor? He'll be so happy you're awake."

"Uh, sure," Lucinda replied in a shaky tone. Laura stood up and left the room slowly. As soon as she was outside the room, Laura's feet moved faster as she speed-walked to Dr. Watkins' office.

She knocked on the doctor's door and heard an echoed reply from within.

"Come in."

Laura opened the door and looked at the doctor with a huge grin on her face. Dr. Watkins didn't even need to hear what the young nurse was about to say to know that Lucinda had woken up. He jumped up from behind his desk as Laura spoke. "Lucinda's awake! Dr. Watkins."

"YESSS!" Dr. Watkins said as he hurried out of his office and down the hall to Lucinda's room. He entered the room and greeted Lucinda with a smile.

"Well, hello there, young lady, I see you're finally awake."

She looked at Dr. Watkins with a puzzled facial expression. "How long was I asleep?"

Dr. Watkins approached Lucinda and placed a hand on her wrist, feeling her pulse as he talked with her. He wanted to ensure that the girl stayed calm and by taking her pulse he would be able to monitor her heart rate.

"You had a nice long seven-day nap. How do you feel?"

Lucinda's eyes grew wide as she considered what she had just been told. "Seven days?" She quizzed.

"How do you feel, Lucinda?" Dr. Watkins repeated. She looked at the doctor.

"Honestly, Dr. Watkins, I'm hungry." The doctor laughed.

"Nurse Laura, do you think you could rustle up some food for our hungry patient?"

Laura was pleased to do so. She left the room and when she walked by Bonnie's desk on her way to get some food, she couldn't contain her excitement.

"Bonnie, guess what?" Bonnie always had a smile on her face and was happy to talk with anyone, especially when that person's sentence started with 'guess what?'

"What, Laura?" said Bonnie, expecting to hear some juicy gossip.

"Lucinda Hall is awake!" Laura said excitedly.

Bonnie shrieked out, "Hallelujah!" The two nurses held hands as they jumped up and down with glee.

"I must get going, I'm getting some food for Lucinda. I'll see you later, Bonnie."

"Ok, Laura. See you later, that's great news."

CHAPTER 31 –

Happy Day

AS NEWS OF Lucinda spread to all the hospital staff, the atmosphere in the hospital became very positive and upbeat. Everyone seemed to be a little more chipper and walked with a bounce in their step.

Dr. Watkins had examined Lucinda several times throughout the day. He called Margaret at home.

"Hello," Margaret said as she picked up the phone.

"Hello, Margaret. It's Dr. Watkins. I have great news."

"Is it Lucinda?" Margaret replied with a modicum of excitement in her tone.

"Yes, Margaret, she woke up this afternoon about an hour ago. I have examined her and she's doing well."

"That's great news, Doctor, thank you." Margaret then hung up the phone without even saying goodbye.

Dr. Watkins heard the phone go dead; he looked at the handset, realizing that the conversation had ended abruptly. He figured that Margaret was just overexcited and forgot to say goodbye.

Margaret rushed over to John's work and talked to his boss, telling him about Lucinda. John's boss then went out onto the factory floor, leaving Margaret in the front office to wait for John.

"John, come over here a second, will ya?"

John walked over to his boss, wondering what he had done to deserve the boss's special one-on-one attention.

"John, your wife's here in the office. She told me your daughter has woken up."

Tears of joy appeared in his eyes as he addressed his boss. "May I—"

John's boss replied, he knew the question already. "Yes, of course, John. Go on, get out of here!" John's boss was overjoyed for him; he gave John a big bear hug. "John, you better get going. Go now!"

John turned and yelled out loud so everyone in the factory could hear. "My daughter woke up!"

Everyone within earshot, which was everyone in the whole factory, heard John's words booming out. They all started clapping and continued their ovation as John walked out.

He met Margaret in the lobby and hugged her. "Praise the Lord, our Lucinda is awake. Let's go to the hospital now, Margaret."

"Of course, John, let's go."

John got in the driver's seat of the car and within a few minutes they arrived at the hospital.

John rushed into the hospital and straight to Lucinda's room. The second he saw her sitting up with her eyes open, he moved in to give her a big hug.

"Oh, my girl, you're awake. I was so worried about you." Lucinda didn't really know how to take this affection from her father. She had never seen him this mushy before.

"I love you, Father." It was all she could think to say in the moment. Margaret stood near the foot of the bed, not overly excited, but happy nonetheless.

When Laura walked into the room, John saw her and he immediately wrapped his arms around the young nurse, giving her an appreciative hug as his eyes were welling up with joyful tears.

"Thank you ever so much for watching over our daughter. You're a special child of God."

Margaret couldn't take any more of her husband's joy. She snuck out of the room just as Dr. Watkins came in.

"Oh hello, Margaret. I guess you've seen Lucinda. She's doing really well. It's a good day."

"Hi, Dr. Watkins. Yes... yes, it's a good day." She half smiled. "I was just going to look for a vending machine, you know, to get a little snack." Dr. Watkins noted that Margaret seemed anxious to get away.

"Vending machines are only in the waiting area of the emergency department. Just down the hall and turn left to go out to emergency."

Helen was the night nurse on shift that night after the family had left and the hospital was quiet; Laura came in looking to talk with Helen.

"Hi, Helen, I just wanted to stop in and talk to you. Have you got a few minutes?"

Helen welcomed the company as the two nurses sat down at a table in the small, empty cafeteria.

"It's great that Lucinda is awake now." Helen smiled.

"That's what I came to talk to you about, Helen. I was thinking that we should both talk to Lucinda at the same time."

"That's a great idea, Laura, but I don't think tonight is the time to do it."

"Oh, heck no, I was thinking tomorrow night. You're still on nights tomorrow, right?"

"Yes, still on nights. We can wait until after visiting hours. Have you told anyone else?"

"No way, Helen, not even Dr. Watkins. Like we agreed, this is Lucinda's choice as to who she tells."

CHAPTER 32 –

Sheer Will

MARY WAS READJUSTING to a new life—a life in which people seemed to have shunned her, or at the very least, they avoided her.

After school Friday as Mary came out, she saw Nathan over near the bike racks. He was surrounded by three older boys whom she recognized as David, Jeff and Karl. They were a year older than Nathan. She stopped as she watched the older boys pushing the younger Nathan around. One would push him into the other, and on it went.

She could hear the boys taunting Nathan.

"W-w-w-why d-d-do y-y-you talk so f-f-f-u-u-u-n-n-n-y-y-y?" They were mocking the timid boy's speech disorder.

"Your m-m-m o-o-o m-m-m- a-a-a must be s-s-s i-i-i- c-c-c- k-k-k-."

Mary started making her way over to the boys, who were no more than fifty feet away.

"Hey!" she yelled. "Leave him alone, you bullies!"

The bullies stopped only for a second to see who had called them out.

One of them replied, "Oh no, look, it's crazy, insane Mary. And she's telling us what to do."

David replied to Jeff's comment. "Oh, don't worry about her, her cheese slid off her cracker. She's a nutcase."

When Mary reached the boys, the largest of them was Karl. He placed his body between her and Jeff.

"Oh, what, Jeff Daniels, you need a body guard?" Mary sniped at him.

Jeff's pride was challenged. He pushed Nathan backwards into David, who grabbed his arms and held him while Jeff engaged Mary.

"No, I don't need a bodyguard. Do you need a head shrink? Crazy bitch."

"Jeff, just leave Nathan alone, please."

"And who's gonna make me? You? What you gonna do? Go loco on me?" The boy laughed at his own joke, with his two friends following their leader; they laughed as well.

Mary moved past Jeff and pushed David before she grabbed Nathan by the arm and pulled him away.

"Nathan, go now, go home."

The bullies were not happy about their prey being set free. As Nathan scampered away, Jeff picked up a rock about the size of a golf ball. "Hey Nathan, run home to m-m-m o-o-o-m-m-m y-y-y." He raised his hand and was about to throw the rock when Mary grabbed his hand. Jeff pushed her away so hard she fell to the ground.

"Stay out of it, bitch, it's none of your business," he warned.

Jeff threw the rock, narrowly missing Nathan, who had already run about fifteen feet away.

"Ok boys, first to bean him in the head wins," Jeff said to his friends. The three boys all picked up rocks and started throwing them at Nathan.

"Stop it, you assholes!" Mary yelled at them as she got up.

The boys were not having much luck with their aim, so they ran after Nathan, getting closer so they could make more accurate throws; the competition to be the first to hit Nathan in the head was on.

Mary chased the boys for a few feet, yelling at them as she did. "Stop it, guys, stop!"

The three bullies cornered Nathan at the chain link fence that surrounded the school's football field. David was the first to actually hit Nathan with a rock, but it was only on his shoulder.

Jeff bent down to pick up a larger rock, about the size of a small baseball, just as Mary caught up with the three bullies. She could see Nathan huddled over with his back turned to the bullies, who were only about ten feet away and well within throwing distance now.

"Stop now!" Mary demanded as she was about to approach the bullies. She saw the size of the rock that Jeff had in his hand. And she saw his arm rear back and the forward thrust of his throw.

For Mary it was surreal; time seemed to be moving in extremely slow motion. She saw the rock Jeff had just thrown was about to strike the back of Nathan's head.

She was mortified; in her mind, she felt exactly how she felt in the moment when she stood up to the light spirit, right before she used her will to break the spirit.

The bullies were laughing. Other kids had gathered around, having seen the commotion.

Mary extended her arm straight forward with her hand out in a stop gesture. She yelled as if she were screaming directly at the rock itself.

"Move!"

Right then, the rock took a right turn like a wild pitch in baseball. The three bullies were shocked. Karl spoke first.

"How?" Jeff and David looked at Karl as he finished his sentence. "How'd you do that?" he asked Mary.

Mary didn't respond as Jeff gave a command to his thug friends.

"Grab her!"

Karl was just over six feet tall and weighed over 200 pounds. Mary's 125-pound small-frame body would be no match for the large boy. Mary turned to face Karl just as he was about to grab her by the arms.

"Back off!" she yelled at Karl as she put her arms out in front of her to push the boy away before he could grab her. She felt something inside her, she felt sheer will just like she did when she broke free of the light spirit.

She pushed Karl so hard that his 200-pound body flew backwards in the air about three feet before he landed flat on his back.

The small crowd witnessed the event. They saw Mary's amazing shove.

"Witchcraft!" Jeff yelled as he pointed at Mary. He and David ran over to Karl, helped him up to his feet and then ran away.

Some of the onlookers started clapping until they heard a voice in the crowd yell out.

"Mary's a freak, a witch!"

At that statement, the crowd became somewhat frightened and backed away from Mary before dispersing.

Mary went over to Nathan, who was now sitting on his butt as he leaned against the fence. Mary offered her hand to the boy.

"Are you alright, Nathan?" she asked as she held her hand out.

The boy was shaking and he started to extend his hand and then pulled it back. He was obviously scared of Mary. In a calm, reassuring voice, Mary said, "Don't worry, Nathan, I don't bite. I won't hurt you."

She watched as Nathan's hand now extended to hers. She added a word to her previous sentence. "Hard." She said with a fun sly smile. Nathan caught onto the joke. As she took his hand and helped him to his feet, he stuttered out a few words.

"T-h-h a-a-a— T-h-h a-a-a n-n-n k-k-k-s M-m-m a-a r-r-r y-y."

"You're welcome, Nathan. You should go on home now. I don't think those boys will be a problem anymore, and if they are, you come find me."

Nathan walked off in one direction and Mary in the other as she walked home.

The story of Mary's witchcraft was all over the town in no time. It had grown to disproportionate levels. The rumor was now that Mary had stopped a baseball-sized rock in mid-air and turned the hard stone to dust, and then, without touching Karl, she used some sort of witch-craft force to knock him flying ten feet through the air.

CHAPTER 33 –

Lucinda Knew

IN RILEY, JUST as Lucinda was about to go to sleep, she had some visitors come into her room. She sat up and greeted Nurses Laura and Helen with a sleepy smile while fighting off a yawn.

"Oh, hello, Nurse Laura, Nurse Helen. I was about to go to sleep."

The friendly nurses were happy to have a night where they could talk to Lucinda alone and uninterrupted. Helen took the lead.

"Lucinda, are you happy to be going home tomorrow?" She watched the young girl's reaction to the question.

"Yeah, I think so," Lucinda said unconvincingly. Laura realized that something was worrying Lucinda.

"Nurse Helen and I have some news for you, but I think you probably already know, and that's maybe why you're not looking forward to going home."

Helen was puzzled at this statement; she looked at Lucinda's facial expression to see that Laura had touched a nerve.

Laura continued. "While you were asleep in a coma, we did an ultrasound on you, Lucinda. Do you know what that is?"

Lucinda paused before she answered. "I didn't know before, but I do now." Helen thought it was a strange response to the question.

Laura continued talking to Lucinda. "We put a wand on your belly that sees what's going on in your tummy."

As Lucinda started to squirm in her bed, Helen said. "And you know what we found, Lucinda?"

"Uhm, yes, I think so."

Helen was shocked to hear her say that. But Laura had already figured it out.

"Lucinda, you already know that you're pregnant, don't you?"

Lucinda's cheeks turned beet red and she became flustered and nervous. She hesitated to answer. Helen's mind was reeling as she tried to catch up, feeling as if she didn't know something that the other two girls knew.

"How long have you known, Lucinda?" Laura spoke in a sympathetic tone.

"Just over a month and a half." Lucinda hung her head. Laura leaned over and gently placed her hand under Lucinda's chin, pushing upwards.

"You have nothing to be ashamed of, Lucinda. Hold your head up high."

The girl smiled and then opened up. "I know it's not my shame to bear. But I haven't told anyone about it." Lucinda seemed to flip a switch and was now speaking in a confident, mature tone. She looked at the nurses; she saw shock on Nurse Helen's face and compassion in Laura's facial expression.

"Who all knows about my condition?" Lucinda asked. Helen saw an opportunity to get back into the conversation now that she had gotten over the shock of finding out that Lucinda already knew she was pregnant.

"No one, Lucinda, only myself and Nurse Laura. We thought it was your choice to tell others." Helen went on to ask, "How did you know you were pregnant? Did you do a home pregnancy test?"

"No." Lucinda answered the second question. "I just knew. I could feel it." It was spooky, the way Lucinda spoke; she didn't sound like a thirteen-year-old child, and she was calm and not panicked at all. "Nurse Helen, Nurse Laura. Please don't tell anyone. I'm not ready yet." The nurses both knew that it wouldn't be long until Lucinda started to show.

"We estimate that you're about six weeks along, so you could still terminate—."

"NO! That's not going to happen, I won't terminate my baby. Six weeks is close, fifty-one days old as of today," Lucinda confirmed.

"How do you know the exact day Lucinda?" Laura asked.

Nurse Helen responded astutely. "Because she only had intercourse once, she remembers the exact day."

"Nurse Helen is right, again, don't tell anyone. I need to do some things before I tell anyone," Lucinda pleaded with the nurses.

Laura spoke. "Lucinda, the reason we didn't tell anyone, not even Dr. Watkins, is because we feel that it's your body and your decision as to who and when you tell people." Laura added, "Lucinda. Mum's the word; we won't say anything. But, you know, before you know it, you'll be showing and people will figure it out."

Helen realized that she needed to cover their asses; otherwise, she and Laura would be looking for new work. "Lucinda, please remember we didn't tell anyone, not even Dr. Watkins. If anyone finds out we did an ultrasound without your parents' permission, we would be fired."

"Nurse Helen. Seems that we all have a mutually beneficial reason for keeping our mouths shut," Lucinda pointed out.

The two nurses laughed along with Lucinda.

"Ok, well, Lucinda, if you ever need anything, even to just talk, come find me or Nurse Laura. We should leave now and let you get some sleep."

Laura leaned over and gave Lucinda a hug; Helen also gave her a hug as Lucinda was thanking them.

"Thank you both." Lucinda smiled at the nurses. "I'm going to go to sleep now, if that's ok."

Both nurses smiled. "It's ok, Lucinda, sweet dreams," Helen said right before they left the room.

CHAPTER 34 –

Finding the Fort

AFTER SCHOOL, DAMIEN was walking home. He decided to take a shortcut through the back alley that had houses on one side and a chain link fence on the other side, separating the houses from the train tracks, which were about two-hundred feet away.

As Damien walked, he noticed a large piece of wood pressed up against the fence. He moved closer to get a better look. Upon further inspection, he thought to himself *that looks like a fort.*

Curiosity got the better of him and he decided to investigate further. The six-foot fence had jagged metal barbs at the top, as was typical of most chain link fences. Damien thought to climb the fence, but hesitated. "Damn, would Mom ever get mad if I ripped my new jeans on that fence." Damien spoke out loud to himself. He continued talking to himself to find a solution to his problem.

"Ok, think, Damien. You want to check out whatever's on the other side of the fence, but you can't climb over." He scratched his head as he spoke to himself.

"I can't go over, but maybe I could squeeze under." Damien remembered seeing rabbits squeeze under chain link fences that were curled up at the bottom.

"Ok, so I don't see anywhere to go under. What the heck, Damien it's just a silly fence. You can do this." He walked along the fence, placing his fingers in the links and pulling slightly. He didn't even realize he was pulling on the fence. As he came closer to the third pole away from where he had seen the fort, he noticed the fence was getting looser.

"What's this all about?" Then he spotted it. Right at the pole, the fence was cut from the bottom up. Neat cuts on each link. He saw a large rock at the bottom that seemed to have been placed there to keep the fence in place.

"You gotta do this, Damien. Go for it," he encouraged himself. He knelt down and pushed the rock away, then folded the fence back to create a space wide enough for him to easily slip through.

Once he was on the other side of the fence, he went to the area where he saw the fort. He saw what was the greatest find of his young life.

"Yes! I was right!" There were shopping carts on each of the four corners. He saw old pieces of plywood stacked on top to create a makeshift roof. Then he noticed in the center was a piece of plywood about three feet wide by four feet tall. He read the words painted on it. "Keep Out!" A poorly painted skull with crossbones was painted below the words.

The temptation was way too much for Damien; he moved the plywood out of the way and went inside. His eyes were wide when he realized that this was the coolest fort ever. A large wagon wheel spool sat in the middle of the one-room fort, the type of wooden spools used by construction or power companies that spooled large-gauge wire on it. Sometimes these spools could be found discarded near the railroad tracks.

Damien had explored near the tracks many times with his ex-friend Todd and others, but never this far down. About a half mile away, the fence was only four feet tall and Damien and friends would go there and put pennies on the track and wait for the train to crush them flat. They also collected small pieces of yellow sulfur that had fallen beside the tracks. Sulfur, when combined with a pack of matches and a home-made wick wrapped in electrical tape, made a great stink bomb.

Damien explored inside the dimly lit fort; he saw a black square box and recognized it as the battery box of a flasher light used in road construction. The top would normally be an orange plastic dome, but on this box the dome was broken off and all that remained was a single small clear light bulb.

He inspected the battery and bulb closer and found a switch on the back side; he flipped the rocker switch and the light came on, illuminating the entire fort. "This is sooo cool," he said to himself.

Looking around, he saw some magazines with a few of them having pretty girls in bikinis or just large pink stars over their nipples. He read the titles of the magazines out loud to himself.

"Playboy. Hustler. Swank. Penthouse. Interesting." He flipped the pages of one of the magazines and saw naked ladies inside. This was the first time in his life that he had ever seen pornography; he felt weird looking at it, but he was also fascinated and couldn't put the magazines down. He flipped through all four of them before he heard a shriek behind him.

"Gggaaawwwttt ooottt!!!" It sounded like jumbled words. Damien turned around and saw a large ginger-haired boy. He could see the boy was older and larger than him. The boy was yelling at him but Damien didn't understand the words.

"Miiineee bbooks!" was the only real coherent thing Damien heard from the boy, who was holding a stick out in front of him, waving it around at Damien.

"Oh, sorry, I didn't know." Damien put the magazines back on the wire spool table where he found them. The older red-headed boy had big orange freckles on his face. Damien felt for the boy as he too had freckles and couldn't even begin to count how many times people called him 'Freckle Face' in his life.

The boy kept yelling and pointing the stick at Damien and then back to the door.

"Ooottt. Ooottt! Gggaaawwwttt ooottt!" It finally clicked with Damien. The other boy was telling him to "Get out." But the problem

Damien now faced was he had to crawl right by the boy to get out and he was concerned about the stick the boy was waving around.

"Ok. Ok, I get it. This is your fort and I'm trespassing. I'm so sorry dude. I'll get out. Can you just move over there a bit?" Damien motioned with his hand to the left, hoping the boy would let him pass without incident. The two boys stayed locked in a stand-off for a long time. Damien kept repeating, "Can you move over there?" he pointed.

The boy finally realized what Damien was saying and he calmed down and moved far enough away to let Damien get past him. Damien crawled slowly; but then he stopped while still in the fort. "Hey just so you know this is the coolest fort I've ever seen."

"Gggaaawwwttt ooottt pplleeeaaasss."

Damien held his hand up in the air. "Really man it's cool, high fives." Damien didn't recognize that the red-headed boy had once again become agitated. "Come on man don't leave me hanging." Damien moved closer to the boy and again raised his hand. "High fives." The boy freaked out and started screaming in an even higher pitched voice.

"Ooottt! Ooottt!" He kept repeating before Damien gave up on the high five idea. The boy raised the stick again and Damien started to crawl towards the exit. He picked up his pace when he felt the stick poke him in the back of his thigh.

"Ooottt," he heard behind him as he exited through the doorway to the outside. Once he was outside, he stood up and before he knew it, the boy had followed him out of the fort.

Damien turned to see the boy waving and swinging the stick at him; he ducked just in time as one of the boy's swings narrowly missed his head. Damien noted the size of the older boy and realized that it was time to run away. He started running for the fence opening with the other boy chasing close behind. As Damien knelt down to slip through the opening the boy caught up with him and swung the stick in a threatening manner, but never actually hit Damien.

Damien turned around after he got through the fence to see the boy was still following him through the fence.

"Sorry. Sorry I went in your fort. I'll never do it again."

The boy now got to his feet, having made his way through the opening. Damien realized that there was no use running—the larger boy would surely catch him—so he turned and faced the ginger-haired boy, putting his hands up to send a signal that he meant no harm. The boy kept stepping forward, occasionally swinging the stick in the air.

Damien was stepping backwards one step at a time while keeping his eyes on the boy and that damn stick. As Damien backed up, he didn't see the large rock behind him that would trip him up, causing him to fall backwards onto the ground, he immediately curled up into the fetal position to shield himself, waiting for the boy to strike him with the stick.

The red-haired boy now stood over Damien. Waving the stick and yelling at Damien. Off in the distance, Damien heard a voice yelling. "Casey, stop! Stop, Casey, stop!" The boy stopped momentarily as the voice kept saying the same thing over and over again. Damien could tell the voice yelling, "Stop." was getting closer and he felt relieved that someone was coming.

"Casey, give me the stick!" he heard the female voice saying. Damien moved one hand away from his face to look up. He saw the woman was standing just above him while she grabbed the stick from the ginger-haired boy. Damien was still on the ground between the boy and the woman who was wrestling the stick away.

After getting the stick, the woman addressed the red-haired kid.

"Casey, go in the house! Go now!"

"Nnnawww, Maaam," the boy replied. Damien stayed on the ground looking up at the two. The woman waved the stick at the kid and threatened him.

"Casey, go in the house now or Momma's going to paddle you with this stick." She waved the stick at the kid. He mumbled something and walked towards the open gate of the house that the woman came from.

She then leaned down next to Damien.

"Oh my. Are you ok?" She spoke gently, offering her hand to help Damien up.

"Yeah, I'm ok, and thanks lady, for stopping that kid."

"That kid is my son, Casey. You must've got too close to his secret fort." Damien started to sit up and the woman helped him to his feet.

"That's your son, lady? Well, you should teach him not to hit people with a stick," Damien scolded the woman.

"Oh no, did he hit you with his stick?"

Damien paused for thought. "Uhm, actually no he didn't hit me, not even once."

"He doesn't really know what he's doing, he's only about four years old mentally. He didn't mean to hurt you, he's only protecting that damn fort, which is his pride and joy. My name's Melissa. What's your name?"

Damien was dusting himself off when he replied, "I'm Damien."

"Ok, Damien, how would you like to come in for some milk and cookies, and I can explain my son to you."

Damien thought about it and decided he would like to know what she meant when she said Casey was mentally only four years old.

"Ok, but no more swinging a stick at me, ok?" Melissa laughed and put her arm around Damien's shoulder as she walked him towards her house.

Once inside the house, Damien sat in the kitchen with the woman; she got him four chocolate chip cookies and a glass of milk. Then she called out, "Casey, come to the kitchen, please. Casey, come here."

Damien felt a little intimidated as he saw the boy enter the kitchen. He also noticed Casey wouldn't make eye contact, even with his own mother.

"Casey, come sit down and have milk and cookies." The boy's eyes grew wide and he awkwardly clapped his hands together—his wrists were actually clapping together while his hands flailed loosely. The woman set Casey up with some milk and cookies, then she looked over at Damien.

"You see, Damien, my son Casey."

Just then, the boy used his right hand and poked at his own chest saying. "I Ca-sey."

It was easy to see the woman had great patience. She acknowledged the boy. "Yes, you are Casey. Yay!" She clapped her hands a few times as if to reward the boy.

"You see, Damien, my son Casey has Down syndrome, which means his brain has developed differently than most. Some people cruelly refer to him as retarded."

"How old is he really?" Damien quizzed.

"He's fourteen and his dad left when he was only three. It's just the two of us here, and I try to give Casey some freedom, but it's hard for him when he meets people; he doesn't communicate so well."

"I can see that, ma'am." Damien was polite.

"Call me Melissa, please. I invited you inside to get to know you and become your friend."

"That's nice, thank you, Melissa, but maybe you're too old to be my friend."

Melissa laughed the offensive comment off. "Well, I don't think so, Damien. Anyone can be friends, no matter how old they are or how very different they are. Casey has a hard time making friends, as you can see."

Damien thought that was hilarious and sarcastically replied, "Oh you think so, huh?" He chuckled.

"Ok, so Damien, can we be friends?" Melissa asked.

Damien thought it was an odd question, but he answered nonetheless. "Well, I suppose so, Melissa." Then Melissa did something that explained to Damien why she wanted to be friends with him. She turned to her son Casey.

"Casey. This is my friend, Damien." She pointed at Damien.

"I like my friend." She put her hand over her heart and made a circle and then pointed at Damien.

Damien watched in fascination as she communicated with her son. She stood up and walked around the table over to Damien; she leaned over and gave him a hug. Damien slowly hugged the woman back as Casey watched the whole scene unfold.

Melissa spoke to Casey again, placing her hand over her heart. "Damien," she pointed at him, "is my friend."

Casey then smiled and replied almost coherently. "Fweend." He then got up and went over to Damien, who instinctively jerked his head back, then Casey leaned over and hugged him awkwardly. As he patted Damien on the back, he said, "Fweend."

"Now we're all friends," Melissa said as she smiled at Damien.

"Friends," Damien said and smiled.

"I should be going; I'm late getting home now. My mom will be worried."

"By all means, Damien, you should be on your way. Don't be a stranger; now that you're friends with Casey, he won't attack you again."

Damien felt relieved as he said goodbye and left the house and went home.

CHAPTER 35 –

Dinner at Casey's

EVERY DAY THAT week, Damien walked home through the alley hoping to see Casey, if for no other reason than to see if Casey would remember him as a friend.

He thought to himself, it must be horrible to have Downs-syndrome. To have no friends. Then a thought crossed his mind that Casey did have a friend. I'm his friend, Damien thought to himself as he felt a warmth inside, as if he were doing a kind gesture by just being Casey's friend.

On the Thursday when he didn't see Casey, he stopped and knocked on the door. He waited for it to open and when it did open, it was Casey standing in the doorway.

Casey looked at Damien and then shrieked loudly back into the house as if to alert his mother. "Fweend!" Then he jumped at Damien and awkwardly hugged him.

Melissa came down the stairs and saw Damien standing outside with Casey hugging him. Damien could see the woman was elated to see him again.

"Damien! Good to see you again. Casey keeps asking where our friend is. Would you like to stay for dinner?"

"Well, I suppose I could. I would have to call my mom and get permission, if that's ok?"

"Sure, come on in." She then tugged on Casey and pulled him back inside the house and she closed the door once both boys were in. "You can call your mom. The phone is on the wall in the kitchen and I can talk to her if she needs me to."

Damien picked up the phone and called home.

"Hello, Mom. I'm at a friend's house. Can I stay over for dinner?"

As Damien said friend, Casey could be heard in the background repeating the word, "Fweend."

"Who is this friend, Damien?"

"His name is Casey; he has a syndrome and his mom invited me for dinner. Would you like to talk with her?"

"Alright Damien, I'll talk to her," Rebecca said.

Damien handed the phone to Melissa and saw that Casey had a blue plastic case; he took Damien's arm and dragged him over to the living room where Casey sat on the floor and opened the case. Inside the case was Casey's collection of Hot Wheels cars. Damien was interested and the two boys looked at and played with the cars as Melissa spoke to Rebecca about Damien staying for dinner.

Melissa hung up the phone and informed Damien, "Your mother is nice. She says it's ok for you to stay for dinner."

"Oh, cool," Damien said and then returned to playing cars with Casey.

⁓

Later that night when Damien got home, Rebecca wanted to have a talk with her son.

"Damien, let's sit and talk."

"Ok, Mom."

"Damien, I talked with your friend Casey's mother. I think her name is Melissa."

"Yup, that's her name, Mom," Damien said lightheartedly.

"She told me that her son has Down-syndrome and how happy he is to have made a friend of you." Rebecca beamed. "She told me that her son Casey doesn't have too many friends because all the kids are afraid of him. She said you are a very special boy. Her Casey has never taken to anyone like he has with you. I just want you to know, Damien, I think it's wonderful that you made friends with that boy. You're a good person, with a kind heart. You make me proud."

"Thanks, Mom. Is that all? I have some homework to do before bed."

Rebecca was happy and it showed. "Sure, Damien. Run up to your room and hit those books."

Damien bounded up the stairs to his room.

CHAPTER 36 –

Getting Stoned

FOR THE NEXT week, Damien would walk through that alley on his way home from school. Little did he know; he was being followed.

On that Friday, though, he thought he heard something behind him. He turned and looked to see Todd there, about five feet away, walking towards him.

"Hi, Todd."

Todd didn't say a word, just came close to Damien and when he got close enough, he started talking. "Damien, me and the boys have been thinking that you probably should quit Scouts."

"No! Why would I do that?"

"Because we don't want you there!" It was then that Damien noticed two more boys that he knew from Scouts had snuck up behind him, and he was surrounded on three sides by the boys.

"No, I'm not quitting Scouts, Todd!" Damien exclaimed.

"That's too bad. You're quitting, I guarantee it." The two boys behind Damien began the attack and grabbed him by the arms. They dragged him over to the chain link fence. Todd took some rope out of his jacket and the two boys held Damien up against the fence.

Damien struggled. "Let me go! Let me go!" Todd punched Damien right in the bread basket, winding him and taking the fight out of

Damien long enough that the other two boys could hold him in place as Todd tied Damien's wrists to the fence.

"Damien, you should quit Scouts. Are you going to quit?"

"No, I'm not quitting," Damien said with conviction.

"Well, then you leave us no choice. We're going to throw rocks at you until you promise to quit."

The three boys threw rocks, some small, some the size of golf balls at Damien as he was bound to the chain link fence. He cried out in pain with each rock that struck him.

"Ouch, stop! Ouch— Ouch— Damn— Ouch— Stop! Untie me!" Damien was trying to get the boys to stop, but they wouldn't.

"Are you ready to quit Scouts yet, Damien?" Todd asked.

"No, never!" Just then, a rock struck Damien's forehead and it hurt badly. "Ouch!" Damien yelled as he struggled to break free of the ropes, but he couldn't. Eventually he turned his head downwards and to the left to try and protect his face from the rocks.

The three Mormon boys stood about seven feet away as they continued picking up rocks and throwing them at Damien. Most of the rocks hit his body, but the ones that were hitting his head were starting to really hurt. Damien felt blood trickling down his cheek.

Todd asked again, "Are you ready to quit Scouts?"

Damien looked up at Todd; the three boys temporarily stopped throwing rocks and waited for Damien's answer.

"No!"

As soon as the boys heard Damien's answer, they resumed throwing rocks again; this time one of the rocks hit Damien square in the eye. Damien had never felt pain like that in his life. His eyes were watering and he could barely see through the one eye. The boys stopped again and asked the same question.

"Are you ready to quit Scouts now?" Damien was in a lot of pain, but his stubborn will was what was driving him now. He would not give in. He lifted his head and tried to look at Todd, but he couldn't see much through blurry, blood-filled eyes. Just as the pain had him at the brink, Damien subconsciously did something remarkable to be able to survive the extreme pain. He didn't know what happened, but he felt as though his spirit had left his body; it went to a safe place while the cruel Mormon boys continued to pelt him, over and over with more rocks.

In his mind's eye, Damien was being guided down a long corridor towards a white light. He saw a radiant blue sparkle to his left and he walked over until he got to the door. A warm loving voice said. "Damien step through the door, you'll be safe my love."

He opened the door, stepped inside and looked around. He saw a cascading, peaceful waterfall, heard birds singing and the smell of lavender was pleasing. He felt a hand on his chin; he raised his head and looked into the eyes of a beautiful woman with deep emerald green eyes and long flowing straight black hair that cascaded all the way down to her ankles. Damien felt peace as the woman ran her hand over his face.

He spoke, "Have I died?" Another woman came into Damien's view, wearing a flowery flowing dress with long blonde hair and the nicest smile he had ever seen. She spoke.

"No, Damien, you're not dead. You willed your spirit here to my sanctuary to disconnect from the pain your body is feeling."

"Where am I?" Damien asked.

"I'm Gaia and this is your ancestor, Malvinia. Your soul is drawn to hers and here in my sanctuary, your spirit is safe."

"So am I dead then?"

"No, Damien, you're safe." Gaia's voice was soothing and Damien never wanted to leave. Just then, a sound interrupted his thoughts. He heard sirens in the distance coming closer and closer. Todd yelled at him.

"Answer me, freak! Are you going to quit Scouts?"

"No!" Damien defied Todd one last time. A few more rocks were thrown that hit Damien, and then he heard a scuffle. He looked up to see, but through blurry eyes he could barely make out the form of the fourth boy. It was Casey and he was waving a stick around in the air at the other boys.

Damien could hear sirens growing louder as Casey chased the Mormon boys away. The next thing he felt was when Casey hugged him briefly and said, "Fweend." Then he felt Casey working to untie the knots.

The sirens were really loud now and Damien realized the sirens were right there. Next, he heard an adult male voice yelling, "Back away from the fence! Get on the ground with your hands behind your back!"

Damien realized that it was the police and they were telling Casey to back away, but Casey didn't understand; he just kept trying to untie the knots. Damien tried to tell the cops. But his words came out severely slurred; his jaw could barely move.

The police came over and grabbed Casey, who screeched at the top of his lungs. "Fweend! Halllppp!"

Damien could tell that Casey was in a panic and he wanted to try to help, but again he found it hard to talk as his jaw was swollen and bruised so badly from where the rocks struck him. He did, however, manage to squeeze out one word before he passed out.

"Friend."

⁓

Casey was yelling and struggling to get free from the policeman who had him by the arm.

"Fweend!" he kept screaming over and over again. Melissa heard the commotion and bolted out of her house, running towards the back alley and Casey's screams.

Casey saw his mother running, as did the policeman holding Casey's arm. As a cop, his focus was always on the greatest danger and in this case he had only a few seconds to assess whether or not the woman running towards him had any type of weapon and what threat she posed. In the officer's brief distraction, Casey broke free and ran over to Damien to return to frantically untying the ropes. Casey managed to get one rope free, leaving Damien hanging from the fence by only one arm. The other policeman tackled Casey to the ground.

Melissa was intercepted by the first policeman.

"That's my son!" Melissa yelled at the cop. The cop stood between Melissa and his partner, who had Casey on the ground.

"Ok, let's all calm down." The officer tried to defuse the situation. That didn't help, especially when Melissa saw the policeman had Casey pinned to the ground with one arm pulled behind his back. Melissa freaked out when she saw the cop put a handcuff on Casey's left wrist.

"What the hell? Don't you cuff my son!" Melissa was losing it. The larger police officer that had blocked her access to Casey was still trying to de-escalate the situation.

"Ma'am, we're only putting on the handcuffs to protect your son and us. Please understand—"

"Screw you! I don't have to understand anything, he's hurting my boy." Melissa tried to push past the big burly policeman.

"Sorry, ma'am, but you leave me no choice." The officer then grabbed Melissa's arm and pulled it behind her back, twisting her body so that her back was to his front. He then used his free arm to put a binding chokehold on the frantic woman.

Talking into her ear softly, he said, "Ma'am, I need you to calm down; you're not helping yourself or your son. If I let you go, will you be calm?"

Melissa saw that the other officer now had both of Casey's arms handcuffed behind his back and was speaking to Casey in a calming voice, telling him to, "Be calm, calm down." Casey just kept yelling until his voice was hoarse.

"Fweend halllppp. Fweend halllppp. Fweend halllppp."

Melissa was slightly struggling as she was held by the officer. She started to calm down and as soon as the fog of instinctual rage left her, she was able to put some pieces of the puzzle together.

"Officer," she said very calmly. "Would you please release me?" The officer was relieved to hear the woman's much calmer tone of voice.

"If I release you, will you be calm and rational?"

"Yes officer. I will." The policeman released her. Melissa wanted to go over and push the other cop off of her son. Against every maternal instinct, she knew that she had to remain calm. She surveyed the scene, registered that Casey was saying two word's over and over again. "Friend help." She looked at the fence and for the first time she noticed Damien with his right hand still tied to the fence, his body hanging limp with blood covering his hair, face and clothes.

"Officer, may I go help Damien?"

The officer didn't quite get it. "Who's Damien? I thought you said your son's name is Casey."

Melissa wanted to smack the officer upside the head for his apparent stupidity. "No! The boy tied to the fence is Damien."

The officer looked back at the fence.

"You know that boy?"

"Yes, of course I do, he's my son's friend, Damien. Now may I go help him please?"

"No, ma'am, we have already called an ambulance, it's not a good idea for anyone to touch the victim right now."

Melissa grabbed her hair with both hands, pretending to pull it out. "Oh my God! You are as dumb as a sack of hammers. That boy clearly needs help, you moron!"

The officer opened his eyes wide at the "moron" comment. He then placed his arm outwards to show the woman he would block any attempt she might make to run to the boy.

Melissa stood there, shaking her head as she heard sirens screaming ever so close. "At least let me talk to my son, please."

The officer looked over at his partner, who now had Casey standing with the handcuffs binding his arms behind his back.

"Hey Upton, is the perp secured enough for his mother to talk with him?"

"Yes, Officer Chernyk, just let me put him in the back of the cruiser."

Melissa watched as Officer Upton walked her son to the cruiser; all the while Casey kept yelling out the words 'friend help', and looking back at Damien. Melissa called out. "He's only worried about his friend."

Officer Upton commented to Melissa, "Some friend." He said very sarcastically.

"You think my son did that?" Melissa said as she pointed to Damien.

The ambulance arrived, distracting Melissa. She then went to the police car and talked with Casey, calming him down as much as she could. She stood outside the door. Casey was seated in the back of the car with the window open.

"Casey, it's alright." Melissa spoke in as soothing a tone as she could muster at that point.

"Fweend halllppp," was all Casey would say, over and over again.

"Don't worry, Casey, he's going to be ok. See, the paramedics are helping him." She pointed over at Damien.

As Damien was loaded into the ambulance, Officer Upton went over and had a few words with the paramedics. He then came back to the car where Melissa was standing. He said to the other officer, "They're taking the victim to the Rockyview." Melissa made a mental note that Damien was going to Rockyview Hospital. Melissa turned her focus back to the officers.

"Ok, so now that it's all over, would you mind releasing my son so I can take him home?"

The junior Officer Upton started to answer in a snarky arrogant tone. "You really think we're going to—" He was then interrupted by the senior Officer Chernyk.

"Sorry, ma'am, that won't be possible. We have to take him to central booking and hold him."

"Hold him? For what reason?" Melissa said in a demanding tone.

Officer Chernyk shook his head slightly. "We'll be charging your son with assault and battery."

Melissa was beside herself. "How dumb can you be? Can't you see that my son is clearly handicapped? He doesn't have a clue what's going on. Come on, Officer Chernyk—it's Officer Chernyk, right?"

The cop confirmed. "Yes. That's correct."

"Ok, Officer Chernyk, that boy that was tied to the fence is Casey's only friend. There is no way on God's green earth that he did that to Damien."

Officer Upton became agitated at hearing the woman's statement. "You're joking, right?"

About ten feet away, Todd and his friends hid behind a nearby bush right after Casey had chased them away. When they heard the junior officer yell at Melissa, Todd whispered to his friends with a chuckle, "We're scot-free. The cops think that ginger kid did it." All three boys snickered.

"You've got to be insane to think that we wouldn't charge your son with assault and battery!" Upton, the younger cop, sneered.

"Ma'am, we're just following protocol—" Officer Chernyk said, but the junior officer cut him off, and from the tone the young cop was using, he was morally outraged.

"We pulled up and clearly saw your son beating on the victim, who was already tied to the fence. Of course we're going to charge your son!"

Melissa again protested. "No, no, Casey would never hurt his friend, it must've been someone else."

Officer Upton wouldn't let it go. "Facts are facts. The victim was tied to the fence and beaten by your son. I found a stick just a few feet away from where I pulled your son off of the victim."

Todd saw an opportunity. He whispered to his friends, "Now's our chance. Let's go. Follow my lead." Todd stood up and hurriedly walked over to the policemen, his two accomplices in tow.

"Officer!" Todd called out. "We saw the whole thing." Todd was still walking towards the policemen. Casey was calm in the back of the police car until he saw Todd and the other two boys come into his view.

Casey started yelling repeating the word, "Baaad!—Baaad!" was about the only thing that the police understood.

"Officer, me and my friends were walking and we saw our friend Damien tied to the fence, and when we went to set him free, that kid," Todd pointed to Casey in the back of the car, "he chased us away with a stick. And then went back to hitting Damien."

Melissa gasped.

"We tried—" Todd started fake crying. "We tried to stop him, but he just kept hitting Damien with the stick." Officer Upton interjected, turning towards and addressing Melissa directly.

"Yes, we will be charging your son with assault and battery. And now we have three witnesses. You might want to get a good lawyer. Your son's in deep trouble."

Melissa was speechless. Young Officer Upton talked to Todd and his friends.

"I need to get your names and addresses. After we book the perpetrator in, we'll need to come by each of your houses and get a statement."

"Of course, Officer," the boys said. They walked over to the front of the car and Officer Upton wrote down their information.

Todd said, "We have Scouts tonight, but we're home by 9pm if you wanna come then. We'll tell our parents."

The boys then left the scene. The young officer rejoined his partner, who was in the process of telling Melissa where they were taking Casey. "Ma'am, we have to take your son in."

Melissa pleaded with the officer. "Officer Chernyk, you don't understand. My son Casey has Down-syndrome, he's doesn't understand what's happening."

"I understand, ma'am. I still have to follow procedure."

Upton was still agitated and wanted to get moving.

"Listen, ma'am, go to central booking, that's where we will be charging your retarded son." Melissa couldn't believe the negative attitude coming from Officer Upton.

"Down-syndrome. Get it right, you moron," she angrily said to Officer Upton.

"Whatever! Your son is going down for assault and battery."

Officer Chernyk stepped in and handed Melissa a piece of paper with the address of the station.

"Ma'am, you really should bring a lawyer with you. We have to go now." The two police got in the car and drove away.

Melissa ran into the house and her first call was to Rebecca.

"Hello, Rebecca, something terrible has happened. Damien has been taken to the Rockyview Hospital and the police took my Casey away. I just thought you should know."

Rebecca's heart raced as she heard the words. "Are you sure? Damien is at Rockyview Hospital?"

"Yes, Rebecca. Rockyview Hospital."

Rebecca was taken off guard and all she could think to say was, "Thank you." She then hung up the phone and made arrangements for her daughters to go to the Lund's house. Her next call was to Alex.

"Alex, hello." Rebecca spoke as calmly as she could. "I don't want to alarm you, something happened and Damien has been taken to Rockyview Hospital."

"Oh my Gosh! What happened?" Alex replied.

"At this point, I don't know Alex! I'll be dropping Cindy and Carla off at the Lund's house and then I'm going to the hospital. Can you meet me there?"

"Ok Becky, first thing you have to do is stay calm, and then—"

"Alex, I am calm, just tell me if you can leave work early and meet me at the hospital."

"Ok, I'll check with my boss and call you back."

"I won't be here Alex, I'm leaving right now, just meet me at the Rockyview as soon as you can. Bye, I love you."

Alex didn't even have a chance to respond Becky had hung up so fast.

CHAPTER 37 –

Bill's Expensive Penance

LUCINDA WAS STILL off from school on Friday. She made a phone call to Pastor Bill.

"We need to talk, Uncle Bill."

"I'll come right over, Lucinda."

"No, Bill, I'll come to your house. Mother is out grocery shopping and she could come home any minute. I would much rather talk in your private study. Come pick me up." Lucinda hung up the phone, not allowing her uncle to object.

As Lucinda waited for Bill to pick her up, she felt a maturity she had never felt before. She thought about what she would say to Bill. A half hour later, when she and Bill walked up to his house, she opened the front door, followed by Bill.

Stephanie saw her niece come in. "Oh hello, Lucinda, how are you feeling?"

Lucinda smiled at her aunt. "Hi, Aunt Steph. I'm fine, thank you. Well, except for this cast," she said as she looked at her arm.

"Lucinda wanted to talk with me, Stephanie," Bill explained. "Come on into my study, Lucinda."

As Lucinda walked towards the study, Stephanie asked, "Can I get either of you something to drink?"

"Not for me." Lucinda answered first.

"I'm fine, Steph, thank you." Bill followed Lucinda's lead.

Inside the study, Lucinda turned and quietly locked the door so that her aunt wouldn't hear the lock latching. She looked at Bill. "Sit down, Bill," the thirteen-year-old ordered.

Bill looked at her and could tell she was different; she had the same confidence and poise that he saw in Mary.

"Ok, Bill, here it is. Only three people know what I'm about to tell you and we're going to keep it that way. Understand?"

Bill was a little put off by his niece's authoritative tone. "What is said in this study stays here. What can I help you with, Lucinda?"

"Great! That's exactly what I wanted to hear, Bill."

He noticed that the girl was calling him by his first name.

"Bill, I'm pregnant." She waited for his response. She enjoyed seeing the relaxed look on his face change to one of pure fright. "You know it's your child. Of course it is; you're the only one who raped me," Lucinda snarled at him.

Bill chortled as he spoke to defend himself. "First of all, it wasn't rape, my dear. You were the one who wanted to play horsey with me, remember? We went through this two-weeks ago and you agreed to keep the confidence between pastor and yourself a sacred one. And secondly, there's no way I got you pregnant, I'm sterile. Do you know what that means?"

Lucinda grinned at the comment. "It means you're a fucking liar Bill. Now tell me more about what we talked about two-weeks ago."

"Well, as I recall, you agreed that our indiscretion was between you, me and God, and that you would keep the confidence. You wouldn't want God to be upset with you, would you?"

Lucinda smiled wider as she looked the man dead in the eyes and he saw her expression; she meant business.

"Listen Bill. Guilt trips don't work on me anymore, the one and only thing we need to focus on right now is our child and what we're going to do about it."

"I agree, Mary." Bill knew he wouldn't be able to prove that he's sterile so he went along. Lucinda quickly corrected the man's oversight.

"My name is Lucinda! Get your women straight, Bill."

He winced at the faux pas. "You're very right, Lucinda, I apologize."

"So, you got me pregnant and you got me into this mess and you're going to figure out a way out for me." Bill sat shaking his head as Lucinda stood beside him, looking down on him as he sat in his chair at his desk. "So, Bill, how are you going to fix this? Keep in mind the following rules: #1. I will not abort this baby. #2. I will not abandon or give up this baby. #3. I will not be made the bad person here; this isn't my fault." She laid it all out for Bill. He thought for a long time before answering.

"Lucinda, I think I have an idea, but I'll need your help."

"I'm all ears, Bill; what's your grand plan?" Bill could hear the maturity in her words and the confidence with which she spoke.

"Well, you can't stay at home much longer. Pretty soon you'll be physically showing and no amount of clothing will cover up the baby bump."

"Exactly, Bill. Go on."

"As for abandoning your baby—"

Lucinda interrupted. "Our baby, Bill!"

"Yes, yes, our baby," Bill placated her. "Ok, so here's what I'm thinking, how you could keep the baby without raising suspicion. If you were to say you had sex with a boy at school and then go away for a year, you could come back with the baby, no one would even second-guess it."

Lucinda laughed at the man grasping at straws. "Ha-ha, Bill, do you hear yourself? You want to throw another boy under the bus, for your sins. Bill, try again! Remember my third rule. I will not be made to be the bad person in this situation."

Bill hung his head and shook it off. "You're right, that was a stupid idea. Sorry I suggested it." He sat and thought for a while. He could feel the girl's eyes staring him down as she waited for him to speak.

"Ok, well, we can get you sent to Hopewell. You would just have to pretend you lost your mind and I could get you voluntarily committed for a time period long enough for you to have your—" Bill stopped himself and made the correction before Lucinda could. "—before you have our baby." Bill finished his sentence properly.

Lucinda noticed the obvious correction and smiled smugly. "See, Bill, you can teach an old dog new tricks," she mocked him. "Go on, tell me more of your new plan, Bill."

"Getting you committed to Hopewell gives us time for you to have our baby. But then we need to come up with a way for you to explain—"

Lucinda interrupted. "Ok, Bill, your plan sucks ass. Listen up, here's what you're going to do. Step by step. Are you listening, Bill?" Lucinda spoke in a demanding tone of voice.

"Yes, I hear you, Lucinda. What's your idea?" Bill was reeling, he didn't believe he had impregnated Lucinda; but the way she was talking he felt that she would be capable of telling others that he raped her.

"Ok, Bill, here it is, step by step. First, I'll do as you said: I'll pretend to go crazy, you'll need to work on my parents and get them to allow me to voluntarily commit myself to Hopewell. But then here's how it's going to go. First you'll find a way to get me a Canadian passport. In Canada you're considered an adult at eighteen-years-old, so once you secure me a new Canadian passport your next step is clear. You'll then buy me a place to live in Canada, paid for in cash; and you'll also set up a bank account for me, and every month you'll deposit one-thousand dollars."

"What makes you think I have that kind of money? And what makes you think that you can pass for eighteen? This isn't going to work Lucinda." Bill shook his head.

"It'll work, everyone always tells me that I look much older than I am, and it's a lot easier for me to wear make-up and pass for eighteen than twenty-one. As for the money, come on Bill, your house is paid for, your cars are all paid for and you get an annual salary from the

Catholic Church which is more than six figures. Everyone knows you have tons of money and that's exactly why this is non-negotiable, Bill."

"Lucinda, it's not a matter of how much I have, but how I could move that kind of cash without my wife finding out."

"Bill, that's your problem."

He tried another way out of the situation. "And if I say no?" he asked Lucinda and was mortified to hear her reply.

"If you say no, Bill, here's how it's going to go down. I'll go straight to my father, your brother; and I'll tell him that I'm pregnant with your child, that the child was conceived when you raped me."

Bill laughed. "You're bluffing. You already tried that and what did you get for your troubles? A broken arm. I don't think you have the courage to try and pull that one again."

"I thought you might say that, Bill, but things have changed. Did you happen to see how sad my father was when I was in the hospital? Did you know that ever since I got home from the hospital, I don't even have daily chores anymore? Oh, and let's not forget how I know for absolute fact that I'm pregnant. There are people at the hospital who are my friends and they did a pregnancy test on me."

Lucinda sat down on the corner of the desk, right in front of Bill, who was sitting in his chair. She rubbed her belly. "And Bill, I'm sure those friends of mine at the hospital would be more than happy to do a paternity test on my baby when it's born." She smiled coyly at him. "And before you say no, Bill, you may also want to take this into consideration: Charley Rodgers. Did you see what my father did to him? Imagine what he would do to his own brother who betrayed him by raping his daughter. Oh, and don't think I don't know that you're also fucking my mother."

Bill's jaw dropped and he slumped in his chair.

"Well, Bill, what's it going to be?" Lucinda paused and when Bill didn't speak, she tightened the screws all the way. "Ok, Bill, I see how it's going to be. So, we move forward. I go home and I tell my father who the father of my baby is. You won't make it to your Sunday services. You'll be lucky to survive at all, once my father gets his hands on you." Lucinda continued berating Bill. "Your way might even be better for me. I wouldn't have to leave my home, my family and my friends. I would have to get a paternity test done when the baby is born, and then your life would get really bad because not only would I have you charged with rape, I would then go after you in a civil suit, suing you for everything you have. Yes, that sounds like a much better plan to me." Lucinda sneered at him.

Bill was completely deflated. "Ok— ok— you win. We'll do it your way, Lucinda."

The girl smiled at him. "So, let's review, Bill. You're going to get me a new name and a Canadian passport, and buy a place for me and our baby to live. Once you have the Canadian passport for me, you'll open a bank account in my new name and you'll deposit two-hundred and fifty thousand dollars in that account."

Bill freaked out. "What two-hundred and fifty thousand dollars? I didn't agree to that."

Lucinda snapped sharply at him. "Bill, I changed my mind. I don't want a thousand dollars a month. I want the money up front; I don't trust you. Be thankful that I'm not asking you to buy me a car too."

"Mary, you're being unreasonable—"

Lucinda cut him off again. "Oh, wow, Bill you must be smitten with this Mary girl. That's twice you've called me Mary. Get it straight, I'm LUCINDA!" She spoke with a confident dominance.

"Fine, Lucinda, two-hundred and fifty grand, but that's it, no monthly deposits. I'll come up with the money. But you have to follow through and leave and never come back, ever."

"Oh, Bill, that won't be a problem. My parents don't deserve to ever see my child, their grandchild. The only love they are capable of is conditional love. I'm done with them; it's time for me to move on, my child is my priority."

Bill corrected her. "Our child Lucinda."

Lucinda became obstinate with Bill. "Bill, this is my child. You're only the sperm donor; you'll never ever see this child. Keep that in mind." She noticed Bill staring at her bare knees as if he were looking up her skirt.

"There's one more thing Bill. I see you looking. Would you like to have more of this?" She slowly lifted her skirt up until she was certain he could just barely see her panties. She saw his eyes fixated.

"Well, Bill, that's never going to happen again. And—" She pulled her skirt back down, slamming the door on the man. "—and just so you know, if I ever find out that you touched any of my sisters—I see how you're starting to look at Suzanne – if you touch any of my sisters, I'll ensure your world comes crashing down all around you. After all, Bill, Riley is a small town, nothing stays a secret for very long here. You see, Bill, this way we both get what we want. You get to keep your life, and I get to build a new one without you in it! Make it happen, Bill, or else!"

Bill was reeling. "You're not giving me much of an option, Lucinda. Give me some time to get it all together."

Lucinda smiled wide, taking the victory. "Oh, and Bill, you can give me a ride home now."

CHAPTER 38 –

Good Mormon Boys

TODD WALKED INTO Scouts with a cocky strut. Michael and Jimmy, his two accomplices, came over to him and moved towards a corner of the gym before Scouts started.

"Todd, that was awesome how you told the cops that it was that retard who attacked Damien," Michael whispered.

"Yeah, good idea, Todd," Jimmy chimed in.

"Did you guys tell your parents yet?" Todd whispered back.

Jimmy spoke first. "Yeah, I told my mom that we rescued Damien from that boy beating him with a stick."

"I didn't have time to tell my mom before Scouts. Did you tell your parents, Todd?" Michael asked.

"Yes, I told my mom on the way. I said the same thing Jimmy said. Mike you gotta tell your parents the same story. We have to stick together; it's our word against Damien's and the retard."

Michael spoke up a little louder. "Yeah, stick together."

Todd immediately shushed him as the scout leader, the Akela, was coming over towards them.

"Ok, boys, it's time to start," the Akela said. Todd stood still as the other two boys went to the center of the gym to join the other scouts.

"Is there something wrong, Todd?" Akela asked. Todd was a master at faking tears; he started to tear up.

"It's Damien, Akela. He got beat up after school. Some older kid tied him to the fence and beat him with a stick. Mike, Jim and me tried to stop the kid, but we couldn't." Akela was in shock and had a sinking feeling in his gut. "The cops came and an ambulance took Damien to the hospital." Todd pretended to be crying more as he put his face in his hands and hung his head. The scout leader put an arm around Todd's shoulder.

"You boys did what you could; all we can do now is pray for Damien. Would you like to inform the scout troop about the incident? We can all pray for him."

"Ok, Akela, I can do that." Todd walked to the center of the gym where the circle of scouts was assembled. Akela walked beside him with his arm around Todd's shoulder.

Akela announced, "Boys, Todd has something to tell us all." Michael and Jimmy both gave Todd a quizzical look. Todd smiled slyly and winked at them. Akela walked Todd to the center of the circle of scouts.

"Go ahead, Todd. Tell the troop." Todd stood still, pretending to be upset; he paused long enough to ensure all eyes were on him.

"After school, we were walking home." Todd's crocodile tears had everyone concerned. Akela patted his shoulder and offered help.

"Would you like me to tell the troop?" Through the fake tears, Todd didn't say a word, only nodded his head yes. "Ok, boys, after school, one of our own, Damien Solez was accosted by an older boy. The boy tied Damien to a fence and beat him with a stick."

There was a collective sigh of concern from the scout group.

"As far as we know, Damien has been taken to the hospital. So let's all have a prayer for Damien."

The group bowed their heads while Akela said a prayer. Afterwards the group went into their Grand Howl ceremony, which is how all the Scouts troop meetings started.

Akela called out. "Pack—pack—pack!"

All the boys gathered in a circle around Akela and yelled back, "Pack!"

The scouts then squatted down on their heels with their front hands on the floor, mimicking the shape of a wolf. The pack then yelled out, "Ah-Kay-La! We-e-e-e-ll do-o-o-o O-o-o-u-u-r BEST!"

Then the cubs jumped up placing two fingers of each hand at the side of their heads to resemble wolf's ears. They yelled out, "DYB DYB DOB! W-e-e-e-e-ll dob-dob-dob-dob" The scouts all knew the ritual and had learned it since they first joined cubs.

Todd was feeling no remorse even through chanting the Scout motto, "Do Your Best! Do Our Best!" In fact, Todd felt triumphant in victory; he was pretty sure that Damien wouldn't ever come back to Scouts now.

Melissa arrived at the police station at the address Officer Chernyk had given her; she went inside to reception and asked the desk officer where Casey was.

"He's in booking, you'll be able to see him in about ten minutes," the officer replied.

"Ok, good, our lawyer should be here by then."

Rebecca arrived at the hospital and went straight to emergency. She was directed to the recovery room Damien was in. On her way to Damien's room, she was intercepted by Officer Upton.

"Hello, ma'am, are you Damien Solez's mother?"

Rebecca stopped to answer the question. "Yes, I am. Is Damien alright?"

"He's pretty banged up, ma'am. I'm Officer Upton; I was one of the responding officers on the scene."

"I'm Rebecca Solez. Is Damien going to be alright?"

Officer Upton felt duty bound to inform Rebecca of the details of the incident and reassure her they had a suspect in custody.

"I'm not a doctor, Mrs. Solez; but this is a great hospital and I think your son will pull through just fine. I need to ask you some questions, if you don't mind. It won't take long at all."

Rebecca's head was spinning, yet she decided to take a few minutes to talk to the officer, despite the fact that all she wanted to do was see Damien.

"Let's sit over here." The officer pointed to some open chairs in the waiting room corner. The pair sat down and Officer Upton filled Rebecca in.

"At approximately 3:45pm we received a 9-1-1 call and my unit responded. Upon arriving, we saw your son Damien tied to a chain link fence with the perpetrator beating your son with a stick. We subdued the assailant and were accosted by his mother." He opened his notebook and searched for the name. "The mother's name is Melissa Henderson."

"Oh my God! It was Casey? And are you telling me that someone called 9-1-1 and didn't bother to go out and intervene?"

"The woman who called 9-1-1 is ninety-years-old, it's probably a good thing that she didn't intervene. I assure you Mrs. Solez, we arrived on scene as fast as we possibly could with the ambulance arriving soon after. We have the assailant in custody and will be collecting statements from witnesses. I would like to get your address and phone number, and set up a time to take your statement. Not now, but when you have time."

"That's fine, officer." Rebecca gave him her address and phone number; she could no longer focus as all she wanted to do was get to Damien. "I need to see my son, is that ok?"

Officer Upton politely replied as he stood up, "Yes, of course. We'll be in touch within a few days."

As Rebecca walked into the emergency room to find Damien, she began crying when she saw him. Damien's face was a bruised-up mess;

his one eye had a big black, blue and brownish yellow welt and his eyelid was swollen shut. She gasped.

"Oh," she said, covering her mouth with her hand. Damien heard the gasp and opened his one good eye.

"Mom," he cried out in relief. "Mom, you're here, thank you, thank you." Rebecca approached the bed and gave Damien a hug. "It hurts all over, hurts to talk. Mom, Casey saved me." He said through his sobs.

"He saved you, Damien? Are you sure?" Rebecca was now very confused.

"Yes, he did, Mom."

"Tell me what happened, Damien." Rebecca needed to get to the bottom of this.

"I was walking home from school. Todd came up to me and told me to quit Scouts. I wouldn't do it, Mom, I didn't want to quit. Mike and Jimmy snuck up behind me and then they all tied me up to the fence. Todd asked me lots of times if I was ready to quit Scouts, I always said no," Damien said proudly. "I stood up to them, even when they threw rocks at me."

"Damien, why would Todd want you to quit Scouts?"

"He doesn't think I belong anymore because you're not my real mom. That I made my parent's divorce." Rebecca's facial expression was one of pure shock.

Just then, one of the emergency doctors came in to check on Damien and upon seeing Rebecca, he introduced himself.

"Hello, I'm Dr. Connors, and you are?" He extended his hand to the woman for a polite handshake.

"I'm Damien's—" She paused in momentary thought. "I'm Damien's stepmother, Rebecca, or Becky, you can call me Becky." This was the first time Damien had ever heard Rebecca tell anyone that she was his "step" mother. She'd never labelled herself as "step" before. He was disheartened to hear her words.

"Well, Becky. Your son has a few nasty bumps and bruises. With welts all over his body and, as you can see, a very nasty black eye and we're monitoring for concussion symptoms. Right now he's on a slight morphine drip, just to manage the pain. He should be fine in a few weeks. The bruising will go away and he'll be back to normal."

"Dr. Connors, do you know what happened?" Rebecca asked. Damien lay in the bed, absorbing the conversation.

"All I was told was that he was beaten by a boy with a stick; but I personally don't think it happened that way."

"What do you mean, Doctor?"

"Come over here." Dr. Connors moved Becky far enough from the bed that he could whisper without Damien hearing. He leaned into Becky and whispered directly into her ear.

"The injuries don't match the report. Multiple welts on Damien's body are more consistent with Damien's account of the incident."

"Damien told you, Dr. Connors?"

"Yes, of course. We always ask our patients what happened, its good practice to do so. Oftentimes the patient is the most informed of what really happened."

"Thank you, Dr. Connors. How long will Damien be in hospital?"

"We'll keep him overnight for observation, but I suspect he'll be good to go home tomorrow afternoon." Rebecca looked at the doctor and held her hand out in appreciation.

"Thank you so much, Dr. Connors." The doctor left the room and Rebecca went and sat with Damien, asking him to tell the story from the very beginning.

At about 6pm, Damien's father Alex showed up at the hospital. After seeing Damien and hearing him tell his story, Alex was enraged. At 8pm, the parents left the hospital and went to the Lund's house to pick up Damien's step sisters, Carla and Cindy.

～

Cheryl Lund answered the door, greeting the parents with a warm reception.

"Come in, come in. Your girls are downstairs playing."

"Thank you so much, Cheryl, we really appreciate you helping out," Rebecca said.

"Well, think no more of it, Becky, we're all good Latter-Day Saints. We help each other out." Rebecca took note of the comment as it played out in her mind over and over for a few seconds. 'All good Latter-Day Saints,' Rebecca thought; she sensed that Cheryl had heard all about the incident by now.

"It's horrible to think that anyone would be so cruel as to tie someone up and beat them with a stick. I blame all the violence on TV," Cheryl said in a sympathetic, condescending tone.

"Cheryl, would you mind if we sat down for a few minutes?" Rebecca wasn't planning on staying long, but she wanted to correct Cheryl and tell her exactly what happened.

The three of them sat at the kitchen table. Rebecca opened up the conversation as Alex sat and listened.

"First of all, Cheryl, how did you find out that someone beat Damien with a stick?"

"Heidi Wells called me. She told me all about it and how Todd, Michael Hamshed and Jimmy Jensen all stepped in to save Damien."

Rebecca's eyes narrowed as she realized that the witnesses Officer Upton spoke of were those three boys. "And when did Heidi call you?"

"About thirty minutes after you called and asked me to watch your girls; I don't mind at all and I'm glad I could help. I hope the police lock that boy up and throw away the key forever," Cheryl added.

"First of all, Cheryl, I agree. I hope the police lock up the boys responsible, and I hope even more that as good Latter-Day Saints, the parents of the boys all repent for the judgmental way in which they have raised their sons."

Cheryl looked dumbfounded. "What do you mean, Rebecca?"

"Cheryl, I just came from the hospital and Damien told me everything. He told me how Todd, Michael and Jimmy cornered him in the alley. That they tied him to the fence and wanted him to quit

Boy Scouts." She glared as she spoke. "Seems that good Mormon boy Todd Wells has been told by his parents that divorce and remarrying somehow makes people less important to God, and therefore lesser Latter-Day Saints than the rest of those who marry only once. Heidi has been sold a bill of goods by her son Todd. Those three boys are all lying through their teeth. They wanted my son Damien to quit Scouts and they tied him to the fence and threw rocks at him until he agreed to quit Scouts. However, my son wouldn't give in, he wouldn't quit and they stoned him like a scene straight out of the Bible. The boy you think beat Damien with a stick is named Casey and he actually put a stop to it. The doctor at the hospital told me that the report of Damien being beaten by a stick is not consistent with his injuries; he went on to say that Damien's account of what happened is in fact consistent with the many bruises and welts covering his entire body. Welts and bruises that would be caused from being struck by thrown rocks."

Cheryl was sitting straight up with a look of complete ignorance on her face. "Becky, that doesn't sound like Todd, he's a good Mormon boy."

Rebecca slammed her hand down on the table. "Cheryl, get your head out of your ass!" She glared as she stared Cheryl straight in the eyes. "That good Mormon boy is a judgmental little prick! Just like his mother. If you're not perfect in the Mormon Church, you're simply not accepted. Damien is my stepson and somehow the simple fact that he's not my biological bloodline child meant he was judged and tortured by other 'good Mormon boys.'"

Cheryl had had enough and she stood up. "I think you should be leaving now, Rebecca." She then called to her husband. "Ross, the Solez's are here to pick up their girls. Can you bring them upstairs now please?"

Cheryl wouldn't make eye contact with Rebecca or Alex. In the few awkward moments until the Solez's left the Lund's house, nothing more was said.

Once inside the car, Rebecca said to Alex, "I'm going to go over and see Heidi Wells as soon as we get home."

"Are you sure that's a good idea, Becky? You're pretty heated up right now."

"Alex, I have to do this now. You heard Cheryl. Heidi is painting her son as the hero when in fact he is the evil little villain. I want to put a stop to this now."

"Ok, Becky. I'll watch the girls."

Rebecca dropped the family off at home and drove over to Heidi's house.

~

Melissa's lawyer arrived at the police precinct and they were taken into a room where they could speak with Casey and Officer Chernyk. The lawyer extended his hand to the officer.

"Hello, I'm Murray Allstrom, attorney at law." He smiled as he shook the officer's hand and passed him a business card.

The door opened and Casey was brought in; he was wearing an orange jumpsuit.

"Hi, Casey. Are you alright?" Melissa hugged her son as the policeman at the door stood and waited like a guard watching his prisoner.

Melissa turned and looked at Officer Chernyk. "Is this really necessary?" She pointed to the guard. Officer Chernyk looked at the officer and nodded. The guard left the room.

Murray got right to the point. "Officer Chernyk, I understand you have charged my client with assault and battery."

"Yes, we have," the officer replied in a professional tone.

"Are you aware that my client suffers from Down-syndrome, and that he is only fourteen, which makes him a minor?"

"We have a physician on the way to evaluate the suspect. Until then, I can't answer that question."

"And when is your physician going to arrive?"

"I'm not sure," Officer Chernyk replied.

Murray was smooth and confident.

"Well, Officer Chernyk, I don't mean any disrespect, but perhaps you would do well to go and get your captain," Murray instructed. The officer stared at the lawyer without saying a word. Murray continued. "The reason I say this, Officer Chernyk, is that…" He paused for effect before laying the hammer down. "…if my fourteen-year-old Down-syndrome client spends even one night in jail, we'll sue you, your commanding officer, and the entire police department for endangering a disabled minor."

"I suppose you'd like me to go and get my commanding officer, then?" Officer Chernyk politely replied.

Murray responded very sarcastically. "Yes, that would be to your benefit to do so right now!"

~

Rebecca knocked loudly on Heidi's door. When the door opened, Heidi smiled wide and ushered Rebecca inside.

"Hi, Becky, how are you and how is Damien doing?"

"We need to talk, Heidi."

"Yes, come in, let's sit in the living room. We can talk there." Heidi was ever the gracious host. "May I get you something to drink, Becky?"

"No, thank you, Heidi. Let's get right to it." Heidi looked a little bewildered. "Heidi, I was at the hospital and I talked to Damien. He told me everything that happened." Heidi instantly perked up and smiled proudly.

"Yes, well, my Todd was just happy to get there in the nick of time. How is Damien doing?"

Rebecca's nostrils flared. "Actually, Heidi, I think your son didn't get the facts straight. As I understand it, Todd is claiming to be the hero that stepped in to save Damien—when in fact Todd is the master-mind monster that was the main perpetrator."

"What do you mean, Becky? Todd saved Damien."

"Not hardly. Todd, Michael Hamshed and Jimmy Jensen all tied Damien to the fence and then threw rocks at him."

Heidi started to argue. "No, that's not true, my Todd would never—"

"Well, he did, Heidi, and he knows it. Ask him yourself."

"I will when he gets home from Scouts."

Rebecca saw red; she had forgotten that it was Friday and Scouts night. "Scouts! That's exactly what this is about. Your son wanted Damien to quit Scouts."

"Why would he want that? They're friends."

"Three weeks ago, Todd told Damien that I'm not his real mom. He told Damien he must be a bad kid because he made his real parents get a divorce." Rebecca watched Heidi's reaction closely. Heidi paused as if she were lost in deep thought. "Did you tell Todd that Damien's parents are less important because they were previously divorced?" Again, Heidi hesitated. "You did, didn't you? You told your son that you're better than us because you've never been divorced, admit it!" Heidi realized where this was coming from.

"That is not what I told Todd. Todd overheard his dad and me talking and took it out of context," Heidi tried to explain.

"Out of context? And what do you call tying my son to a fence and throwing rocks at him? A justified religious stoning, maybe?" Rebecca's tone was very condescending and in your face. Heidi gathered her thoughts and fought back.

"Todd didn't do what you say, Becky! And when the police come to take his sworn statement, you'll see, he didn't do it. He saved your son Damien, something you should be grateful for and not even question."

"You're really something, Heidi. You think the whole word revolves around you and your perfect family. Well, let me tell you, your son is a monster. A misguided, evil, judgmental child."

"Stop right there, Rebecca Solez. You have no right to come into my house and make these accusations."

"I have no right?"

"You have no right! This is my home and you come in here making false accusations."

The doorbell rang. Heidi stood up and went to the door. She opened it and gleefully invited the guest in. Becky could hear the happiness in Heidi's voice.

"Officer Upton, I assume. Come on in, I'm glad you're here." The officer stepped inside the door.

"Hello, you must be Heidi Wells. Is your son Todd home? I have come to take his statement on the incident that happened this afternoon."

Rebecca heard the officer's voice and stood up and went to the front door to join the conversation.

"Hello, Officer Upton. Remember me from the hospital? I'm Damien's mother, Rebecca Solez."

"Oh yes, I remember you. How's your son doing? I'm hoping to take his statement tomorrow."

"He's very badly injured as you know; but, I've spoken with him about what happened, and to be honest, you have been lied to. You don't have your facts straight."

"With all due respect, Mrs. Solez, I have a suspect caught red-handed by the police and backed up with three eyewitnesses. I'm pretty sure I have all the facts straight." Heidi looked over at Becky with an, 'I told you so facial expression.'

"Officer, when you talk to Damien, he'll tell you the whole story and it will be the truth. Even the doctor backs up Damien's account of what happened. Dr. Connors, talk to him, he'll tell you the truth."

"Well, it was nice seeing you again, Becky," said Heidi, "but I think you should get going. Go home to your family. I'm sure the officer will get to the bottom of the absolute truth once he talks to Todd."

"Oh, you're dismissing me, Heidi. That's fine; I don't need to cause a scene in front of the police. I'll go, but this isn't over, not by a long shot."

As Rebecca was leaving, she heard Officer Upton's radio go off; she didn't think anything of it.

⁓

Officer Chernyk returned to the holding room with his captain in tow.

"Hello, I'm Captain Greenwood. You must be Mrs. Henderson." She offered her hand to Melissa.

"Ms. Henderson, I'm not married." Melissa shook the captain's hand. Murray offered his hand and introduced himself while he shook the captain's hand.

"I'm Murray Allstrom, attorney at law; I represent Ms. Henderson and by extension her son, Casey Henderson."

"What can I help you with today?" asked Captain Greenwood.

"Well, for starters, you can release my client forthwith. And then we want all the charges dropped and expunged from Casey's record."

The captain laughed mockingly. "Not asking much at all, are we?" Before Murray could go into another spiel, the captain laid down the law. "Mr. Allstrom. I'm sure that you're aware that as the police, we can hold a suspect for up to forty-eight hours. In this case, we have a written report from a decorated police officer stating he saw your client's son beating the victim with a stick." Officer Chernyk hadn't seen Officer Upton's report, but he knew that was incorrect.

"Furthermore, we're currently in the process of collecting statements from three eyewitnesses. This seems like a case the district attorney would definitely want to prosecute." Melissa could see her lawyer's heavy-handed tactics were not working.

"Captain Greenwood, with all due respect, I wonder, do you have any children?" Melissa asked.

"Yes, I have three kids."

"As a mother, you can understand why I'm here trying to get my son released."

"Of course, Ms. Henderson, I completely understand; however, my hands are tied. I have Officer Upton's report that clearly outlines that he witnessed your son beating the tied-up victim with a stick." Officer Chernyk shook his head, hearing his captain's words.

"Captain Greenwood. My son Casey has Down-syndrome. He's not capable of handling a night in jail; he's never in his life spent a night away from home. Please, you must understand."

Officer Chernyk pressed a button on his police radio so that it would make a sound. He then tapped his captain on the shoulder.

"Captain, we need to step outside, this is an emergency," he said after tapping his radio.

"Sorry for the interruption, folks. Police business. We'll be right back." The Captain was polite but annoyed as she and the officer stepped out of the room.

～

"Captain. I haven't seen Officer Upton's report, but you said twice that the report states he saw the suspect hitting the victim with a stick."

"Yes, that's exactly what the report says. Is there a problem?"

"We didn't see the suspect with a stick, Officer Upton only found out about the stick after talking with the eyewitnesses. His report is incorrect."

"Get Officer Upton on the radio now, please."

Officer Chernyk did exactly as instructed and radioed Officer Upton.

"Officer Upton responding. What's the emergency?"

Captain Greenwood took the radio from Officer Chernyk. "Officer Upton, are you alone?"

"No, I'm at the Wells residence, waiting to take a statement from Todd Wells."

"You need to excuse yourself and step outside where you're alone, Officer Upton."

The officer excused himself and stepped outside; he saw Rebecca Solez about to open her car door.

"Officer Upton. I need you to think very clearly on what I'm about to ask you. Do you understand?" the captain radioed."

"Yes Captain Greenwood I understand."

"Did you actually see the suspect Casey Henderson hitting the victim Damien Solez with a stick? Think very carefully, Officer Upton! Did you actually see the suspect hit the victim with a stick?" The captain was very deliberate in her tone.

Officer Upton thought for a few seconds. "Captain Greenwood. No, I made an error in my report. I didn't see the suspect hit the victim with a stick." Hearing radio silence, Officer Upton knew he was in for a reprimand. He tried to save his ass. "Captain Greenwood. The victim's mother is here, I could bring her down to the station to give her statement. That might clear things up."

"Did you say the victim's mother is at the Wells residence? Repeat, please."

"She was here when I arrived, she's currently sitting in her vehicle, I could ask her to come down to the station."

"Yes, do that, Officer Upton."

Officer Upton ran over to Rebecca's car, almost slipping as he ran out onto the street and slid on some loose gravel on the pavement. He knocked on her car window. Rebecca rolled the window down as Officer Upton was catching his breath.

"Mrs. Solez, would you mind coming down to the station to make a statement on Damien's behalf, please?"

"And why would I do that at this time of night? Surely it can wait until tomorrow."

"No, really, Mrs. Solez, we have a young man in custody and we really need your statement tonight."

"Which young man do you have in custody?"

"We have Casey Henderson—"

Rebecca interrupted. "You have the wrong guy, you bumbling morons. Let's go down to the station. I'll follow you."

⁓

Captain Greenwood and Officer Chernyk returned to the holding room. Immediately the lawyer started to speak. "My client—"

Captain Greenwood held her hand up in a stop motion. "Mr. Allstrom, if you could both be a little patient. At this moment, we have a witness coming to the station to make a statement. It's our hope that this witness will provide the clarification we need in order to release Ms. Henderson's son. I'll be back in a bit."

"Thank you very much, Captain Greenwood," Melissa answered.

Five minutes later, Officer Upton arrived at the police station with Rebecca Solez. He led her to one of the interrogation rooms where she could make a written statement.

Captain Greenwood intercepted them in the hall.

"Officer Upton, I presume this is Mrs. Solez?" She stepped closer to Rebecca and offered her hand.

"Yes, I'm Rebecca Solez. I'm here to give a statement."

"Right this way, Mrs. Solez." Captain Greenwood led her to a room, opened the door and ushered Rebecca inside. When Officer Upton went to follow her in, his captain put her arm on the doorframe stopping him from entering. She whispered to him, "You won't be interviewing this witness, Officer Upton. In fact, I want you to go to the break room and wait there for me." Officer Upton's shoulders slumped and he walked away.

Captain Greenwood went into the room and shortly thereafter was joined by Officer Chernyk.

"Mrs. Solez. First of all, thank you so much for coming to the station so late at night. We really do need to get this cleared up right now."

"No problem; I want to make a statement." Rebecca was eager to tell the truth of the incident. She retold everything that Damien had told her.

"I'm very thankful and happy that you came here and cleared that up for me. Let me assure you that Officer Upton, who made an erroneous report, will be admonished. In your detailed report, Mrs. Solez, you said the doctor at the hospital confirmed that the injuries your son suffered could not be from a stick. Is that correct?"

"Yes, Dr. Connors said that Damien's account of the story is more consistent with his injuries."

Captain Greenwood looked at Officer Chernyk. "After Mrs. Solez leaves, will you please go over to the hospital and have a talk with Dr. Connors?" She looked back to Rebecca. "It's the Rockyview Hospital, right?"

"Yes, the Rockyview Hospital," Rebecca confirmed.

"Mrs. Solez. Thank you for your statement. Would you mind taking a few minutes to write it down on paper and sign it?"

"Not at all, Captain Greenwood. I hope my statement helps to get the right offenders punished."

Captain Greenwood left the room, leaving Rebecca to fill out her written statement. She went directly to the room where Melissa was. She opened the door and stepped in.

"Thank you for waiting so patiently. We've just interviewed a witness that refutes the statements of other witnesses—"

Murray interrupted with a gleeful tone. "Great, then I will get my client and we'll get out of here."

"Hold on, counsel, it's not that simple. Let me finish."

Melissa glared at her cocky lawyer. "Murray, you're not helping, just let the captain speak first."

"I was—" Murray blurted before Melissa said,

"Shush, I told you. Let the captain speak. You work for me; now hush!"

Captain Greenwood smiled and nodded at Melissa. "As I was saying, we have a witness with opposing testimony. The victim's mother came in and gave a statement in which she tells the victim's side of the story. As such, we will release your son Casey to your custody, but you aren't to leave the city; we're still investigating. Does that work for you?"

"Yes, yes, that's great," Melissa said with a gleeful smile.

"I'll have an officer escort your son to a room where he can change back into his civilian clothes, and then we'll bring him back to the front waiting area. You can wait for him there."

Melissa joyfully agreed. "Yes, that's good, thank you so much." Melissa then went over to Casey. "Casey, you go with the officer. Change your clothes and I'll see you soon."

Melissa, Murray and the captain left the holding room. The captain turned left and headed to the break room where Officer Upton had been ordered to wait. Melissa and her lawyer went to the right towards the waiting area.

~

Rebecca finished writing her statement and handed it to Officer Chernyk. "Thank you, Mrs. Solez."

"You're very welcome. Now you can go get the boys who really did this to my son."

"The investigation is still ongoing; we'll keep you posted."

Rebecca walked down the hall out into the waiting area. She went to the front counter where the desk officer was.

"Do I need to sign out?"

"Yes, Mrs. Solez, please sign here." She handed a clipboard for Rebecca to sign. Melissa had overheard the brief conversation and she realized that must be Damien's mother. She waited for the woman to turn around.

"Are you Damien's mother?" she asked Rebecca.

"Yes, I am." Before Rebecca could say any more, Melissa was hugging her tightly and crying tears of joy.

"Thank you... thank you... for coming tonight. I'm Melissa Henderson, Casey's mother."

"You're welcome. Call me Becky, please. How's Damien doing?"

"Damien is doing ok, I guess. They're keeping him overnight for observation, but he should be fine—a few welts and bumps and bruises, one big black eye. The doctors tell me he'll take some time to heal."

"Thank God for that." Melissa released the hug sounding very relieved. Just then, Casey came through the doors and ran to his mother, hugging her as he sobbed.

"And this must be the famous Casey I keep hearing about. Damien really likes him."

Melissa was patting Casey's back as she hugged him. "Yes, this is Casey, but he's a little rattled right now. Sorry."

"No problem, Melissa, I completely understand. You should go and get him home now."

"Yes, that's a good idea. Good luck to you, and please let me know how Damien is tomorrow. Can you give me a call, please?"

"Of course. And be sure to thank Casey for me. He's the real hero here."

Rebecca left the station. After signing out, Melissa also left with Casey. As they walked out, her lawyer was just pulling away; she waved goodbye and loaded Casey in the car and went home.

CHAPTER 39 –

Hunting Mary

PASTOR CONRAD HAD an excellent service on Sunday. After the service when everyone was gone, he was sitting in his office when a knock came on the doorframe. The door was open and Pastor Conrad looked up to see two tall men in black suits standing in his doorway.

"Hello, Pastor Conrad. May we have a few minutes of your time?"

"Why, yes, of course. Come in, have a seat." Conrad stood to shake the men's hands.

"I'm Agent Smith and this is Agent West." The men each shook Conrad's hand in turn and then took a seat.

"Agents? You mean like the FBI?" Conrad quizzed. Agent Smith laughed.

"Well, kind of; we don't carry badges but we are authorized by the Vatican to investigate issues that could present a danger to the church or its parishioners."

"Authorized by the Vatican, how interesting. This isn't some sort of prank is it?" Conrad chuckled.

"No, this isn't a prank." The agent reached inside his suit pocket and produced a black business card with white scripted letters. He handed it to the pastor, who read the card out loud.

"Agency of the Light." Conrad read further. "Authorized by the Prelature of the Holy Cross." Conrad was stunned to read that part. "You're Opus Dei?" he questioned the men.

"No!" Agent Smith responded. "Our agency is authorized as the official investigative branch of the Prelature of the Holy Cross. Contrary to popular belief, Opus Dei sprang from the Prelature, but it did not replace it."

Agent West also chimed in. "The Agency of Light is necessary to protect the Roman Catholic Church in all areas, we use the acronym of AOL, it's just easier that way."

"Come on, you're shining me on?"

Agent Smith looked at Agent West and nodded his head. In unison, the men reached into their inside jacket pockets.

"Oh no, please tell me this isn't some kind of mob hit," Conrad jested right before he noticed the butt end of the gun in Agent Smith's jacket. Conrad swallowed hard.

"Not a mob hit, you're a very funny man, Pastor Conrad." Agent Smith passed Conrad the item he had removed from his jacket; Agent West also handed over his identification for the pastor to examine. "Take a look; you'll see."

Conrad opened and read Agent Smith's identification first. It read very clearly:

Senior Agent: Sergio Michael Smith

Issued by the Holy See

Agency of Light

Conrad also saw the official Vatican seal, which he easily recognized.

"Ok, I'm convinced, and I have to say I'm also a little bit nervous and scared. Agents, you must forgive my ignorance, I had no clue your agency existed."

Agent Smith spoke in a tone of condescending forgiveness. "Pastor Conrad. We get that all the time; we're used to taking our identification out for verification. AOL is a very well-kept secret, even within our own church."

"Ok, so what can I help you with, agents?"

Agent West explained. "We're here to investigate a report of a young girl who used 'witchcraft.' The Vatican received a phone call a few days ago in which it was reported that a young girl is possessed by a demon and performing witchcraft. It's probably nothing, but were tasked to investigate nonetheless."

"You're talking about a witch hunt. I thought the Roman Catholic Church stopped doing witch hunts when they denounced the use of the Hammer of Witches book."

Agent Smith raised his eyebrows. "The book you refer to is actually called the Malleus Maleficarum, it was written by AOL. And you're correct, the church has long ago denounced the book, mostly because society doesn't understand the lengths we must go to in order to protect the church. Make no mistake, Pastor Conrad, there are instances of official demonic possessions; as well, there have been actual proven cases of witchcraft. Witches pray to, and derive their powers from demons who will often possess the witch's body. We've personally investigated actual instances of witchcraft."

Agent West added. "It's not something the church wants the public to panic about, we heard about this girl in Champion, Mary—" He stopped to thumb through his notebook. "Mary Jones. Do you know her?"

"Yes, Mary Jones, is one of my parishioners, but I can assure you she's no witch."

"Pastor Conrad, nevertheless we need to interview the girl. We came to see you first as a courtesy."

"But why Mary? What's the complaint?"

"Off the record, the accusation is that she used supernatural powers to stop a thrown rock in mid-flight by turning that rock to dust. This is a serious sign of witchcraft."

"I can't believe what I'm hearing. You're saying Mary has the power of telekinesis."

"No, not exactly telekinesis; it's more like casting a spell in which the witch's imagined thoughts become reality. A person with this power is very dangerous; they can basically use their mind to project their will onto objects or even people."

"Well Mary recently had an accident; she was out of sorts for a few days; but she was examined by an experienced parish priest who found her to be free of demonic possession. Champion is a small town, if there were witches here, I'm sure I would've heard about it."

Just then, the phone rang. Conrad just allowed it to continually ring.

"Go ahead, answer your phone, we're in no hurry," Agent Smith said.

Conrad picked up the phone. "Hello, Pastor Conrad speaking."

"Hi, Conrad, I was just calling to check up on Mary. How's she doing?"

"Yes, Pastor Bill, good to hear from you. No, I haven't found a junior pastor yet."

"What are you talking about, Conrad?"

"Well, you know, Pastor Bill, it's harder than you think to find a good junior pastor. They all want to go to Hopewell, because they feel it's safer. Safer to be in a big city than in a small town like Champion."

Pastor Bill realized that there was a masked sense of urgency in Conrad's voice. He figured it must have something to do with Mary so he started asking yes/no questions.

"Is Mary in danger?"

"Yes, of course, Pastor Bill," Conrad said, relieved that Bill caught on.

"Is there someone there with you right now?"

"Again yes."

"Is Mary there with you?"

"No, Pastor Bill, that's not as easy as you think." Conrad's heart raced, hoping the agents wouldn't catch on to his cryptic conversation.

"Is Mary in immediate danger?"

"Most definitely, Pastor Bill."

"How can I help, Conrad? Do I need to drive out there right now?"

"No, Pastor Bill, there's not enough time."

Bill was getting a picture in his mind. "Ok, Conrad, I understand. I'm going to call Sally and James and have them bring Mary to Riley. Will that work?"

"Yes, Pastor Bill. As soon as we can. The sooner the better—I really need a holiday." Conrad paused as if he was listening to the caller. "Oh right Pastor Bill, I forgot to place the order for the hymnals, I'll do that right away, thank you for reminding me, bye now."

Conrad hung up the phone and looked at the agents still sitting in his office. "So, you want to interview Mary Jones?"

"Yes, we would like that very much, Pastor Conrad."

"They were at church earlier. As I recall, the family goes out to the local diner after church every week."

"We appreciate your cooperation, Pastor Conrad. Where is the local diner?" Conrad wanted to stall the men as long as he could, hoping that Bill would get a hold of Sally and James to give them a warning.

"If you can wait for a few minutes, I have to make a phone call and then I can take you to the diner."

"Yes, that would be great, it would save us time driving around." Agent Smith smiled appreciatively.

～

Bill hung up the phone and immediately called Mary's house. James picked up.

"Hello, James. It's Pastor Bill."

"Hello, Pastor Bill, what a pleasant surprise."

"Listen carefully, James. Don't argue, just do exactly as I say, and do it quickly, ok?"

"Whatever you want, Pastor Bill, we owe you so much."

"James, are Sally and Mary at home with you?"

"Yes, they are."

"I want you to go pack a few overnight clothes and get out of your house right now. Leave Champion and drive to Riley. All three of you!"

"What? Why?"

"James, there's no time to explain, I need you to do it now! Pack some things and get out of the house. Make it look like you haven't been home for days and get out of there now. Drive to Riley and go to the church. I'll be waiting for you there."

"Ok, Pastor Bill, we will."

"Don't hesitate James, do it now, please. Trust me, do it, get out of there now."

"Will do, Pastor Bill, see you soon."

Conrad made his fictitious phone call to his own house, where he knew the answering machine would pick up.

"Hi, it's me, Conrad, just calling to talk to you about the quote for hymnals." He paused to pretend that someone was speaking to him. "Oh yes, fifty will be fine. When should we expect the hymnals to arrive?"

Agent Smith and West were in the hallway just outside Conrad's office; they could hear the pastor talking on the phone.

"Ah, come on, we don't have all day," Agent West said impatiently.

"Just relax, West. Having the local pastor as our guide will save us time and effort. It's worth the wait."

"It's been almost ten minutes, Smith, I think he's taking his sweet time."

"Sometimes in these rural small towns, they don't have the same sense of urgency that us big city people have; they take things slow and easy."

At that moment the phone hung up and Conrad called out from his office.

"Ok, gentlemen, I just have to go to the washroom and then we're out of here. I'll take you to the diner."

"Finally!" Agent West whispered to Agent Smith, who just shook his head at the impatient junior agent.

"Sally, Mary, come here now!" The two women rushed out of the kitchen, sensing the urgency in James' voice.

"What's the emergency, James?"

"I just got a phone call from Pastor Bill."

Mary smiled wide. "How's he doing?" she asked.

"It was the strangest phone call I've ever had. He told me to get the two of you and pack an overnight bag and get out of Champion right now."

"What?" Sally was bewildered.

"He sounded very serious and made a point of telling me how important it is we leave now, and we have to make it look like we've been gone for a while."

"It's probably because people around town think I'm some sort of demonic witch. I think we should do what Pastor Bill said. He wouldn't steer us in the wrong direction. How about I go out to the garage and get some of the recent newspapers and put them on the front porch?"

"Great idea," James commended Mary.

"I'm going to go clean up the kitchen," Sally said.

"We don't have time to clean the kitchen, Sally."

"James, if someone came into the house and saw dirty dishes in the sink, they'd think we left in a hurry. It'll only take a few minutes, and then I'll go pack my bag and we'll be out of here."

"Ok, let's get moving, everyone."

~

Conrad rode shotgun with Agent Smith sitting in the back while Agent West drove. Once they reached the diner, Conrad scanned the parking lot for the Joneses' car. He was relieved that it wasn't there. He thought to himself, *Thank God.*

"Ok, let's go in and see if they're here." Conrad opened the car door. The men all got out and went inside the diner. Conrad took his time looking around.

"Do you see them?" Agent West asked impatiently.

"No, I don't see them. I could ask the waitress if they've been in today."

"Ok, you do that, Pastor Conrad," Agent Smith implored. Conrad walked to the counter and addressed the waitress behind the counter.

"Hello, Janice. Have you seen Sally and James Jones today?"

"No, Pastor Conrad, they didn't come in today. Were they at church this morning?"

Conrad smiled because the girl was helping him to stall. "Honestly, I thought they were, but I could be wrong. Maybe they went to Oklahoma City for the weekend. Ok, thank you, Janice, we'll head over and see if they're at home."

Agent Smith whispered to West, "Now aren't you happy we waited for the pastor to guide us? This'll save us lots of time."

West grumbled, "Yeah, ok, it was a good idea to wait."

Conrad approached the agents. "Agents, would you like me to take you to the Joneses' house, to see if they're home?"

"That would be great, if you could, Pastor." Agent Smith smiled.

As they got closer to the Joneses' farm, Conrad fidgeted with his hands. He was getting nervous and hoped and prayed that Pastor Bill had got a message through to the Joneses family.

As they turned onto the road that would lead to the Joneses' home, Conrad saw a car turning out of the Joneses' driveway coming directly at them on the opposite side of the road. He thought quickly.

"Turn right here, that's the Joneses' driveway." Conrad paused and waited for the car to make the turn. "At least I think it's their driveway, it's either this one or the next one." He smiled.

Agent West made the turn just seconds before the Joneses' car drove by. Conrad glanced over his shoulder to the left and saw James Jones driving the car.

"Oh darn. I got the wrong turn. It must be the next one. Sorry, agents." Agent West turned the car around and headed back to the main road, turned right and then took the next driveway, which was the Joneses' driveway. Once they reached the house, the three men got out and went to the front door to ring the bell. They stood waiting.

"I don't think they're home right now. They must've gone to Oklahoma City," Conrad said.

"Ring it again." Agent West listened as he heard the bell chime inside the house. "Ok, let's walk around and check out back in case they're outside."

"Good idea, Agent West." The three men then walked around the house. Agent Smith peered into the kitchen window. "Looks like they haven't been home recently, the kitchen is clean."

"What a waste of time," Agent West complained.

"Pastor Conrad, we'll drive you back to the church. Just let us know if you see the Joneses; we really need to speak with Mary."

"Thank you, Agent Smith. I appreciate that and I'll let you know if I see them."

They dropped Conrad at the church and drove off. Conrad went into the church to his office and thought about calling Pastor Bill, but he was concerned that maybe the AOL agents had his phone tapped or something. He decided to take a trip to Riley the next day.

CHAPTER 40 –

Hiding Mary

PASTOR CONRAD LEFT Champion at 4:30am to avoid any chance that the agents would find out he left town. He made the one-hour drive to Riley. When he pulled into the church parking lot, he saw no other cars around. He then reclined his car seat as far back as possible and took a nap.

At 7am when Pastor Bill drove into the church's parking lot, he noticed the stray car. He parked in his normal reserved spot and walked over to the car. He looked inside and saw Conrad sleeping. He tapped on the window.

Conrad's body jolted as he awoke, startled. "Oh snap!"

"Well, good morning, Conrad." Bill chuckled. "Didn't mean to scare you out of your wits. I see you're here nice and early. When did you get here?"

"Morning, Pastor Bill. I got here around 5:30am, I believe."

"Why so early, Conrad?"

Conrad seemed a little anxious. "Can we go somewhere private, Pastor Bill?"

"Well, yes, let's step into the church."

Conrad replied immediately. "No, no, not the church, somewhere private, Pastor Bill. The church may not be safe."

Conrad's paranoia was obvious to Bill. "Ok, Conrad, get in my car. I know just the place."

They drove across town to the local massage parlor. Bill parked the car and got out. The two men went to the front door and Bill took out his keys, unlocked the door, walked inside and disarmed the alarm system.

"A massage parlor, Pastor Bill?"

"It's all good, Conrad. I'm part owner in the business. I have an office in the back. We can talk there."

The two men sat down in the office.

"Pastor Bill, I assume you understood my cryptic phone call and you contacted James to get his family out of Champion."

Bill grinned. "Yes, Conrad, you were pretty keen in that phone call. Who were you with that you had to be so cryptic?"

"I'll get to that, Pastor Bill—"

Bill interrupted. "Conrad, let's not be so formal, just call me Bill."

"Ok, Bill. So where are the Joneses now?"

"I have them stashed in the local hotel under false names. Their car is in my big shed at my acreage, it's out of sight." Conrad let out a sigh of relief and began to relax a little.

"Ok, great. Thanks, Pastor Bill."

"Just Bill, remember?" Bill reminded Conrad. "Now how about you fill me in on everything?"

"Ok, yes, Bill. Ok, so yesterday after services, two visitors come to my office. Bill, have you ever heard of something called the Agency of the Light?"

"Is that who visited you, Conrad?"

"Yes. Do you know of such an agency?"

Bill looked Conrad directly in the eyes. "I've heard whispers of them, yes."

"Bill, they said their agency is the investigative arm of the Prelature of the Holy Cross, with a mandate to protect the Catholic Church's interests. They had guns in their jackets Bill. What do you know about them?"

"Conrad, what they told you sounds accurate to what I've heard, yes. I don't know a lot about the internal workings of the Prelature of the Holy Cross, but there's a lot of conspiracy theories surrounding the church. This is one of them. Rumor has it that AOL is the Catholic CIA."

"Bill, I believe this is more than a conspiracy. They showed me their identification, which said they were agents of the Agency of Light, and it had the official seal of the Vatican."

"Fascinating, Conrad. So, let's say you're correct. What interest would AOL have in Mary? I assume they came to talk to you about Mary, which is why you wanted them out of Champion so quickly."

"Bill, I'm ninety-nine percent certain that these men were legitimate and they told me they were there to investigate Mary Jones for performing witchcraft."

Bill looked at Conrad with focused attention.

"The rumor around town is that Mary used supernatural powers to disintegrate a thrown rock in mid-air. I asked the men if they meant to say that Mary had telekinesis powers. They said that they have seen people with powers like that and more. They said that the powers come from witchcraft."

"Conrad, witchcraft is a serious accusation. If those men say they are AOL, then they're on a witch hunt."

"They mentioned that, Bill. They said something about their agency authoring the Hammer of Witches book."

"Conrad, it's rumored that the Prelature of the Holy Cross wrote the Malleus Maleficarum. It was originally used as an AOL internal guide for their agents; but then the book got out and members of the church used it as a step-by-step guide to hunting down, interrogating and disposing of accused witches."

"Yes, they said that, and that's when you called and I decided that we needed to protect Mary. I know that she's not a witch; you know she's not a witch."

"I agree, Conrad. Witches derive their power from demons. I interviewed Mary for two days and she never once showed any signs of possession in the slightest. She's not a witch. You did the right thing." Bill's eyes grew wide as his mind turned.

"Ok, so what's our next step, Bill?"

"Conrad, here's what we're going to do. First, we're going to tell James and Sally about AOL and that AOL is looking for Mary. We're going to check Mary into Hopewell under an assumed name."

"I like that Bill, tell me more."

"We send James and Sally back home and they will surely be contacted by the agents who visited you. They'll tell the agents that Mary has been sent away to Europe on an exchange program."

"What about Mary, Pastor Bill?"

"Yes, we should include Mary; she should know that these men are looking for her and that they are very dangerous."

"I agree, Bill."

"One thing about God is that while he presents us with challenges and hurdles to overcome, he also provides us with solutions to all our problems." Bill's excitement was hidden behind his poker face.

Conrad smiled, happy to be working with Pastor Bill again. "Ok, let's go see the Joneses."

They left the massage parlor and went to the hotel. Bill knocked on the door in a secret code type of knock. Mary opened the door. "Pastor Bill! And Conrad," Mary said with a huge smile.

The two men stepped inside the hotel room. Mary hugged Bill.

"Good to see you again, Pastor Bill." Mary whispered in his ear during the hug, "I missed you, Bill."

Sally and James also greeted the two pastors. Conrad spoke first.

"James, I wanted to thank you for listening to Pastor Bill and getting out of Champion."

DOORS OF THE VEIL

"What's this all about, Pastor Conrad?"

"We'll tell you, but maybe we should all sit down." There weren't enough chairs for everyone, so they all just sat on the beds.

"Yesterday after church services, I had a visit from two men. They're from the Vatican, from an organization known as the Agency of Light. It's a secret investigative branch of the Catholic Church." Sally, James and Mary listened intently.

Bill added. "AOL is publicly denounced and secretly supported by the Roman Catholic Curia; and they want to speak with Mary,"

"Why our Mary? There must be a mistake," Sally said.

Conrad turned to Mary and asked her some direct questions. "Mary, did you happen to have an incident at school recently? Involving someone throwing a rock, and you stopped the rock's trajectory, freezing it in the air or something?"

Mary laughed at Conrad's question. "That's the rumor, Pastor Conrad. But it didn't quite happen that way."

"Well, what happened exactly, Mary?"

"Some bullies, Jeff, David and Karl were throwing rocks at Nathan. Jeff threw a rock like a baseball pitch and the rock curved and missed. He was embarrassed and started calling me a witch."

"And what about the boy you pushed, Mary? Did he go flying through the air ten feet like the rumor said?" Conrad asked.

Again Mary chuckled as she answered. "Pastor Conrad, you know how rumors are. Mountains out of molehills, you know."

Bill followed up. "Well, Mary, there was a report made to the Vatican. They dispatched two agents from AOL."

"So what? I have nothing to hide, Pastor Bill."

"Mary, these men, this organization is serious business. They do more than just investigate instances of witchcraft. Kidnapping, interrogation and torture are minor compared to what they have been suspected of doing. AOL is rumored to have assassinated world and religious leaders. I've heard these people are a group that operates autonomously from the Roman Catholic Church. They answer to no one and they don't hesitate to torture and kill those they interrogate. We need to take this as a serious threat." Bill was convincingly scary.

"What should we do, Pastor Bill?" Sally's voice trembled.

Conrad answered, "Sally, we have talked and we think the best thing would be for Mary to go to Hopewell under an assumed name."

Bill nodded affirmative as Conrad explained. Mary thought to herself, *Bill, you dirty dog, this is all just to get me into Hopewell.*

Bill added, "The point is that Mary needs to be kept out of the reach of AOL, if they really want her they'll likely have a bounty on her."

"Oh my God." Sally gasped at Bill's statement. "What kind of bounty?"

"Depending on how badly they want her, the bounty could be well into the six figures." Bill sounded serious.

Conrad spoke up. "James and Sally, the plan is for the three of us to return to Champion and continue on with our daily routine."

James asked. "If those agents do come around, they'll ask where Mary is. What do we tell them?"

"You tell them that Mary is away in Europe on a student exchange program, and whatever you do; don't act nervous or scared. You have to act as natural as possible so they buy the story that Mary is away." Bill answered.

Sally looked at James. "I don't know, James. What do you think?"

"Sally, I think that it's really up to Mary. But my vote would be for Mary to stay here. At least we know Mary is safe here with Pastor Bill."

Mary wasn't quite sure if there was truth in what was being said or if Bill had cooked up this elaborate plan just to get her back into bed. She was certainly curious to find out, so she played it up.

"Mom, Dad, honestly, I'm scared. If those men think I'm doing witchcraft and they're as bad as Pastor Bill says, I would be afraid. I think we should go with Conrad's plan."

Bill was very pleased; everything was falling into place.

"Ok, then, I'll make the arrangements with Hopewell. Mary, stay here at the hotel. I'll come back and get you as soon as I get the arrangements made. I can drive Conrad back to his car and take James and Sally to their car. The three of you need to get back to Champion as soon as you can. And remember, James and Sally, act natural, don't show any fear."

Everyone agreed to Bill's step-by-step plan. They all left Mary in the hotel room alone as Bill drove Conrad to the church first and then took James and Sally to their car.

James and Sally arrived home around noon. As they drove up, they saw a black sedan parked in their driveway.

"Look James; that must be the agents Pastors Bill and Conrad warned us about." James noticed the car as well.

"Listen, Sally, I don't think we should tell them that Mary is an exchange student, I was thinking that on the drive home. If we tell them that they might be able to check if she went on a flight. We'll tell them Mary is at Aunt Peggy's which is in the Ozarks."

The couple got out of their car and the agents did the same. James and Sally walked towards the agents who were standing at the walkway to their house.

James decided to take a comical approach and he called out to the men, "If I've told you Jehovah Witnesses once, I've told you a thousand times, we're devout Catholics and we don't need your Watchtower pamphlets." He chuckled. The taller of the two men laughed along with James while the other didn't seem all that amused.

"No, sir, we're not Jehovah's Witnesses. Close but not quite; in fact, we're rather happy to hear you're devout Catholics." Agent Smith smiled at the couple as they approached.

"What can I help you gentlemen with today?" James said cordially.

"Well, we would like a few minutes of your time, Mr. Jones. I'm Agent Smith and this is Agent West. We're with, coincidently enough, the Roman Catholic Church." He pulled out a black business card and handed it to James.

"Look, Sally, such a nice card. Oh, and look, on the back is the official Vatican seal."

"May we come inside?" Agent West wanted to cut through the small talk and get down to business.

"By all means, the Catholic Church is always welcome in our home. Come on in." James opened the door; all three men waited for Sally to walk in first.

"Can I take your jackets, agents?" James opened the front hall closet.

Agent Smith declined. "We'll just keep our jackets on, thank you Mr. Jones."

"Would you gentlemen like some tea?" Sally offered. Agent West started to decline but was interrupted by Agent Smith.

"Yes, ma'am, that would be nice." He smiled.

Agent West began to protest. "But I don't—" Agent Smith gave him a sharp elbow. James noticed the elbow, but pretended not to.

"So, what brings you to our tiny little town? To our home, agents? And how do you know our names?"

Agent West was taking the silent approach after receiving the sharp elbow. Agent Smith replied, "Well, Mr. Jones, as the card says, we're from the Vatican. We have been sent to meet with you."

"Sent by who?" said James.

"Vatican City. You see, James, we're with the Agency of the Light. Our mandate is to protect the Roman Catholic Church and all its members from forces that would be harmful." Agent Smith was polite and cordial. Sally walked in with the tea and four teacups on a silver platter. She set the platter on the coffee table.

"Would you like cream and sugar, agent?" She looked at Agent West as she poured into the cup she had set in front of him. Agent West looked at Agent Smith and turned his hands over exposing the palms, as if to ask, *what should I have?*

"You look like you could use some sugar, agent. Two lumps or three?" Sally enjoyed mocking the frowning agent. "Three lumps it is." She opened the lid to the sugar-cube jar and used a set of dainty silver tongs to remove each sugar cube. One at a time, she dropped each cube in turn into the teacup in front of Agent West.

"You don't need any cream, agent, wouldn't want it to curdle in your tummy, would we?" Agent West could tell the woman was mocking him.

"And for you, agent, how many lumps?" Agent Smith raised his hand as if to gesture stop. "Only cream for me, please."

"I see, agent. You must be sweet enough already." Sally continued to jest and poke fun at the agents. James did everything he could to hold back his laughter at his wife's clever teasing. James reached over the table, offering his hand.

"I'm James Jones and this is my lovely but sassy wife, Sally." He emphasized the word sassy to let Sally know he had caught on to her subtle mocking of the stoic-looking agent. "But you already knew who we were, didn't you?"

"Of course, Mr. Jones, it's our job." Agent Smith spoke as lightheartedly as he could.

"We're in the area investigating a potential threat to the church. We've heard news that a satanic cult is planning on coming to Champion and setting up shop in your peaceful little town."

"That's terrible," James said as he looked over at Sally and rolled his eyes so that only she could see. "Go on, Agent Smith, we're listening."

"The cult I told you of is targeting young teenagers, and we understand you have a sixteen-year-old daughter. I think her name is—" The agent opened his notebook and pretended to thumb through it to find the name. "Her name is Mary."

Mary's parents were keen people; they could both tell that the agent was full of it. They played along anyways.

"Oh dear, so you think our Mary is a target of this awful satanic cult? What about all the other teenagers in town, have you talked with them?" Sally made her lips into an 'O' shape and then covered it with her hands to feign fear.

"You jest Mrs. Jones, but trust me, this cult is serious business; they lure teenagers with the promise of unimaginable gifts and powers they will receive, and in the end some of the children become human sacrifices for their satanic rituals."

"That sounds really bad," James interjected.

"It most definitely is, Mr. Jones. We'd like to meet your daughter. To find out if this cult has contacted her."

"How will you know if she has been in contact with the cult, Agent Smith?"

"We would simply interview her and tell her everything we know about the cult. Once she knows the potential danger, she would surely tell us if she was involved. Would you mind if we spoke with her?"

Sally was on a roll. "We don't mind at all, agents."

Agent West smiled as he thought they'd get down to business once they talked with Mary.

"Great! When can we speak with her?" Agent Smith asked in an excited tone.

Sally chuckled as James answered. "Well, Agent Smith, our Mary is not at home right now. She's visiting with family in Arkansas."

Agent West finally spoke. "Would it be possible to—"

Sally interrupted Agent West. "Actually, it's not possible to contact Mary right now. She's with family deep in the Ozarks. They have no phones, no TV and no electricity where she's at."

"When will she be back?" Agent Smith asked politely.

"Honestly, agents, it's a personal family matter. We sent Mary away because of an incident at school where some boys were throwing rocks at her and calling her names." James was testing the agents.

Agent Smith said. "So sorry to hear that, Mr. Jones. I hope she returns home soon."

Agent West started to speak again and Agent Smith interrupted. "Well, Mr. and Mrs. Jones, we thank you for your time. We should be going now." He stood up and looked at the other agent. "Let's go, Agent West."

James showed them to the door. As the men were leaving, James mocked them with a snippy comment, "Come again, just not too soon, y'all hear?"

The agents got into their car and Agent West started in on Agent Smith. "What was all that, Sergio?"

Agent Smith shook his head. "They were onto us before we even sat down. They knew we were coming."

"Do you believe that Mary is in the Ozarks?" West asked.

"Not a chance. She's close by. Like I said, someone tipped the parents off," Agent Smith stated.

"It had to be the pastor. And why does he call himself a pastor? Isn't he a Catholic Priest?" West was clearly annoyed with the Joneses.

"West, out here in mid-America, the Catholic Church is not so rigid. Many of the churches here were once Baptist or Protestant churches that the Catholic Church bought and converted. Entire rural towns changed over to Catholicism. It's not all that unusual for a Catholic priest to be called pastor. Some of these rural priests are even married."

"History lesson aside, Smith, why did you make up that stuff about the cult?"

"I could just tell that they were already onto us, West. They knew who we were before we even got there."

"It was that Pastor Conrad who tipped them off, it had to be," West fumed.

"Exactly, West. That's why I made up the cult story; I wanted to give them conflicting information, just to see their reaction. Did you notice how they didn't have a serious reaction?"

"No, they didn't at all, Smith."

"That confirmed for me that they were expecting us, that they probably think we're there to check if their daughter is a witch."

"I think we should pay that Pastor Conrad a visit."

"Not until we have new orders from command, Agent West."

CHAPTER 41 –

Arms of Mary

BILL WENT BACK to the hotel where he had Mary stashed. He opened the door with his key.

"Bill!" Mary rushed to his arms as he closed the door. She was all over him and he accepted her affections; the two embraced and were locked in a passionate kiss. By the time they both fell on the bed their hands had removed most of each other's clothes. After having a mind-blowing round of hot erotic sex, they laid in bed naked with only a thin sheet covering them.

"Bill, was this all part of your plan to get me back into bed?" Mary jested.

"Not entirely, Mary. Although I must admit I'm very happy to see you again."

Mary placed her hand on his crotch. "You're not the only one, Bill." She winked.

"Mary, you need to be serious about the AOL threat. These agents were sent to interrogate you, they're on a mission to find you and they won't rest until they do. AOL is absolutely relentless and ruthless, and they have connections and agents all over the world."

"Bill, you're scaring me, tell me it's a joke." She slapped his chest. "It's all a joke, isn't it, Bill?" She looked into his eyes and saw he was serious.

"I wish it were so, Mary."

Ring... Ring... The phone in the room rang loudly, startling both Bill and Mary.

"Answer it, Mary. Say only the word 'hello'; don't give your name."

Mary leaned over Bill, grabbed the phone and pulled it back over to her side of the bed with the coiled phone cord across Bill's body. "Hello."

Bill listened closely.

"Yes, this is Mary. I'll take the call. Thank you."

Bill put his hands on his head and silently mouthed words to Mary. "*I-told-you-not-to-say-your-name.*"

"Hi, Dad." Mary looked at Bill and smiled like she knew exactly what she was doing. Soon after, her smile disappeared. Bill watched her cheeks turn from an excited rosy-red to white as if she had just seen a ghost.

"Ah— Oh— ok— Dad— I'll tell Pastor Bill." She kept the phone to her ear and then in a somber tone she said, "Tell Mom I love her. Love you, Dad."

Mary didn't even try to hang up the phone; she just let it fall out of her hands. The phone fell in Bill's lap, narrowly missing hitting him in the family jewels.

"What is it, Mary?" Bill asked as he reached for and hung the phone on the receiver. He turned to look directly at Mary; she was in a trance. "What is it, Mary, tell me?"

Bill placed a hand on each of Mary's shoulders and he shook her back to reality.

"What is it, Mary? Tell me, please!"

"You weren't joking, Bill. Those men are real agents of the Vatican and they want to interrogate me."

"What did your dad say?" Mary was in clear and obvious shock. "Did the agents visit with your parents?"

"Yes." Mary said still in a daze.

"What happened Mary, tell me!" Bill wasn't getting an answer. He leaned over and took the girl in his arms, then lay back, dragging her upper body on top of his as he kept his arms wrapped around her. He stroked her hair slowly, running his fingers through her long straight brown hair.

"Ok, Mary, don't worry, you're with me, and I'm not going to let anything happen to you." He thought he heard the girl crying softly; it was confirmed when he felt a teardrop fall on his chest.

After a long period of time just being comforted by Bill's hands caressing her hair, neck and shoulders, Mary spoke in a sad tone. "Bill, he said that the men visited them and were over-anxious to see me. He said that he and Mom wanted me to be committed to Hopewell and they would come get me when this all blew over. He said they felt the men were very dangerous." Mary started crying. "I'm going to be all alone in Hopewell while these dangerous men are after me."

"Mary, you'll always have me. I'll come see you as often as I can. This is for your own safety." Through her tears, Mary tried to joke herself out of crying.

"Well, it's good to think you'll be close and that this wasn't just a big fat scheme for you to get back into my pants." She chuckled.

"Never, Mary. I wouldn't even dream of putting you in a cage that you didn't want to be in."

"When, Bill?"

"When what, Mary?"

"When do I go into Hopewell?"

Bill thought for a moment. "I think the sooner the better, Mary. I could take you there tonight."

"No, Bill. Stay with me tonight." The tone in Mary's voice was fearful and Bill wanted nothing more than to stay with and soothe her.

"Ok, Mary, I'll be back later and I'll stay the night with you. Ok." Mary cheered up a little at hearing that.

Bill went home and had dinner with his wife. He gave some excuse as to some church business that would keep him away overnight. He then drove back to the hotel and parked his car in the back so it wouldn't be seen. He then spent the night in the arms of Mary.

CHAPTER 42 –

Circle the Mormon Wagons

ON MONDAY OFFICER Chernyk let Rebecca know he'd be stopping by to give her an update. When he arrived at Rebecca's door, she brought him into the house.

"Come on in, Officer Chernyk. Come have a seat in the living room."

"No, thank you, ma'am. I won't be able to stay long."

"What's the update, Officer Chernyk?"

"Mrs. Solez, I'm happy to report that we have dropped all charges against Casey Henderson."

Rebecca smiled. "That's good to hear."

"But, Mrs. Solez, we have also wrapped up our investigation of the other three boys. We've also dropped all pending charges against them. We simply don't have enough evidence to proceed further."

"What about Damien's statement? Did you take that into consideration?"

"Yes, ma'am, we did, and we also talked with Dr. Connor at the hospital, and all signs support Damien's claim that the boys tied him up and threw rocks. But—"

Rebecca rudely interrupted. "But what? Arrest those little buggers and throw them in jail."

"Sorry, Mrs. Solez, we simply don't have enough evidence to go to court. It's their word against Damien's."

"So what? Three liars get away with murder?"

"Not quite murder, but yes, Mrs. Solez, they're going to get away with it, there's nothing we can do. I'm very sorry to be the bearer of bad news. I must be going now; thank you for your time." The officer opened the door and left the house.

Rebecca closed the door, went and sat in her living room, fuming mad.

~

The next morning, Bill woke up beside the beautiful young woman. He gazed down at her sleeping form. He rather enjoyed having her arm wrapped around him as she slept.

When she finally woke up, Bill smiled at her. "Good morning, sleepy head." Mary looked up at him with dreamy eyes and stretched her arms above her head.

"Good morning, lover." Mary beamed.

Bill sat up and got out of bed. He went to the washroom and returned wearing his shirt and starting to do up the buttons.

"We should get moving, Mary."

"Bill, make love to me one more time before we go."

"We don't really have time, Mary." Bill pulled the covers off the girl, staring at her naked youthful body. He was tempted, but he knew they had to get going. "Up and at 'em, Mary, let's get going."

"Bill, I want you now. Come take me."

Bill turned around and without saying a word, he did as he was commanded.

"Come take me, lover!" Mary said in an aggressive tone as she spread her legs and lay back on the bed. Bill was powerless; he couldn't resist and he jumped on the girl like a hungry lion pouncing on its prey.

"Oh yes, Bill, yes, yes, yes!" She cried out in ecstasy as the man did exactly what she wanted and took her to the heights of orgasmic bliss.

Rebecca had tossed and turned all night long. She was thinking about what Officer Chernyk had told her. Her mind was spinning.

She woke up feeling more exhausted and tired than she had ever felt before. "I need a pick me up," she said to herself.

As she went about her day, she had an idea. She muttered out loud to herself, "If the law won't give justice to Damien, maybe the Mormon Church will." She went to the phone and dialed up Bishop Graham.

"Good morning, Bishop Graham speaking," the man answered in a kind, cheerful voice.

"Good morning, Bishop Graham, this is Sister Rebecca Jones. I was wondering if I could make an appointment to see you?"

"Well of course, Sister Rebecca. I'm free this afternoon around 1pm, if you're available."

"That would be great, Bishop Graham. I'll meet you at the church at 1pm."

"Sister Rebecca, how about you come to my house we can meet in my home office. It'll save us both some driving time."

"Sounds good, Bishop Graham. I'll see you then." Rebecca hung up the phone with a feeling of relief and hope. She wondered to herself, *'Why didn't I think of this before?'*

Bill watched as Mary got up and out of bed, Bill watched her strut to the washroom and he for sure didn't miss it when she looked over her shoulder and blew him a playful, sexy kiss.

"I'm going to shower, Bill, and you're next after me."

"Make it a quick shower, Mary, we're already going to be late." He muttered under his breath to himself, "She hates when people are late, damn."

After Mary got out of the shower, Bill jumped in as Mary did her make-up and spoke to him through the shower curtain.

"Bill, I have to say, you were amazing, I'm sure going to miss you when I go into Hopewell."

Bill called out from the shower, "Oh, don't you worry your pretty little self, Mary. I plan to see much more of you than you expect. You might even get sick of seeing me."

Mary grinned. "Glad to hear it, Bill. I have to say a part of me is really excited."

~

They drove to Hopewell. Bill walked Mary inside and to the front reception area. He greeted the woman at the counter.

"Well, hello there—" Bill looked at the triangular wooden name block on the counter in front of the woman seated behind the counter. "Hello, Karen. And how are you today?" Mary stood beside Bill with a pleasant grin on her face.

"I'm fine, sir. And, how are you?"

"Life is good, Karen. We're here to check this lovely young lady in. Would Dr. Williamson be available by any chance?"

"Of course. I'll page her to reception. One moment please." She picked up her phone, "Dr. Williamson, you have a couple of visitors." She put her hand over the mouthpiece of the phone, looked at Bill and asked, "Who may I tell her is here?"

"You can let Veronica know that Pastor Bill and Mary are here to see her for an admittance interview."

"Dr. Williamson, it's Pastor Bill and Mary here to see you." She hung up the phone and addressed Bill. "The doctor will be right out, Pastor. Feel free to take a seat in the waiting area."

Bill smiled and nodded. "Well, Karen, thank you very much."

Mary and Bill waited for about five minutes. They spoke softly to each other so as not to be overheard by the receptionist.

Mary looked around at the brightly lit room; the marble floors in the hall were shined to a polished mirror finish. "Bill, this place looks really nice. I think I'll like it here. Maybe I won't ever want to leave." She chuckled.

"Hopewell is a top-shelf, very professional institution. I have brought a few patrons here over the years."

"What about my clothes, Bill? I don't have very many clothes, only enough for three or four days."

Bill laughed. "Three or four days, Mary – that's what you call an overnight bag?" In response, Mary lightly punched Bill in the shoulder.

"Well, Bill, you know a lady can never have enough outfits." Mary teased with a wink and a sensual lick of her lips.

"William Hall!" Mary heard a voice booming as it echoed through the waiting room. She turned to see a tall blonde woman dressed in business slacks, a low-cut, almost see-through blouse with four-inch stilettos, wearing a pristine white lab coat over it all.

Bill leaned over and whispered in Mary's ear. "This is all your fault little lady, just remember that." He poked her in the ribs.

"Hello, Veronica—"

The doctor interrupted Bill before he could hardly get a word out. "You're late by two hours!" She was walking towards Bill, who stood up out of his chair to meet the woman. Mary half expected the woman to slap Bill.

"Veronica, please forgive me. We had an unexpected but pleasurable delay." Bill used cryptic language. Mary liked it when he did that, sending out secret messages to her that only she would understand. She stood up to stand beside Bill as she watched him lean in and hug the woman.

"Pleasurable, huh? I get it," Veronica said with a knowing wink and a sly smile. After the two broke the hug, the woman looked to Mary, smiled wide and in a softer yet still commanding voice, she introduced herself. "And you must be the beautiful smart young lady that Bill has raved to me about." She offered her hand to the now blushing girl. Mary thought to herself, *Bill told this woman I was beautiful and smart.* She extended her hand and felt the woman's hands were soft yet her handshake grip was quite firm.

"Yes, I'm Mary. Not sure about beautiful and smart, but I'm Mary."

Bill injected himself into the conversation. "Don't sell yourself short, Mary. You are—"

Again, Veronica interrupted Bill. "Zip it, Bill. You're already in the doghouse for being late. Don't add to it by interrupting me while I speak with this obviously stunningly beautiful young lady."

Veronica smiled at Mary as Bill objected, "But it wasn't my fault."

The woman took Mary by the hand, looked at Bill and jokingly pushed her chin up and turned her head slightly away from him in a mockingly playful gesture of snobbery.

"Yes, well, Bill I don't want to hear another word from you. Its Mary I want to talk to. I can hardly wait to get to know this intriguing young woman." Mary found herself blushing uncontrollably.

Dr. Williamson walked Mary down the hall; the doctor's stilettos could be heard echoing loudly throughout the hallway. They walked into the doctor's office and the three of them sat down and talked.

"Mary, it truly is a pleasure to meet you. I understand you would like to commit yourself to Hopewell. Is this true?"

"Yes, Dr. Williamson, from what I see so far, I'm impressed, and I feel it would benefit me to come to Hopewell."

"Mary, call me Veronica, or Dr. V, all the girls call me Dr. V. We're really casual around here."

Bill smiled at Mary as Veronica spoke.

"Well, let me tell you a little bit about Hopewell." She paused and looked into Mary's eyes.

"I would very much like that, Veronica— Oops, I mean Dr. V."

"Either one is fine, Mary. I don't mind as long as you don't call me Dr. Williamson—that's my father." She winked at the girl. She sat up and placed her hands on the desk, clasping them together and apart again.

"First of all, we have a registered functioning school that accommodates Grades 1 through 12. You'll be expected to attend classes Monday through Friday. Do you like school Mary?"

"Yes, Dr. V, very much so. I love to read and write."

"We have breakfast, lunch and dinner in the cafeteria. The food here is amazing. Our chefs get rave reviews for the delicious dishes they cook up and the eatery is more like a fancy restaurant than a cold dingy cafeteria."

Mary's eyes were wide as she nodded her head up and down.

"At Hopewell we strive to build up our members. To give them the skills and tools to be happy and successful in life. In addition to educational classes, we have optional group activities and field trips to visit outside of the institution. Do you like sports, Mary?"

"I guess that depends, Dr. V, on the sport."

"Fair enough, Mary. Saturdays we have a cinema night, complete with peanuts, popcorn, pop, hotdogs and all the things you would find at a regular movie theater."

"I like what I'm hearing." Mary beamed. Veronica smiled and continued with her Hopewell sales pitch.

"We're very proud of our prenatal wing. All our expectant mothers are housed in this wing. We have bi-weekly prenatal courses as well as access to the best birthing rooms south of the Canadian border."

"Oh, Dr. V, I won't be needing that." Mary chuckled. "I don't plan on getting pregnant any time soon." The doctor gave Bill a funny expression that Mary picked up on. "Dr. V, did you think I was pregnant?"

The doctor didn't answer, again looking at Bill and waiting for him to say something. "Ok, Bill, you can speak now. I forgot I told you to zip your lips."

Bill laughed at the comment, turned to Mary and explained. "Mary, I have brought quite a few young ladies like yourself to these halls. Many of them are good Catholic girls who have become pregnant and simply needed a safe place to go for the duration of their pregnancy. Some of those girls I rescued from abusive religious families and brought them here for protection. Hopewell is a safe haven for young ladies."

Veronica added, "It's also for young men, and anyone who is being persecuted, be it socially, religiously or even politically. We're a safe haven for everyone who needs it and can live by Hopewell rules."

"But Bill, I'm not pregnant and I have a wonderful home life. My parents treat me good."

"Yes, Mary, I know." Bill then turned to the doctor and explained, "I brought Mary here because she had a traumatic experience and is here to rest, recharge and become the amazing woman that she is meant to be. In her hometown there is a big rumor mill and the gossip about Mary is unbelievably cruel."

"Mary, tell me more about what Pastor Bill is referring to, please."

"Well, Dr. V, I got hit by a car, fell down and hit my head, and now everyone thinks I'm crazy." Mary paused and looked at Bill.

"Veronica, there's no major drama here. Mary's not crazy. Her town is just unbearable and to be honest, I felt she would be a good fit here in Hopewell." Bill stated.

"Mary, do you have any questions?" Dr. V asked.

"Yes, Dr. V. You said 'members'; don't you mean 'patients'?"

"Ssshhh, Mary! Don't tell anyone. Hopewell is not an actual asylum. It used to be, but when my company bought it out, we changed from an asylum to a safe haven for young and promising ladies and men." She smiled as she completed her sentence.

Mary didn't know what to say. It was quiet for a second when Veronica broke the silence.

"In all seriousness, Mary: we didn't change the name, as it adds to the building's security. No one wants to break into an asylum. And rest assured, Mary, our security here at Hopewell is second to none. Our members are well cared for and protected. How does this all sound to you, Mary?"

"I love it, Dr. V, where do I sign?" Bill and Veronica both chuckled at Mary's comment.

"Oh, Bill, you're absolutely right. Mary is very bright and the perfect fit for Hopewell. I sincerely hope that she chooses to stay."

"Dr. V, I'd like to stay!" Mary said very excitedly.

Rebecca was getting ready for her meeting with Bishop Graham. She looked at herself in the mirror and decided to change her skirt to one that didn't show as much leg. She changed into her favorite skirt that drew down just below the knees. She wore a nice red blouse to contrast her black skirt. She carefully applied her make-up and did her hair. The last thing she put on was a little bit of perfume.

She drove over to the bishop's house and arrived fifteen minutes earlier than the arranged time. She walked up and knocked on the door. The door opened and Bishop Graham smiled and invited her inside.

"May I take your jacket, Sister Rebecca?" She turned her back to the bishop giving him better access to take the jacket. She wiggled out of it as he took it from her shoulders.

"Thank you, Bishop Graham." As they walked into the home, Rebecca noticed that it sounded quiet.

"Where are your wife and kids, Bishop Graham?"

"Kids are at school and the wife is out shopping; no one will be home for a few hours, Sister. Would you like a refreshment? Juice, water?"

"Sure, Bishop Graham, I'll have a water, please and thank you."

The Bishop walked in front of Rebecca to the door just off to her right. He opened the door. "That's my study, Sister Rebecca, feel free to make yourself comfortable. I'll be right in."

Rebecca walked into the beautiful room. One whole wall was all oak bookcase with every shelf filled with neatly placed books. She looked at the big desk and wondered if it was mahogany or oak.

There was a large high-back leather chair behind the desk and two regular leather chairs on the opposite side of the desk where Rebecca was standing.

Off to Rebecca's right was an all-glass rectangular coffee table in front of the three-cushion leather sofa. Rebecca, having completed a check of her surroundings, sat down at a chair across from the bishop's desk.

The Bishop came in with two glasses of water. He went over to the coffee table and placed two coasters before putting the glasses of water on the table.

"Sister Rebecca, why don't you come over and sit on the sofa? This is a relaxed meeting, no need to sit at the desk."

Rebecca stood up and walked over to the sofa, picking a seat on the left. The Bishop sat down beside her, leaving about six inches of distance between them.

"Sister Rebecca, what is it I can help you with today?"

"Well, Bishop Graham, I wanted to come to you to find out if the church would step in and punish the three boys who attacked my son, Damien. I assume you've already heard what happened."

The Bishop looked into her eyes. "Yes, such an unfortunate incident indeed. Is that why you weren't at church yesterday?"

"No, Bishop, it wasn't unfortunate. Todd Wells planned the whole thing and, for a lack of better words, he was judge, jury and executioner in a trial where my son was found guilty and convicted and nearly stoned to death. And yes, we didn't go to church yesterday as Damien is still quite bruised and I didn't want to subject him to his three attackers until I have a resolution."

The Bishop listened without any response. He did, however, move a little bit closer to the woman and now his knee was within a half inch of Rebecca's knee.

"We went to the police and they have decided not to press charges because it's those three boys' word against Damien's word. That's not right to me at all and I thought that if the police won't help me, maybe the church will. So here I am."

"Yes. Here you are, Sister Rebecca," the bishop said with a gleam in his eye. "And how do you think I can help, Sister Rebecca?"

"Well Bishop Graham, I thought that maybe you could take my complaint and perhaps then my son would get some justice. At the very least, maybe we could get Todd and his two friends and their families moved to a different ward. It's just not fair for my boy to have to see his attackers every Sunday at church."

"Well, Sister Rebecca, you certainly give a convincing argument." The Bishop now rubbed his knee against hers and every time Rebecca moved her knee the bishop would move even closer."

~

Mary finished signing all the admittance paperwork. Veronica then led Mary and Bill to the room where Mary would be staying.

"We're here, Mary. This is your room." Veronica opened the door and stood to the side as Mary walked in, followed by Bill.

"Wow, Dr. V, this is great!" She opened the bedroom closet. "Yeah, I'm going to need some more clothes."

Bill assured Mary, "I'll get more of your clothes from your parents. I'm sure a young lady like you can fill this closet."

"Oh, I don't know, Bill. This is a pretty big closet." Mary looked to the other side of the room where there was a door beside the large picture window with rolling blinds and beautiful curtains.

"Where does that door go to?"

"Go ahead, Mary, open it. See for yourself," Veronica encouraged her. Mary opened the door. "Oh my God!" she screamed excitedly.

"Is this mine? All mine?" Bill looked over Mary's shoulder to see the glistening clean bathroom, complete with a large soaker corner tub with rain frosted windows allowing in natural sunlight, a stand-up glass shower, a toilet and a double sink counter.

"Wow, Mary, it's nice," Bill said.

"It's more than nice, it's amazing!" Mary beamed.

Veronica spoke up. "Yes, Mary, this is all yours. Here at Hopewell, your room is your sanctuary. The kitchen, cafeteria lounge and three

TV rooms are all common share rooms, but your bedroom is yours and yours alone. But there is a downside, Mary." The girl was still very much excited.

Veronica took a few steps to just inside the bathroom. She opened first a larger closet about two feet wide.

"Here's your towel closet and laundry collection." She then opened the slightly smaller closet beside it to reveal a broom, dust pan, small upright vacuum and cleaning supplies. "You're responsible for keeping your own room clean. And here at Hopewell we have high expectations that our young ladies and men will be responsible and keep their rooms clean at all times. Can you do that, Mary?"

"Oh yes, oh yes, Dr. V, I surely can. Thank you. Thank you."

Bill stepped back as Mary walked back into the room, looked around again and smiled widely.

"Ok, well, Mary, I'll get going and get out of your hair. Enjoy your new home." Bill turned and opened his arms to the girl.

She stepped forward and gave him a hug, whispering in his ear, "Thank you, Bill, I love it all."

"Mary, I'll show you around the facility and introduce you to some other girls." Veronica turned towards Bill and they exchanged a hug.

"Thank you, Veronica, it's always my pleasure."

"Bill, the pleasure's all mine."

Bill left Hopewell and headed straight for his office at the church.

~

Rebecca explained everything that had happened to her son in great detail. The bishop paid attention not so much to the words Rebecca spoke but more to the V-neck blouse and the modest cleavage that she was showing. His eyes would ogle her from her legs to her chest and back again as she told Bishop Graham the entire story of how her son was assaulted.

"So, Bishop Graham, you can see why I think it would be very uncomfortable for the Wells to remain in the same ward as my family." The Bishop was lost in his ogling and didn't really realize it was his turn to speak. "Bishop Graham, what do you think?" He snapped out of it and recovered nicely; his knee was still slowly rubbing up against hers.

"Well, Sister Rebecca, I completely understand and I think that we could work something out, but I would need a quid pro quo." Rebecca looked at him, puzzled. "I can help you, Sister, but I need you to help me out as well. You're an attractive alluring woman, and I'm a handsome virile man." She half smiled at the compliment. "I scratch your itch, you scratch my itch, Rebecca. Do you get my drift?"

"I think so, Bishop Graham," she agreed although she wasn't absolutely certain if she really understood what he wanted.

He then placed his right hand on her knee as he put his left hand on her right shoulder.

"I'm very happy to hear that you agree, Becky." He grinned as his left hand moved behind the woman's head; his right hand moved upwards from her knee to her mid-thigh as his hand massaged her bare flesh.

"Bishop Graham—" she started to say before being interrupted.

"Call me Steve, we're all good here." His hand moved really far up her skirt and he now leaned his head towards her as his left hand gently pulled her forward. He opened his mouth, turned his head to the side and kissed the woman square on the lips.

Rebecca pulled her head back slightly. "Bishop Grah—" He pulled her head forward and kissed her hard on the mouth, interrupting her words. Rebecca was surprised and her body froze. At this point she was in shock and couldn't think straight; she just let the man kiss her. As soon as he felt her resistance wane just a little bit, he took that as a sign of permission.

His hand pushed all the way up her skirt and his left hand began undoing her blouse. Rebecca felt as if time stood still and she was powerless as this man took what he wanted from her body.

Within seconds he had removed her undergarments, pushed her skirt all the way up and opened her blouse, exposing her bra-covered breasts. The next thing she knew, the man was on top of her and she couldn't breathe as he entered her body.

She cried out, "Please stop!" The bishop ignored her words and continued with his sexual assault.

"Stop— stop— stop— Bishop, stop, no!" Rebecca yelled out. Her screams only served to urge the man on more. When he finished, he got up off the woman, looked at her with an expression of disgusted satisfaction.

"Becky. You liked it and you know it. Don't try to pretend otherwise."

"No, I didn't! I told you to stop."

"The way I see it, Becky, you came to my house in the middle of the afternoon when you knew my wife and children were gone. You came with the express purpose to seduce me. Wearing that low-cut blouse, the skirt, the make-up and that perfume. Mmm," the bishop cooed.

"I didn't want that," Rebecca said.

"You came over here with the express purpose to seduce me in order to convince me to remove the Wells family from our ward. You planned to use your feminine wiles to get exactly what you wanted, and when I declined to remove the Wells family, you became agitated and threatened to accuse me of rape."

"You raped me!" she yelled at the bishop.

"You say rape; I say you seduced me with a very specific purpose. It's your word against mine and I'm a decorated, long-standing bishop in the Mormon Church. You— you—" Rebecca started crying. "Well, put it this way, Becky. You're a woman with a past. An alcoholic who couldn't keep her first marriage together and has only gotten sober long enough to hook a good man like Alex Solez. You probably did to him exactly what you did to me. You seduced him and put him under your sexual spell and convinced him that you've changed."

"I didn't." She spoke through her tears.

"Yes, you did! And on the many occasions that I have counseled you, you've told me how much you crave the alcohol, how you miss it. If you insist on saying I raped you, I'll have to reveal that I believe you to be drinking again and unstable. An unstable Mormon and an unstable mother; you'll lose your children."

"No— no— I'm not drinking." Rebecca had no idea how easily the bishop had manipulated her.

"Becky, this could have been a nice thing, but then you had to go and cry rape. I suggest you get your drunk whore ass out of my home this very second."

She stood up and straightened her clothes, leaving her ripped undergarments laying on the floor as she headed for the door.

"Oh, and Becky, I think it's you and your family who'll need to look for a new ward. The Wells will be staying right here in this ward."

She left the home of the bishop more dejected now than ever before.

CHAPTER 43 –

Bill's Betrayal

THE FIRST THING Bill did when he got into his office was pick up his phone and make an important call.

A female voice answered the phone. "Hello, you have reached the Offices of the Vatican, how may I direct your call?"

Bill replied, "I would like to speak to Cardinal Ad Lucem."

"Who is calling, please?" the woman asked.

"This is Father William Hall of Riley, Oklahoma."

The line clicked and sounded like it went dead. A moment later, a male voice came on.

"Cardinal Ad Lucem's office. Compromise is a word found only..."

Bill knowingly replied to the cryptic sentence. "...in the vocabulary of those who have no will to fight." The phone clicked again and another voice came on the line.

"Father William Hall, please state your member ID and code."

"Father William Hall 23767, code word: Archangel."

"You have reached the Agency of the Light. How may I be of service, Father William?"

"I understand the agency is looking for a young lady named Mary Jones. I know where she is."

The voice paused and Bill could hear keyboard clicks.

"Father William. Where are you?"

"I'm in Riley, Oklahoma."

"We have agents near to you in Champion."

"Yes, I'm an hour away." Bill stated.

"We can have our agents meet you at your church in one and a half hours."

"I'll be there, is there a reward for Mary Jones?" Bill asked.

"There is a substantial reward for information leading to the capture of Mary Jones."

Bill smiled as he hung up the phone.

⁓

Rebecca went home and went straight to the bathroom, got in the shower and scrubbed her body from head to toe.

After a long shower, the hot water had run out. Rebecca got out of the shower then dressed in a pair of flannel pajamas. She went to the kitchen freezer, dug around in the back and found a full bottle of Amaretto. She took a swig and placed the bottle back in the freezer.

⁓

That afternoon at just before 4pm, Bill was in his office at the church when he heard the doors open and two sets of footsteps walked through the church. He stood up and by the time he reached his doorway, the two men were standing just outside the door to Bill's office. Bill noticed they were wearing finely tailored black suits, as he expected."

"Good evening. How may I help you gentlemen?"

The taller of the two men spoke. He pushed his left arm out, revealing a large gold watch on his wrist. He placed his other hand on each side of the watch and wiggled it slightly.

"Would you happen to have the time? My watch seems to have stopped, Father."

Bill watched as the man started to remove his watch and Bill looked down, pushing his left arm forward to reveal his own watch. A black one with gold face. He wiggled his watch in the same manner.

Bill saw the man turn over his watch; the back side of the watch contained the official Vatican seal.

"I do have the time, agent." Bill removed his watch to reveal the exact same Vatican seal on the underside of the watch.

"I'm Agent Sergio Michael Smith and this is Junior Agent Matthew Julius West, my junior apprentice."

"I'm Pastor Bill Hall. Pleased to meet you, agents. I have much to tell you. Come have a seat." The agents looked happy and relieved to finally get a credible lead in the Mary Jones case.

"Agents, I understand that you're looking for Mary Jones."

"Yes, we have been looking for her for days now," Agent Smith replied. Bill smiled like a Cheshire cat that just caught a mouse. Agent West became excited at Bill's smile.

"Pastor Bill, please tell me you know where she is!" Agent West exclaimed.

"I most certainly do, agents. However, she's in a secure facility and you'll need my help to get her out."

Agent West's excitement turned to immediate frustration. "We can get into any secure location there is," he said in an admonishing tone.

"Agent West, let the man speak. He sounds like a man with a plan." The wise Agent Smith was right on the money. Bill went on to explain the plan he had come up with to deliver Mary to the agents.

Bill handed Agent Smith a piece of paper with an address written on it.

"I'll call you in the morning between 7am and 7:30am, and somewhere between 9:30am and 10:00am, I'll bring Mary to the address on the paper I handed you. I'll drop her off in the secluded parking lot at the rear of the bus station. When I drive away you can snatch her up and our business is concluded."

Agent Smith laughed and stated, "And forty-eight hours later your agency bank account will get a healthy two-hundred and fifty-thousand dollar injection of funds."

Bill smiled at the two agents, licked his lips slightly and replied, "Damn right it will. But the money is not the reason I do this. It's all about doing the Lord's work. The Light shall Shine Eternal."

Both the agents replied at the same time as if they were saying Amen. "And the Light shall Shine Eternal."

"Thank you, Father William. We'll be there at the appointed time." Agent Smith expressed his gratitude.

"But remember: you must wait until I drive away. I can't be implicated if you are seen. Do you understand?"

Agent Smith assured Bill, "We absolutely understand, Father William. Thank you once again."

The two men stood up and exited the church. Bill sat in his office with dollar signs in his eyes.

It was Tuesday and Alex had bowling league and wouldn't be home until later. Rebecca made dinner for the children, put them all to bed, and that evening she went back to the freezer, dug out the bottle, took a glass out of the cupboard and went to the living room to sit in the darkness.

The only light in the room was the moonlight from the half-moon that shone in through the front window. It gave just enough light for Rebecca to see enough to be able to pour the alcohol into her glass.

It was just before 10pm when Damien woke up with a tummy ache. He went to the kitchen to get a glass of milk to settle his stomach. Just then, he heard the front door open and he knew his dad was home. He stayed in the kitchen, leaving the light off.

As Alex walked by the living room, he thought he saw Rebecca sitting in the chair. He flipped the light switch on the wall which turned on the lamp between the chair and sofa.

"Becky, what are you doing?" he asked as he noticed the bottle of Amaretto on the side table beside the chair she was sitting in. He saw the glass in her hand and instantly his heart sank. "Becky, what are you doing?" he repeated a little louder. His wife didn't answer. He walked over to her and sat on the sofa beside the chair. He looked at her face and could tell she had been crying as her mascara was running down her cheeks and her eyes were all puffy and bloodshot. "Becky! Answer me! What are you doing?" She just sat there in a daze; she wouldn't even look at him.

Alex shook his head and grabbed the glass from her hand. "What's this?" He sniffed the liquid in the glass and recognized that it was exactly as he thought, alcohol. "Why, Becky, why?" Alex's tone was full of disappointment.

"Geave thaaat bayck to mae." Becky slurred her words.

"No, Becky. You don't need to drink. Now tell me what happened. Why are you drinking again?"

Damien could clearly hear his parents from the kitchen. He leaned with his back against the wall, just about ten feet from the living room where his parents were.

"Becky, tell me now! Why are you drinking again? This is getting annoying, answer me!"

"Why Aleeeeeex? What does it mattttaaa anywwwaayss?" she yelled back at him, still slurring her words.

"It matters, Becky. This isn't the woman I married, not the woman I love. Why are you drinking again? Why now?"

"You—" she slurred.

"What do you mean me?" Alex demanded to know why he was the cause of her drinking.

"You only love me if I'm the perfect little Mormon wife."

"That's ridiculous, Becky, I love you—"

Becky went on a drunken tirade, interrupting Alex. "Everyone—
everyone— you— the police— the bishop— everyone is against me.
You only love me if I fit into your perfect little world."

She then stood up out of the chair on wobbly legs and grabbed
for the glass Alex had placed on the coffee table. Alex reached for the
glass and got it first. Becky became irate and slapped him across the
face. *SLAP!*

The loud slap worried Damien as he listened, wondering if he
should run out and tell his parents to stop.

"Give me that, Alex."

"No, Becky, you don't need it."

"Fine!"

Becky then grabbed the entire bottle and stumbled three steps
away. Alex put the glass down and gave chase. Becky moved the wrong
way and was cornered.

"This is mine. Get away, Alex," Becky warned.

"Give me the bottle, Becky."

"No."

"Give it to me now, Becky!" Alex barked. Her reaction was to place
the bottle to her lips and take a big swig, so big that some of the alcohol
dribbled from the corners of her mouth.

"Stop that, Becky!" Alex demanded.

"No, it's mine!" Becky was intent on keeping her bottle. Alex
pushed his body against hers, trying to isolate her arm that was holding
the bottle. Before he knew it, her other hand slapped him across the
face really hard. *SLAP!*

Damien was very worried and he wanted to jump up and go into
the living room, but instead his back slid down the wall. As his butt
touched the floor, his knees drew to his chest and his arms wrapped
around his knees. He continued listening to his parents fight.

"You bitch! Stop slapping me!"

"Then get away from me, Alex. This is mine." She clutched the
bottle tightly in her hand.

Alex tried again to grab the bottle and once again Becky slapped him. *SLAP!*

This time Alex lost it. He grabbed Becky by the throat and pinned her to the wall. He raised his free hand as if he was about to strike her with his fist. Becky saw this and cried out, "No! Please don't hit me." Alex froze, with his hand firmly gripping the front of her neck pushing her back against the wall. He came to his senses and released her. He turned to walk away, but before he got three steps, she called out.

"I was raped!" Becky then dropped to her knees on the floor, falling back on her heels and eventually landing on her butt as her back banged into the wall, making a loud thud.

Damien was trying his hardest to hold back his tears; he didn't want his parents to hear him crying.

"What did you say?" Alex couldn't believe the words she had just said. He stood with his back to her. She wouldn't answer.

"What did you just say, Becky?" Alex yelled, trying to prompt the woman to repeat it. Still no answer.

"Ok Becky. I'm done with—"

Becky interrupted. "I was raped, Alex. Please don't hate me." He turned to face his wife, but didn't approach her.

"What do you mean, you were raped? Who raped you? When?" Alex was asking so many questions that Becky didn't have time to gather her thoughts. "I can't tell you."

Alex became enraged. "Who raped you, Becky? Tell me now!"

"It doesn't matter, Alex. Please, I love you," Becky pleaded.

"Becky, I'm going to give you to the count of five to tell me who raped you, and if you don't, it's over, I'm leaving! Five— four— three—" Alex paused. "Two— one— goodbye, Becky!" Alex started walking away.

Becky panicked. "It was Bishop Graham," she sobbed. Alex was still walking and she raised her voice. "Bishop Graham raped me!"

Alex felt weak in his knees. He turned and punched the wall, making a loud noise and putting a hole just a little bigger than the size of his fist through the drywall.

The noise his dad's fist made when he hit the wall both startled and scared Damien. He felt paralyzed to move.

Becky was bawling her eyes out now. "Alex, please— please— please— don't go. No one loves me. I need to be loved— Alex, please—"

Alex heard his wife's pleas, but they fell on deaf ears. He went to their bedroom and slammed the door. A short while later, he came out of the room with a suitcase in hand; he headed for the front door.

Becky saw him but she was too drunk to stand. She leaned against the wall, begging. "Alex, pleeeaaassseee don't go. No one loves me."

Damien looked over and could see his dad's hand on the door; he saw the door open and his dad leave. The door slammed and Damien jumped up and ran to the door. He opened it, yelling at his dad. "Dad, please don't go!"

Alex didn't even turn around, he just kept walking away. Damien closed the door, went over to his stepmom, knelt down beside her, and looked up into her red puffy eyes. He reached up, wrapped his arms around her neck, and put his head on her chest.

"I'll always love you, Mom."

CHAPTER 44 –

Mary Makes a Friend

BILL LOOKED AT the time; he phoned his brother John.

"Hello, Margaret Hall speaking."

"Hello, Margaret, it's Bill. Could I please speak with John?"

"Of course, William, he's right here." Margaret handed the phone to John.

"Hello, John speaking."

"Hi, John, it's Bill. I was wondering if I could stop by for a few minutes to speak with Lucinda."

"Yes, of course, Bill, if it's not going to take long. She goes to bed at 10:00pm."

"Oh, it won't take long, John. I need to talk to Lucinda about youth group; it shouldn't take longer than fifteen minutes, and I'll be right over."

Bill hung up the phone and headed over to John's home. Once he arrived, he greeted the family. He looked at John. "May I have a few words with Lucinda in your study, John?"

"Of course." "Lucinda, come in here," John called out. Lucinda walked into the hall, saw Bill and scrunched her face a little.

"Lucinda, Pastor Bill would like a few words with you about youth group. You can use my study for privacy."

Lucinda walked into the study with Bill following behind. Once the door closed, she spoke.

"I thought you almost forgot about me, Bill."

"Never, Lucinda," Bill said in a pleasant tone. "I'd never forget about you, darling."

"Uh, Bill. I'm not your darling, angel, or any other cute words you want to call me. Just tell me that you've done what I told you to do."

"Yes, I've done everything you asked, Lucinda." From his jacket he took out a passport, a bank book and an envelope. Lucinda reached for his hand and he pulled it back. "Not so quickly, Lucinda."

"Bill, don't try me. My father, your brother, is just outside that door. One word from me and—"

Bill interrupted Lucinda. "Listen, Lucinda, I just want to make sure that this is what you want to do. That you're absolutely certain you want to run away from your family, your friends, your home."

"What family? My mom is a bitch. My dad has never shown me love and as for friends, I don't have any friends. The most important thing to me now is my baby." Lucinda sounded resolute.

Bill handed her the envelope. She took it from his hand. As she looked inside, she saw cash and a bus ticket.

"Lucinda, that's two-hundred dollars cash for your trip across the border and a bus ticket to a city in Alberta, Canada, called Calgary."

"And what about the rest, Bill?"

"I've secured and paid for a condominium for you. Here's the bill of sale. Bought and paid for in full." The girl took the piece of paper and read it. The paper said "Calgary, Alta."

"And the quarter of a million dollars, Bill?" He opened the bank book and showed her the printed balance showing $250,000.00.

She reached for the bank book and Bill pulled it and the apartment deed away.

"Bill!" she said in anger.

"Look, Lucinda, you can keep the envelope with the bus ticket and the two-hundred dollars; but the rest I'll give you when I drop you off at the bus station and you're on your way. And that's how it's going to be or the deal's off!" Bill's poker face was solid.

Lucinda reluctantly agreed. "Ok, fine, Bill. We'll do it your way. What's the plan?"

"You'll have to tell your parents that you are leaving for school early and that you're walking."

"That's easy, Bill, ever since the accident with the bus I've been walking to school. I leave fifteen minutes before the bus picks up my sisters. Oh, and remember, Bill: hands off my sisters. If I find out—"

Bill interrupted; he didn't want her to finish her sentence. "You have my word. I won't touch your sisters, Lucinda."

"Never, Bill, never. Swear it."

"I swear. Never."

"Ok, so I leave early, walk to school and then what, Bill?"

"What time do you leave for school?"

"I leave at 7:00am sharp, Bill."

"Tomorrow morning, I'll be waiting for you in the alley near the playground. You get in my car and I'll drive you two hours northwest to the town you'll be catching the bus in. I'll give you the passport, apartment deed and the bank book. You get on the bus and start your new life as a whole new person."

"And what's my new name going to be?"

"Lucinda, that's a surprise we'll leave for when I give you your new passport."

"Fine! Bill, I'll see you tomorrow morning in the alley. Don't blow it."

Bill smiled and stood up. They exited John's study. Lucinda was smiling wide. John saw the smile and commented to Bill, "Well, you must have given Lucinda some good news about youth group."

"Yes, brother, it's really good news. Lucinda is going to be asked to become a junior leader." He smiled.

"That's great news, Bill." John moved closer and shook his brother's hand. "Thank you for stopping by."

Bill left the house and went home.

~

Mary was having breakfast in the cafeteria when a girl about her age with long straight blonde hair asked if she could join her.

"May I join you for breakfast?" The girl smiled at Mary.

"Of course, have a seat." Mary patted the chair next to her and offered her hand. "I'm Mary."

The girl shook her hand. "Norma-Ann," she said as she sat down. "So, you're new here. How do you like it so far?" Norma-Ann asked.

"So far it's great. School's been an adjustment, but it's been one day. The food is good, I love my room and the people all seem really nice."

Mary took a drink of her milk and felt nauseous. She covered her mouth, jumped up and ran to the cafeteria washroom directly into one of the stalls.

Mary didn't realize that Norma-Ann had followed her into the bathroom and come up behind her. Norma-Ann took her hair in her hands to stop it from getting wet or vomited on. Norma-Ann held her hair and Mary appreciated it, but every time she would try to say thank you, she heaved and vomited more.

"Don't worry about it, Mary, I got you," Norma-Ann said in a soothing voice.

After a few minutes, Mary felt like she was done voiding her breakfast. She got up and apologized.

"Sorry to run off and sorry for the— ah—"

Norma finished her sentence. "For the stinky vomit smell." She laughed.

"Exactly!" Mary said as she walked to the counter where the sinks were. She saw a bottle of mouthwash and some paper cups right beside the bottle.

"I think you should probably get used to that, Mary, at least for a while."

Mary was now rinsing her mouth out and after spitting out the gargle, she followed up with a cup of water, gargled and spit it out.

"No, Norma-Ann, the food is great. I don't know what came over me. It just kinda—"

"Oh, Mary." Norma-Ann took each of Mary's hands in her hands, and when she did both girls felt something electric. They both paused and looked into each other's eyes. Time seemed to stand still as they were lost in thought.

Mary felt incredible urges that shocked her. She'd never thought of girls in this way before. Her blood was pumping and she could feel her loins getting warm as the two girls were holding hands, staring into each other's eyes.

"Mary, Mary, Mary..." Norma-Ann said, trying to get her attention.

Mary finally heard the third time the girl said her name. She realized that she was frozen as if something had hypnotized her.

"Yeah, ok," Mary stammered out with a little thought still stirring in her mind.

"Mary, it wasn't the food, girl. You have morning sickness. Pretty soon you'll be just like me." Norma-Ann removed her right hand, leaving her left hand still in the palm of Mary's right hand. Norma-Ann rubbed her belly, indicating to Mary that she was pregnant.

"Oh, oh, oh, no, no, I'm not pregnant, Norma-Ann, it was just weird." Mary could barely focus as her feelings for this girl were growing more intense by the second. She felt like her libido was on fire; she wanted so badly to just lean over and kiss Norma-Ann.

"Oh, yes, Mary, you're most definitely pregnant, even if you don't know it yet. I can tell. I got a feeling for these kinds of things."

"Well, you've got it all wrong, Norma-Ann. I should be getting to classes now. Maybe I'll see you at lunch."

"It's a date," Norma-Ann said with a smile. Mary left the washroom and headed for her second day of classes.

CHAPTER 45 –

A New Life

THE NEXT MORNING, Lucinda was excited as she woke up early. She got herself ready and packed an old rucksack full of all the clothes, shoes, jackets and bathroom items she needed. She opened the bathroom window, threw the rucksack out the window to the ground below and then she went downstairs to have breakfast.

After breakfast, Lucinda went through her regular morning routine.

"Mother, I'm going to school now. Goodbye."

Margaret called out from the kitchen, "Have a good day at school, Lucinda."

She was excited as she walked out the front door; as soon as she stepped off the last step, she ran around the side of the house, grabbed her rucksack and headed towards the alley. She thought to herself, *Bill better damn well be there.* As she entered the alley, she saw Bill's car and was excited that he had come through for her. She got in the car, threw her bag in the back seat and closed the door.

"Good morning, Lucinda. Are you ready to start your new life?"

"Absolutely!" she replied.

"I see you're happy today." He smiled at her. "Have you got everything packed that you'll need?"

Lucinda shook her head in disgust. "Listen, Bill. It's a long drive and I don't want to listen to you yapping all the way. Let's just not talk, please."

Bill cringed. "If you say so, I just thought maybe—"

Lucinda interrupted Bill. "Don't expect me to say thank you, don't expect me to forgive you. What you did to me is reprehensible. So just shut up and drive."

"Ok, fine." Bill pursed his lips and didn't say another word for the entire drive.

~

After the two-hour drive, Bill pulled into the secluded back parking lot of the bus station. He parked the car, turned the radio off and turned to face his niece.

"Lucinda, this is your last chance to change your mind. Are you absolutely certain?"

"Yes, Bill, I'm one thousand percent sure." Just then, something changed in the girl's attitude. "Uncle Bill. I'm sorry for being so mean. I just really need to start a new life. My baby deserves to be happy and have a happy mother. I just don't think my life will be too happy in Riley when people find out I'm pregnant."

"I'm sorry, Lucinda, I do feel guilty for putting you in such a bad position."

Her eyes lit up and she hugged Bill. "It's ok, Bill, I'm looking forward to my new life. Thanks for setting it all up for me."

When the girl released the hug, Bill reached into his jacket and took out the bank book, apartment deed and passport. He handed them to Lucinda. She took the documents, grabbed her rucksack and exited the car. She waved at Bill; he waved back and drove away.

Lucinda opened the passport, excited to see her new name. She read it out loud to herself. "Mary Jones, Date of Birth: 23-Feb-1978. Place of Birth: Champion, Oklahoma."

"Bill, stop!" She turned around to see his tail-lights driving away. She talked out loud to herself. "That idiot screwed up, this is an American passport."

As Bill drove out of the parking lot, a black sedan drove past him heading towards the secluded back parking lot. He nodded at the two men as he drove past.

The agents parked close enough to Lucinda that they would be able to grab her, but not close enough to scare her away.

They got out of the car, looked around to see no one in sight and the parking lot deserted of any cars. There was a chain link fence twenty yards from the building that ran the length of the bus station.

Agent West could hardly contain his excitement at finally acquiring Mary Jones and completing their mission.

As the agents approached Lucinda, West quickened his pace with Smith trailing slightly behind. "Mary Jones!" West called out. "Mary Jones, we'd like to talk with you."

Lucinda was lost in thought and it didn't register with her that according to her new passport, she was now Mary Jones.

It startled Lucinda when Agent West grabbed the sleeve of her left arm. She snapped back to reality when she realized that these men were calling for Mary Jones and that was the name on the passport Bill had given her.

"I'm not Mary Jones. I'm not Mary Jones! Let me go. Let me go!" Lucinda pulled hard and broke free from the loose grip West had on her jacket, she headed towards the building trying to find an entry door at the back of the bus station. West gave chase and when he tried to grab her, she tripped and fell near a garbage dumpster with her rucksack flying from her shoulder landing three feet away from her as she cried out from skinning her knee on the pavement.

Agent West closed the gap and gripped the left arm of her jacket much tighter this time. Agent Smith picked up the rucksack. "That's mine, give it back." Lucinda screamed loudly. "Help! I'm being robbed!"

West laughed. "She thinks we're robbing her Smith. That's funny Mary, you're coming with us." As West pulled the girl to her feet Smith had started back towards the car. He turned around just in time to see West take hold of Lucinda's left wrist.

Lucinda pivoted her body around a hundred and eighty degrees. In that moment of fear and adrenaline rush Lucinda felt as if time stood still, a feeling she had only felt one other time. She closed her eyes tight, saw green lightning bolt flashes and with all her will focused, she used her casted right arm to swing down onto Agent Wests right forearm. A loud snap was heard the instant Lucinda's cast struck the man.

Agent Smith saw what happened, but he was now twenty feet away when the girl broke free. Agent West was holding his arm as he turned to see the girl running away. Lucinda ran as far and fast as she could, faster than she ever thought she could; with Agent West and Smith in pursuit she ran out of real estate when she came to the end of the parking lot there was an eight-foot-high chain link fence with a gate that was padlocked with a heavy iron chain.

She came to the fence and tried pushing the gate open, but it was chained and locked tightly. Just then, she heard Agent West's footsteps come to a slow trot behind her and she turned to see him walking towards her as he held his arm and breathed heavy.

She closed her eyes and focused on the heavy chain. Again, time stood still for Lucinda. Agent West watched in disbelief as the chain rapidly froze solid, became brittle and crumbled to dust.

Agent West reached out with his left hand to grab the girl as she pushed the gate open. He caught her by the jacket, causing her to wheel around and face him. The palm of her left hand contacted his chest and he flew backwards through the air, landing on his back. He couldn't breathe; he was winded and it felt as though a cannon ball had just been shot directly into his solar plexus.

Lucinda turned to go through the now open gate and she felt a bite on her neck. She held up her hand to feel a feathered dart just before her eyes rolled up in her head and she fell to the ground.

Agent West looked up from the ground to see Agent Smith's gun pointed at the girl and he realized that his partner had just shot the girl with a tranquilizer dart.

Agent Smith briskly walked over to West.

"You alright, West?" The agent on the ground, still out of breath, waved his partner over to the girl. "Get her. I'm ok."

Agent Smith went to the girl's limp body, picked her up in his arms and carried her back to the car. As Agent Smith was carrying Lucinda, Agent West got to his feet and started to walk towards the car, rubbing his forearm. "Do you need help, Smith?"

"I got this, West, just get her rucksack and let's get going."

Once inside the car, Agent Smith drove. He looked at West holding his right forearm.

"It hurts, doesn't it?"

West growled back, still rubbing and touching it gingerly. "Yeah, getting whacked with a cast doesn't hurt at all," he snapped at his partner sarcastically.

"No worries, the agency doctors will fix you right up, West."

Agent Smith then took out his satellite radio and contacted head-quarters as he drove.

"This is Agent Smith reporting. We have the girl Mary Jones in custody." He released the talk button and waited for a reply. A voice came over the radio.

"Agent Smith, where are you at this moment?"

"We're on the way to the AOL airfield in Tulsa. We should arrive within ninety minutes."

"Copy that, Agent Smith. Did you encounter any trouble?"

"We ran into some issues. I request a medical unit to meet us at the air strip. Agent West was injured in the apprehension."

"Copy that, Agent Smith."

"Command, there is something else I should report."

"We're all ears, Agent Smith."

"Command, I believe that we have apprehended a bona fide VP who has manifested her powers. Please advise."

The radio went silent.

"Command, did you copy that? We have a proven VP in the back of our vehicle. Please advise!" He repeated himself with a tone of sudden urgency that piqued Agent West's curiosity.

"We heard you, Agent Smith, and we have sent the info upstairs; we'll advise as soon as we can. Hang tight."

"I understand, command. I have the girl sedated at the moment. By all means take your sweet time." Smith sniped.

Command came back with instructions. "Agent Smith. We're sending an escort to meet you on the highway."

"Copy that, command." Agent Smith put the radio down.

West was curious. "Smith what was that all about? And why is command sending an escort?"

Agent Smith looked over his shoulder into the back seat where Lucinda was drugged; he then looked back at Agent West.

"West, that girl is why they're sending an escort."

"Why?" Agent West was now very concerned and annoyed that he didn't understand what was going on.

"West, they'll send an escort that will include another agent vehicle as well as state troopers to escort us to the agency air strip as fast as possible."

"What's the rush, Smith?"

"The rush is we don't know how long Mary Jones will stay sedated."

"I don't understand what all the secrecy is about, just tell me what I need to know, Smith! And what exactly is a VP, Agent Smith?"

Smith didn't answer. "Look there." Smith pointed up ahead at the intersection. Two state troopers were behind another car. Just then, command came on the radio.

"Agent Smith, your escort has arrived. You're clear to fly."

"Copy that, command." Agent Smith pinned the pedal to the floor and the three cars joined them on the road with one state trooper leading the way, followed by Smith and West, the second agency car and then another state trooper taking up the rear. Both troopers had their lights and sirens on.

"What is a VP, Agent Smith? Tell me!"

Agent Smith again looked over his shoulder into the back seat at the unconscious girl.

"What is a VP, Smith?" Agent West was clearly agitated. Smith decided to answer him, if only to shut him up.

"A VP is short for Veil Piercer, West, and don't even try to ask me to explain; it's way above your pay grade. You're only a junior agent; I would be reprimanded just for telling you that. I can tell you this much, you're damn lucky she didn't sheer your arm right off."

At that moment, neither of the agents saw Lucinda's left pinky finger twitching.

CPSIA information can be obtained
at www.ICGtesting.com
Printed in the USA
LVHW110845150421
684499LV00010BA/96

9 781525 598449